D0279453

The Obelisk Of Time
By
Turneramon

(Being Book Two In The Trilogy Of Nethertime)

Copyright Richard Turneramon 2005

No part of this book may be reproduced, stored in a retrieval system
or transmitted by any means without the written permission of the
author.

This book is a work of fiction and any similarity to persons alive or
dead is purely coincidental.

Cover design by Richard Turneramon, digitised by Jason Duggan

British Library Cataloguing In Publication Data

A Record of this Publication is available
from the British Library

ISBN 1905363931

Published December 2005 by

Exposure Publishing, an imprint of Diggory Press,
Three Rivers, Minions, Liskeard, Cornwall PL14 5LE
WWW.DIGGORYPRESS.COM

To Christopher Luke... Though You Are Far Away From Me, Your Cherished Memory Lives On In The Pages Of This Book...(Unlike Luke In This Book, We Had Some Good Times At Park House)

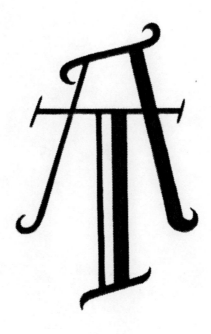

Contents

*** PROLOGUE ***

The sun had just set behind the Theban Necropolis near to the Valley of the Kings on the West Bank of the Nile. An indigo shadow, cast by the ever-watchful Gurn, that natural pyramid-like hill which dominated the skyline, moved across the barren desert wadi and the tomb entrances which were dotted haphazardly about the face of the limestone cliffs were extinguished one by one as the purple shroud moved across them.

Only the tall palms and the higher crumbling mud-brick walls of the distant village were brushed by the rouge of sunset as the desert air of upper Egypt turned chill and a turquoise afterglow seared the clear sky.

Standing on the chipped terracotta tiled floor of the rest house, his dirty galabiya fluttering in the breeze, a small boy turned to look in the direction of the noise.

Stones were rolling down the steeply inclined cliff as a minuscule figure teetered on the top, silhouetted against the shimmering crepuscular sky. The boy's eyes narrowed, crow's feet puckering his leathery skin as he marked the man's progress down the rocky slope, his wild strides accompanied by an avalanche of rocks and sand.

Seeing his quarry of that morning returning from the desert and now in obvious difficulty, the boy called out to his mates in an ululating high-pitched voice. He ran to join them at the base of the cliffs; a pointed flint in his hand and the small boys took up their stations and watched the stranger's descent down the tortuous path.

The man was half way down now, his Egyptologist's pith-helmet askew, sweat streaking his dusty face and running down in rivulets onto his khaki fatigues.

'Yer kh'wager, yer magnoon!' The boys shouted at him 'you foreigner...you crazy man!'

The taunts of the village boys assailed his ears as the Egyptologist desperately tried to slow his fall, and swinging his staff at the nearest urchin, he somehow managed to dodge the hail of flints that the gang of boys launched at him.

Using the momentum of his frantic descent he was able to outrun them and gain the sanctuary of the resthouse as a bombardment of missiles hit its tiled floor.

'Mahmoud! Talla, Mahmoud!' The Egyptologist shouted as a bleary eyed man in dirty galabiya appeared from behind a torn curtain.

'Ouse Eh, magnoon... what do you want crazy one?' he asked, the yawn becoming a scowl.

'Beer, give me beer!'

His rasping breath subsiding slightly, the Egyptologist perched his wiry frame on the barstool, picking at the dried blood on his legs. He reached into his khaki shorts and started filling a pipe.

'Birah.' Mahmoud slammed a cold beer on the marble bar, scowling at the crazy explorer; he was not pleased at being woken from his siesta.

He walked out onto the veranda and threw the beer bottle top at a sleeping dog. The boys, lurking still at the base of the cliffs and hopeful of another chance to berate the crazy foreigner, retreated at seeing Mahmoud, slinking back to their hovels.

Why, Mahmoud thought, did these mad Egyptologists have to come to his country, digging and poking about? They were more trouble than the tourists, and penniless to boot! Mahmoud scowled into the Egyptian afterglow as he recalled his various attempts to extort money from this discredited Egyptologist. No, the tourists were an easier touch, he thought, rubbing his unshaven jaw, and what might have passed for a smile flittered briefly across his course features as he thought of his recent philandering: the girl from the Swedish tour, lost and penniless...

His thoughts were interrupted by the voice from the bar.

'Mahmoud... get me Luxor Police H.Q....I want to report a murder!'

Chapter One
*** The Burial ***

Park House, lying in its own grounds on the edge of the Royal Borough of Kirkcudbright on the Solway coast of Scotland, was host to a strange gathering of people this early autumn morning as various cars drew up into its capacious driveway.

Luke Slater, straightening his black tie and buttoning the jacket of his morning suit, grimaced into the mirror at the ill-fitting garment he had hired from the local outfitters, wondering how his father would have handled this.

In fact, he thought, as he gave a final glance over his athletic frame, pushing back the blond curl on his forehead, his father would have been in his element. Irreverent of authority to the point of anarchy, and despising of tradition, he would have found all this rigmarole laughable. A faint smile crossed Luke's clean-cut face as he thought of how his father would have loved to have witnessed this imminent event – his own funeral!

Not that Luke believed this recent nonsense! A few days ago in Egypt, an Egyptologist had found the remains of a body. Instead of a new tomb for which he was looking, he had discovered a corpse lying at the bottom of a tomb shaft near to the Valley of the Kings. On raising the body, the local Egyptian authorities had discovered that the Caucasian male had been the recipient of foul play – evidence of his throat being cut from ear to ear being adequate testament to this. On conducting a murder enquiry, the local police had identified the body as Luke's father, Jock Slater, who had disappeared over two years ago in that area. Naturally distraught, Bridget, Luke's mother, had put away her old grievances with her estranged husband and demanded the authorities return his father's body to Scotland for a Christian burial.

Mulling over this bizarre event, Luke's thoughts went back, recalling vivid memories of his father's 'carrying ons'. At the time of Jock's disappearance, some two years previous, there had been a certain amount of gossip as to his whereabouts. This had been contained mainly to his drinking buddies around the small Scottish town until someone had written an article in the local press, wondering where the larger than life character, the sometime Artist and Egyptologist, Jock Slater had got to.

Then it had escalated when some London hack had done a little research and unearthed a few juicy titbits about his father's life, writing an implausible, yet newsworthy - and therefore saleable story about the philanderer Jock Slater. Luke remembered all too well reading an account of the wild allegations of antiquities thefts and even drug smuggling levied at his father, and some later accounts had him either rotting in an Egyptian jail or taking time out to paint a harem.

There was something almost tragic, Luke thought sadly, about the knack his father had for attracting bad press - even before his disappearance. As a painter his work was controversial and 'difficult' and at best had come in for scathing criticism. Seeming almost to wallow in it, Jock Slater had heaped more and more scorn upon himself as he almost purposefully, it seemed, locked horns with the media.

Luke remembered reading through copies of old reviews way back in the eighties. His Father had inadvertently left his studio door unlocked, and Luke - then a belligerent little so and so - had sneaked in one day with a school friend. They had sniggered over the news clippings that showed paintings of naked women, and read about how his father had stripped off at one of the openings to make a point about the beauty of the human body. Naturally the press had had a field day, and Slater's nude body had graced the tabloids' front pages, receiving more coverage than his work.

Later, when the galleries got fed up with his pranks and his prices slumped, Slater had become a recluse, wandering around the London bars telling tall tales of his journeys into foreign lands and even lost dimensions. One article that Luke had read had called his father "Mad Jock" and the lad remembered how livid he felt on reading of the character assassination of his eccentric, though cherished dad.

This period of failure though had put a great strain on his father's marriage, and his relationship with Bridget, Luke's mother, had been put to the test. She had gone her own way, and after one last row Jock had stormed out of the house. The next thing the Slater family heard of him was in a letter from Luxor, Upper Egypt.

Jock had got his old job back, working as an artist with the University of Chicago's Oriental Institute in Luxor, where he had been re-employed in recording the scenes on the walls of the temples and tombs in and around the Valley of the Kings. He had written reams of letters to Luke, all of them stored in the studio-come museum that Jock had made in this beautiful old house, Park House; a gift it appeared from a patron and admirer of Slater's work, though from some old letters Luke had found as he snooped around his father's studio, there was a hidden dimension to his dad's past: something mysterious as to his genealogy.

'Luke, hurry up!' It was Bridget shouting up the stairs. The youth was brought back to the present as the recent events since the news of his father's demise came painfully back.

The body, officially identified as Jock Slater, had been flown back from Egypt and Luke was bracing himself for the funeral; although he simply could not believe it was his father in the casket downstairs, he would go through the pretence for the sake of his mother and the relatives - who had of course turned up like bad pennies. Running the gauntlet of the press he could handle; his father had been a good example of that: if the news-hounds wanted to make up wild stories of an ex-patriot who had been murdered by a smuggling cartel, then let them - for he knew something that they didn't.

Descending the great gothic staircase, Luke was suddenly brought back to the grim reality of the situation. In the main hall were a number of sombrely dressed people who discharged their collective condolences in a mechanical and perfunctory fashion. Acknowledging these as briefly as protocol would allow, Luke walked along the main hall and out through the French windows onto the patio.

Outside, the camera flashes of the few newsmen who pressed about in the cobbled courtyard eclipsed the bright sunshine as they spotted the tall, handsome son of the formerly much maligned "Artist;" a good subject for a photo shoot if they could just get a statement from him. They had obviously been doing their homework regarding Jock Slater's chequered career as they all asked the same fatuous questions.

'Can I verify your father was a Russian spy? Was he murdered by the antiquities smuggling mob, the Abdul Rasool Clan?' Did he find a new tomb...?'

Luke countered the wild accusations with a shake of the head as he strode down the drive towards a black Rolls Royce Shadow that was parked outside the stables block.

'Bloody Vultures!' he oathed as he stepped inside the limo, putting his arm around his trembling mother who had just run the gauntlet herself, 'these people want blood, don't they?'

The Rolls had been a good idea; it threw the press off the scent. After the brief but private memorial service at the local Kirk in the nearby Scottish town of Kirkcudbright, the car, followed by a small coterie of close friends and relatives returned via a circuitous route to the house. Unaware that this small, private service was a red herring, a blind to throw the press off the scent, the odd couple of reporters at the main gate hardly managed the obvious question. 'But where is the coffin...what happen to the body?' before the main gate of the estate was closed and locked and the small procession wound round to the west of Park House.

A black hearse was standing on the gravel crescent in front of an avenue of Lime trees. Bearers, their black top hats askew, awkwardly lifted the coffin from the car. The black and purple-robed minister led the procession to a small wood of Scots pine, through which the path wound before opening into a lozenge- shaped clearing, in the centre of which was a large white marble sarcophagus.

The group stood silently, Luke supporting his mother, as a tall, gaunt man, the lawyer to the deceased, handed the minister a sealed wooden box. As the minister pulled open the waxed paper seals and proceeded to read out a lengthy eulogy, Luke noticed a glint of light in the dark of the pinewood. Squinting into the shade, he saw a tall man dressed in black and standing alone, an errant ray of sunlight catching his dark glasses. The minister had started reading the lengthy document couched in the incomprehensible vernacular of Scottish legalese. It sounded like the last rites, with Ancient Egyptian mysticism thrown in for effect - where were

11

the temple dancers? Luke thought, as he suppressed a wry smile. Yes, his father had retained that surrealistic touch right to the end, though Bridget wasn't holding up as well; she was trembling.

As Luke hugged his mother's shoulder, somehow he could not accept that this was actually happening - though the last two years had irrevocably brought the family to the conclusion that Jock Slater, artist, traveller and practical joker, had finally met his end. This however was not too soon for the rather puerile side of his mother's family, who viewed his father's work with disdain, nay contempt.

A strange silence hung over the wood as the men strained with the weight of the coffin. It was lowered down into the darkness below and Luke comforted Bridget Slater who shook visibly as her husband's last remains vanished from human view.

Almost surprised that there was no resurrection trick, and the deceased wasn't about to pop up out of the sarcophagus dressed as Tutankhamen, Luke led the funeral party back to the house; the man who Luke had seen earlier followed at a discreet distance behind.

'Master Slater,' it was the man behind him who had caught up, 'may I have a word with you?' Luke turned to face him as the man took off his sunglasses. He was of Arabic origin, distinguished looking, with a finely chiselled face and a streak of grey running through his otherwise dark and neatly combed hair - Luke thought a diplomat perhaps.

'I had the pleasure of knowing your father' he said, a faint smile revealed a gold tooth set in almost white teeth. 'Permit me to introduce myself. My name is Harran Rachid.' The man peeled off a calfskin glove and extended a strong, but well manicured hand. Luke grasped the proffered hand, feeling a firm handshake and said to the stranger: 'Please come to the house. We have a few family matters to discuss first, mainly legal, but I would like to talk to you afterwards, if that is suitable?'

The man bowed. 'I understand' he said, 'I don't want to interrupt a family affair. It's just that I have something of your father's that I would like to return to his estate.' Rachid turned and gestured to the white Mercedes at the gate. 'If you like, I can have it brought in...it's quite large.'

'Thank you' Luke replied, resisting the temptation to ask what this item of his father's might be. 'If you would like to have it brought into the hall, it would be most helpful,' he pointed to the main double doors of the house through which could be seen the massive hall. 'I will keep the doors open.'

Rachid bowed and headed for the car as Luke entered the house. Walking across the hall he heard the sounds of raised voices coming from the sitting room. He entered and saw Abrams, his father's agent and a gallery owner, who was in a heated argument with Mr. Havers, his father's lawyer.

'He was under contract to me, I tell you. These paintings are the property of the gallery!'

'Mr Abrams!' the tall, emaciated lawyer stood glaring down at the fat little man. 'It says quite distinctly in Mr Slater's will that all his work is to be held in trust until his return...'

'*His return...his return*!' Abrams spluttered, his beady eyes blazing with rage.

'Excuse me mister solicitor, but we have just done *burying him*!' Luke moved to where they were arguing

'Gentlemen please,' he said politely but firmly, 'I will not have voices raised in this house on such a day.' He turned to look at Abrams. 'I have seen the will and this gentleman is correct...everything in this house including the paintings will stay put...until Father's return. That is what the will says!'

Abrams' eyes stood out like piscine globes as he looked angrily at Luke, his voice almost reaching falsetto. 'You don't mean that you believe this crap. It's a cheap trick to cheat the gallery, not to mention myself, out of our rightful share of the paintings. After all the time and money we have put into promoting him... and now his prices will be going up...I knew your father was a shyster, but...'

'*How dare you*!' A deep cultured voice cut through Abrams' whining tones as they turned to look at the man standing in the doorway; it was Rachid. 'How dare you insult the name of my dear friend' he moved into the room, his black tie and white collar immaculate. 'Forgive me Master Slater' he said looking at Luke, 'I do not mean to intrude but I cannot tolerate such slander...'

'That's alright.' A feminine voice spoke as Bridget entered, 'Any friend of my former husband is welcome in this house.' She looked disdainfully at Abrams as if to say that he was not included in that group. Luke introduced the elegant foreigner to his mother who coloured slightly as she shook his hand.

Please' she said, 'Sherry or something stronger is being served in the dining room, please go through and let us hear no more of this bickering.'

***

The logs crackled in the large ornate fireplace as Luke stood in front of it sipping a glass of sherry. The solicitor had done his formal reading of Father's will and most of the small group of family and friends had gone. Luke was trying to relax after the stressful events of the morning, although there had been one persistent reporter who had recorded the extraordinary contents of the will before Luke had realised that he had infiltrated the house, and kindly asked him to leave, making sure to rip out the top pages of the man's notebook before showing him the door. Abrams had tried to intervene saying 'any press is good press...we need all the coverage we can get.' Yet Luke saw through the Art Dealer's motives, for now that his father was "officially dead," his prices would rise; and who would be beneficiary of that?

There had been a lot of disappointed face at the reading of the will. "Everything to be held in trust until his return..." What a way to treat people! Not that most of them had come for handouts. But the few that had, after consuming sherry, wine, scotch and a variety of delicacies from the generously apportioned buffet, had paid their begrudging respects and left.

Luke smiled as he recalled the sour expressions of certain family and friends alike, as they shook his hand at the door; it did seem like everyone wanted a piece of the trickster Jock Slater.

Abrams had feigned dizziness, no doubt due to his over indulgence in the dining room, as the scotch had been almost totally depleted. He had been ushered into the large sitting room where he was still asleep. Bridget had finally condescended to finding him a bed for the night in one of the many bedrooms of the house, and Rachid and his manservant Jaff had been accorded the same privilege, though not so begrudgingly. They and the rest of the household had retired, but Luke was restless as he mulled over the events of the day.

He walked into the large oak panelled hall and looked at the object which Rachid's strong servant had carried in. It was a six-foot long roll of what could only be paintings. It was carefully wrapped in polythene and bore stickers of airfreight from its point of departure; Luxor, in Upper Egypt. Luke could see the edges of the white linen canvas through the polythene as his curiosity grew. He had agreed however to wait until the following day so that Abrams and Rachid could be present in the opening of the mysterious parcel. Yawning, Luke made his way to bed; he would have to wait until the morning to satisfy his curiosity.

Breakfast was an odd affair. Abrams, groggy from his over zealous personal wake in the name of his least cherished of stable artists, sat looking moodily out at the landscape. The bucolic scene of cows and sheep grazing in the adjacent pastures to the grounds of the house didn't hold much charm for him; he had a distaste for the country, and he couldn't think of one landscape painting in his collection.

Rachid sat, inscrutable and impeccable as ever as he talked politely of his various interests in history and travel and Luke gathered that he must be quite wealthy. His manservant Jaff, who had obviously never seen a knife and fork before, sat uncomfortably at the table, his eyes downcast as breakfast was served. Luke tried not to look at the brutish man with his shaven head and one golden earring; he looked like a villain out of the Arabian Nights, Luke thought – a genie in an ill-fitting suit.

Bridget tried hard to keep the conversation going but was aware of what was uppermost in Abrams and Luke's minds and she breathed a sigh of relief, rising first from the table. 'Right,' she heard Abrams say, 'can we have a decko at Slater's recent work.' He has had had a good look at the parcel in the hall, Luke thought, and it hadn't taken him long to divine it's contents.

'How did you happen to come by these paintings?' Abrams said as casually as he could, looking at Rachid as he tapped the long roll with his foot. Rachid took a deep breath as he attempted to explain. He was trying very hard to disguise his contempt for the Art Dealer, who saw only in Jock's work the means to advance his own pecuniary interests, and would perhaps understand these paintings about as much as the theory of relativity.

'Some of them, the older ones, I acquired from a Captain Mustapha Sawat' he started hesitantly. 'They had been impounded for several years after a strange event occurred in Luxor...'

'*The disappearance!*' Luke interjected.

'Just so' Rachid rejoined, looking at Luke. 'This information should be by rights for your ears only,' he added, looking suspiciously at Abrams as he continued with his account.

'Captain Sawat was very puzzled by the case. Jock had vanished into thin air. And the old lady who owned the old monastery where the alleged crime took place had also vanished. These paintings were found in Jock's studio, the old Monastery, and the local police kept them for evidence in the light of new information. There was none forthcoming, and so those paintings were put up for auction...I, myself brought them for a pittance,'

Luke watched Abrams as his eyes lit up.

'So.' The art dealer said to Rachid 'these older paintings are your property...they must have been the ones Slater did on his original trip to Egypt.' Luke thought he could almost see the calculating mind of this 'art collector' - art thief more like - working out his percentage.

'Well then,' Abram's made his pitch, a vapid smile of condescension gracing his smarmy face, 'If they belong to you... do you want to sell them? I will offer you a good price...'

'*No!*' Rachid cut the fat man short. '*I do not!*' I do not wish to sell them. I wish to return them to Jock's estate!' Abrams excited expression deflated somewhat.

'What about the others?' Luke asked Rachid.

'These were done more recently' Rachid replied, 'As you know Jock came once more to Egypt, to work for his old employer, the Oriental Institute of Chicago University. He told me when we met up again that it had given a new impetus to his work. He used to miss the magic of Egypt terribly you know, but he also felt guilty about leaving you and your Mother behind.'

'I know' Luke said, 'He wrote us enough letters.'

'Well' Rachid continued 'Before his disappearance for the second time, although we may have to regrettably conclude that the body found in the tomb was indeed your father's, he handed me a roll of recent paintings...but there was something very odd about them....'

'Odd?' Abrams exclaimed. 'Odd? All Jock Slater's paintings are odd! *That's why they don't sell!*'

Rachid smiled contemptuously at the dealer. What did he understand of his former friend's work; he had about as much soul in his character as a block of granite.

'What was odd about these recent ones in particular?' Luke asked, trying to ignore the detestable little man.

'Well' Rachid hesitated. 'If we could unroll them, I will be better able to show you.'

'Now you're talking' Abrams rejoined 'Lets have a look at them!'

'Alright' Luke agreed, producing a large key and unlocking the door of his father's studio.

They dragged the heavy roll inside and Abrams deftly cut the polythene package, his eyes alight with greed as Luke's curiosity rose. Abrams' eyes brightened as he scanned the studio, seeing the stacks of canvasses neatly piled up against the walls. He was standing in a veritable treasure chest - if only he could get his hands on them - the artist dead with all this work still unsold! He controlled his baser instincts and got to work carefully peeling off the heavy plastic wrappings and unrolling the paintings onto the floor.

'My God!' Abrams exclaimed excitedly as the top painting was revealed 'Is this one of his recent ones?'

'Yes.' Rachid replied in a measured voice. 'I would like to tell you a story about this particular one. Is it possible to re-stretch it?' Abrams looked around the studio. Slater mainly worked on the same large size. He saw an unused stretcher in the corner, and his beady eyes noticed a staple gun on the desk. 'Leave it to me,' he said 'Give me an hour or so. I'll have it done by then.'

Luke took Rachid's arm and they walked down the hall, 'would you like some coffee,' Luke said. He was a bit wary of leaving the grasping dealer alone in his father's studio, but Abrams *did* know what he was doing; no one could doubt that. Bridget had gone somewhere in the car, and the housekeeper was not to be seen; perhaps she had gone back to her cottage.

Luke sat down at the large dining room table as Rachid sat across from him and Jaff stood awkwardly at the door. Luke looked out through the large bay-windows – the autumn colours were wreathed in golden sunlight as he glanced up to the near hills which were clothed in purple heather and crowned by an Obelisk; one of several in the area which he had walked up to many times. The Obelisk caught the golden autumnal light, seeming almost to wink at him.

'I noticed that Obelisk' Rachid said, as if reading his thoughts, 'there are quite a few on these beautiful Scottish hills.'

'Yes' Luke rejoined, 'I have been up there many times, you can see them all from the top of that hill.'

'Does the Obelisk bare an inscription?' Rachid asked casually.

'No, all the Obelisks around here are devoid of inscriptions.'

'For what purpose were they erected?' Rachid asked, a curious light in his eye. 'Are they funerary monuments?'

'I don't think so' Luke replied. 'They are not near any burial grounds. I think they were erected to Mark out the territory of the land owners; a sort of Arcadian cult of Antiquity which was fashionable at the time of the enlightenment, but no-one seems sure.'

'Do you have a plan showing their positions?' Rachid asked as Luke began to wonder at Rachid's interest.

Luke went to the drawer of the oak writing desk and brought a roll of foxed paper over to the table. He opened it and pinned it with small glass weights on the table as Rachid poured over it. 'Do you have a ruler?' he asked as he studied the plan 'Is it all right to draw on it?'

'It's been in that drawer for ages' Luke said. 'I don't think anyone would mind.

Rachid used the proffered ruler and with an expensive gold pen, made connecting lines between the positions of the obelisk, as Luke studied him. 'Do you know about such things?' he said after a while. Rachid looked up and gave Luke his full attention. 'I was the inspector of Antiquities of the Theban Necropolis, across the river from Luxor...I should know a little about Obelisks, yes.'

'That was how you met father?' Luke asked, in the Valley of the Kings...'

'Yes.' Rachid regarded the youth with his candid, yet deep black eyes, 'Not in the Valley of the Kings though, but in and around the various temples where he worked for the University. I had of course to check that no damage was being done to the walls of the temples. But this is interesting,' he looked down at the plan again. 'Is it possible to keep this plan, or have it copied?'

'Keep it' Luke said 'I don't think anyone will miss it' Rachid rolled it up carefully and slipped the elastic band back over it, handing it to Jaff. 'Put it in the car,' he ordered him, 'in the boot...make sure it is locked!' Jaff bowed and hastened away.

'This story I have to tell you' Rachid turned back to Luke, 'is also about an Obelisk...and it concerns your father...' But Luke would have to wait as a strident voice interrupted.

'Finished!' Abrams called down the hall. 'The painting's stretched and what a cracker...any chance of a coffee?' Luke took Abrams a coffee to the studio and Rachid followed - then both of them stopped dead in their tracks as they beheld the most recent work of Jock Slater that Abrams had stretched up and hung in a prominent place over the mantelpiece of the large room.

'Wow!' Luke exclaimed, 'this is something quite different.' He walked towards it.

'Just think what it would look liked framed' Abrams enthused, rubbing his chubby hands.

'It is as I thought' Rachid added looking in awe at the painting. 'It is a facsimile of the missing Obelisk, the Obelisk of Time!' He approached it and felt the surface of the canvas. 'Don't touch it' Abrams rasped, 'It's a masterpiece...'

'My friend' Rachid retorted, turning to Abrams, 'I know it is a masterpiece, and why? Because it is the only surviving copy of the inscription on the face of the lost Obelisk, The Obelisk of Time!'

'*The Obelisk of Time?*' Luke and Abrams exclaimed almost simultaneously as they gazed at the ecstatic expression on Rachid's face.

There was no reply forthcoming from the scholar for his enraptured eyes were fixed on the painting. Luke turned from Rachid; his eyes also drawn magnetically back to the last of his father's paintings. This one was different to most of his other works: it was more detailed, and in essence it was a topographical scene. There were some nude figures in the foreground; one of Slater's trademarks, but the focus of the painting was not about the quasi-erotic cavorting of neo-classical figures – the landscape itself was the principal subject. The familiar neo – classical scene of an antiquity backdrop to grace the interactions of naked women, which disported themselves in the space - filling compositions of his former work, had been subjugated into a landscape 'portrait' of a scene that as Luke looked harder, became so real that he imagined he was there.

But it was the central configuration, which drew Luke's attention, for in the middle of a complexity of different styles of temples - the likes of which he had never seen before - arose a golden Obelisk. Its pointed cap seemed to glow with real gold, reflecting the raking light; another one of Slater's trademarks, which he used again and again in his paintings.

'Look at the inscription' Rachid urged. Luke looked at the hieroglyphic inscription on the painted Obelisk and frowned

'They are not the usual style.' Luke whispered as he tried to tear his eyes from the towering golden Obelisk; it was if it reached out and filled the whole room.

'Not only are they atypical' Rachid stated, 'they are unparalleled...'

'Will someone please explain.' Abrams interjected. 'What do these inscriptions have to do with this painting... and what in the name of Beelzebub is the *Obelisk of Time?*' he coughed and looked at the painting. 'We can all see that this is a masterpiece of fantasy...it is not of this world...'

'Precisely' Rachid cut in 'It is a true to life painting of another world...'

'What world?' Luke asked, his heart skipping a beat, '*Nethertime?*'

'I see, Master Slater,' Rachid looked keenly at the youth, 'that you are not unfamiliar with your father's travels, or is it his fantasies? But no, this painting does not depict the mystical, though questionable lost world of the Nethertime. What it *does* depict is of far greater import.' Rachid moved to look at the painting as the others listened with baited breath.

18

'This painting shows us the Mythical world of Aiyu, the Land of the West, or the Paradise of the Ancient Egyptian, which is supposed to exist only in legend.' Rachid turned from the painting and paced the room.

'You see,' he continued, 'how could such a place, viewed from the precepts of our own so- called modern world, with its origins in the concept of definable time, be considered possible? It is, after all, only a belief; a superstition in the mind of a primitive people. And yet this painting in its clarity shows that Aiyu *does* exist!'

'How could father paint such a world' Luke asked though he knew the answer.

'Because, my fine looking youth' Rachid's eyes were bright, 'Because *he has been there*!'

'Yes, Luke said, tearing his eyes from the painting, 'that's right. His journals describe some fantastical world... that of Nethertime...but I always thought they were of his rather fanciful imagination...'

'Journals?' Rachid and Abrams exclaimed simultaneously. 'You have them here?' Rachid's eyes were bright 'May we see them?'

Luke went to his father's plan chest and unlocking the top drawer, he brought out a pile of plans and a folder; he opened the folder on the oval table.

"The Sacred Eyes of Time" by Jock Slater "My journey into Nethertime - a remembered account," the title of the first page read. Rachid perused it in the manner of a man who has found gold whilst Abrams scowled at the neat writing, muttering: 'Slater is a painter...not a bloody novelist!'

'All I know is' Luke said, scowling at the gallery owner, 'that when my father returned from his first stint in Egypt, he was changed man. Mother told me so. And if he tried to recount his memories, and his alleged journey into a mythical land, then so be it'

'Yeah,' Abrams agreed reluctantly, 'but he was a graduate of the Royal College of Art, and they don't get any better than that. Are you trying to tell me he actually did this little trip, or did the heat of Egypt sap his brain?'

'Now listen to me you little schmuck!' Luke's patience with this arrogant, rude and grasping art dealer had finally snapped as he grasped the fat man around the throat.

'You may think you can talk ill of the dead with impunity, and you may see in this work of genius a way of bettering your own ends, but I tell you one thing...as I have breath in my body, you will never take any of my father's work out of this house...Do you understand?' Abrams recoiled from the physical threat of the strong youth as he was released from the stranglehold and stood in the centre of the room.

'So be it' he croaked, his voice choking with anger and a constricted larynx. 'So be it my fine friend,' he whispered as he made his exit, but I shall see the reputation of your beloved father rot in hell...'

'Where you shall join him!' Luke shouted as the art dealer staggered back into the hall and Luke heard the principal doors to the house slam shut.

✳✳✳

Abrams was without a taxi and on foot as he set off through the late autumn sunshine towards the little town of Kirkcudbright. His experience at Park House had ended in a nightmare as he wrestled with the tenure he had lost as Slater's sole representative. Did that arrogant youth know with whom he was dealing with; obviously not!

Of all the people who could have helped that family, perhaps in their hour of need, he was the one – why, he could have sold that last painting for a fortune!

The wind gusted in the tall trees and the light, slanting and golden, glanced from the dells and clefts of the low hills as he made his way through the countryside towards the town.

Glancing upwards, he saw the sunlight flickering on the Obelisk on the far hill. Why could they not accept his summation of that final Slater painting as being a masterpiece? Abrams passed the Stewartry museum with its archaic relics of Celtic craft displayed in local pride, and shuddered. All he wanted to do now was to return to London and be in the company of real people – not heathens.

Finally he reached the town, and saw a sign: The Selkirk Arms. This small hotel and pub would do for the night until he decided on his next move. He checked that his wallet, stacked with credit cards, was still in his blazer pocket, and unloosened his black tie as he gained the door. The formal proprietor showed him up to a single room as Abrams tore off his tie, washed and descended to the bar.

The hotel lounge was empty, but he heard the sound of animated voices from the taproom and headed for that. Wary of the sea of eyes observing him guardedly from their tables, he sat on the barstool and ordered a double scotch and soda.

The barmaid was a pretty young thing with long tresses of blonde hair and he quickly struck up a conversation with her. 'I am a stranger to these parts' he half-lied, 'Do you know anything about Park House?'

'Park House?' a stranger came out of nowhere and planted himself on the adjacent stool, 'Park House is it? I can tell you a thing or two about that place...for a start, *it's haunted...*'

✳✳✳

I'm sorry about that' Luke apologised to Rachid, looking through the hall windows at Abrams staggering up the steps to the road-gate. Without a backward glance, the art dealer was gone and Luke returned to the studio.

'Now,' he said to Rachid who stood looking at the new painting of his father's, 'perhaps we can continue. You were yet to explain what the

Obelisk of Time is and how it is connected with father. Is it to do with his hypothetical journey to the Nethertime... or Ancient Time was it?'

'I don't know if it is connected' Rachid said 'It may well be, but there is something strange going on regarding the Obelisk. Let me try to explain...' Rachid tore his eyes away from the painting with obvious difficulty and continued.

'I was trying to explain that this last painting of your father's is of great value, not just for its intrinsic beauty, but because it is the only record I know of the lost inscription on the so-called Obelisk of Time. And now that you have brought Jock's journals to my attention, could I ask you a favour?'

'Ask away,' Luke said

Before I attempt to explain to you the complex nature of the Obelisk of Time, could I bring Dr. Labachi, the leading authority on Obelisks, here to visit Park House and see this painting... also your father's journals. I would also like to show him the plan of these local Obelisks which you have been so kind to give me, so we may try to shed some light on this mystery?'

'Yes' Luke replied, 'certainly Mr Rachid'

'Thank you Master Luke,' Rachid smiled, his gold tooth glinting 'may I make a phone call?'

Luke was in the studio whilst Rachid spoke volubly and excitedly in Arabic, then putting the phone down, his tone changed harshly as he spoke to Jaff.

'Dr. Labachi will be on the next flight to Glasgow,' Rachid turned to Luke, I am sending Jaff to pick him up. Jaff returned briefly with the plan of the local Obelisks, which had been locked in Rachid's car. Then they heard the Mercedes leave the house at speed.

'So now can you give me some explanation as to the Obelisk of Time?' Luke was getting irritated by these interruptions and was itching to hear Rachid's story.

'Yes,' Rachid looked at Luke, and then at the painting 'you may find this hard to swallow,' he said, 'but this Obelisk was not discovered or excavated. It just appeared one day...standing on the site of the former temple of Amenophis the third, near to the colossi of Memnon on the West Bank of the Nile, opposite Luxor. I had a frantic phone call one morning. Some poor farmer working at dawn in the nearby fields suddenly saw it materialise- no noise, nothing – it was just there! I was at the house of the Inspectorate, the former house of Howard Carter's expedition, who as you know, discovered the Tomb of Tutanhkamen.'

Luke knew of Carter's discovery of course and nodded as Rachid continued.

'I was the first Egyptologist on the scene, though I had left word that all the other specialists from the nearby University digs should be alerted. I cannot describe what a spectacular sight it was, though the local fellahin were out of their minds with fear, and who could blame them...for this was powerful magic! Rachid, who had been pacing the room, stopped to look at the painting as he continued.

'I could not at first believe that this phenomenon could be real, but as I walked up to it and touched it, it was solid, and there was no doubt, it was there! I looked at the inscription and I could not understand it. It was totally alien to any form of hieroglyphics I have seen... it was in a word, indecipherable! This was also the opinion of all the other experts – locally resident Egyptologist's who had arrived on the scene in response to my summons, some in overcoats thrown over their pyjamas...can you imagine their faces?' A hint of a smile flittered across Rachid's face as he recalled the momentous event.

Luckily the American team had brought your father with them. He was working for them as an artist; this was two years ago, and I shall never forget the date. It was the twenty first of June – the dawn of the summer solstice! They had cameras of course, but your father was able to make an accurate facsimile drawing of the inscription from the ground, though we were making preparations to rig up scaffolding.' Rachid turned to look at Luke.

'But before any real work could be done on it, it started to crumble...'

'What!' Luke gasped.

'Yes' Rachid sighed, 'as the sun came up over the eastern desert and its rays hit the Obelisk, it started to disintegrate. There was nothing we could do. It had been like a brand new block of granite, its surface polished and without a trace of erosion...but it just crumbled into pieces in front of the team. Jock had just finished copying the last of the hieroglyphics before he was ordered back and we all watched as slivers of the hard rock fell down to the base and the whole megalith lay in rubble at our feet.

'My God,' Luke exhaled in a whistle of surprise, 'how, could that be possible?'

'Oh, don't think we didn't try to find a logical reason – pollution, internal fusion, ultra-violet ray damage, but no one could ever explain its disintegration just as no one could explain its sudden emergence....it was a supernatural event! So of course, as all the evidence had gone, we decided there and then to keep it quiet. We all had our reputations to think of and we didn't want to lose our funding on the basis of being cranks. The press were never informed, and the locals who had seen it were bribed to keep their mouth's shut.

'What about the copy of the inscription which Father made?' Luke asked.

'Now' Rachid started pacing again. 'That was the next strange thing. 'Your father took the hand-drawn facsimile of the inscription back to his studio at Chicago House, the expeditions headquarters in Luxor, and made blue prints of them. They were handed out to all the Egyptologists who had been present that miraculous morning, but before they could begin to decipher the strange text, although they all agreed that it said something about Time, the image faded and they were left staring at a blank sheet of paper...

'And the original?' Luke asked.

'Please' Rachid put his hand on Luke's shoulder. 'What I have to tell you is an assumption, and I may be wrong...I hope I am wrong, but it does cast a shadow over my good friend, your father. Please hear me out before you throw me out'

'Go on' Luke said cautiously, not liking the sound of what was to come.

'I believe' Rachid said, 'and I may be wrong – that your father used the original to transcribe onto this painting,' he looked at the large canvas over the mantelpiece. 'For whatever reason, he encoded the text of the phantom Obelisk onto this painting, for the original drawing just disintegrated...'

'What!' Luke exclaimed. 'You mean Father mislead everyone...'

Rachid raised his hand. 'Perhaps he was disenchanted with his work; he was paid to pittance you know. He once described himself as an intellectual's labourer. Perhaps he wanted to rejoice in the knowledge that this, his copy, was the only one extent...it happens in all professions, not just impoverished artists. To be in sole possession of some fact or object is what drives collectors to collect...reflected glory I think it is called.'

'So he doctored the blue prints so they faded, and did something similar to the original, after he had made his own copy? Luke summarised.

'Yes' Rachid said 'Perhaps... though of course he professed all ignorance of it.'

'Well he would, wouldn't he' Luke stated the obvious.

'Yes of course' Rachid conceded, 'but I was never to see him again, for he disappeared shortly afterwards.

'So that was when he went missing!' Luke said, his eyes brightening, 'after the discovery, if that is the right word, for the vanishing Obelisk! I mean all we got here was a telegram stating that he had left the headquarters of the University at Chicago House.

'Yes' Rachid said, 'that was very unfortunate. The Director thought he had left, possibly to take the news of this mythical Obelisk to the Western press and in the light of the duff blue-prints, they had all his things packed up from his apartment, and I got a phone call...could I store them. They were very upset about his walking out, as they put it.'

'Oh Father,' Luke groaned, looking around the room with Slater's painting and effects piled up. 'Why do you have to be such a flake!'

'So it is that I bring Jock's paintings back to his estate,' Rachid interrupted Luke's thoughts, ' and I am sorry that it is on this sad occasion of your Father's funeral... but', he said grasping Luke's shoulder again, 'I *do not believe he is dead*!'

23

'What!' Luke was knocked back into the present.

'I think he did not die, and that was not his body found in the tombs at The Valley of the Kings, for the corpse was unidentifiable. And I believe you have buried someone else!'

Luke's eyes watered as he clutched Rachid's arm

'Thank you, friend of my father. Thank you for those words. For I too know he is not dead. But where is he?'

'I have been pondering on this ever since Jock disappeared' Rachid said, 'and I have come to the conclusion that he did not destroy the copies of the Obelisk's text for his own ends.' 'He did it to protect the Egyptologist's who were in receipt of this information.

'Protect?' Luke exclaimed, his face a blank

'Yes, I think he discovered something... something which I am not sure of, but which *may* be capable of doing harm... *some evil force!*'

'To do with the inscription?' Luke guessed

'Yes, I do believe it has the power to destroy.' 'Was it not itself destroyed when its own message was copied?'

'Hum' Luke thought for a while, as he turned to look at the painting.

'So, by implication, this painting of father's carries a dangerous message.'

'I think it is an inscription of evil which is part of a force of which we have no, or very little knowledge.' Rachid stated flatly. 'And I suggest that *you destroy the painting!*'

Chapter Two
*** Ishtar ***

Luke was walking around the grounds of Park House. He loved the views across the estuary that was turned to gold as the ragged clouds raced across the wild windy autumn sky and their shadows moved over the hills, sunlight glinting from the Obelisk standing solitarily atop the hill of the Rhinn O' Doon bay. The kellstone, the locals called it, yet no one knew who had built it or for what purpose.

Still a guest of the house, Rachid had gone to his room, having talked sbout a migraine coming on, and Luke had to admit that all that talk in father's studio had given *him* a headache. Still he felt better to be out in the fresh air as the wind tugged at his blond hair.

On arriving back at the house, there had been a phone call for Rachid who had stood in the hall talking again animatedly in Arabic, after which he had told Luke that Dr. Labachi and his assistant would be at Park House within the hour. Bridget had returned from her trip, her hair windswept, and having overheard the conversation, had in a strangely tremulous voice asked Rachid if he would like to bring his famous guest to dinner, afterwards whispering to Luke to dress for dinner; Bridget was obviously taking these new guests a bit too seriously.

Suitably attired, Luke went into the sitting room and poured himself a scotch. The nights were drawing in, and he was glad that Hanna, the housekeeper had made up the fire.

The gong for dinner went and Luke walked through into the dining room. Hanna had done her best, no doubt on Mother's instructions. The long table was laid with silver service and the log-fire crackled in the carved stone fireplace. The shutters had been closed and the flicker of firelight on the pinewood lent a warm effect to the room. Two of Slater's small paintings hung on either wall facing each other and the whole scene had a calming atmosphere about it.

Luke stood behind his accustomed chair at the head of the table as Bridget came in, carrying some flowers for the centre of the table. 'Luke,' she whispered, would you mind letting Dr. Labachi have the head of the table,' Luke coloured slightly at the suggestion but moved readily enough. 'Hanna' Bridget shouted towards the kitchen, can you hold on for a few minutes.'

The doorbell went and Bridget dashed along the hall as Rachid came down the staircase. Together they greeted the famous Dr. Labachi and his assistant, taking their coats and Luke heard the sounds of laughter as the guests walked towards the dining room, feeling a bit hurt at being left out of the greeting ceremony, particularly after vacating his rightful place at head of table. Bridget led the way into the dining room and showed them in and Luke looked in curiosity at the imminent arrival of the legendary archaeologist.

Rachid entered first, he was dressed in a black evening suit with a diamond pin holding a spotless white shirt at the collar. He stood to one side and ushered in a man in similar attire, yet whose long white hair was windswept and unruly; he looked like a genius, or a mad professor. Luke shook Dr. Labachi's hand and stood aside as the Egyptologist, his hand around her shoulder, presented his assistant.

Luke stood there with his mouth open. She was a woman of indeterminate age, and yet of pure complexion. Her hair was jet black and combed into a fringe which was held by a silver band on which was mounted a silver crescent moon. Her dark expressive eyes were outlined with black kohl extending in a line to each side; she was the epitome of an Ancient Egyptian, except for the lotus flower.

She wore a transparent gown of pleated white which revealed in every detail the exquisite beauty of her body as Luke, moving in a trance, took her proffered hand and she smiled at him. He could smell her perfume of Oil of Lotus, and his hand trembled when she squeezed it in a strong grip.

'Allow me to introduce Ishtar,' Dr. Labachi said, 'my daughter and my assistant.'

Luke mumbled something stupid as the professor laughed, saying: 'Don't worry, Ishtar normally has that sort of effect on the opposite sex...beautiful she may be, but she is also a gifted scholar.'

'I don't doubt that' Luke affirmed finding his voice at last.

'Come' Bridget said. 'Let us sit down and eat. You have had a tiring journey.'

Dr. Labachi nodded. 'That is so, but this bit of the countryside is a refreshing change from the antiquities of the British Museum' he laughed again.

'Though,' he continued, his manner becoming serious, as if in compensation of his misplaced levity, 'I do want to give you both my heartfelt condolences on the loss of Jock. He was a good friend and a talented artist. Please accept this small token in our memory of him.' He handed Bridget a small package of expensive-looking embossed green paper, tied neatly with a golden ribbon as Luke watched in fascination.

'Thank you,' Bridget replied, her eyes were starting to water a little and her hand shook, 'may I open it now.' She untied the cord and unfolded the green paper, which was embossed with small hieroglyphics. Inside was a black oblong box. She lifted the lid and gasped, picking out the object from the padded box; it was a solid gold Obelisk!

'I don't know what to say,' she turned to Luke 'it is truly wonderful' she said, her voice trembling as much as her hands. 'Thank you...I will treasure it...in Jock's name...'

Bridget placed the golden Obelisk in the centre of the dining table and dabbed her eyes with an embroiled handkerchief, trying desperately to recover her composure. Soup was served and the others engaged in small talk as Bridget brightened.

Ishtar was seated opposite Luke and he found it very difficult to keep his mind on the conversation, for the radiance of her beauty beneath the black Egyptian hairstyle seemed to fill the whole room. He asked her about the flight from London to Glasgow and about her work, and she replied in impeccable English. It transpired that though she was born in Cairo, she had spent most of her life in London, where her father Dr. Labachi had been doing most of his research into Obelisks at the British Museum.

'Do you go back to Egypt very often' Luke asked.

'Now and again' Ishtar replied. 'Though I prefer to travel to Ancient Egypt... it is far nicer.' Her voice was casual, a hint of a mischievous smile played about the corners of her sensuous mouth.

'Of course' Luke concurred thinking she was joking.

'No' she said 'I am serious. I go back in my dreams. I astral travel!'

Luke was silent, not sure what to say. He didn't know if this haughty beauty was taking him for a ride or whether she was serious; serious in her own mind.

'What about Nethertime' he said finally, 'ever astral travelled there?'

'I have never tried' her expression was enigmatic, her eyes unfathomable, 'I think it would be a bit too medieval for me, all those Djinns and evil spirits; you know.'

Dr. Labachi laughed. 'Please forgive my daughter,' he apologised on her behalf, 'but she does have a penchant for sounding mysterious.' Ishtar continued with her meal, unperturbed at her father's slight.

Dinner finished, Luke rose and going to the oak cabinet, poured brandy for the men, and liqueurs for the ladies. Dr. Labachi was talking volubly from the head of the table about his experiences in Egypt, as Bridget, her face flushed, listened attentively, laughing at his stories. Luke couldn't help feel a little jealous; Not only was the Egyptologist sitting in his father's rightful place, but he was stealing the limelight...if only Jock Slater were here, Luke thought, he would out-story tell this self important, over confident man.

'But this find is amazing' Dr. Labachi's arms embraced the room, 'that Jock's painting should incorporate a copy of the vanished Obelisk.'

'You know of this then' Luke asked from the drink's cabinet.

'Yes' he said 'Haram has of course told me the news. I was one of the first to witness this strange occurrence.'

'I phoned him' Rachid said 'He was in Luxor at the time, didn't I mention it...' Luke frowned, perhaps he had, he shrugged 'You may have' he said.

'What is this vanished Obelisk?' Bridget asked and Rachid explained his theory to her.

'Your husband was some man' he added. 'We thought the copy of the text was lost forever.'

'Gentleman' Luke said, getting a bit tired of the conversation 'Would you like to bring your brandies to the studio, and look at the painting.

Dr. Labachi rose, not accustomed to being ordered about, but nevertheless bowing. Bridget noticed that the ladies were not included in the viewing; there was something of the male chauvinist about her son that she did not like.

Luke strode down the great gothic hall and unlocked the door to his father's studio. Rachid ushered Labachi in and clutching his brandy, the professor walked up to the painting. He muttered something under his breath in Arabic and Rachid stiffened.

'May the Prophet be merciful.' Labachi exclaimed as he stood mesmerised in front of the painting 'Jock Slater. Your name will go down in history!' His eyes were ecstatic as he read the inscription on the painted Obelisk aloud. Luke glanced at his watch, noting it was nearly ten o'clock, and turned to look at the academic.

'I thought you said it could not be translated' Luke queried, looking at Rachid

'Dr. Labachi is an authority on these hieroglyphics' Rachid replied weakly, 'only he is able to decipher them.'

'But this is outstanding' Labachi exclaimed 'this is without parallel...it is the precursor of all the Obelisks of Oblivion...'

'What?' Luke interjected incredulously, *'Obelisks of Oblivion*. What in the name of God are they?'

'We can use this!' Ignoring the youth, Labachi turned to Rachid. 'We can use this to stamp out the *Order of the One Dimension*!' Luke's mind was in a whirl.

'Do you have paper Master Luke?' The professor asked, his face bathed in a fine sweat, 'Can I make a hand-copy?'

'No!' Luke replied emphatically. 'You cannot! Not until you tell me what is going on!' He ushered them to the door and led them down the hall.

'You have some explaining to do,' he said as they joined the ladies in the sitting room, Ishtar exchanging meaningful glances with the culprits.

Luke stood in the doorway as the men sat down; his face was resolute.

'Please explain your recent remarks to everyone here,' he insisted as he looked with concern at Bridget and Ishtar.

'Allow me' Ishtar rose and beckoned for Luke to be seated. He closed the door and sat on one of the several settees, colouring slightly. Ishtar stood in front of the fire, its lambent glow throwing her lithe body into silhouette as Luke swallowed hard at the beauty of her figure.

'You are obviously talking about the Obelisk of Time' her voice was mellifluous and soothing, 'and of its properties in its ability to resurrect the Obelisk of Oblivion, are you not...?'

'We were' Luke said weakly, 'or they were' he gestured to Labachi and Rachid 'Though I do not know how you could be aware of it.'

'It matters not' Ishtar continued, 'let me try to explain,' she looked around the room as the back light from the low- burning logs radiated through her pleated dress of fine linen and Luke tried to keep his mind on the subject under discussion.

'The Obelisk of Time is a marker. An ancient people erected it, to protect and forewarn of catastrophe and it is connected to others through channels of power that are incomprehensible to our modern world. It reappears on the summer solstice every three thousand years, so it has never previously been recorded, well not in modern times. Its physical status is of no import, as it reasserts it presence, and then crumbles into an alien, or unknown to us, form of energy...'

'How can you know all this?' Luke asked, his eyes transfixed.

'I and my father have studied it, as we have all the known Obelisks in the world...and believe you me, there are many thousands of them.' Ishtar replied, her dark eyes like magnets into the otherworld.

'What about the order of the One Dimension' Luke threw at her, remembering Labachi's words. Ishtar froze. Her smile, painted onto her face, slipped, to be replaced by an expression of anger mixed with hatred. 'You have a lot to answer for; she spat at her father. 'You have opened your mouth beyond the limits of caution...'

Labachi's face was abysmal as Bridget and Luke, startled at the sudden change in the beautiful woman's face, exchanged anxious glances. Luke's mind was racing.

'I am sorry' Ishtar composed herself, smoothing down her sheer gown. 'I have been working too hard, so have we all... I am a little overwrought, please forgive my silly outburst.' She looked around the startled faces and continued in her enrapturing vein.

'We believe that the Order of the One Dimension is an arcane cult, which goes back beyond recorded history. The Ancient Egyptians were aware of it, and it was the evil powers of this cult that corrupted them into their darker passions... the scenes of carnal desires, copulation between hybrids and mutants on the walls of the crypt at the Temple of Dendera, for instance....'

'So why do you need the inscription?' Luke interrupted. There was some hidden agenda here and he was going to get to the bottom of it.

'For scholarship only' Ishtar replied disarmingly, staring into Luke's eyes as he felt the room swim in front of him and her will bore into his.

'I see,' he said feebly 'well that's all right then. Forgive me for being so protective of Father's little find' he felt as weak as a kitten.

Bridget rose, her eyes half-closed. 'It is late,' she said, her voice distant. 'Please be our guests for tonight. Your rooms are prepared. Perhaps we will talk tomorrow.' She walked heavily to the door and pausing for a moment, looked back uncertainly, and then went up the stairs.

'She has had a gruelling day' Ishtar said, looking at Luke. 'Thank you for your hospitality and I hope you will accept our apologies for broaching such difficult subjects.' Luke felt his eyes devour her as he looked at the divine figure standing in front of the fire. 'Can you find your way,' he said 'I must sleep now, I am very tired.'

'Goodnight' Labachi and Rachid said, but as Luke stood at the door he could hear them talking in Arabic, their voices though heated, were lowered to a whisper.

✳✳✳

In the Solway Firth, a trawler battered its way through the breaking waves. The lights of Kirkcudbright harbour could be seen in the distance as the skipper stood, a solitary figure at the wheel. They had been out for three days, trawling for queenies, the only shellfish left in these overfished waters. The Spaniards had come in beyond the three mile exclusion zone and taken all that remained of the flounders and catfish, and had gone back to their own country with never a word of rebuke from the bloody government; how were the Scots supposed to earn a living if foreigners were allowed to fish in their rightful territory? It was hard enough in the old days when there *were* fish to be caught, but dragging for queenies was the end of the line; the skipper, Dougal thought, smiling at his little pun.

The sea had calmed a bit during the dogwatch and Dougal leaned on the wheel, rolling up a cigarette. The mist was coming down now though as the ebb tide drew the strands of cloud out into the shallow waters of Kelpie Bank; the lights of the town grew dim and faded as Dougal steered an approach course based on his uncanny knowledge of these treacherous waters.

Just to be sure, Dougal switched on the antiquated decca navigator, and relaxed as he saw his position verified by the radio beacons. In the old days, fishermen had steered this difficult estuary blind, and he couldn't help but be reassured by the green light vectors on the screen that gave him a fairly accurate plot of his position.

He puffed on his roll up, sure in the fact that in an hour or so he would be with his cronies in the Harbour Tavern, downing a pint or two and recounting the endless stories which abounded in this remote, yet tightly knit fishing community.

From the bridge he could see the black waters of the estuary coursing past the vessel and the white froth of the bow wave became more directional as the waves abated. Dougal tapped the Decca Navigator; it was not showing the radio beacon from the Kellstone atop the Rhin O' Doon hill, the local fishermen's marker for a safe entry into the channel. He looked out form the small bridge deck yet could see nothing but a white mist surging towards the trawler's bow. He glanced back at the wheelhouse chronometer; it showed one minute to ten – should he ring six-bells or take the vessel in himself and let the other's sleep; God knows they were exhausted after the recent three days at sea.

Dougal looked out again into the swirling mist. Suddenly, it parted and he caught a glimpse of the kellstone, but it wasn't right – there was something odd about it – it seemed to radiate some sort of unnatural and spooky presence that sent a chill shiver down his neck. Dougal checked his position – was this the same marker that he had used time and time again? As the mist cleared, to be sure, it *was* the kellstone, but it was glowing in an otherworldly golden light, its straight vector cutting through the swirling fog. He stepped into the wheelhouse and adjusted his course; he had a visual. What a story he would have for the lads in the Harbour Tavern this night. Yet he could not help but wonder at the weirdness of that golden light, and he took a stiff draught of scotch from the near empty bottle.

Chapter Three
*** The Coven ***

Luke awoke, his body running with sweat. He had experienced a nightmare more terrifying than any he had previously known. It had been about the Obelisks and their powers to destroy, and he was shivering in the memory of it. The mesmerising words of Ishtar had riddled his brain and he sensed that there was some force, something inhuman and evil about her; yet he could not get the image of her bewitching face and body out of his mind.

He got out of bed and threw on his clothes; he had to get some fresh air, and try to pull himself together. The landing was dark except for one errant ray of moonlight that shone down from the casement at the end of the long gallery. Luke crept silently down the gothic staircase and let himself out into the grounds of the manor house, walking towards the topiary gardens.

The moon lit his way, like a white beacon moving through silver-edged clouds that floated across the blue-black velvet of night as he wound his way though the formal gardens towards the copse of Scot's pine. The wood was silhouetted jet-black against the windswept sky as he walked along the leaf- strewn path and up to a wooden bench situated on a slight rise.

The silver moon sailed out from behind torn fragments of cloud and bathed the clearing in the copse in a sparkle of white light, hitting the edge of his father's sarcophagus, the white marble gleaming in the ethereal light; it was difficult to imagine that the remains of Jock Slater were inside that giant, almost vulgar edifice. Then his thoughts were interrupted. As Luke watched from the bench under a large yew tree, he heard subdued voices and saw three monk-like figures walking through the topiary gardens towards the pinewood. They came into the clearing and walked up to the sarcophagus and Luke's eyes narrowed as he tried to identify them, but the cowls of their black robes were up, hiding their faces.

As he watched, hidden from view by the overhanging branches of the yew tree, he saw one of the figures throw off her robe and Luke recognised the white flowing tunic of Ishtar, her transparent costume fluttering in the breeze as the moonlight picked out her sylph-like form; the other two must be Rachid and Labachi, Luke deduced.

Luke focussed on the divine shape of Ishtar and he watched in fascination as she started to dance, but a dance like no other dance he had ever seen. Her back arched unnaturally and her hands touched the ground behind her, the curve of her body thrown into silhouette. She straightened; the tempo of her dance increased and Luke's ears were confounded by an unearthly singing that seemed to permeate his whole being. Ishtar's movements grew increasingly erotic and as Luke watched her lascivious gyrations, he was torn between desire for her and outrage: outrage that she should dare disport herself so near to his father's tomb – even if he were not resident in it. This dilemma was avoided when suddenly the ethereal figure stopped dancing and the singing was cut dead; now all Luke could hear was the rustle of leaves blowing along the ground, although his ears were ringing with the celestial music.

Luke pinched himself to make sure this was still not some continuation of his nightmare, watching mesmerised to see the silvery figure, her arms outstretched, leave the ground slowly in an effortless, gravity-defying 'drift', to 'float up' onto the top of the sarcophagus, her sensuous form a ghostly emanation as her body lay stretched across the white marble tomb. This compounded his outrage against the memory of his father and Luke vacillated once more between the conflicting emotions of family loyalty and curiosity; yet he bided his time.

He heard the hooded figures chanting and the otherworldly singing return as Ishtar lay supine on the gleaming monument. Luke's attention was drawn now to a ray of light behind him, and turning, he saw the Kellstone on the far hill glowing in an eerie glare.

Simultaneously, Luke scarce able to believw what he saw, a giant transparent golden obelisk arose from the sarcophagus and towered up into the dark stormy sky, its translucent tapering shape shimmering and dancing along its gilded edges; it without substance. The volume of the angelic choir increased and Luke's ears started to bleed as he saw the spectral shape of Ishtar rise up the narrowing column of the shaft of golden light, disappearing gradually from sight as she reached the top. The sound stopped, the Obelisk and Ishtar were gone as the two figures walked slowly back to the house. Luke sat on the bench, his body shaking in spasmodic convulsions; he felt a warm trickle of blood running down his jaw from his bleeding ears; his body was a block of ice, he was petrified with terror!

Hugging his arms around him, Luke sat for a long while, his fear gradually subsiding and his shivering now due as much to the cold and a growing anger as to the terror he had recently felt. He tried to rationalize what he had seen but there were no rational explanations to be had; he had witnessed a supernatural event! If he had disbelieved Rachid's account of the sudden apparition of the Obelisk of Time as he had described it to him in the studio, then that doubt had been swept away - for he too had seen just a moment ago the ghostly emanation of a terrifying and unnatural force.

He had to throw away any modern concept of physics, for unless it was all hallucination, he had just witnessed magic – and black magic at that! Ishtar had said she astral travelled, and Luke had thought she was trying only to make an impression, but that was not the case; she was for real!

As he got up slowly and walked cautiously back to the house, he wondered where she was now. She had faded at the top of that spectral vortex of shimmering golden light and had vanished into some unknown dimension. That was it...he had it! The Order of the One Dimension! They were of the cult. Hiding behind the respectability of their professions... they were cultists!

The landing was dark and quiet as he gained his bedroom and locked the door. He bathed his bloodied ears in the wash hand basin, being as quiet as he could, and got into bed. They hadn't seen him in the pinewood copse and that was one slight advantage he had over these frightening people; but he was going to find out more!

✳✳✳

Abrams had decided to stay on another night at the Selkirk Arms, though he didn't relish too much being in the land that time forgot. His ears had burnt with the salacious gossip about the goings on at Park House in the bar the previous evening, and although he was not at home in this neck of the woods, he was not going back empty handed; he was going back to London with the new Slater painting!

He had eaten a good meal at the up-market hotel, and now fancied a walk around the town before retiring. He had walked along the High Street with its neat little rows of houses painted in their pretty colours of grey – green and ochre's, and past the Tollbooth, the old jail in which, or so he had read, John Paul Jones, the founder of the American Navy had been imprisoned, and which now stood in foreboding and neglected darkness. He passed the Hornel Gallery, and made a mental note to visit it in the morning. Hornel was a renowned Scottish colourist, one of the Glasgow boys, and had recently enjoyed a bit of revival - perhaps he could pick up some small paintings on the cheap.

Passing a ruined castle: Maclellan's Castle, the rusty sign said, and looking out onto the harbour and river Dee, Abrams saw a trawler making its way up the estuary. Ribbons of white mist lay across the muddy waters and it looked like some sort of phantom ship from another age.

Across the square Abrams saw the lights of the Harbour Tavern beckoning, and thought he would have a nightcap. All eyes turned in his direction as he walked into the dingy bar and ordered a large scotch. At the end of the dilapidated snug were some rum-looking characters regarding him with hostile stares, but Abrams was pretty thick-skinned and he struck up a conversation with the pretty barmaid.

He told her about the stories he had heard about Park House the previous evening. She listened whilst she polished glasses, her blue eyes wide as Abrams embellished them with tales of nude orgies and devil worship and she broke off to serve a customer, still listening.

'Mad Artist used to live there,' Her customer, a thickset fisherman offered, getting the gist of the conversation. 'Painted naked woman as if they were going out o' fashion! He winked at the barmaid. 'Does nay surprise me yin wee bit' he said; he was a man of the world.

'All tha' galavantin' aroond in their altigither...anywa', the mon's deed now...so may tha geed lord bless him!' The fisherman downed his pint, looking at Abrams for a top-up; Talk was not cheap. Abrams begrudgingly obliged.

Just then the door burst open and a man staggered in. His yellow fisherman's oilskin shone wetly in the murky tavern as he staggered up to the bar 'Geet me a bottle!' he ordered breathlessly, curtly cutting in from Abrams' order. The barmaid obeyed. The entire bar was silent as they watched the man take a hefty swig of the neat Scotch whisky, his hands shaking.

'Jees Dougal' the thick set man said, standing away from the bar, 'what's tha matter wi yer mon? Ye look as if yer've seen a ghost!'

'Tha Kellston' Dougal blurted. 'It's no right. It's bewitched 'o something...it was lit up like a golden torch 'o the very De'il himself!'

Abrams left the bar and the mad old boys. They were of a different time, and he just wanted to get back to his own little world of gallery openings and deals, yet he would not go without the painting. The town was silent as he retraced his steps and headed out into the dark countryside towards Park House. Why he was the one who had supported Slater in his mainly thin years. He was the one who had stretched up that strange, yet valuable painting, and he was going to have it!

As he retraced his steps of the previous evening, the moon broke through the ragged cloud and bathed the road in a snaking ribbon of moonlight; in the distance he could see the forbidding silhouette of Park House; all was in darkness. He tried one window, then another; it opened and he felt his way through the laundry room and into the dark hallway. The studio door was locked but this did not deter him. Unwinding the key ring with a bit of difficulty, he inserted it into the antique keyhole, and jemmied the door.

Moving cautiously into the darkened studio, he saw the painting he was after still in place over the mantelpiece. He was about to lift it off when he saw a flicker of something. He stepped back, not sure what he had seen and watched, his piscine eyes bulbous - then the Obelisk in the painting started to glow. At first he thought it was a trick of the light, some reflection from a passing car headlight through the window, but as he watched, Abrams was transfixed, for a blinding golden light shot out from the painting and the Obelisk hovered in realistic detail in front of his incredulous eyes.

Abrams backed away, a preternatural feeling of horror knotting his bowels and as he turned, he saw through the window the giant glimmering Obelisk of Oblivion rise up from the nearby pinewood. It was too much for him, and like a drunken man, he stumbled out the way he had come; out through the window and onto the road, his body shaking in a contortion of terror as he ran back to the town. The last taxi was just pulling out to go home. 'The station,' he shouted desperately, 'take me to the bloody station in Dumfries!' his hands trembled as he got in. 'It'll be double, this time o' night.' the Taxi driver said cynically. 'It doesn't matter' Abrams shouted, 'Just get me away from this infernal place!'

Chapter Four
*** The Obelisk ***

Luke woke early. The grey light of dawn was peeping through the gap in the shutters. He lay for a moment, his mind recalling the events of the previous evening; the shining golden Obelisk, the lascivious dancing of Ishtar bathed in moonlight, and the sinister chanting of the hooded figures of the cult.

He was about to get out of bed, his mind was awhirl with the strange and macabre ritual he had witnessed the night before, when the door of his bedroom opened slowly - though he was sure he had locked it. He feigned sleep and saw a lithe figure attired in a pleated white gown of transparent gossamer move silently into the room. She went to the shutters, opening the central one of the three windows, and stood for a moment silhouetted against the grey light. Her hourglass body was revealed through the thin linen shift; in its centre, the dark triangle of her pubis, and Luke felt his passion rise as he devoured the divine form of Ishtar.

The ghostly figure moved towards his bed, as with eyes nearly closed Luke saw the perfect oval of her ivory face framed by lustrous black hair bend over him as she placed her full warm lips on his. Her hard black nipples pushed into his nightshirt as she pressed her firm breasts against his chest and he smelt the arousing scent of her oil of Lotus perfume and the natural musk of her body and his loins hardened with desire.

'I will teach you to travel with me' she breathed onto his lips as he pretended to sleep. 'You and I will be one, and travel to the ends of Time,' she stroked his pulsing temple with her delicate fingers and pushed back his damp blond hair.

Then she was gone, and Luke cursed himself for not taking her body to his own, which was now on fire and longing to be united with her flesh. He did not care about her affiliations, her membership of the cult, or her supernatural powers, which had terrified him. All he knew was that he was consumed by desire for her and that he would travel to the ends of the earth with her, or do anything she bid. His aroused manhood gushed out onto his tight stomach and down onto the sheets as he held the memory of her dawn visitation in his mind's eye - and then he drifted into a strange and languorous sleep in which she and he were riding upon the ether, high above the world, embroiled in an embrace of carnal lust that saw the sun and moon rise and set.

Bridget was up just after dawn and quickly washed and dressed, she was feeling a lot better - energetic in fact, and put her torpor of the previous evening down to stress: the awful stress of the funeral and perhaps a little too much sherry. She descended the great gothic staircase and made her way to the kitchen; she would prepare breakfast for her famous guest, Dr. Labachi.

Luke would be down soon, for he usually rose early and did his run around Saint Mary's Isle before coming back for a hearty breakfast.

Hanna would not be in for an hour or so and she relished being in control of her own kitchen again. Soon a griddle of haggis, bacon, sausage, eggs and tomatoes were under her expert control; she would give her scholarly guests a good send off.

Dr. Labachi was the first one down, sauntering into the vast, Bavarian-style kitchen in a casual dress of tracksuit and trainers. He approached the busy woman and grasping her around the waist murmured: 'What a delicious smell, my dear, are you cooking the breakfast of all time?' Bridget flushed and busied herself with the eggs. 'Sit down Dr. Labachi, I'll get you some coffee.' Labachi released her and wondered around the kitchen. 'You remember Cairo, don't you, my dearest?'

It was a memory that Bridget had been trying hard to forget. It had been her first time in that mysterious country of Egypt, when she had been young, and pregnant with Luke. Jock had mistaken her flight time, arriving only minutes too late to greet his wife, whilst Dr. Labachi had, by some strange coincidence, been at the arrivals area and made the connection that she was the wife of the new artist whom the University had recently employed. He had introduced himself, ordered her luggage speeded through customs, and swept her into a taxi to the Garden City Hotel in Cairo.

Jock had stood at the airport for hours looking at the flight lists, only to be told by an official that his wife had arrived and had been met by a prominent Egyptologist, and was now, presumably, somewhere in Cairo.

In those days immediately following the six-day war with Israel, communications had not been good, and the professor had shown her the sights of Cairo as she waited for word of her husband. Jock had finally tracked her down to the Garden City Hotel, but by that time it had been too late and his wife had succumbed to the youthful charms of the handsome scholar. Bridget had experienced deep pangs of guilt about their intense, but brief affair, and she had kept it a secret all these years from the one she had always loved; her estranged husband, Jock Slater.

As her ex lover stood there now in the country kitchen of this remote house in Scotland, looking at her as he had done all those years ago, she felt as if the old memories were rekindled and a deep rouge rose up her neck and onto her face.

'You are still as beautiful as the day I first saw you at Cairo airport, my dearest' Labachi intoned in his silk- smooth voice.

Bridget turned from the breakfast array and walked into the embrace of her former lover, as the eggs griddled themselves to a frazzle on the stove.

A discreet cough proceeded Rachid's entry into the kitchen. He looked elsewhere as the couple disentangled themselves; he was such a gentleman.

'Please' Bridget said trying to compose herself. 'Please sit down in the dining room...I have a Scottish breakfast for you...' Rachid took Labachi's arm and led him away, muttering something under his breath in Arabic, as Bridget tried to resurrect the breakfast.

Bridget's eyes were downcast, as she brought in the near-cremated remains of her Scottish breakfast, but Labachi and Rachid tucked into it as if it were heaven sent. Ishtar arrived halfway through the meal, her body draped in a solemn black cloak; she smiled briefly at Bridget and drank a glass of orange juice. Luke was nowhere to be seen.

'My dear,' Labachi addressed Bridget after finishing the last scrap of the burnt meal, 'that was the most delicious breakfast I have ever eaten!' Bridget nodded, casting an embarrassed glance in the direction of her ex lover's daughter. Labachi continued: 'I realise your difficulty in retaining this superb estate, particularly in the light of the demise of our beloved friend.' His voice was contrived and deferential as he steeled himself for the big question.

'Could we ask you to part with the recent painting?' he emphasised 'part.'

'I would like to purchase it from you. I will give you ten thousand pounds for it...' Bridget's eyes flickered. That sort of money would be very useful to a woman in her predicament, yet she felt a reciprocal pull against selling; it was, after all a masterpiece. 'Twenty' she said nervously.

'Agreed' Labachi affirmed, taking an embossed chequebook from his tracksuit, he had obviously come prepared.

'On two conditions' It was Luke standing in the doorway, having overheard Labachi's and his mother's agreement, 'One is that is you explain your real interest in the painting... and two, that you help me get to Nethertime... so that I can bring father back!'

Labachi, Rachid and Ishtar jumped nervously in their seats on hearing the unexpected voice behind them, and cast each other meaningful looks before Labachi recovered his equilibrium.

'Very well,' the professor smiled ambiguously 'would you allow us an hour in the studio' he looked at Bridget, who nodded, colouring slightly.

The three men and Ishtar walked down the hall. The studio door was ajar. 'Have you been in here?' Luke asked turning to Rachid and Habachi. 'They shook they heads, in obvious consternation 'The painting!' they exclaimed simultaneously. It was still there on the wall, as Luke shook his head. 'Maybe I left the door open last night' he said limply, but he knew he hadn't.

The Academic moved into the centre of the room. 'To business.' He spoke curtly. 'You ask about my interest...my *real* interest in this painting,' Labachi was looking intently at it. 'Let me try and be as brief as possible. You may not accept what I have to say, but so be it.'

'This scene represents Aiyu, the Ancient Egyptian concept of Paradise. Now the artist could only have painted it if he had actually been there because it is too detailed to be purely from imagination....So how did he get there? The only way that we know of projecting the physical body through time and space is that of astral travel...where the exponent summons up a ka, or spiritual double and projects it into a conceptual time and space.' Labachi ran a hand through his unruly hair.

'The Ancient Egyptians practised astral travel, but we believe they learnt it from a much older civilisation which is lost to all records. I believe your father learnt the skill of astral travelling whilst he was in Egypt, and did it principally to enhance the other-worldliness of his painting. But, and this we can only guess at, he either *chose* to remain there, in Aiyu, or in Nethertime for reasons unknown, or, he got lost or trapped and could not find his way back.'

'So you really do believe father is alive and is lost out there somewhere and can't get back.' Luke gestured at the painting.

'Yes.' The professor acquiesced and Rachid nodded. 'We have said as much previously.'

'Now Labachi turned to look at Ishtar who stood still as a statue in her long black cloak, her face immobile. 'Will you teach Luke the art my dear....will you teach him how to astral travel and help him reach his father?'

'I will gladly do that.' Ishtar said impassively.' She was a good one at disguising her feelings, Luke thought; himself torn between an overriding desire and utter loathing for her. He was remembering the scene of the previous evening as she floated up that transparent golden monolith, that spectral obelisk, after lying on his father's tomb, but more so, her visitation to his room in the early hours of this morning. A flush of confused allegiances stole across his face at that memory and its outcome, and that surreal dream he had drempt afterward.

'Very well.' Labachi broke into Luke's thoughts. 'That concludes half of the bargain. Now regarding the other of your two conditions, namely our interest in this painting.... This is a little more complex.' The longhaired genius started to pace.

'Now what I have to tell you is for your ears only, and I do not blame you if you scorn my theories... because they are so far fetched that at first your mind will reject them out of hand. All I can ask you to do is to listen, and not to judge what I have to say until I am finished.' Labachi fixed the youth with his intense brown eyes and continued.

'As you are well aware, I am the foremost authority on obelisks in the world, having published many books and scholarly papers. In my research into the obelisk, I made a plan connecting all the known obelisks throughout the world... and there are many! From this research I found that there was a pattern to them. Not a random grouping, but an ordered design as to their positioning, and a point of convergence. This seemed to indicate that there should be a Master Obelisk, a central kingpin if you like, which was missing... until that is, the emergence of the phantom obelisk on that fateful morning two years ago! Now that spectral obelisk we call the Obelisk of Time because it seems to control ancient, and perhaps even modern vectors of time that we believe were used to stabilise, or to keep ordered, unknown forces in the ancient world that could destroy time itself. The inscription on the vanished Obelisk of Time said something to that effect, though we are not exactly sure of its meaning.'

'So the Obelisk of Time is the marker or beacon which controls the others.' Luke asked, trying to get his head around this preposterous theory.

'That's what we believe' Labachi replied. 'But there are dissident forces at work...enemies of this ancient civilisation.'

'The Order of the One Dimension' Luke conjectured.

'Yes, just so' Labachi looked out of the window to the pinewood. 'And some of these dark forces, these dissidents, have also the power to astral travel, though they have another word for it. They have an interest in the Obelisk of Time, and they want to subvert it to their own ends – for in its changed state it becomes the Obelisk of Oblivion!'

'To do that, they need the inscription, hence our great interest in protecting the painting. But there is another copy of the inscription...' Labachi turned to look at Luke.

'Can you tell me who made that magnificent sarcophagus of your father's

'It was made by a stonemason at the Brig'O Dee, Luke said frowning. 'It's about ten miles from here, a remote farmhouse where he has a workshop.

'And who supplied the plans?'

'I did' Luke went to the plan chest in the corner of the studio and leafed through some large drawings, bringing out a vellum drawing and laying it on the table. Labachi and Rachid bent over, scrutinising it then straightened.

'Your father was a canny man' Labachi said 'He sent you this drawing for his own tombstone from Egypt didn't he.'

'Yes' Luke was beginning to get a drift of the conversation, 'It, along with other documents which were quite specific about his own funeral, were sent by the University after he disappeared, though in a sealed roll which he had addressed to me.' Luke rummaged in the pile of the artist's effects and brought out the roll.

'That's Jock's handwriting' Rachid said flatly

'Very well' Labachi picked up the transparent vellum and held it up against the painting, muttering under his breath in Arabic as he correlated the two inscriptions.

'You mean' Luke had finally got it 'Father had the inscription carved onto his tombstone?' Labachi nodded, 'but I do not know why' he said as he put down the plan.

'I have a confession to make' it was Ishtar who spoke, her black hair and cape made one silhouette against the window, like a black widow spider, Luke thought. 'Last night I transgressed. I travelled into Aiyu via the spectral Obelisk. We wanted to see if the inscription on the tomb worked. 'We desecrated your father's grave; I am deeply sorry.'

'I know,' Luke said 'I saw you...'

'You saw us...how?'

'I was there in the grounds, under the yew trees and I was very, very afraid.'

There was a heavy silence as the three stared at Luke. Ishtar walked from the window and put her hands on Luke's shoulders. Her black liquid eyes looked into his and he smelt the musk of her body as he remembered the magical dawn.

'Luke' she breathed, her face close to his. 'Do you believe us?' 'Do you believe in the truth of our mission, or do you think we are devotees of the black art?'

Luke felt his resolution ebb and his will cave in as he looked into those lustrous pools of infinite blackness and he knew that he would float upwards with her into eternity.

'Yes' Luke's voice was distant. 'Yes I believe your mission is just.'

Labachi and Rachid were muttering again in Arabic as Ishtar hugged the entranced youth to her breast and he felt her warm breath against his ear.

'Join us,' she whispered as she held him to her. 'Join us in out fight to overthrow the dark forces of the One Dimension, and I will show you how to reach your father; and I will also show you Paradise!'

'I will' Luke said, his voice choking on the emotion of his infatuation with this enigmatic woman who consumed his body and his mind. 'I will...'

Labachi and Rachid laid their hands on Luke's shoulders. 'It is good my boy.' Labachi said. 'Its good that we have your trust, because we must now strike out the inscription on your father's tomb.'

'What' Luke broke away from their embrace and struggled to reassert his will. 'Why,' he asked 'For what reason?'

'In case it falls into the wrong hands' Labachi answered 'those of the One Dimension, who may use it to destroy the Obelisk of Time...'

'I cannot desecrate my father's tomb.' Luke wrestled with his conscience. 'Even if it is not occupied by him it would be sacrilege!' He looked at Ishtar - into her fathomless dark eyes, feeling his will crumble. 'I will phone the stonemason now,' he said, his voice vacant,

'There is no need' Ishtar held him with her eyes 'I will do it, come...'

They walked out of the studio, into the hall and through the principal door as morning sunlight struck Luke in the face and he squinted against the brightness. They walked through the grounds to the pinewood and up to the blinding white marble effigy; the sargaphagus of his father.

Ishtar stood in front of the inscription, an Eddie of wind tugging at her long black hair that fell over the black cloak. Holding out her hands, she started to incant in a strange unearthly tongue as the end of the inscription started to crumble and fall down onto the yellow and red leaves covering the gravel.

'*Desist!*' a deep voice echoed around the Pinewood.

'By the order of the Eon, the Sacred Writ of Time, *I command you to stop!*' Ishtar froze, the words of the incantation she had been uttering hung aborted on the air as she spun around, her black hair and cape swirling and the others turned to look in the direction of this new voice.

A man in a long blue robe was standing under the yew tree. Long white hair and a beard that swirled across his face softened his stern, gaunt features. In his hand he held a staff that bore a golden ankh at its head. On his feet were golden sandals graced by small wings protruding either side.

'Neb-Ankh' Ishtar muttered to Labachi and Rachid 'Why comes he now?'

'You tamper with the forces beyond you control...forces that will destroy you.' The old man shouted. 'Desecrater that you are...you efface the commands of time...you will perish in the Eternal Void if you extinguish the written word of the Obelisk of Oblivion...'

'Go back Neb-Ankh' Rachid shouted 'resume your dimension. You have no jurisdiction here' Ishtar returned to her backward incantation of the inscription.

As Luke looked at the prophet-like figure, two spectral jaguars appeared at his feet, their transparent muscular forms tensed as they waited for his command.

'I warn you' Neb-Ankh shouted from the yew tree 'You bring down on yourselves the wrath of the Prophets of Time.' He whispered a command and the phantom Jaguars bounded across the leaf-strewn lawn and leaped up in a powerful arc towards Ishtar's back. She turned and faced them, her black eyes fixed on them as they froze, suspended in mid-air, their slavering jaws almost closed upon their prey as Rachid, Labachi and Luke stepped backward, terror written across their faces.

'Enchantress of the underworld' Neb-Ankh called across the lawn. '*Enchant this!*' He pointed the staff with the golden ankh symbol at the two Jaguars, their transparent crystalline forms winking in the sunlight as they metamorphosed into real live beasts - and with white fangs bared against their mottled, sleek heads, they dropped to the ground and paced to and fro waiting for the moment of attack.

Ishtar recited the last of the long inscription as the carved stone disintegrated and dropped down to the floor. She looked at the fierce animals that paced in front of her and murmured some reassuring words as the Jaguars sat and then licked her out-stretched hands and she stroked their sleek heads.

She knelt down and looking into their eyes whispered something unintelligible and the beasts turned and bounded towards Neb-Ankh, snarling, their fangs bared. The old man shouted across the lawn. 'You will perish in your own mischief, you Peddlers of Time,' and with his white hair swirling about his face, he de-materialised into a mist of sparkling silver particles whilst the Jaguars returned to their spectral form, likewise to vanish into the same Time-Void.

Ishtar and the others looked at the spot where Neb-Ankh had disappeared, as Luke exhaled his breath; he wasn't quite sure what or whom he had just seen.

'Who or what in the name of Heaven was that?' he exclaimed.

'That was Neb-Ankh... one of the so-called Prophets of Time of the Order of the One Dimension' Ishtar answered 'and I don't think he will be back. He saw that I destroyed the inscription. He was only here to try and stop me.'

'So that he could copy it?' Luke asked

'Either that or transport the entire sarcophagus into his Dimension.'

'He can do that...'

'Yes...oh yes...he and his kind can do that...and much more if they are so minded. How do you think the giant sarcophagi of the Bulls of Apis at Saquara in Egypt were located in their underground vault when they are larger than the doorway' Ishtar's voice was assertive and Luke didn't really feel like arguing anymore, but he was a stranger to this alternative world that his father's 'friends' had so abruptly dragged him into, his only knowledge of such astonishing events coming from fantasy novels - and this, his very own life, was turning into one!

'What about the Jaguars?' Luke could not hide his curiosity.

'Astral projections' Ishtar replied as if it were a commonplace occurrence.

'Can you do that sort of magic?' Luke asked though he knew the answer.

'If I have to' Ishtar said 'But I prefer mesmerism or atropine...'

'I know of the former, I should do,' Luke rejoined, 'but, what is atropine?'

'It's a crystalline alkaloid extracted from the deadly nightshade or Belldonna berry ... it's a mind bender...' she laughed

'Alright' Luke smiled 'So you have a sense of humour as well as your other dubious gifts.' In spite of himself he was starting to trust her. She was, after all on the side of right...*against* the evil Order of the One Dimension!

'So when are you going to teach me how to astral travel? 'He asked.

'When the moon is full; that's the best time to learn' Ishtar confirmed. 'And there is one tonight!' Luke was about to ask her how she knew but the question seemed too obvious 'Can you stay another night?' he asked, his heart in his mouth, Ishtar turned and spoke rapidly to her father and Rachid in Arabic.

'Iowa, wahed belail bass' Labachi replied, 'one more night.'

'There you are!' It was Bridget carrying a silver tray with five glasses, a decanter of Zabibe and a jug of water 'This has been the longest hour ever, its almost time for lunch.' She put the tray down on the table, unaware of the recent events or their import, and invited her guests to imbibe the aniseed flavoured liquor of the East. 'I don't know how you like, it this Zabibe ....Jock brought it back from his last trip and its been kicking around the place for years; Arak isn't it?'

'Dear Lady,' Labachi rose and bowed 'You have no idea what a joy it is to have a drink like this once more, it costs a fortune in London.'

They filled their glasses 'To Jock,' they toasted, looking at the slightly redressed sarcophagus. After some reassuring small talk, Bridget turned to Labachi and said: 'Last night you were explaining about the Obelisk. Well Hanna has come back with some strange stories from the town. It seems that all the folk of Kirkcudbright are prattling on about the Kellstone...how a fisherman claimed it lit up with a golden glow last night...'

'Ah' Labachi interjected, forestalling Luke who was about to relate his own experiences to his mother, 'A little knowledge is a dangerous knowledge,' he misquoted, looking at Luke and bidding him to be silent, his fingers to his mouth.

'As I was trying to explain to Luke' Labachi rose, his expansive gestures honed in the lecture theatre, encompassed imaginary space.

'Imagine if you will, a people of the Ancient past who discovered something precious – or, who were handed on some arcane knowledge from an older source.' Bridget was trying to imagine it as she sipped the Arak and the bright sunshine dappled the topiary garden and pinewood, reflecting off the white sarcophagus.

'They discovered a secret so profound that they knew if it got into the wrong hands it would wreak havoc upon themselves and any future generations. How would they protect it?' Luke's mind turned over endless possibilities as Bridget frowned in baffled concentration.

'They would make it invisible' Luke answered for his mother.

'Precisely' Labachi turned, like a conjurer or a game show host, which held captive the attention of his audience – poseur - he loves it, Luke thought.

'But first, the professor continued, they would encode it in a set of ciphers so complex as to render them incomprehensible to ordinary people.'

'Like hieroglyphics.' Bridget guessed. 'Writing by and for the priests, which only they could understand; and in that they retained their power.'

'Exactly.... Excellent, Dear Lady' Labachi replied as if he were congratulating a third former with his first attempts at a simultaneous equation. The master of ceremonies continued: 'Well, that is the enigma of the Obelisk of Time. For even though it is no longer visible, we know where it is located ... on the West bank of the Nile... and that it reappears every three thousand years.'

'Unless...unless...the inscription that these ancient people tried so hard to encipher is read out.' Luke supposed.

'Well it *was* read out' Labachi stopped and turned on his heel, his unruly hair flying. 'We read it out last night...and we the grid by doing so.'

'*The grid*?' Bridget asked, her face flushed with confusion helped by the liquor.

'All the inter-linked Obelisks "lit up",' Labachi used the gesture indicating parentheses with his index fingers. 'Yes they lit up, and from the plan I have studied of these local Obelisks, they are connected to the grid...a bit like an electricity grid, only infinitely more powerful' he strode up and down

'And that' he said, pointing across to the Kellstone on top of the distant hills, is what your poor fisherman saw...about ten o'clock last night, was it?'

Bridget nodded. She was in awe of this strange man who once had held a place in her heart and as Luke noticed the expression of rapture on her face everything clicked into place. Father's feckless and disorganised life had led to the direst of consequences; his own mother had been seduced by this man, and still carried a torch for him - but worse; he himself was madly in love with his daughter!

The gong sounded for lunch and they all got up, Rachid offering to carry the tray. 'I don't suggest you tell any of the locals this' Labachi said to Bridget 'They would probably burn us at the stake.'

'Strangely enough' Bridget retorted. 'The last witch to be burnt at the stake was only one mile from here, just beyond Saint Mary's Isle, at Mutehill.'

'I must visit the sight' Labachi said offhandedly, but Ishtar had overheard the conversation and her eyes were alight with a strange glow.

✳✳✳

Hanna was in a state of nervous apprehension as she served lunch. Her hands shook as she struggled to retain her composure. She had learned to live with the strangeness of the situation at the big house. For years she had had to look at the monstrous great paintings of the cavorting harlots and kelpies in foreign lands which hung in the spooky gothic hall, and had peeked into the so called studio when Luke had left it unlocked. There were more of them in there, all stacked up as she prised them apart to wallow in the gratuitous sexual frenzy of a mad artist who should have been given a dose of bromide long ago.

Last night she had been forced to serve the devil incarnate himself as he brought in his tart of a daughter in her flimsy underwear that showed everything she had got; had she no pride!

The other one with his slick hair and fancy car was a mystery. She had even had to find a bed in the stable block across the courtyard for his swarthy shaven-headed servant, (rent boy, more like). Him with his big golden earring that should by rights be on a curtain rail. No these were not the sort of people welcome in this God fearing part of the world; even the "white settlers", the English, who had made a killing down south by selling their property and came up to Scotland to lord it over the locals, had packed up and gone home when they realised they had entered the land that time forgot.

And now there was witchcraft afoot. The poor man Dougal was not a liar, and he was still traumatised at the evil goings-on with the Kellstone. Lighting up all by itself and she had heard more: Roy, the local taxi man had told the whole town about the fare he had taken to the train station at Dumfries. The man had told him of some great obble-isk thing, which had just appeared over Master Slater's tomb; and him just laid to rest. No there was some witchery afoot and she wanted no part of it. She recited her catechism as she lay down the cheese board and her hands shook as she placed the knife on the board. Her duties done, Hanna went back into the kitchen and uncorked the bottle of Sherry she had saved for herself; she needed something to steady her nerves.

Bridget sat at the walnut dressing table, looking ponderously at her reflection; she felt tired and confused with seeing Wabib Labachi again after all these years. He and his beautiful yet terrifying daughter had gone with Rachid to look at the local Obelisks in the area. Jaff had washed and polished the Mercedes and Wabib had promised to return for dinner, kissing her hand. Luke had gone out for a jog, and Hanna had returned to the town; Bridget was alone in the house.

Bridget unbraided her long auburn hair and let it float freely over her shoulders. She ran a finger down her finely furrowed brow, tracing a course across the merest beginnings of a fleshing-out of the angular cheek bones, her hazel eyes looked back at her in the mirror; was she not still an attractive woman?

She sighed deeply as she ran her hands across her firm breasts, feeling her nipples engorge to the touch under her silk slip. She was weary; tired of waiting for the man she had given her life to. It was as if her whole life stretched out before her: those frantic times in Egypt, the excitement of it all as Jock's enthusiasm had urged her along; the strange places they had visited, the people they had met, all rushed back to her in vivid memory - that mad bastard!

He had charmed her with stories of a noble birth. Said he was James Merebrook, and the heir to Merebrook Manor on the Devon coast, though he had never taken her there, claiming that his father, Sir Geoffrey disapproved strongly of him becoming and artist and was always threatening to disinherit him. Even so, he did get mail with an official looking seal on it, and cheques from time to time, so perhaps it was true.

Jock had always reminded her of the "Gingerbread man" by J.P. Donleavy, which she had read in the six-form at school. This character was always getting into scrapes, always confrontational, and lived from hand to mouth, eternally looking for the next thrill - like a child, only with the desires of a man. Her own gingerbread man had told her that he had changed his name to Jock Slater by deed poll when he got a place at the Royal College of Art. The reason, he had said was because he wanted to disassociate himself from his staid family origins, and to strike out on his own; he thought the name 'Sporty'.

Jock had been an athletic youth when she had first met him at the teashop in the Victoria and Albert Museum. She had been an impressionable young girl of seventeen in her first job in the city, and he had swept her off of her feet. After he had laced her Tea with whisky and got her half-cut, he had smuggled her into his domain through the interconnecting passageway to the Royal College of Art to show her his paintings.

She had been suitably impressed, considering her state, and he had taken her to the large mural room, which was conveniently empty, and seduced her on one of the mattresses used for life modelling. After that, she was hooked and she would have followed him to the ends of the earth. Bridget became aware of her protruding nipples as they pressed out of her silk slip and the sweat aroma of her arousal permeated her nostrils as she remembered the first time.

After graduating with an honour's degree, Jock had taught for a while and tried to engage the interest of some London galleries in his work, though not very hard. He had become restless and had heard of a job as an artist with the University of Chicago in Luxor of all places – that had been the beginning of the change in him and the start of the slippery slope. At first it had been fun- travelling to Egypt, the well-paid job, the round of receptions at diplomatic functions – but Jock had become distant, obsessed by the idea that he would become the painter of all time, and his work and life became stranger and stranger.

When Bridget was aware she was with child, Jock was ecstatic, and they lay awake until the early hours in the University's compound, going through all the possible names – like most couples do. They had been married the previous year, yet none of his family had been invited, and this saddened her and her own doting family.

But the beginning of the end came when Jock failed to show up at the airport and she, six months pregnant, was met by the striking academic, Dr. Labachi. She had been swamped by his affection and had succumbed in her loneliness to his affections. Jock had realised what had happened and a gulf had grown between them as he carried out his menial tasks for the University and locked himself into his own painting and alcohol at night.

They had rented cheap flats in London when they had returned from Egypt for the summer break and Luke had been reared partly in Luxor and partly in London. The reprieve came when an anonymous patron of Jock's work gave them Park House and here they had found some sort of stability for a time. Jock had held down various lecturing posts though never for very long and always hankered after Egypt, you could see that in his work.

After hard nights at the bottle, or down in the town carousing with friends, he had become delirious, shouting out in his sleep about his meeting with an old lady who was a reincarnated Ancient Egyptian Queen or something ridiculous, and about his adventures in some imaginary place called Nethertime, and wishing he could go back. Bridget had put this down to the delirium tremens as she mopped his sweat- bathed face. But she now realised, he was not a normal person, and that he had had some very strange experiences in the years she had not accompanied him to Egypt.

Finally he had got his old job back in Luxor, and the rest was history, but as she lay down in the double bed alone and lonely, she remembered the old days as she felt the haunting memories of those lost days of passion come back to her, and she stroked herself to sleep.

CHAPTER FIVE
*** ASTRAL TRAVELLER ***

Luke was on the home stretch. He had run all the way around the peninsula of Saint Mary's Isle, and Park House was in view. His breath came easier now and his stride lengthened as he pressed himself into the last mile. He was thinking of a good soak in a hot bath, a glass of good malt whisky, and then once more beholding the beauty of that dark mysterious face which swam in front of his eyes.

And it would be a full moon tonight. Perhaps, finally he would learn the secrets of Astral Travelling and be able to pursue his dream; that of finding his beloved father - with these thoughts racing through his mind he hurled his body into the last hundred meters.

Luke descended the large gothic staircase. His hair was still damp and he felt refreshed after a long soak in the bath. The nightmares of the night before seemed far off now, and he was certain that these houseguests, though possessing some arcane knowledge and supernatural powers, were on the side of good; he felt even guilty for thinking otherwise.

Luke walked into the dining room, up the oak cupboard and poured himself a large scotch. His athletic body felt relaxed after the run and he moved to the bay window, seeing the full moon rising just behind the Kellstone. Close to it, the Dog Star, Sirius twinkled in the clear yet dimming twilight; it would be a good night to start his pilgrimage.

Bridget came in through the other door, her face was radiant and her hair held back in a chignon secured with an ivory clasp. She poured herself a sherry and came up to her son 'You know, don't you?' she whispered, her ivory face colouring and an ugly red blotch creeping up her neck. 'But you do not understand. You cannot understand all I went through with your father...'

Luke felt awkward, not really equipped to consider that his own mother might have very similar feelings to his own. She was after all flesh and blood like himself, but he found the concept of her chequered history embarrassing. Steeling himself, he embraced her. 'Please' he said, 'it was a long time ago... before I was born...let him who is without blame cast the first stone. Forgiveness? I forgive you Mother, if that is what you want.' Bridget blinked away a tear and shook her head, moving to the window.

'It is a beautiful night' Bridget observed.

'It will be a night to remember' Luke rejoined, for his mind was on other things.

They heard the gravel crunch as the Mercedes drew up in the driveway. Bridget went to greet the guests and Luke looked expectantly, hoping to see the woman of his dreams, but the ravishing vision of sensuality he was expecting was not to be seen – instead Ishtar was dressed very conservatively.

'What news on the Obelisks?' he asked Labachi, trying to disguise his disappointment.

'They are still there.' The professor replied rather flippantly, it was as if nothing strange could ever, or would ever happen. Dinner was a perfunctory affair as they engaged in small talk, the mysteries and the supernatural events of the last twenty-four hours were glossed over, and even Hanna was reassured. The brazen hussy was dressed in a high bosomed Stewart tartan dress, and her hair was tied back in a bun, eliciting a tight-lipped smile from the staid housekeeper - this is the way she liked to see women dressed, particularly those younger than herself.

Even so, as the rest of them talked in animated fashion about the financial and political climates, world heath, sport and even horse racing, Bridget's eyes focussed on Wabib. Her daydreams of a few hours ago returned as she remembered how after 'finding' her at the airport, apparently stranded and helpless, he had shown her the sights of Cairo on that first night at the Garden City Hotel.

Stepping out onto the balcony of the hotel, Wabib had pointed out the busy suk, which it overlooked, and brought her attention to the sweep of majestic domes and minarets of the citadel, the old quarter. That evening, in a whirlwind tour of Cairo, Wabib had enumerated many historical facts about the citadel and its famous names from history: Richard the first, Saladin etc. They had entered the sacred mosque, barefoot and she had looked in wonder as the knowledgeable man had reeled off a list of historical events, which had set her mind reeling. Jock would never have done that; he would never have spared the time to share his little knowledge with her or anyone else for that matter. She felt a bitterness burning inside her when she thought of the difference between her estranged husband and her former lover. Bridget shook off her morbid thoughts and joined the rest in their conversation, until the brandy was served and they retired to the sitting room. Before they got there Labachi and Rachid excused themselves to get something from the car whilst Ishtar went up to her room promising to meet Luke in ten minutes at the studio.

Taking advantage of a few minutes alone with his mother, Luke approached her and took her hand.

'You know what I must do.' He said looking at her earnestly. 'It is tonight that I shall learn to travel, learn the ancient secrets... and if I am successful...find Father!'

'Luke,' Bridget looked into the eyes of her beloved son. 'You know what I am going to say, don't you?' She held her one and only son in a tight embrace as she looked into his eyes. 'And that is ... be very careful! I don't know if I totally trust these people,' her voice was a whisper, 'I have seen the way you look at Ishtar...I do not trust her...' Bridget's eyes were a mystery of apprehension but her warning was cut short as Labachi and Rachid walked in.

'Here you are my dear,' Labachi said offering a large wrapped bottle to Bridget. 'Whilst my little winged Priestess is showing your Knight in shining armour a bit of black magic, I have brought you a bottle of your favourite Egyptian vintage,' Labachi laughed and Bridget coloured again.

Suppressing a pang of protective anger at the familiarity with which this overly self-confident man addresses his mother, Luke was distracted by the sudden appearance of a figure at the top of the stairs.

Ishtar walked down the great gothic staircase, Luke's eyes noting her every move. She had changed back into her Ancient Egyptian costume; its white pleated tunic swishing as she walked down the stairs, her black hair held by a small crescent moon that glinted silvery in the hall lights. Her eyes were made up with black kohl into the elongated Ancient Egyptian, Ujot eye-style, her heavy lids eyelined with turquoise mascara.

She took Luke's hand and led him down along the hall into the studio. The moon was bright, white and full, shining down through the high windows of the room as Ishtar directed his attention to the painting: Jock's last painting of the Obelisk. 'Look at it' she said. 'Hold that image in your mind and tell me where you want to go to' Luke stood in front of the hypnotic painting, the reflection of the moon's rays, glinting from the glass- plated table seemed to illuminate the central Obelisk.

'I want to go to Nethertime.' Luke whispered, feeling a lump in his throat.

'For how long' Ishtar said, standing behind him. 'Because you can either go temporarily, leaving your corporeal body here, or you can go forever; in which case it is far more difficult to return!'

'Can I try temporarily?' Luke asked, feeling nervous about the second option. 'I will instruct you and accompany you' Ishtar said, 'but you must always remember the incantation in your mind...so that you can return.' Luke nodded.

'You must repeat this until you remember it...until it is engraved upon your soul.' Ishtar's voice was urgent. 'Or else you will be lost, like your father, and not able to return. Do you understand?'

'I do' Luke swallowed hard, 'what is it?'

'Turn around and look into my eyes' Ishtar said, 'I will transfer it to you, for it cannot be said aloud, only when you wish to travel.' Luke turned and looked into the jet-black eyes of the enchantress as he heard strange syllables form inside his mind.

Neb-Ankh-Sar-Eff-Jded-Rhekit

Luke's eyes were locked on those of the mesmerist as she held him by the shoulders and willed the arcane symbols into his mind.

'Have you got it?' she whispered, 'are you ready?' Luke nodded, feeling Ishtar wrap her arms around his waist and close her eyes so that he felt the warmth of her body press into his.

'Recite' she said, 'on my command, incant.' Luke heard the first syllable spoken and his mind remembered the phonetics and pronunciation of this magical spell when he said it out loud. On the last syllable, he felt his body gripped by some demonic force; then it started to rise up out of the room. Locked in Ishtar's steely embrace, he saw as if from outside himself and his mentor, their two corporeal bodies clutching each other as their ka's ascended, slowly at first and then upwards at a terrifying speed. The house grew small, the estuary below and the distant mountains receded until they formed into the landmasses and continents of the world, plumed by swirling feathers of moonlit cloud that itself became minuscule and was gone as the habitat which he knew was swept from view and they hurtled into the void of blue-black space.

A chilling fear gripped his bowels as the astral traveller held him in her inhuman embrace and he lost consciousness, aware only that his astral body was being hurtled through time and space.

✳✳✳

Luke felt warmth on his face. His body felt as if he had run a thousand miles; his insides were cold as if he had been immersed in icy water for an eternity. He felt a gentle slap on his face and his eyes flickered open; Ishtar was looking at him, a smile hovering about her lips. 'We are here my lovely boy' she said. 'We have arrived...Do you remember?'

Ishtar knelt over him, her silver crescent-moon glinting in the flurry of her black hair as a warm wind ruffled her pleated white tunic. He looked around him, propping himself up on one arm. They were on the top of an enormous sand dune that curved down in a zigzag shape from its cornice, to be lost in the folds of wind – driven dunes, the light breeze blowing particles of fine sand into his face. Above, the sky was a shimmering cerulean blue from which the overhead sun burned down upon them. In the distance could be seen the glint of a river as it wound its way through a broad flood plain, and Luke detected buildings, mere specks at this distance but either dwellings or temple structures of some sort.

'We have missed our spot' Ishtar said, 'over run our landing site by quite a bit...never mind.' 'How do you feel?' her voice was enigmatic.

'Very very weird' Luke answered, 'that was the most terrifying experience of my life... *ever*!'

'Yes,' Ishtar rejoined, 'the first trip is always the worst, but you are a good little apprentice.'

'Are we in Nethertime or Aiyu?' Luke asked. He couldn't quite remember which destination he had decided upon before his Ka left his body.

'The amnesia of the astral-traveller.' Ishtar smiled, gazing down on the the disorientated youth. 'Can you remember your name?'

'Luke' Luke replied, he wasn't that frazzled

'Good' Ishtar's voice with ambivalent 'Can you remember the incantation?'

Luke's mind was fogged by his recent out of body experience as he grappled with the phonetics of the strange arcane inscription.

'Neb – Ankh – Sar...'

'Oh what a pity.' Was Ishtar's voice mocking, Luke wondered, sensing the irony of his situation and squinting up at her smiling face, haloed and obscured by the bright sun.

'I thought you had drummed it into my head' he said, feeling a nagging doubt stirring in his breast. 'Didn't you mesmerise it into my mind?'

'Oh dear, my poor little cherub.' Ishtar clasped her hands around his neck and pressed his head to her breast. 'You are so trusting...' She released him as his head flew back onto the sand and she stood up, her legs either side of his shoulders as he looked up to her lithe thighs and the mound of her womanhood beneath the wind-tugged pleated tunic; she spoke:

'I will be going now...I have kept my side of the bargain and shown you the arcane secrets of Astral traval. I have brought you here to where you wanted to be...the hidden dimension of Nethertime. I hope you find your dear Papa, though this territory is somewhat vast. I enjoyed our bit of romance, but if you cannot remember the most important words you will ever learn in your life, then that is not my fault...Goodbye!'

Ishtar stood over him, her arms locked and folded against her breast, and he heard her incant:

'Neb – Ankh...'

The rest of the precious incantation was muttered in silence and as Luke looked up at her splayed legs into the cradle of her womanhood, he heard a sound like the of ripping silk as she momentarily hovered above him, her lascivious smile raking his brain, to be borne upwards on the astral wind and become a diminishing dot in the clear blue sky. And as the sand eddied around his face, the image of her form haunting his mind, Luke grappled with the appalling realisation – he had been tricked!

'*Traitor*!' Luke's voice was horse and choking, as he shouted into the blue void. 'You trickster of my heart!' His heart-renting words echoed around the yellow sand dunes as he lay back on the crest of the cornice, the echoes of his lament fading up into the empty vault of the sky.

Luke lay there for a long time, contemplating the enormity of his folly as the sand particles slowly formed a ridge about his head and the overhead sun burned into his brain...he had been tricked - tricked by one whom he had finally resolved to trust; and a bitter tear ran down his cheek.

Finally, when he realised that there was no one about to come to his aid, and that he had been abandoned in a strange and hostile land, his sorrow turned to rage! Rage against Ishtar and her co-conspirators, Labachi and Rachid - and a resolution to get back to his own time metalled his nerve. He would, for a while, have to abandon his search for his father, for if these people could be so duplicitous to *himself* then what plans did they have in mind for his *mother*?

Cursing his gullibility, Luke pulled himself out of the near-engulfing sand dune and stumbled to his feet. He realised that he had forgotten the correct incantation, and that he must try to remember it, in order to get back. But more pressing was the need to find cover from the overhead sun that was unbearably strong.

He tore off his studded denim shirt and covered his head, feeling the poppers, red-hot against his flesh. The withering coldness in his gut had subsided, and the shock of going from freezing cold to boiling hot played strange games on his body as he girded his faculties about him and started the dizzying descent down the sand dune.

He focussed on the vast plain below the ochre desert with its glinting ribbon of winding water that could only be the Nile. Yet was it the Nile of Nethertime, or of Aiyu, or was he still in contemporary time and would he soon encounter a group of eager tourists flocking into the valley of the Kings.

Still he could not remember the correct phrasing of the incantation, paramount to his ability to 'get back but he sensed somehow that his unconscious mind may have grasped it!'

Luke's feet grew lazy as he catapulted himself down the endless dunes of wind-driven sand, his cowl of a shirt shading his eyes from the glare of the over head sun, though he felt a sunburn on his back.

With his body dehydrated in the glaring heat, thirst soon became a problem of the uttermost concern and he closed his mouth, retaining what saliva was left and breathed the scorching air of the desert in through his nostrils.

The plain of the river was getting closer as Luke descended the great desert escarpment and he saw the blue mountains on the other side of the vast rift shimmering in the heat haze. The huddle of dwellings or temples he had seen from his high vantage point seemed to take on more detail and he tried to ascertain their identity; they were unlike any structures he had ever seen.

Luke's legs, though strongly formed and honed into solid muscle by his running, were at the end of their tether, and he felt them buckle as he collapsed onto the last dune and felt himself slide into the soft sand to be borne downwards in an avalanche of cascading ochre waves. He relaxed and let the sliding morass of moving sand carry him downward, oblivious to the approaching edge of the cliff. A gully of jagged rock swam in front of his sweat - beaded brow, as he looked down at the floor of the valley many metres below.

Luke jammed his feet against the projecting buttress of rock which protected him from certain death and the sand slide skewed around him and poured down into the gulf below. As the liquid yellow river of sand grains slowed and then stopped their passage over the ledge, he saw a way down, a narrow chimney that could be traversed by a climber, which he was, but now one on the verge of exhaustion - yet there was no other way!

Luke lowered himself cautiously into the narrow cleft of the chimney, and the strictures of his climbing days all came back to him. He braced himself in the three—hold technique, the first commandment of the rock climber, and lowered himself, arm by arm, leg by leg, down the sandstone shaft.

The inevitable chock-stone he negotiated, recalling previous challenges of the climbs he had made in those not to distant days of his youth. The sandstone was fragile and broke off in his hand as he looked for those impossible holds and saw the plain of the valley swimming far below him.

Something akin to instinct took over as Luke pitted his skills against the fragile rock and he inched himself down; the base was nearer now.

"Oh dear, my poor little cherub...you are so trusting," Ishtar's treacherous taunts were all that Luke could think of as he climbed down a wider section of the chimney. How could he have been so trusting of the woman whom he had thought he had loved, and whom he had trusted? But his determination gathered momentum and his jaw set in a ridged line of defiance as he lowered himself down into the opening jaws of the gully; he would have his revenge!

The chimney widened now, its width impossible to bridge, and as Luke perched precariously on the vestiges of a foothold, his arms and legs trembling in exhaustion, he decided to jump the rest - for he was at the end of his endurance. He threw his body outwards into space and plummeted down from the sandstone crag, seeing the degraded remnants of the cliff face rise up to meet him. He hit the slope below with some force, rolling down it in a jumble of arms and legs, until his momentum slowed - then he felt the black void of unconsciousness overtake his senses.

✳✳✳

Ishtar arced up from the realm of sunlit Nethertime into the blue-black vault of the heavens. As she looked down upon the poor youth who she had tricked into flying with her, she felt no remorse. Of course he could not remember the correct incantation for she had blocked his memory with the weapon of her womanhood and his mind was a confusion of desire; could it be so easy?

As his pathetic figure, groping in the sands of Nethertime diminished and was lost to view, she felt not one qualm, not one scrap of guilt, for he was expendable in the larger view - the conquest of time.

Her pleated kilt glowed golden in the last rays of the sun and her supernatural figure straightened out like an arrow to be was raised up into the astral void of space. The astral traveller intoned the incantation for her reciprocal voyage across the cosmos and down to the site of her take-off.

The realms of the outer ether engulfed her and she felt a charge of invincibility as she cleaved her way through the dimensions of time and space; soon she would be with her own people.

The intense chill that Ishtar felt as she hurtled on in her unworldly flight only intensified her feelings of righteousness. She had not tricked or misled the hapless lad, for it was only his own desire to find his father which had led to him into accepting her guidance in helping him gain the hidden dimension. And now that she and her cult had the inscription - there was no limit to their power. How gullible were mere mortals.

Ishtar zoomed down out of the ether and into the black night of reality that was now studded by the known stars of the Zodiac and by the full moon. She recognised the territory of her landfall and noted the estuary of this remote Scottish outpost, the moonlight gleaming along its muddy banks, as she started her descent. Park house was below her and she slowed her pace, her mind reciting the arcane law of reciprocal motion. As the full moon glinted on the black waters of the bay, an errant gust of wind blew her slightly off course; no matter she would land close by. As she slowed her speed, she saw the flames of a bonfire on the foreshore of the estury nearby, this would be her marker. She incanted the command for a landing and started to fly down towards the flames of the bonfire: The Astral traveller was only a mile or so distant from her destination - she would walk back to Park House.

Flickering, orange light illuminated the loutish-looking faces of a group of youths, as they passed around the bottle of whisky, warming their hands on the bonfire they had lit on the beach. They had been thrown out of the Harbour Tavern, which was the last place tolerant of their abusive behaviour, and had driven their battered Skoda to this deserted spot to stupefy their already meagre brains a little more with alcohol.

They had shouted jeers and taunts as they passed the last house before Mute Hill - Park House, which they knew from the local gossip in the bars was a den of iniquity and devil worship. Talk had been rife in the tavern about giant glowing obelisks or some such thing, "gay muckle stanes wi fairy-lights all glowing around 'em." "'Ye ask Dougal," the fishermen in the harbour tavern had said; but they had jeered at his stories. Finally they had grown rowdy and had been thrown out of the bar by the hefty fishermen who believed every word of Dougal's story.

'We'll gan tae Mute Heel an see ef tha Deil's aboot.' The drunken louts had said, aware that it was a site shunned by the God-fearing people of the town, being the place where the last witch had been burned at the stake. It was a lonely spot on the Dee estuary, and as the youths danced around the fire, they re-enacted the ritual of the burning in their demented and especially fermented minds.

But their imagined apprehension quickly turned into superstitious horror as they saw a figure, all white, her tunic fluttering about her naked legs come flying out of the night sky, the firelight from their fire bedecking her strange face, framed by whirling black hair, her silver crescent moon emblem catching the orange glow.

'Tis the weetch!' one of them jabbered, his hands shaking as he held the near-empty bottle' This yins the weetch o' mute heel! They backed away to the car, their eyes wide with fear as the apparition landed, looked at them with her demon eyes and spun around to stride quickly in the direction of Park House 'She's ganning ta tha hoose. She's ganning ta tha weetch's Sabbath....' One said as they staggered towards the battered car. 'Thas a can o' petrol here, dae ye have ye litchter Tam,' the youth asked, his voice thick, 'lets gan tae Park Hoose... We haive some work tae do!'

Ishtar walked up to the Mercedes on the driveway. Jaff was putting a large, carefully wrapped parcel into the capacious boot. 'You're late!' Rachid barked. 'We should be gone by now!'

'You have the painting?' Ishtar asked and Rachid nodded. The rear window of the car wound down and Labachi said, 'how did your little lesson go, did you teach him not to meddle.' Ishtar looked at the slumped figure of Bridget, in the rear seat, her head leaning on Labachi's shoulder.

'He is out of harm's way' Ishtar's voice was icy. 'He has forgotten the incantation, he will not be back...'

'Get in' Rachid ordered as Ishtar walked around the car and squeezed in next to Bridget. Jaff lowered his bulk into the driving seat, the moonlight gleaming menacingly from his bald head and giant earring.

He reversed the white Mercedes down the driveway and turned. The car proceeded up the drive as an old shabby vehicle swerved in through the gateway, nearly hitting the Mercedes. Jaff shrugged, turning onto the road and accelerating into the night.

They took the winding country road up over the hills of Auchencairn, swerving around the moonlit bends that shone white against the dark purple heather. Rachid glanced in the rear view mirror and ordered Jaff to pull over. Looking back they could see Kirkcudbright bay and the lights of the little town twinkling in the distance. The kellstone atop the Rhinns a Kells shone white against the black velvet of the sky and further down and across they saw the orange glow as flames engulfed Park House.

'Is seems we have some little helpers down there' Rachid said as Labachi and Ishtar smiled, their faces lit by expressions of pure evil. 'Drive us to London' Rachid ordered Jaff, who had turned and was looking at the drugged face of Bridget, still slumped in the back seat. 'And get us there before morning' Jaff nodded and the white Mercedes sped off across the moor and towards the M6.

✳✳✳

Lying at the foot of the sandstone cliffs, Luke's consciousness slowly returned, and with it, his memory; the fall had cleared his head. He could see the words of the forgotten inscription in his mind's eye, the one that Ishtar had mentally recited to him whilst she mesmerised him with her feminine charms, and he could hear her careful articulation of the arcane words that comprised the incantation. These he repeated to himself, memorising their difficult pronunciation as he checked his body for broken bones.

Now he felt a little more empowered and he had to decide what to do – the first thing was to find out where he was. Looking at the distant landscape, he tried to discern signs of habitation. Down in the lower valley there grew clumps of palm trees dotted around the ruins of various temples, but the scene was devoid of human presence. He vacillated between trying to orientate himself in this unknown world or trying to get back to his own time, constantly repeating his newfound memory of the inscription and determined not to let it escape him again.

Also the plight of his mother weighed heavily in the equation. If Ishtar's deception had led her to these lengths in order to get rid of him, then what had the cult got planned for her; for he knew now that they were of the cult of the One Dimension. All the reassurance they had given him about working to destroy the cult was a pack of lies, and he cursed himself for being so gullible; it was the desire he felt for that treacherous enchantress that had lured him into this predicament.

Luke had made up his mind. He adopted the astral-travelling position of arms folded as the words and their arcane inflexion hung on his lips and he formed a mental picture of where he wanted to go...to Park House.

Neb-Ankh-Sar-Eff-Jded-Rhekit

Luke felt a rush of air as his feet left the scorched desert rock and he was blasted upwards into the blue sky, his ka speeding through the ether to join his corporeal body as a numbness of cold enveloped his senses. The firmaments swam around his dizzy mind – then he lost consciousness and was hurtled back into real time.

Confusion overtook his faculties for Luke saw himself standing in the studio of Park House. But the house was on fire; sheets of orange flame engulfed the entire building. As his ka re-entered his body, he felt the heat of the inferno, hearing the windows crack as they fractured in the intensity of the fire. The sudden jolt from his place of departure to this unfolding catastrophe was almost too much to take on board and Luke summoned all the strength he could to nerve himself against his own impending doom: death by fire! Panic overwhelmed him and he wrestled with two choices: to try and save his father's work, or to get out. Even as the shock of seeing the stacks of his father's paintings in flames registered on his numbed mind, Luke noticed the recent picture of the Obelisk of Time was gone! This grave realisation was eclipsed by the flaming ceiling descending on his head, and Luke hurled himself through one of the fractured windows and rolled onto the lawn and away from the burning house.

As Luke used the momentum of his forward roll to propel himself into a standing position, one thought suddenly hammered on his disorientated mind as he stood staring in total disbelief at the raging inferno. 'Mother! for god's sake, Mother!' He was not to know that she had been spirited away by Labachi and the others moments before his inopportune 'landing.' Red flames burst through the windows of the first floor bedrooms and he watched in a frenzy of bereavement, seeing the roof cave in whilst the flames gutted the attic bedrooms roaring upwards into the dark night.

Luke collapsed onto the damp lawn and buried his hands in his face as the wail of a fire-engine's siren pierced the crackling of fire-consumed timbers and the crash of the chimney-breasts as they sunk into the fiery rage of orange flames. 'No,' Luke sobbed,' No, please God. This cannot be....' He was dragged back from the gutted house by strong arms as the firemen looked at each other hopelessly. The pumps were on and the hose hissed as the water cannon sprayed across the roof, but it was all in vain; the house and its contents were doomed. The fire was out of control and it consumed the entire building.

Luke opened his eyes, looking blearily around the white, Spartan room. Though vivid images of a fire and a desert landscape raced through his dizzy mind, he saw now that he was in a hospital ward; he seemed to be the only occupant. There was a numb pain in his head he realised it was bandaged, then looking down, he noticed his bare feet sticking out of the white open-weeve hospital covers, seeing that one of them was also bandaged. A saline drip stood next to the bed and he felt a variety of tubes attached to his nose and mouth and some more to his arms. His eyes roamed around the small room and he saw two figures through the doorway in the reception area. They were nurses, and their blue uniforms and white starched caps sent a chill down his spine as he remembered the terror of the fire and how he had tried to return to the house but had been beaten back by the flames. 'Mother,' he whispered, his mind awhirl at the recollection of the terror of that moment when he realised she was beyond saving. His body jerked up and the tubes tore from his face and arms as he straddled one leg out of the bed and started to get up. 'No, Master Slater' one of the nurses rushed in and held him down on the bed. 'No, please, stay put!' and she shouted out into the reception hall. 'He's come to, he's conscious!' Two more nurses rushed in and restrained him as they gave him a sedative. He saw the hypodermic sink deep into his arm and he slipped back onto the pillow and the blackness overtook him again.

✳✳✳

Luke regained consciousness some days later, and he saw through the cloud of his blurred vision two men standing over his bed, peering down at him. One was a doctor, judging by a white mask under his chin, and the other was his father's lawyer, Mr. Havers, who had officiated in the reading of his dad's will only days previously; they were talking to each other in whispered words and their expressions were serious.

'Master Slater' the doctor spoke 'Are you well enough to talk?' a nurse propped him up in the small bed, plumping up the pillows as he fought with the nausea caused by whatever kind of drug they had administered - some sort of sedative no doubt. Luke nodded his head and tried to retain his focus on the two men.

'You have been in a coma for five days.' the doctor said. 'It is imperative that you rest now, but Mr Havers here has a few questions for you...are you feeling up to answering them?' Luke nodded and then coughed as the nausea returned 'Mother,' he gasped, did you find Mother? The two men exchanged meaningful glances. 'Your Mother was not in the house' Mr Havers said, taking Luke's arm. 'The fire department has gone through the remains of Park House and has found no trace of anyone. Nobody died in the fire...'

'Are you absolutely sure!' Luke's voice was on the verge of hysteria as he clutched the solicitor's hand; 'can you be certain?'

'It is a certainty' Havers repeated 'no one perished in the fire.'

Luke coughed as a wave of relief swept over him, and he whispered 'Thank God!' Then as the inevitable question formed in his mind he stammered 'where... where is she? Has anyone seen her...is she?'

'We do not know Master Slater' the solicitor said quietly. 'She has not been seen locally, and you may be able to throw some light on her whereabouts, but I can confirm, she was not in Park House at the time of the fire.'

Luke's mind was racing. His relief at the news that Bridget had not perished was uppermost in his thoughts and he rejoiced at that; but it led on to the obvious question, 'where is she?' He was about to tell them of the strange visitors who had arrived for his dad's funeral: Labachi, Rachid, Ishtar, of the cult of the One Dimension, but thought better of it and bit his tongue. He was trying to imagine how they would take his account of his little trip with Ishtar – if the father was an eccentric, then the son was a luny....Mad? They would have him certified and sectioned and taken off to an asylum before you could say Jack Robinson!

'I don't know where she can be' he half-lied to Havers, trying hard to resurrect the memories of before the fire. He had been seduced by that temptress Ishtar into astral travelling to some unknown destination. Why? To get rid of him so the cult could abduct his mother? But they hadn't counted on his memory of the spell returning, and they certainly had underestimated his resolve. His search for his father would have to be put on hold for a while longer, but he was going to move Heaven and earth to find and rescue his mother! Even so he would have to be careful!

'We will involve the police if you wish, in order to try and find Mrs. Slater' the solicitor said, 'but you must give us your consent in this matter? Havers looked earnestly at the youth who seemed to be relapsing. 'In the meantime,' Havers continued 'there is the matter of the insurance' he looked at Luke again. 'Are you well enough to continue?' Luke came out of his faked relapse and raised himself up onto the pillows, 'go on' he said, feigning disinterest.

'It is a little complicated' Havers prevaricated. 'It seems that Park House was not in your father's name, but registered under the name of James Merebrook.'

'Jock Slater was a pseudonym, Luke retorted. 'He is the son of Sir Geoffrey Merebrook, even though he disguised his true identity.'

'Um, yes...' Havers frowned slightly. 'Well the insurers will pay the sum of four hundred and fifty thousand pounds, the full valuation of the property if it were to be totally destroyed by fire. Their assessors have been up here and they have been to my office...there is no doubt about the total loss, and they will pay.' Havers brought out some documents from his briefcase.

'But,' he continued.' To whom do they pay it? Your father is dead and buried and your mother is missing.... and though we hope she will be found soon and in good health, the insurers need to know...'

'What does the law say?' Luke asked, 'and does that figure include any of the valuable paintings in the house at the time of the fire?' Havers frowned, a line of fatigue moved across his forehead.

'Err...sadly...no,' he continued. Their value cannot be substantiated, and the list of contents does not include such valuable items! 'But' the solicitor added. 'In the light of your mother's absence and in view of the fact that you are the de facto beneficiary, they are willing to pay the sum to yourself... are you in agreement with this?

Luke yawned and started to slump into the pillows 'yes,' he said indifferently. 'Let them make the cheque out to mother's and my own joint account.'

'Very well' Havers stuffed the unread paperwork into his briefcase, 'he needs to rest still' he said to the doctor who bent over and felt Luke's pulse. 'Yes,' the medic agreed, 'he should rest now!' The two men departed and Luke opened one eye and watched them leave; he was trying not too feel too elated. Though both of his parents were now in unknown locations, this money, invested in their and his joint names would give Luke the freedom to pursue the quest of all time, and as he rested up in the hospital bed, he could not help but feel a sense of excitement at the adventure that lay ahead.

✳✳✳

Two weeks later, Luke discharged himself from the little country hospital of Kirkcudbright, and walked out of the door. Limping on a walking stick, his wounds partially recovered from the secondary burns on his head and legs, he made his way towards the local solicitors in the high street. He pushed open the door with his good foot and went up to the small counter, saying: 'Mr Havers if you would be so good.' The female clerk looked at the fresh bandage around his temples and went to the back of the small building, whispering to her colleague. The crippled youth was ushered into the tiny office as Havers got up from his desk. 'I didn't know you were discharged,' he said as he helped Luke into a chair. 'Are you feeling a lot better then?' Luke cut through the feined concern.

'The cheque' he said bluntly. 'The cheque from the insurance company...'

'Oh that,' Havers stalled, and then with a slight frown of irritation crossing his gaunt face, he unlocked a drawer in his filing cabinet.

'Here,' he said handing Luke a large white envelope. Luke tore it open and disregarding the letter, looked at the cheque... four hundred and fifty thousand pounds, it was printed. 'And your fees?' Luke eyed the little man as he saw his forehead bead with a fine sweat. 'Ah yes, let me see.' Havers filed through some paperwork on his desk. 'Err, yes, here it is.' Luke took it from his proffered hand. Five hundred and thirty-five pounds, it said. 'A bit steep isn't it? He asked, evenly enough.

Havers eyed him up and down. Luke was dressed in ill-fitting baggy trousers and a knitted pullover that hung down almost to his knees, the best that the charity shop had to offer in the light of his recent discharge; his own clothes having perished in the fire. The Solicitor's hand hovered on the bell below his small table, though he knew there was not much help to be had from his secretaries, should this discharged youth turn nasty.

'Make it five hundred' Luke said coolly. 'It will have to be a promissory note as I have no cheque book available to me at this time, as I also have no clothes, no lodgings and nothing apart from this cheque!'

'Five hundred?' Havers enquired.

'Yes' Luke said 'if you give me the names or descriptions at least of the arsonists who burnt down Father's house and destroyed his work of a lifetime!'

'Ah' Havers replied, I see. How did you know about these... these...'

'Arsonists...thugs!' Luke helped him out. 'I heard the gossip well enough. I have had ample time to listen to the nurses talking... I know what the're saying around town ... a can of petrol on a very drunken night, and no one is talking...but all I want their names!' Luke shouted, his contained anger erupting into the tiny room. 'I want to know who they are!' The little man hovered with his finger on the button as Luke grasped his hand and crushed it in his strong grip. Havers was catapulted into his chair as the beads of sweat that studded his forehead turned into rivers.

'Tam...' he spluttered, 'the talk around the town is that it was Tam and his cronies....' 'Where?' Luke asked as if he didn't already know 'The Harbour Tavern?' Havers nodded as Luke wrote a promissory note in large shaking handwriting and pushed it into the solicitor's hand. Clutching the cheque, he stormed out of the office and to the door, his rage setting within him as the two receptionists cowered at the back of the tiny reception area.

Luke limped down the High street and into the Royal Bank of Scotland. He came up to the counter and presented the cheque as the manager rose from his seat. 'I want to pay this into the account of James and Bridget Merebrook,' he said, 'and I want a new cheque book.' His voice was terse as he looked around the bank.

'Yes Master Slater,' the bank manager replied, looking over his glasses at Luke's bandaged head and charity shop cast-offs. 'I see you are also a co-signatory.' Luke was trying to calm himself.

'That's right.' Luke confirmed. 'So can you cash me a cheque for one thousand pounds?' The bank manager looked keenly at the dishevelled youth and reluctantly nodded his head. Whilst he entered the information into the computer Luke was tapping his stick, looking at the waning daylight outside and his mind whirled in the knowledge that the perpetrators of this crime against his father's lifetime's ambition were just a few meters away.

'One thousand pounds, Master Slater.' The bank manager handed him the bills, smiling weekly. 'I do hope you are on the mend and all the staff here extend our deepest sympathies.' Luke took the money and shoved it into his ill-fitting cast-offs

'Thank you for your concern.' He replied. 'I am on the mend and I shall be feeling a whole lot better in a few minutes!' Luke limped towards the door as he heard the girls behind the counter whisper, 'Poor thing.'

The sun had set in a crepuscular display of orange magic as the tapestry of the quick-following autumn night invaded the small Scottish town and Luke limped down the street towards the Harbour Square. In his raggedy pocket he had a thousand pounds, and another four hundred and forty eight and a half thousand to draw on - but it was not the money that brightened his soul. No! It was the strength of his resolve that sped him limping along the cobblestones of the Harbour Square; that and his overriding desire for justice. Then he would find his mum, for he had a good idea of where she had been abducted, and after that, he would find his dad!

The entire bar was silent as the invalid limped in. The denizens of the Harbour Tavern whispered amongst themselves as they eyed the son of the mad artist who had got his comeuppance. Luke reached the bar, and plonking down his oddly-dressed frame on a barstool, ordered a large scotch whisky. Looking at the blonde haired barmaid who held a glass up to the optic and poured out a double measure, he placed a Twenty-pound note on the counter and sipped the liquor - the first he had tasted in as many a long day.

'Keep the change,' he said loudly as the barmaid caught her breath. 'But, it's tweenty poonds!' she gasped as Luke held her hand down on the bar. 'There is a forfeit,' he said, looking at the bemused girl. 'Which one is Tam?' he whispered in her ear. The girl flushed and tried to withdraw her hand but Luke had it in a tight grip. 'The one in the corner,' she whispered, her voice betraying her fear 'the one with the earring.'

'Thank you,' Luke replied, letting her arm go as she looked concernedly in the youth's direction. Luke imbibed the malt liquor, feeling the strength of his battered and burned body return and he swivelled on the barstool.

'Here is a thousand pounds!' Luke shouted at the onlooking men in the tavern who regarded him with hatred: the young Laird of the former manor, here, back from the dead and flaunting his ill gotten gain around... still... a thousand pounds!

'A Thousand pounds, or very near-like for he that gives me the name of the bastard who burnt down Park House!' Luke was clocking Tam and his mates who were colluding together on the far table, their eyes flickering in malice at this unscheduled development to their drunken rampage; a grim silence hung in the dim, tobacco-filled gloom.

'I'll tell ye.' Tam, of the dark hair and glittering earring rose from the far table as the whispers circulated around the dingy room. Tam walked up to the youth who dared to come into this, his bar, sitting, all brazen, in that cast-off clothing, his head bandaged, and his stick at the side of the barstool.

'Yes' Luke's voice was steady as he held his palm over the pile of money. 'Then tell me!'

'Twas I.' The dark haired youth said, approaching the bar. 'It was I, myself, and me.' Luke saw the youth's hand come up as he flicked a switchblade, glinting in the light from the bar, and Luke froze as the lout swiftly held it against his neck.

'So' Luke said calmly, thought the adrenaline was racing through his body. 'Twas, just you then... What about your friends, don't they deserve a little bit of this.' Luke raised his hands as Tam's eyes devoured the money. Why don't you invite them over.' Luke said loudly so the whole pub could hear as the denizens sat mutely at their tables, transfixed by the glittering blade at the young Laird's neck.

The other three youths rose from the table and proceeded to the bar. 'I mean,' Luke said disarmingly, as he felt the knife begin to cut into his jugular vein, 'fair's, fair.' He slid his hands along the top of the bar and the tangle of notes fell down onto the floor. Tam's eyes became transfixed by the cascading flow of notes and he disengaged the blade at Luke's neck momentarily as he saw his fortune fluttering onto the beer-sodden flags - and then Luke struck.

His good hand slammed into Tam's temple bone with his knuckle braced into a rigid karate strike that propelled the knife-wielding ringleader backwards to reel across the tables nearby. The others, not so sure now, hesitated, and a tense stalemate ensued as they eyed up their chances with the cripple. One of them went for the fallen knife that had skidded along the floor, but before he could pick it up, his hand was delt a hammer of a blow by the crutch that Luke wielded so effectively. Before the remaining two could make up their minds whether to rush this not so crippled youth or retreat, their temples were given a hearty thwack as Luke used the crutch as an extension to his arm; the karate strikes being the more devasting. The accomplices staggered backwards to join their half-conscious mates, groaning and holding their broken hands and heads in similar fashion.

The bemused company in the Tavern stared in disbelief to see Luke gather up the money from the floor and slap two twenty-pound notes on the bar, and shout. 'Drinks are on me and keep the change!' The Tavern was silent, its denizens watching the limping figure make his way to the door and exit into the sea mist that rose up from the nearby estuary into the dearth- like room.

CHAPTER SIX
*** MOLLY ***

An errant ray of sunshine struck through the ragged banks of grey cloud, illuminating the stone lions atop the steps. A figure sat on the top step to the side of one of the lions, watching from the cover of a broad brimmed bushwhacker-style hat. His barely discernible face was blotchy around his forehead and a beard of several days gleamed ginger in the brief sunlight.

The tall youth could pass as any student or young tourist on a budget trip as he sat reading an A to Z street map of London. His blue denim jeans were new looking, as were his trainers and grey and yellow chequered coat, and the youth reached into his rucksack, pulling out a bottle of orange juice and taking a long swig.

Luke had been in London for several days now. He had found a cheap B+B not far from where he sat, on the steps of the British Museum, and had been coming here each morning in the hope of sighting Labachi and Rachid. He was wary about going into the Museum and asking for the eminent Dr Labachi by name, for he wanted to remain incognito as long as possible. He was not so much interested in where the professor worked, but more so where he lived; for that was the vital clue he needed to find his mother.

As his mind went back to the recent events at Park House, he had to admit that Bridget may have gone off with Labachi of her own will – or, and he hoped desperately this was the case, that she had had been abducted. He knew now that she had had a brief affair with the academic whilst in Cairo. For whatever reason, she had fallen for the then possibly handsome, and certainly charismatic man, for Luke had noticed her face on those two evenings that they had dined together at Park House, and was certain that she still carried a torch for him. He preferred to think that she had been seduced by the charms of this man in Cairo, whilst his father, in his pathetic way had tried to find her - his chaotic life-style having caused him to mistake the day of her arrival - only to leave her stranded at the airport. She had intimated as much in their conversations at Park House, before he was seduced into astral travelling with that duplicitous enchantress, Ishtar.

There was no doubt in his mind however that she was, either willingly or not, in evil company, for Luke was sure now that Habachi, Rachid, and Ishtar were members of the cult, the Order of the One Dimension. He had paid his respects to the low-lifes who had burnt down Park House and with it, almost the entire life's work of the unfortunate Jock Slater. His mission now was to seek out the cult, and release Mother, and to settle the score with that perfidious temptress – Ishtar.

Throughout all the travails of these recent days, and especially when he had recovered consciousness in the tiny country hospital of Kirkcudbright, Luke had hung onto the correct form of the incantation as he rehearsed it in his mind daily, and before going to bed – almost like a catechism; for he was determined not to loose it ever again. After all, once he found mother, it was clear in his mind that his next mission was to find dad. He smiled in grim satisfaction that there was at least the cushion of the money from the insurance payout which was earning interest even as he sat there, which would provide a nest egg for his parents to start up again in the future. That was possibly the only ray of light in this dark and tragic tangle of improbabilities.

A white Mercedes swung in through the high gates of the British Museum as Luke buried his face in the A to Z. The car screeched on the gravel forecourt, pulling up in a reserved parking bay. Two men got out and walked to the front entrance. Luke looked up briefly to see Rachid and Labachi in animated conversation, before he lowered his head again. As they walked through the front doors, Luke got up - his limp barely noticeable now - and followed them. He saw them walking down the main Ancient Egyptian gallery, and casually made his way down it, keeping the large statues in front of him. The two men stopped at the bottom of a spiral staircase and Luke hid behind the massive clenched fist fragment of a Ramesses the second statue, in the pretence of reading the label.

There were other visitors in the gallery; some of them obviously students or young sightseers as well as the occasional uniformed attendant. But no one paid any heed to him in his slightly 'hip' outfit, and he was sure Rachid and Labachi had not recognised him –why they still probably thought of him as lost in some arcane dimension, like nethertime. The two men climbed the spiral staircase and Luke heard Labachi sorting through a ring of jangling keys as they approached the door at the top of the stairs. They entered, and the heavy door slammed shut. Luke looked around - the attendants were out of sight and he quickly ascended the spiral staircase, crouching down to be less conspicuous and read the sign on the door – "Department of Ancient Egyptian Antiquities: Restoration Room." He tried the heavy Chubb door handle quietly, but it was locked. Moving carefully along the small mezzanine corridor, he came to a narrow window at the end; it opened - so much for security - and Luke stepped out onto a narrow ledge that ran along the building. Looking down, he saw an array of skips and bins, and he saw that the facing wall of the adjacent wing was devoid of windows; he would not be detected.

Luke inched along the ledge and came to a window on his side. The thick, antiquated glass had been whitewashed on the inside, but a small round patch had been missed at the bottom and as Luke pressed his eye to it; he could see most of the room inside. There was a long central table with various white plaster casts and moulds scattered along its length.

Then, squinting through the hole in the paintwork, Luke saw something else that made his quest seem more attainable: two scholars that he knew well were in consultation with each other.

Labachi and Rachid were deep in conversation as they gestured at the white plaster cast of an Obelisk standing in the centre of the table. A young woman walked up to join them. Her long wavy red hair fell onto her white lab coat, whilst her hands were covered in plaster. The lab technician stood as Labachi said something, and she bent down to look at the cast of the Obelisk; he could not hear the conversation. An idea was forming in Luke's mind as he stepped carefully backwards along the ledge and through the small window, closing it and heading down to the spiral staircase. He looked at his watch; it was nearly twelve-twenty – nearly lunchtime.

There were more visitors in the gallery now - helping to preserve his anonymity - as Luke took out a note pad and walked around the various artefacts in a studious gait, scribbling nonsense onto the pad - his eyes always on the spiral staircase. His patience was rewarded, for after a few minutes, the red- haired lab technician that he had glimpsed just now, came out of the Restoration room door, the clicks of her high-heels on the spiral staircase reverberating around that end of the gallery.

Luke checked the position of the attendants who were looking at a crowd of unruly children, whilst he waited behind a statue of Ra-Hotep and gauged the progress of the woman by the sound of her heels on the wooden floor. Purposefully walking backwards from the statue, he felt himself collide with the woman, and he turned; a fake, startled expression on his face to see the lab technician lying sprawled on the floor.

'Please' Luke said, taking off his ridiculous hat. 'Please forgive me...' he bent down to assist the distraught young woman, pulling her to her feet with a strong hand. 'I am so sorry,' he said as he looked into her face. 'Are you alright?' He noticed a flush steal up from her neck to colour her face, as she brushed herself down. A file of papers was strewn across the floor as Luke hurried to retrieve them, saying:

'Please allow me to make amends... can I buy you a coffee or something...I was just going down to the restaurant ...are you permitted?'

'*Permitted*' the young woman laughed, and the few people who had noticed the collision lost interest and moved on; the attendants hadn't even noticed, as Luke looked around cautiously.

'Do you think I'm some sort of prisoner here' she continued as Luke took her arm and carrying her file, asked. 'Are you hurt, can you walk alright?' The woman laughed again and looked strangely at him. 'You're not trying to pick me up, are you?' It was Luke's turn to blush as they reached the end of the gallery and walked into the vast entrance hall.

The young lady gave Luke an odd look, then said: 'As a matter of fact, it's my lunch break and I am on my way to the restaurant, so yes you *can* buy me a coffee... but only if you tell me what happened to your face.' Luke's hand went up to his burn and he quickly put his funny hat back on.

'My name's Molly by the way.' The young woman said as they went down the stairs towards the restaurant. The smell of stewing coffee and doughnuts pervaded the air as Molly guided Luke to an empty table, looking concernedly at his forehead, though most of the burn was now hidden under his hat. She was more familiar with the layout of the restaurant and obviously a few years older than Luke, and she took charge now - for he was a stranger in her territory. 'What can I get you?' she asked, turning the tables on his offer to buy her a coffee. ' I'll have a steak Dijon and a bottle of the finest champagne' Luke jested as Molly laughed 'you'll have what I get you' she said, her eyes engaging his as she pulled rank, seeming to revel in it.

Luke realised that he must look like the archetypal starving and impecunious student and he smiled back warmly. Whatever he was doing was having the desired effect on this attractive young lady - he was even feeling his limp coming back. Well, if she wanted to play superior, then let her, for he had tricked this lab technician into talking to him for one purpose only; information!

Molly returned from the buffet counter, carrying a tray of doughnuts and coffee. Her white lab-coat was a little too tight for her and Luke eyed her ample figure as she sat down at the table.

'Is this the new designer diet?' he asked, as she laughed again. She liked laughing, Luke thought, and it was doing him the power of good; he needed some laughs.

'So,' Molly said devouring a doughnut as if it were about to go out of fashion. 'Tell me about yourself,' her pale green eyes looked meaningfully into his own. 'Were you really trying to chat me up back there in the gallery?' Luke thought about that for a while, and it did seem like a good ploy to disguise his real interests, and perhaps may provide a possible clue to the whereabouts of Labachi and Rachid.

'Yes' he lied. 'I saw you coming down the spiral staircase, and I saw your lovely figure and heard the rat-a-tat-tat of your high heels, and I was overcome with lust...I am sorry.' He looked up and into her eyes as he saw the incredulous expression on her face, as the colour rose up from her neck to blotch her cheeks with a red mottling.

'I see' Molly said, struggling to regain her composure. 'So...it must mean that you really fancy me?' She said it as if it were the last thing possible in the world. 'Well' Luke had to be careful now,' 'it's not just that, but I thought that I might be able to talk to you...you see,' he said working himself into the part. 'I am all-alone in this big city, and it.... overwhelms me...it is so, impersonal.'

'You silly boy' Molly reached out and took his hands in hers as some as the luncheon guests turned in their seats, smiling at this uncommon display of affection. 'Luke,' she said, 'I am flattered that you fancy me, and I would like very much to talk with you. The only thing is,' Molly looked at her watch, 'that I have to be up in the lab at one thirty.'

'Okay' Luke squeezed her hands, hardly believing his luck. 'I'll see you on the steps of the entrance at....'

'Five thirty' Molly finished the sentence as her pale green eyes gazed searchingly into his. She rose, smoothing down her ill-fitting lab-coat and with an enigmatic smile she walked confidently out of the restaurant, clutching the file.

Luke got up from the table, feeling slightly claustrophobic, and made for the entrance of the British Museum, his mind in a whirl. As he sat down once more next to the stone lions on the steps where he had been just one or two hours ago, his mind raced with the implications of this new liaison. All he had wished to do was to find out the private residence of Labachi and Rachid, so he may be able to effect the release of mother, and his spying on the restoration room had proved effective to some extent, though mainly accidentally; for surely Molly must know where her boss lived. Still he had to be cautious.

He had engineered a situation where he might derive some knowledge as to the whereabouts of the cult, who he knew held Bridget captive. And yet he had precipitated a possible liaison with the one person who may be able to help him; for there was no doubt that a very physical chord had been struck between Molly and himself.

With four hours to kill, Luke stood up and walked down the steps of the British Museum and out through the high metal gates to wander the streets and the bookshops that graced the road outside the greatest repository of Ancient Archaeological knowledge ever to be stored under one roof.

As a thunderclap echoed above and the rain pelted down onto the grey pavement Luke ducked into the nearest bookshop, noticing the man behind the desk eyeing him with an expression barely short of contempt. The raindrops dripped from the absurd hat as Luke perused the bookshelves and the proprietor watched him as a cat watches a mouse. Luke's eyes were downcast as he noted the titles of the expensive books: " for collectors only."

Amid the array of prestigious authors, one stood out on the neatly stocked shelves, Dr Wabib Labachi; A treatise on the known obelisks of the world – an impressive sounding title, but to Luke's mind, written by an even more impressive and ambiguous author. Luke plucked the book from the shelf, and deposited it on the counter as the weasel eyed him suspiciously.

'Ninety Five pounds' the proprietor announced, a cynical smile of contempt hovering about his lips; there was no way that this ragamuffin could afford that.

'Totally absurd price' Luke said, rummaging in his wallet , 'the price on here say's twenty pounds.'

'It is a deleted copy' the bookseller voiced, in a hurt sort of way, 'it has been struck, I mean, it is out of print' Luke was waiting for the tears.

'My friend' Luke grasped the little man by his Oxford tie, 'it says on the sleeve, twenty pounds. Are you going to engage me in an argument, or will you accept this!' Luke pushed a twenty-pound note into the nose of the book dealer as he tightened his grip on the man's tie.

'Take it' the bookseller choked. 'It is yours,' and I hope you have many happy hours of reading.'

Five thirty finally arrived and Luke saw Molly exit the Museum from his position just outside the gates. The white Mercedes was still in its allocated parking space, so Labachi and Rachid must still be inside. He waved to Molly as she looked around for him on top of the steps and she joined him at the gate; they walked off towards Russell Square as the weasel-faced man in the bookshop, having observed them with interest, pulled the blind of the shop door window down.

Molly, having discarded her lab-coat was wearing a smart, two- piece tartan suit, a big improvement on her technician's outfit Luke thought, as she led the way through the maze of narrow streets.

'Where are we going?' Luke asked, looking at the bright-eyed young woman. 'Surprise' Molly replied as she bounced along the pavement, almost skipping. She had been thinking about the tall blonde haired youth all the afternoon, and though she was secretly flattered that he found her attractive, she was buoyed by the prospect of talking to someone she thought she could trust. Though Molly was an attractive (if slightly on the heavy side) young woman, her bubbly nature was suppressed for most of the time as a result of working in that dreary lab with two men who communicated in Arabic, and spoke to her only to bark orders.

'Nearly there' Molly slapped Luke's shoulder, running ahead and up the steps of a terraced house. She let herself in with a key and Luke followed as she ran up the dark stairs to the top-floor flat.

'Entrée' She stood at the open door as Luke pushed past her, looking at her bright eyes and smelling the light fragrance of her perfume. He felt his arm brush against her breasts as he walked through the narrow doorway and saw her excited breathing as her bosoms heaved under her tartan suit. 'You're out of breath' Luke said, taking her hand and feeling her pulse. Molly closed the door and put her other hand up to Luke's head. 'Let's take this silly hat off' she said. She pulled it off, standing on her tiptoes to reach and threw it onto the settee. She grasped his neck and pulled his head down to her full red lips and kissed him and Luke put his arms around her, feeling her narrow waist as her green eyes searched his face.

'I've been thinking of doing this all afternoon.' Molly said as she suddenly broke off the embrace and pushed Luke away. She was an impulsive young lady, Luke thought as he smiled at her and replied nonchalantly. 'Oh, I generally have that effect on woman!' She laughed and went into the tiny kitchen. 'Tea or Coffee' she asked. 'Whisky' Luke shouted over his shoulder as he looked around the flat, 'I mean it is permitted isn't it?' 'It is after six...'

'There you go again... using that word permitted again.' Molly said as he heard the clink of glass; she was taking him seriously.

'I like your African art,' he shouted as he looked around the tiny flat. The lounge was literally given over to ethnic artefacts: drums and a variety of musical instruments hung from the magnolia walls; carved mahogany elephants and naked African figurines were dotted around the room, making walking a rather hazardous experience.

'Do you travel much?' Luke asked as he moved carefully to the window and looked out into the late autumn landscape of nearly denuded lime trees and artisan terraced houses that curved neatly around the crescent in their grey-ochre London brick façade. The sky was an overcast pallor of lead and the streetlights came on as he looked at the late October evening.

'Do you have any lighting here?' he wise-cracked, 'or do you like to feel your way around' Molly appeared from the kitchen holding a tray with a bottle of single malt, a decanter of water and two glasses, which she set down on the table. She came to stand beside Luke and put her arms around him, kissing him again fully on the mouth. 'You do ask a lot of questions' she said as she came up for air and stood looking into his eyes.

'What happened to your face' she asked gently touching his burn. 'I will tell you' Luke said, squeezing her hands then sitting down on the settee and pouring himself a drink. Molly joined him. 'You don't really drink scotch, do you?' Luke asked. 'No' Molly said, 'it was a present from someone.' She left it at that, but poured herself a glass anyway and they clinked glasses reciting the inevitable. "Cheers."

Luke launched into the story of how he had come by the burn on his forehead, and watched Molly's face as she stared incredulously at him whilst he described the strange events since his father's funeral. A frown of confusion or disbelief hovered about her brow as he told of Labachi's and Rachid's involvement and how he thought them to be disciples of an evil cult and responsible for his mother's abduction.

'You poor, poor, boy,' Molly sympathised, 'and I thought you were just a student. 'My God, you have been through the mill.' She stood up and walked to the window, turning his incredible story over in her mind.... It seemed so implausible that it might be true.

'Do you believe me?' Luke asked after a while. Molly turned from the window and the scene of the streetlights below and looked at the scarred and strangely dressed youth.

'I don't know she said.' I would like to trust you but I cannot quiet take onboard the astral travelling bit....'

'What about Labachi and Rachid? Luke asked her. 'Do you think them capable...?'

'Is this why you chatted me up?' Molly's voice was sad, 'so you could get information about Dr Labachi and Mr Rachid.' She was trying to fight back the old feeling she often got of being used. 'I thought you said you fancied me,' she added limply. 'I mean,' she said coming to sit beside him on the settee, 'it's all so fantastic.... It's difficult to know what to say. You just wanted some information from me, isn't that it?'

Luke took her shoulders and swung her around to face him as he looked into her hurt, green eyes that brimmed with tears on feeling this sense of betrayal. Luke also felt that negative feeling of guilt...was he just using her to try to find his mother?

'I did say that' Luke admitted, 'and I knocked into you on purpose.... Because I would do anything to find mum...wouldn't you? He looked into the tearful face. 'But that was then; before I came to know you a little better...and what I feel for you now I cannot tell you... because it is too obscene! He felt his loins course with suppressed desire as he hugged her to his chest. Molly's eyes were wet and her sense of this handsome youth's duplicity brought the bottled-up ardour of her longing to the surface and she wept openly as Luke held her tight.

'I am sorry' Luke continued, 'I only know that I have found in you a true friend, and more than that, but I need you to trust me. They embraced on the small settee and Molly felt her previous feelings of mistrust dissipate as she relaxed with Luke's strong arms around her.

'Will you stay with me tonight' Molly's watery green eyes probed his face as she attempted a smile, wiping away a tear as Luke held her tight and felt a warmth and closeness which he had never before experienced.

'Yes, my love' he said, 'I will stay with you, and protect you from the bogeyman.'

'This is Friday' Molly clutched him to her breast. 'It means that we can have a lie in...'

Luke picked up the young woman, and pushing the door to what he guessed was the bedroom, carefully laid her down on the single bed.

✳✳✳

'Do you believe me?' Luke asked, sipping a cup of freshly made coffee as morning sunlight streamed into the tiny flat. Molly had risen before him and was busy with breakfast as Luke sat on the edge of the single bed, his hair knotted into blonde curls as he looked through the open door.

'I believe that you're a good bullshitter' Molly shouted back, her face ecstatic as she busied herself with the frying pan. 'Oh, and I believe you're good in bed, but the rest...' She clicked her tongue, 'the rest I will have to think about.' Luke showered and dressed and sat down at the small kitchenette breakfast bar.

'Here,' Molly said, 'get this down your neck. We can't have you pleading hunger as well.' Luke laughed; her light touch was reassuring as he tried to suppress the demons which haunted him. Molly's breasts were peeking out of her nightdress as she bent over him, setting the plate of bacon, eggs, and waffles under his nose. Luke grabbed her and kissed the warm flesh, smelling the natural scent of her body. 'You are like a mother to me,' he whispered as he sought her lips and they kissed a long and satisfied kiss of requited love.

'Silly boy' Molly scolded, 'Your eggs will get hard.' She tore herself away as they both laughed, seeing the mutual expression of ardour on each other's faces.

'Um'. Luke exclaimed as he devoured the breakfast, 'this is good, what do you charge for B+B.'

'It's free' Molly giggled 'so long as you do the washing up.'

'Suits me' Luke said with his mouthful.

The meal over, Luke was as good as his word and he busied himself in the kitchen, thoroughly washing the greasy pans and dishes. Molly sat on a stool patting her tousled red hair in the triple mirror and examining her slightly bruised breasts. She peeled off her nightdress and showered in the tiny blue and white tiled en-suite and then came back to the dressing table, combing her long wet hair.

Molly marvelled at the events of the previous day and in particular the long night of love making and realised that she would have to be careful. She was not in the habit of going to bed with casual strangers and wondered if her passion she felt for this strange, handsome youth was prudent. Yes, she had been very lonely in recent months, and her job was not as fulfilling as she would have liked it to be. But the stories Luke had told her about the cult, and his experience of Astral travelling were like something out of a gothic horror story and she still could not bring herself to believe them.

Perhaps her slight seniority, she was seven years older than him, had engendered a maternal feeling towards him, for she could see that he had been through the wars; the burns on his face and body were testament to that. She felt a close bond with him, not to mention physical attraction – but was that healthy? Was it all too fast, too sudden?

She hummed an Irish jig as she talced herself and put on her bra; she had to stop feeling negative. What had happened, had happened, and she felt like a woman again. She decided to keep a check on her emotions, but she owed him enough to trust him; he had made her feel happy again

'So, my beautiful, green eyed, red haired Irish beauty.' Luke camped it up a little as he sat on the breakfast bar that now was as clean and tidy as a whistle. 'Where shall we go today?'

Molly came out of the bedroom, ruffling her almost dry locks as the sunlight emblazoned their red-gold sheen. 'I'm going to take you to the market,' she said, 'to see what I can get for you...'

'To buy for me, or to sell me?' Luke jested, his blue bright eyes gleaming under the tumble of blonde locks.

'I'm going to sell you into slavery,' Molly retorted, 'to the highest bidder,' she tapped a shoulder bag which hung against her Indian cotton print dress. 'But I will be doing the bidding!' her voice was assertive.

'Then,' she continued, her voice coming down a tone. 'I'm going to show you where Dr Labachi lives!' She was serious.

'Thank you' Luke said as he leaped from the breakfast bar. 'Thank you my love.' He embraced her and felt her warmth through the cotton fabric and the fragrance of her freshly washed hair wafted over him.

'But, we had better go now unless my humble slave mistakes his station' She pushed him away. 'And I'm putting you on a diet of bromide!' Molly said sternly as she tossed her hair and made for the door.

Portobello Road was awash with people. Every colour, creed, ethnic origin and social status mingled together in the jostling crowd, as they walked down the open market from Notting Hill Gate. Luke's arm was around Molly's waist as they threaded their way through the noise of animated conversation and the press of bodies, looking at the stalls, which ranged from knick-knacks to valuable antiques, prices jumping from mere pennies to thousands of pounds within the space of a few feet. All was a jumble of bartering frenzy and multi-coloured commotion, as the poor mingled with the rich and the young rubbed shoulders with the old.

'I love this market,' Molly said brightly, 'you can find anything here.'

'Except devotion.' Luke added, pinching her bottom through the Indian smock. Molly slapped his hand in a strangely prudish gesture. 'Don't forget,' she said, 'my boss lives near here.'

They brought a few trinkets, and Luke placed a cheap set of Indian beads around Molly's neck. 'Now you're really ethnic he said,' as she scowled at him. The weather had improved, and the sunshine felt warm as they took a drink and a sandwich outside onto the patio of a pub, watching the throng of people wind their way up and down the narrow road. Suddenly Luke's eyes were drawn to the figure of a tall woman in a black cape who walked purposefully down the street - most of the crowd who saw her stepped out of her way, or looked at her in awe. She had jet-black hair cut into a fringe and very strange eye make-up.

'Come on' Luke said, taking Molly's hand and leaving the half-finished sandwich and drinks as he literally dragged her down the steps back into the throng of people. 'You don't have to show me Labachi's house,' he said 'so you won't have to feel like a betrayer. See that tall woman ahead,' he gestured to the black-haired figure who was having more success than themselves in cutting through the jostling melee. 'That is Ishtar, of whom I told you. She is Labachi's daughter...and she must be going to the house.'

Ishtar had swung into a side street and was heading for Ladbrook Grove. There was less cover here and they dodged behind parked cars and tradesman's vans, but she didn't look back. She crossed over the Grove into Elgin Avenue and Luke stood at the corner, hidden behind a high wall as he watched her go swiftly up the steps of a terraced house. He noted the position of it, and then pulling his crumpled hat from his pocket and knocking it out into shape he put it on. 'Wait here, he said, I'll be back in a mo.'

Luke had visualised the position of the house that he saw Ishtar enter and walked casually by on the far pavement noting the number: 100, he could remember that. Now all he needed was to wait for darkness, for he had some visiting to do. He walked around the block, singling out the back garden of the house from the footpath, which led through communal gardens. Apart from the ground floor, all the blinds were drawn on the windows of the four-storey house as he glanced carefully up at it, but he couldn't detect any movement from the downstairs window. He circled around and came up behind Molly who was still peeking from behind the wall. He pinched her ribs as she froze, and spun around, her face registering alarm.

'You little rat!' she spat at him. 'Don't you ever do that again!'

'Come on' he said, 'let's go and finish that drink, if it's still there.'

Luke tried to enthuse about the rest of the afternoon as they pottered about the bookshops and craft stalls dotted around the area, but his thoughts were on the sighting of Ishtar, and his finding of the house, and the time dragged by.

'You know what I have to do' Luke held Molly as they stood on the platform of Ladbrook Grove station, 'and I have to do it alone...'

'Just be careful.' Molly cautioned, handing him a card with her phone number on it. 'Will you please phone me as soon as you are done... and then come back?' 'Yes, my love.' Luke kissed her, watching her board the train; then he was gone, bounding up the steps back up to the road, three at a time.

CHAPTER SEVEN
*** THE SATANIC HOUSE ***

It was almost dark as Luke walked out onto the road and headed towards Elgin Avenue. An autumn mist had come down and he welcomed the grey blanket of cover, walking cautiously along the path at the rear of the house.

The gate to the garden of the house was locked and the privet hedge was high, but not too high for Luke to vault over. He crouched down and made his way stealthily to the narrow space at the side of the house, seeing the lights come on through the large patio doors. He ducked down, and peered carefully upwards in time to see Ishtar drawing the curtains. He thought he saw the gleam of her silver crescent moon atop her black hair.

It was the top floors of the house Luke was interested in and he saw that his only way of getting up to them would be a sturdy but rather rusty waste pipe that ran from a toilet on the second floor; the other drainpipes were too insubstantial to take his weight.

He hauled himself up onto a couple of discarded old tea chests and tugged the pipe; it seemed sound enough. He climbed carefully up to the top floor, glad of the misty drizzle, and perched just under the toilet window; it was open a crack. He levered the window with his strong fingers and it slid upwards stiffly. It was just large enough for him to squeeze through and he dragged himself over the sill doing a slow forward roll over the toilet seat and onto the floor. He listened, but the house was quiet; he had not been heard. Luke opened the toilet door and peered into a dark corridor; there didn't seem to be any lights on upstairs at all. He listened down the stairs and could hear the sound of voices and the tones of strange music; he also smelt the acrid smell of some sort of incense: the cult must be making ready for one of their gatherings.

Luke decided to do a search of the second floor, which he was on, and then the third floor, which he guessed, was the attic. As there were no lights on up here, he would have to move carefully. He crept along the corridor, opening the door to each room slowly before he inched into the dark interiors. They were mainly bedrooms, but he did not stop to ascertain whose, only to check they were empty.

One room however, did intrigue him, as it could be non other than Ishtar's. In the dim light from the streetlights, which filtered through the closed blinds, he saw the tools of the enchantress' trade neatly arranged. Jars of ointments, small glass jars of lapis lazuli mascara and black kohl eyeliner were grouped in front of the dressing table mirror, whilst her jewellery and hair bands were laid out in antique dishes of Jade and Onyx. Her robes and sheer tunics were hung on the tall mahogany wardrobe and the room was filled with her strange and exotic perfumes from the East.

Luke felt his groin constrict as he remembered that erotic hold which she had exercised over him those weeks ago, and kneeling at her bed he pulled down the soft satin duvet and placed his head on her pillow, aware of that indescribable desire sweeping over his body once more. He cursed himself for his weakness: was she not the demon who had tricked him into astral travelling, only to abandon him in some alien landscape? He rehearsed the inscription, deriving comfort in the knowledge that he still had the mastery of it, for he felt a premonition that one day he would need it to escape or avenge himself of this treacherous woman.

'Molly, forgive me,' he muttered to himself, walking out of Ishtar's room and trying to free himself from that unwholesome shackle of lust that he still felt for the temptress.

The rest of the rooms were devoid of human occupancy and Luke moved up the narrow flight of stairs to the third floor, the attic. Finally, in the last of the four smaller bedrooms, his heart raced in the knowledge that he had found mother. Though all the clothes and various feminine effects were new, he could sense Bridget's presence and his heart rejoiced as he recognised her antique silver bracelet on the table.

So, she must be downstairs. He searched the room once again but could find no trace of drugs or restraints that would confirm his assertion that she was a captive in the house. Nevertheless, she could have been hypnotised or brain washed into joining the evil cult and this would make her a prisoner in an equal sense. Overjoyed at the prospect of being reunited with his mother, yet aware of the danger he was now in, Luke edged his way down the stairs to the lower floors.

As he descended the staircase, Luke could hear the voices and music coming from the ground floor. On the first floor he passed a door from which a red light emanated, its eerie glow spewing out across the carpet of the landing. Luke pushed the door and as it opened, he gasped out loud for the whole of this floor had been knocked through and it was now one enormous room with a beautiful polished parquet floor illuminated by soft amber-red wall lights. In the middle of this foreboding room, bathed in the unnatural red light, was an imposing-looking throne. Sculptured from some precious stone, jade perhaps, this elaborate artefact rested on a plinth, the whole structure sparkling subtly, causing the translucent green stone to glow in an ethereal presence.

A back rest supported by intertwining arms held a life-like cobra, its hooded head flared out in striking attitude; the eyes of the serpent were made of large red rubies that glowed menacingly, seeming to penetrate Luke's gaze as he withered under its preternatural stare. He closed the door abruptly and blinked; how could a sculpture of stone have the power to mesmerise?

This then must be the Godhead - the inner sanctum of the cult, Luke thought, and it was a place of pure evil! He shuddered, and started to walk silently down to the ground floor, the human conversation seemed to be becoming louder - like a chant - and the astringent acrid smell of incense burned his nostrils.

The ground floor hall was empty and as he looked along the tiled Victorian passage he saw that the double doors to the large room at the rear of the house were slightly ajar - this was where the sound was coming from. Luke crept stealthily from the bottom of the stairs and placed his eyes against the crack in the door. The large room was filled with people, sitting in a circle on the floor. They were dressed in orange robes and sat silently, their eyes fixed on four figures in the centre of the circle: Labachi, Rachid, Ishtar and...*Mother!* Luke's mother was there, standing half facing him, her eyes bright as she stood silently dressed in an orange robe.

His pulse racing, Luke caught a snippet of the conversation: 'And let us be thankful...' it was Labachi who addressed the others. 'Let us be thankful this day that we have a new member to our Order. We have a distinguished lady who has seen the light and joined us, this illustrious group of the Order of the One Dimension.'

Bridget stood silently, her dilated eyes fixed on Labachi whilst he introduced her to the cult. Ishtar stood at her side, her Egyptian hair and eye make-up were immaculate in the light from the soft wall-lights that illuminated an astrological design on the large sweep of curtains drawn closed around the bay windows.

The chant continued: 'So let us connect in astral projection to our Lord, the Esoteric Oracle and tell him our news...let us adjourn to the inner sanctum of the Oracle...'

As they turned towards the door, Luke shuffled back along the corridor, and crouching, ran back up the stairs as the followers filed through the double doors and into the hall. Luke watched from the landing of the second floor as Labachi silently led them into the room with the bizarre serpent headed throne. After the last of the 'congregation' had entered, the door closed, but not quite. Luke tiptoed down the stairs and pushing the door very carefully and slightly, peered again into this vast room. What he saw made his gut rise up in an abhorrent surge of repugnance.

Bridget was seated on the sepulchral jade throne, her hypnotic eyes looking upwards at Labachi who held out his hands in some arcane gesture of supplication, the orange robed acolytes sitting around cross-legged in a circle.

'Master' Labachi spoke slowly, his accent thick and full of awe. 'Accept this neophyte into thine Order. Grant her the fortitude to fight the oppressor, and to remain with us until the end of time...!'

'Aye, it is so' the circle of followers chanted; their eyes shut. 'For she brings us great treasure, oh Master of the One Dimension...'she brings us the inscription of the Obelisk of Time...' Luke shuddered, yet he watched entranced.

Ishtar went to the wall and took hold of the purple cord attached to a similar cloth. She pulled the cord and the purple cloth fell to the floor to reveal Jock Slater's painting of the Lost Obelisk,

'Look now and behold, oh Brethren.' The followers opened their eyes and inhaled together at the strange beauty of the landscape and Luke himself gasped out loud, his voice unheard by the awed members of the cult.

Bridget looked at the painting but her eyes registered no response; Luke knew now that she was drugged or mesmerised. She didn't know what she was doing, or where she was.'

'This painting,' Labachi was speaking again, 'represents a new horizon in the understanding of our Master's great design. It represents, not just the vanished Obelisk of Time, but gives us the power to travel to his bosom at will...to travel to the Kingdom of Paradise in the Grand Master's Temple at Aiyu.'

'Ooh...a hallowed coo of recognition arose from the seated acolytes as they gazed up at the painting, 'may the Oracle be all-powerful, our gratitude to the Oracle...!

Luke wanted to vomit as he heard their ingratiating chants of simpering nonsense.

'Are you ready my dear?' Labachi asked, looking at Bridget's fixed eyes, their piscine globes registering infinity. 'Are you ready to travel to our new domain at Aiyu? Are you ready to go to our holy Esoteric Oracle, there to deliver to him the arcane inscription lost for time immemorial...the inscription as foretold by the Prophecy of Time, but one which only *you* can pronounce. Go now and consummate your order of neophyte. 'I am...I will' Bridget intoned, her voice distant and trance-like.

What was this? Luke tensed as he knelt at the door. Go where? Consummate what?

'You know the command?' Labachi asked

'I do' Bridget concurred. 'Neb...Ankh...'

'*No!*' Luke's desperate voice echoed around the room as he lurched into the middle of the assembly. 'No, Mother! Do not say the incantation...'

'You!' Labachi snarled, his eyes a menace of hatred. 'I thought you were disposed of. Seize him, he is not one of us!' he ordered. Four burley men arose from the floor, securing Luke in a grip of solid steel, rendering his struggles in vain and a large hand was clamped over his mouth.

'Continue!' Labachi ordered, to the woman who was unaware of her son's intervention, her glazed eyes fixed unseeingly on her husband's painting as she recited:

Neb – Ankh – Sar – Eff – Jded – Rheckit

The Obelisk in the painting started to glow as Luke watched in horror as his mother completed the inscription and he strove to break out of the

Herculean grip of the four men, but to no avail. Luke's incredulous eyes protruded in shock as the corporeal body of Bridget faded from view and he saw now only the grotesque chair with the red eyes staring out from the hooded cobra back; there was not a trace of its former occupant!

'No,' Luke sobbed inwardly, 'what have you done?'

'You!' Labachi spun to face Luke. ' I do not know how you managed to return whence you were deposited...it is of no consequence now ... for we have the painting and the inscription. Your mother has gone to learn of our ways in the temple of the Esoteric Oracle... and I warn you on pain of your life... *do not darken this sanctuary of light again!*'

'Throw him out!' Labachi ordered the bodyguards and Luke was dragged from the room. The last thing he saw before a neck chop rendered him unconscious was the venom glowing from Ishtar's black eyes, hearing at the same time the sibilant chants of hatred rise up from the circle of cultists.

✷✷✷

Molly was pacing up and down the small flat. It was midnight and there was still no phone call from Luke. It was almost six hours since she has bid him farewell at Ladbrook Grove station. A myriad of possibilities ran through her mind as she checked the phone to see if it was still working, for the nth time. Perhaps he had found his mum and taken her home - perhaps he was a total liar and his stories had all been mendacious fabrications, making her the victim of a one-night stand.

She doubted this however, and she was about to get her coat on and take the last train to go and find him, when the phone rang. 'I'm on the way back' it was Luke. 'I'm at the station,' I'll see you in half an hour; but expect the worst...' The phone went dead as Luke hung up and Molly's mind raced with a new set of endless possibilities. The doorbell went half an hour later and Molly pressed the remote door lock and heard giant footsteps on the stairs.

As she looked at Luke on the threshold, Molly didn't know whether to laugh or cry. His face was bruised and blood ran down from the corner of his mouth; he had straw sticking out of his rumpled hair, and his clothes, new-looking that morning, looked as though they has been dipped in a vat of multi-coloured paint.

'What on earth happened?' Molly exclaimed, pushing him into the room. Are you all right? You look like you've been pulled through a hedge backwards.

'Something like that' Luke mumbled, his gums sore. 'I was beaten up and dumped in a builder's skip.' Molly's mouth vacillatedbetween sympathy and hysterics; the latter won out which she later explained away as a release of anxiety as she guffawed in Luke's face, dropping to her knees and clutching his plaster and straw covered coat as she choked with laughter.

It wasn't quite the reception Luke had been anticipating, and he felt a bit hurt until he looked in the mirror and saw his appearance; it was as if he had been tarred and feathered, only with paint, plaster and straw.

'So much for heroics' he said as he changed into one of Molly's kimonos that ended just short of his underpants; 'what I need is a new wardrobe.'

The calming effect of Molly's laughter as she cleaned him up before they went to bed didn't last for long as Luke's nocturnal thoughts returned inevitably to the plight of his mother.

'So, let me get this straight' Molly reiterated Luke's account of the events of the previous night as they stood sipping coffee and looking out of the window at the foggy morning.

'You're saying, that it was not just Bridget's ka that astral travelled but her whole corporeal body...she just faded into the air? Molly was trying to believe in Luke's implausible stories, but with difficulty.

'Which means that either the place, the incantation, or the effect of the magic painting was different' Molly summarised, looking at the distracted expression on the poor youth.

'*The throne!*' Luke suddenly had it. 'It was that chair...it had some sort of power...' he left the window and started pacing the room. He stopped and turned to look at Molly.

'You know what I have to do, don't you?' he approached her and grasped her shoulders, looking into her eyes. 'I have to get into that room somehow, and do what she did.... you know! I have to follow were Mother went ... sit in that chair, and then recite the incantation.' He squeezed her shoulders in a strong grip. 'Will you wait for me?' his voice was serious.

'Yes,' Molly said 'I'll wait for you...*but please be careful...*'A tear welled up in Molly's eye as she looked dolefully up at the harrowed face of the handsome youth.

✱✱✱

Luke gained access to the house in Elgin Avenue by the same means as the previous night, having noticed the white Mercedes absent from the driveway. He could detect no sound in the large dwelling as he climbed up to the first floor and was into the room of the cult without a problem; the door was unlocked. He placed himself in the Jade seat of the strange throne as his spine chilled to the preternatural tingle that seeped into his inner being on making contact with this device for transporting living matter from one dimension into another. He remembered the events of the previous evening when this same repository of evil had been filled with orange-robed acolytes. So the cult had sent her to Aiyu, that mythical place of Ancient Egytian legend. Also Labachi had uttered some mumbo jumbo about her knowledge of the inscriotion for astral projection, which he didn't fully understand.

So Aiyu was his destination then - that mythical place that somehow his father had been able to capture on canvas – and a dazzling thought swept through Luke's mind: perhaps that was where his father was, and he would arrive in that arcane dimension to see them reunited. But he cast this fallacious glint of hope aside, telling himself not to be silly and just to get on with the task in hand. Then looking at his father's painting on the wall facing him, he drew strength in the knowledge that this was the only link to his family that was left; everything else had perished in the abomination of the fire at Park House.

As he rehearsed the incantation in his mind, his thoughts went back to Molly and the closeness that they had shared in the short-lived time they had known each other. She was the antithesis of Ishtar; everything that evil trickster was not. He had wished that he could delay this voyage into the unknown, that he could spend more time in her company, but his need to try to save his Mother was pressing, and he could defer no longer.

Neb – Ankh – Sar – Eff - Jded – Rhekit

The snake-headed chair became threaded with a myriad of electric particles that tingled through his own body as Luke recited the incantation aloud, seeing the painting shake and tremble and the Obelisk in it glow a molten gold, its light shining out from the picture. It seemed to project into the very space in which he sat, and he felt his body lift off from the chair to start its corporeal journey into time and space. He held fast the images of his mother in his mind's eye, hoping that this would be the correct method of controlling when and where he was to be sent in his astral projection from the known world into the terrifying prospect of the unknown. As the blackness of space engulfed his senses, he felt once more the stupefaction of numbness and cold caused by his body's tranfer into another dimension.

Chapter Eight
*** Zalkina ***

It was not like the last time. It was not at all similar to the easy ride, (well almost), which Luke had experienced in the guiding arms of Ishtar. He was on his own in this trip into an unknown time/space continuum... and this realisation brought with it all the horrors!

As the vectors of time and space locked his body into some predetermined course, a nightmare of delusions pervaded his subconscious mind as he fought with the dictates of an alien force. It seemed as if his ka and corporeal body were trying to be separated; as if some diabolical navigator were attempting to wrest his will from his grasp. Luke could only imagine that the seat in which he had so trustingly sat as he incanted the formula for astral projection, was imbued with a greater will; one that sought to wrest his own identity from him. All the negative forces of his subconscious were paraded in front of his unseeing eyes, as the devourers of his soul sought to strip away his nerve and tear his ka from his body.

Yet Luke remained brave; adamant in holding in his mind all the precious memories of his family, even the scriptures he had learned as a boy, as the phantoms of the underworld clawed and tore at his very being; ghoulish spectres that tore of the very fabric of his soul with their satanic messages – the wails of the damned – repelled now by the conviction in his breast. Holding fast to what he knew was right, Luke felt their unwholesome force languish and retreat, and breaking free of their evil influence, he knew now only the joy of 'travelling' as he re-entered the ether and recognised the signs of his imminent 'landing.'

His landfall was not too short from the mark, although Luke didn't know it. The howls and screams of the un-dead and yet unborn were still ringing in his ear as his resurgent belief fought off the devourers of his soul.

As Luke came out of the stygian blackness, aware now that he had outwitted the enemy, an ecstatic sense of victory pervaded his disorientated mind. He had fought off the emissaries of the Esoteric Oracle, He of The One Order. He had conquered the satanic perversions of the evil cult by thinking on wholesome thoughts, on good and beauty. He had followed in the path of his mother, or so he hoped, and was standing on the threshold of a new world were the challenge of finding her would become his epic quest. High on this feeling of victory over evil, Luke did not realise the difficulties that lay ahead, but they would become evident all too soon.

Luke opened his eyes and looked around him, feeling a gentle warmth of sunlight on his face, a warmth that caressed his cold and air-worn body;

the deep, deep cold of the Astal Traveller. He saw that he was sprawled out on a ridge of soft turf that formed the top of an escarpment. It was thinly covered by pine trees and large ferns - he could feel the pine needles digging into his hands. A scented breeze cooled his fevered brow, bringing the aroma of sandalwood, and he guessed that those trees also graced the escarpment.

Sunkissed by a rosy, raking light, a deep valley was in front of him. From its distant blue slopes, tendrils of white mist floated whilst at the bottom a small stream meandered, its minuscule waterfalls glinting in the angled beams of sunlight. But it was the view across the valley that fired Luke's imagination; for it was of something very familiar. From the steep sides of the valley, crags rose up, their serrated buttresses forming an arbour for a variety of strange structures, temples perhaps. Above the rim of this part natural part manmade bastion, a pointed tip glowed golden in the raking light. It could only be one thing – an Obelisk, The Obelisk of Time. And then it suddenly dawned on Luke that he was looking at Aiyu, that scene depicted in his father's painting – but viewed now from behind. It was the reverse side of the mythical Paradise of Aiyu that he beheld - he must have missed his mark in a marginal time/space slip, though he was close, very close – he could walk that distance in a day, or maybe less.

So that was the legendary land of Aiyu, Luke thought as he lay still and tried to slow his racing mind in order to take in the beautiful aspect of this distant city of paradise - the hope of him landing not too far from his mother's destination spurring him on – for Aiyu was were she had been sent by the cult, if his memory served him well.

From this distance Luke could detect no sign of human activity, and if this were where his mother, (and hope against hope), his father might be, then he had to work out some sort of strategy. Was this citadel friendly, or was it enemy territory – was it in fact the seat of the Order of the One Dimension? Surely it had to be as that was where mother had been sent, hadn't Labachi mentioned this in his little speech just before Bridget recited the incantation and disappeared from view. And then it dawned on him: they, the cult, didn't just want the painting for the inscription - but equally because it portrayed their intended port of arrival – Aiyu: the very place he himself had just travelled to!

As Luke's thoughts ranged from the sublime, in the rapture of the beauty of the place, to the realistic - the grounds for any future plans were suddenly voided when he felt sharp abrasions to his skin as a course rope net enveloped his body. He was yanked from his crouched position up into the overhanging trees to hear the jabber of strange tongues below him as he dangled in space.

After more jabbering from down below, Luke felt the net in which he was ensnared start to descend. His feet touched the ground and yet whoever controlled the trap was not disposed to let him go, and tightened it once or twice to make sure that his prisoner understood this.

Luke looked through the mesh of the net and saw a host of diminutive men, clad only in loin clothes, who jabbered and chanted, gesturing and pointing like little gerbils – that is if gerbils could do all of the above. Luke, after his descent from the ether, could not help but feel a sense of superiority when he compared his stature to that of the natives, realised that they must feel in total fear of someone of his size - whatever the case, he was certain that these natives were not the cult.

'I am Luke, I am a man.' He knelt in the rope cradle of his prison and tried in his best possible manner to make gestures of supplication, or at least, tacit friendship to them, but as he beat his breast in an opening up sort of ceremony, the little men backed away, chuntering amongst themselves.

'Take me to your leader' Luke tried in his best Arabic, but it only engaged a similar response as the tribe went into a huddle and seemed to be hatching some sort of plot. Their eyes had become malevolent as they advanced towards the net. The tallest of them, reaching up to about Luke's navel, had a menacing sort of spear, (like a stone-age flint tied to a stick that Luke had seen in museums). Growing a little weary of their pathetic response to his parlaying, Luke tried the only available last resort as he started the incantation.

'Neb – Ankh – Sar – Ef....'

The effect could not have been more miraculous than if Luke had delivered ten tons of salt to their pygmy's huts, for the leader of the group dashed his spear to the ground and joined the others as they trembled on the black earth, their hands over their ears and bowing down in fearful homage to this alien being - the Demon from the stars – big magic! The net-master in the tree above cut the strands of the trap and jumped, in an amazing feat of gymnastics, to the ground where he joined his terror-stricken tribesmen.

'Me, Tarzan!' Luke shouted as he prized open the slack ropes and walked away from the net to confront his enemy.' The little men huddled in their groups but did not back away as this giant with the strange garb approached them. He knelt in front of them and extended the palms of his hands, as they cowered in their communal bunker of flesh. Luke noticed that one of the small brown natives seemed to be older: his curly hair was white and white hair sprouted also from his chin and his shoulders - perhaps he was the headman.

Luke padded towards him on his knees and saw the man's beady eyes watching his every move. The man did not withdraw as Luke reached out and tweaked the man's white whiskers, and then did the same to his own light stubble. Luke saw the light of recognition dawn in the small man's eyes - he was playing a game – he was not the Devil!

The white haired native stood up, the other natives groaning in dread, and Luke grasped his shoulders; the two of them were, with Luke kneeling, roughly about the same height.

'Me' Luke said as the group swayed and moaned 'me, Luke' he pointed to the brown man.

'Ima...Zalkine' the man said, pointing to his stomach.

'Zalkine huh...Good.' Luke said as he smiled into the man's face.' We are going to get to know each other.' Luke rose and took the old man's hand in his. He pointed upwards to the stars which now blazed from the blue – black vault between the over hanging trees 'Me, from the stars!' Zalkine prostrated himself again as he trembled and a low communal moan rose up from the group of terrorised men - not a good move, Luke thought.

Presently a new member to the group of natives arrived and Luke breathed a sigh of relief - anything to help him out of this impasse. A man of very curious demeanour indeed stepped into the grove as he approached Luke without any apparent fear whatsoever.

He was slightly taller than the natives, who rose in obvious relief at his presence, and stood watching as he approached the Demon from the stars. He had long red hair that fell down in natural ringlets from his bald dome of a head and his costume was sackcloth, although a motif of faded patchwork of indistinct origin was emblazoned upon his breast. In his hand he carried a strange device, which looked like an ancient Egyptian Systrum. However, as Luke was to find out, it was not an instrument for making music with, though it did emit some sort of sound. The curious old man talked into the device and then shook it as a strange language issued from it. Then it was the white haired one, Zalkine, who took a turn. This little party trick continued for a while and Luke grew more and more puzzled, whilst the natives watched in the awe – this was entertainment!

'Let me try' Luke said stepping towards Zalkine, but the man bid him to stay with his index finger raised as he spoke again. He shook the instrument. 'How do you do... I am Zalkine.... Take me to your leader,' a voice from the implement spoke and the little man's eyes lit up in expectation as he looked questioningly at Luke, his white curly eyebrows arched in the wizened nutshell of a face.

'How do you do' Luke replied. 'I am the leader' there was a pause as their eyes studied the machine and then the strange tongue of Zalkine's language was translated from the systrum. Zalkine's eyes turned back to Luke and the little men cooed in respect, bowing onto the pine needle-strewn earth.

'I come here to look for a woman' Luke used his best pigeon English, 'red hair,' he pointed to the taller man's locks. 'About so tall' he used his hands as a measuring rod. The natives listened carefully to the translation from their very superior voice box, then chattered wildly. Zalkine beckoned for Luke to follow and they set out along a path that led through the forest, away from the escarpment and the fabled city of Aiyu. They soon arrived at a cluster of huts made from branches bound together and covered with animal pelts. Luke was shown inside, sitting down on the soft skins of gazelle and wildebeest (or similar), whilst shouted instructions around the camp.

After a while, a deputation arrived and the natives, their faces beaming, thrust a figure clothed in a stitched rabbit-skin in front of the hut. Zalkine approached and peeling off the mottled furry cloak, exposed of a girl of great beauty to the gaze of the man from the stars.

'You come here for woman' Zalkine said speaking into his translator. 'Please accept my daughter...'

'No, No!' Luke scrambled out of the hut and placed the fur pelt back over the poor girl's shivering body. 'I don't mean *any* woman....I come for *my mother*!' Zalkine's face dropped as he realised his error. 'I am sorry' he spoke through the voice box, ordering his daughter to be led away - though not without a backward glance from her at the tall handsome stranger - as her father paced up and down muttering to himself, almost as if cursing his own stupidity. His face brightened after a while and he spoke into the translator.

'My daughter...she came from the stars as well' he gestured up into the trees where a few specks of white starlight could be seen through the dense foliage. 'Come' he said and led the way along a trail through the forest as Luke ran to keep up with the old man who shambled along on all fours like a primate.

After a while, they reached a clearing in the trees and Zalkine pointed at a dark pool in the centre. The white stars could be seen reflecting from the black surface of the pool, and as Luke followed the direction of the old man's gnarled finger, he saw a gleam of something down in the water. At first he couldn't make it out, but then the shape, half buried in the mud at the bottom of the pool, seemed familiar and it dawned on him that it was the top section of an Obelisk, the pointed cap lying just below the surface of the water.

Zalkine pointed upward and speaking into the systrum –like device, explained, 'It came from above, from sky...long time ago...it came from star people.'

'Do your people worship it?' Luke asked, bowing down to enact his meaning. 'Is it sacred?' Zalkine thought for a while and then shook his head. 'No, he said pointing whence they had come towards the distant city of Aiyu. 'My people worship yonder one...the one that breathes fire...' Luke thought for a minute. 'You mean lights up' he said 'it looks like fire... a sort of burning light?' Zalkine nodded and gestured excitedly, the strange foreigner understood.

The chief's daughter had followed them, and she sat bare-backed on a zebra, her long brown legs resting easily against the animals withers and she tossed back her black hair, looking at Luke as the zebra drank. Her rabbit skin pelt was wrapped around her torso and tied with a string of cowry shells. Luke sensed from her posture that she was strong, athletic and a very confident horsewoman.

'Was there a temple here' Luke asked, thinking that normally obelisks are situated near temples, but that was in the land of logic, not here, wherever here was.

'Yes Zalkine' replied with aid of the translation device, there are many temples in the swamps. It is dangerous, but my daughter knows the paths better. She will show you...she know places better than rest of my people, the Zalks. She first daughter of Zalkine, she called Zalkina.'

'Zalks, Zalkine, Zalkina...I can handle that,' Luke muttered.

'Zalkina' the old chief spoke to his daughter in gruff tones and she nodded her head. He handed her the translator, and suddenly Luke's mind made a bizarre connection.

'Did you find it here? He asked the old man, 'the magic voice...'

'My father find it over in the temples' Zalkina spoke through the futuristic mouthpiece... follow me... I show you!' The old man turned and walked up the trail, soon he was lost in the dark shadows.

'What your name' Zalkina talked into the systrum; Luke replied.

'Come Luke, come strange one, and follow me.' The girl set off around the edge of the pool on her zebra, and Luke did as he was bid.

✳✳✳

The remnants of the forest changed rapidly into a swamp proper as the tall trees leaned against each other, covered in moss and intertwining lianas, which hung in strange patterns above and trailed down to the boggy black ground. Large orchids grew from the rotten trees that littered the track, glowing in the half-light like strange fallen stars. Giant fungi spread their striated mushy forms out into their path as Zalkina dismounted, leaping from the zebra. In a flurry of rabbit-skin, she led the animal carefully over and through the obstacles as Luke followed; how she could see her way in the half-light, he had no idea.

The swamp was strewn with the remains of an old temple now, as blocks of stone and covered lintels rose from the bubbling black ooze or were leaning half-submerged in it. Zalkina turned and pointed to a sort of tall, familiar looking structure as she led the zebra up a flight of slippery stone steps that ended in an oblong, slightly sloping platform. Gaining the top, Luke realised that he was standing on a pylon, or ancient gateway, and looking down he saw a dark pool, its black waters pinpricked by white reflections of stars. Although the pool was a different shape to the one they had just come from, it seemed to be constructed in various interlinked curves to form a shape similar to a giant flower, a Lotus flower perhaps.

'This pool,' Zalkina said, holding up the systrum, 'is where the Gods bathe' she pointed upwards to the stars. She stood on the edge of the high plinth, her long black hair flowing across her face in the light breeze as her zebra nuzzled her and the beauty of her profile struck Luke. He recalled Molly's face though and counselled himself to keep a firm grip on where he was from, and what he had come here for.

All around the submerged Lotus pool were the remains of temple structures: columns; some still leaning melancholy in the starlit glade, others broken and lying across the dark swampy earth and overgrown with wild honeysuckle and other creepers. A dragonfly of immense proportions glided across the clear waters, its phosphor glow leaving an iridescent trail as it zigzagged away and was lost to view.

'You want to see the lost city?' Zalkina said suddenly, her voice cutting into Luke's thought's of Molly, and his recent journey from the house in Ladbrook Grove to this strange and beautiful place - for not even Jock Slater had painted anything as stunning as this starlit monument to a lost civilisation.

'Lost City!' he repeated 'where?'

Zalkina pointed down into the dark twinkling waters. 'Can you travel through water?' she said.

'Swim?' Luke retorted. 'You mean swim... you bet ya!'

Zalkina shook the systrum and frowned. It wasn't too good on some specialist words. Luke had a better idea. He was a fair linguist and he reckoned he could pick up the basics of this seemingly simple language. He suggested that the girl teach him and they sat crossed legged on the top of the sloping pylon as Zalkina gave him a grilling in the rudimentary words they would need to communicate. With sign language and certain key words, Luke found it more direct to talk to the beautiful native girl than using the translator.

'Tell me' Luke asked, looking into her dark, unfathomable eyes, 'why you afraid of speaking...Neb – Ankh – Sar...'

Zalkina jumped up, her eyes wide at the mention of that forbidden utterance. Luke sat mute until she sat down again, facing him as she tried to explain. 'It is big magic,' she said, simplifying her language so Luke could grasp her meaning. 'It is what the slave–masters say to bring the anger of the gods...'

'Slave-masters' Luke had to resort to the systrum for a while as he handed it to the girl to assist in the translation; it was getting complex.

'They come from the city,' she pointed back to where Luke had stood when he first arrived in the strange land. 'They come and take our people... to make slaves.'

'What are they called, these people?' Luke asked as Zalkina held the systrum to her mouth.

'They called people of the one...' her voice trailed off as her body shook.

'*The Order of the One Dimension!*' Luke helped her and she nodded, trembling on the edge of the pylon. Luke moved to her and took her shoulders as he saw the fear in her eyes. She clutched him and sobbed into his chest as he felt a bond, more like a brother and sister, grow up between them.

So the order of the One Dimension *did* control the fabled city of Aiyu –he had thought as much; from Labachi's words, he had guessed it, and now it was starting to become clearer - they had captured these poor people to take into slavery in their city of occupation. What fate the original dwellers in the city had suffered was only to be guessed at, though Luke wasn't going to press the girl further in her obviously distressed state.

Luke stood, trying to change the tone a little and stroking the zebra's head as it whinnied and snorted, clattering its unshod hooves on the stone surface, not too sure of the stranger,

'What call you he?' he asked Zalkina

'Kina, he called Kina.' Well that wasn't too difficult to remember either, Luke thought, and asked: 'You got brothers ...Sisters?' The girl shook her head and she rose and looked at him. Her black eyes were large globes in her brown face, the starlight emphasising their liqidity. She put her arms around him and he held her close - he would have to explain that he was like a brother – it could be difficult!

'So' Luke perched on the edge of the pylon, stripped down to his underpants. 'Show me the lost city.' Zalkina was naked; her fur wrap lay on the floor as Kina nuzzled it - he did not like his mistress leaving him.

'You must take in much air!' Zalkina gestured, inhaling. She was learning his language well, Luke thought as he looked at her brown body poised on the edge of the pylon, the starry glow from above painting her silhouette with an eerie, surreal blue light. 'Take a deep breath' Luke corrected, watching Zalkina who paused momentarily on the stone cornice and then plunged into the lotus pool, her body a graceful arc and her lithe, slim shape penetrating the dark waters like an arrow - without a ripple.

Luke followed her and cleaved the waters in a neat swallow drive as he went straight down to the bottom of the pool, seeing the sandy floor lit by the twinkling starlight above. He saw Zalkina's shape swimming towards a submerged rock-face and followed her, touching her feet with his hands as she cut through the star spangled waters in a strong breast-stoke ahead of him. He saw the fuzzy shape of an arch and followed close on her as the darkness of the tunnel cut off his vision, but such was his trust in her that he kept up with the fleeting water-wraith, but swimming behind her, touching her feet to reassure her he was still there.

Luke sensed her momentum glide upwards and he followed as they broke surface and trod water, taking in deep breaths. The chamber they had surfaced in was black, apart from a thin streak of starlight that entered into this secret aquatic world through a crack in the broken side of the pylon above them. Zalkina held onto Luke's shoulders as she floated, getting her breath and he felt her warm body press against his, trying to resist the temptations that paraded themselves in his mind.

'We go through tunnel now' she said 'Suck air, many air' Luke nodded and squeezed the girl's arm in acquiescence. She dived down and he followed, swimming one after the other through the tunnel of carved sandstone, he tapping her feet and hoping that she knew the way - though it was pretty obvious that she had done this many times before. Luke's lungs were about at bursting point; he tapped his leader's feet more urgently and she increased her stroke and they were catapulted through the subterranean passage to rise to the surface. Luke felt the reassurance of sandy ground under his feet as he gasped for air. My God he thought, she was some kind of swimmer! They were in a small chamber carved out of rock and what Luke couldn't quite grasp was how it was lit. For as he beheld Zalkina's face and looked into her excited eyes, feeling her body taking in deep gulps of air as she stood next to him on the shallow floor of the pool, the small cavern was sparkling with an iridescent light. Then he had it - it was natural fluorescing feldspar or some such crystal that glowed of its own accord and from which the subterranean cavern was made.

'Cave of light' Zalkina's breath was a white vapour as she pointed,' 'me call this...cave of light!'

They rested for a while, recovering their breath and Luke looked into the girl's lustrous eyes. She saw this as a great adventure and he was just as excited, though he knew not why!

Zalkina was shivering as they stood in the underground grotto. She placed her arms around Luke as they hugged each other to restore their body warmth; she seemed to be shivering more and more – it must be the cold, he thought.

'Come' Zalkina said, 'We go to pool of hot now,' she jumped up gracefully onto the overhanging stone ledge and extended her hand as she pulled the less athletic strange one up. Holding hands like childen, they ran along the corridor in the underground grotto and ducked under the fluorescing crystalline stalactites, which graced the ceiling. The passage opened into a vast chasm that disappeared from view and Luke saw a hand-carved lotus-form pool in the centre of it. From the rock wall of the cavern gushed two waterfalls that cascaded into the green waters. Zalkina squealed with delight as she threw her naked body into the underground geyser of steaming, fluorescent water. Luke followed and they sat on the floor of the shallow rock - cut pool and let the luxurious heated waters that cascaded from some geothermic source engulf them, warming their chilled bodies.

'I not see this...' Luke tried to communicate, his shivering body warmed by the waters, illuminated from all sides as the Fluorspar cast its shadowless light over them.' 'I no see this before.' He smiled at the girl who lay soaking in the heat of the thermal waters, oblivious of his attempt to converse. They lay for a long while in the pure green restoring waters, luxuriating in their regenerative powers. Luke tried not to look at the totally unselfconscious native water nymph as she stretched out in front of him and her brown lithe body floated up to the surface, her eyes closed and unaware of his adoring gaze.

'Come' he said, dragging himself from the aphrodisiac effects of the waters, 'Come,' we have the lost city to see! Zalkina opened her almond shaped eyes and reluctantly stood up without a trace of modesty as to her naked body, squeezing her hair and sleeking it down along the nape of her neck as she stepped from the pool. She shook herself like a dog emerging from water and started to run along the tunnels in an animal-like way and Luke caught his breath trying to keep up with her. She is like no athlete I have ever known, he thought, marvelling at the graceful motion of her body.

They ducked and dipped under the numerous crystal projections as they sped down the subterranean tunnel until they ascended rock-cut stairs and stood in an underground vault. In the centre of this partly rock-cut cavern was a structure, the likes of which sent a horror of recognition running down Luke's spine, yet he could not explain this, for he had not seen anything like it before. It was similar to a giant bell, yet sunk into the rock and slanted, as if it had reposed there for a very long time. Atop the bell that was covered by green verdigris, was a massive gantry of poles, which towered up into the blackness.

'Who made it? Where did it come from?' Luke asked.

'Come from stars...Come from your people.' Came the cryptic reply.

Luke didn't want to lower his status in her eyes, so he elected to omit the truth of his origin, though he argued with himself as by way of an excuse, that they were all really star people by modern definition.

Luke had to admit, as he looked at the strange bell-shape, that it bore some similarity to those absurd photos of flying saucers that he had found in an old book as he had poked around in an antique bookshop back in the real world, which seemed like an age away.

'So where is the lost city?' Luke asked trying to focus his mind on what they had really come to see. Zalkina beckoned and walked under a low natural arch and held Luke's arm as he almost walked out into sheer space. He gasped as he looked at this massive cavern, which was like a gigantic inverted dish, or a sort of flattened dome. So vast was it that the other side was lost in distant mists as the natural light of the feldspar glowed around the walls way above their heads.

They were standing on a narrow ledge and the walls of the cavern fell away below their feet as Luke looked down at the sickening space below them. But it was what stood in the centre of this vast, dizzying scene that grasped Luke's imagination – for there was the lost city! Its domes and minarets, temples, large and small, and some architectural structures that he had never seen before but which all appeared to be made from ivory coloured crystal, were there for the stupefaction of the senses as Luke let out a long low whistle of disbelief. The whole complex was bathed in shimmering, incandescent, silvery light scintillating from the electrum cap of a giant obelisk that stood in the middle of the complex.

'It is truly magnificent' Luke exclaimed; Zalkina smiled at the stranger's awestruck face. 'I wonder what happened to the people...'

'People go to Aiyu,' Zalkina pointed back to the other fabled city, the one above ground, 'no one live here now.' And it was true; not a sign of human activity or occupation could be seen. It was as if the beauty of the lost city were to be forever held in a well of non-being, never to be glimpsed by human eye unless they were to make this almost impossible trek that Luke and the girl had made.

There were many questions on Luke's lips, which he wanted to ask Zalkina, but they would have to wait, for the girl made a naïve sign with her hands, indicating tiredness and took Luke's hand as they retraced their steps. Luke, his mind in a whirl and marvelling still at the Lost City, followed Zalkina back along the miasmic caverns as she strode purposefully and silently onwards to the underground pools.

'Deep Breath', she looked back at Luke, an enigmatic smile on her face, obviously pleased with her new addition to the star-boy's language. When they surfaced from the last pool and held on to the masonry of the pylon to catch their breath, they saw the moon was up and glinting yellow through the trees. Zalkina whistled a low-pitched whistle and her Zebra's head appeared above them, his whinny encouraging them to return as they climbed up the eroded limestone pylon with the help of the overhanging lianas and she embraced the ecstatic animal.

Zalkina re-robed, shivering as she put her put on her rabbit-skin cloak and Luke also dressed, then they lay on the top of the limestone pylon, watching the moon climb across the velvet sky, its creamy reflection mirrored in the dark pool below, finally to fall asleep in each other's arms. As he held Zalkina, Luke's mind was restless with the many imponderables posed by this strange ruined world: why had such a beautiful city been built underground... where had the abandoned bell-shape device come from, and what did it do...and many more imponderables, until he finally drifted off to sleep.

An errant ray of sunshine hit the yellow pylon and shone on the sleepy figures, locked in each other's arms. Zalkina awoke and sat up, looking at the strange youth to whom she had felt some sort of emotion she had never known before, and which she could not explain. She would have to go and see the medicine man and ask him why her heart hurt...was she sick?

She tickled Luke's nose with a blade of grass and he opened his cornflower-blue eyes, looking up at her. He stood up and lifted her up off the ground and when he threatened to throw her into the pool, she squealed in mock fright. They set off through the swamp to the village, talking animatedly and by the time they reached the camp of the Zalks, Luke and Zalkina had a good grasp of each other's language without the aid of the systrum. Zalkine embraced his daughter and after a lot of jabbering, which Luke interpreted as 'why did the chief's daughter have to take all night to show the stranger the Lost City,' they ate the staple breakfast of the Zalks: the fire-burnt carcass of the desert hyena, which tasted like over-cooked Camel dung - but Luke didn't complain.

'You see Lost City?' Zalkine asked Luke diplomatically, or was it that he was unaware of the obvious physical attraction between his daughter and the strange youth.

'Yes' Luke replied as he tried to chew the rock-hard meat. 'Have you seen it?'

'No Zalkine shook his head,' me to old to go through the water...Zalkina tell me of it...very pretty place.'

'I want to take Luke to see Joruck?' Zalkina said to her father. 'He will know many things which man-boy want to know!'

'You go take him' Zalkine nodded his head, 'but take water, and watch out for the slave-masters.' He tapped his forehead and pointed to his eyes.

Zalkina went to her hut and after a while she came out in a different attire. Her long legs were bound with sliced and twisted liana rope that looked like leg warmers. Her feet were shod in goatskin mules and a stitched ensemble of large plantain leaves graced her upper body, their ends forming a large collar encircling her head.

'Desert thing' she pointed at her surreal dress mode and gestured to Luke's creased and mud-stained jeans. 'It's not good for desert' she stated emphatically. An elder woman of the tribe gladly offered her skills in the re-robing of the blond giant, as with her eyes shining, she stripped him of his clothes, (though he fought to retain his underpants), and dressed him a similar fashion. Finally they were ready and Luke was awarded the odious task of carrying the goatskin flagons of water and a lump of hyena meat, sun-dried into hard tack, which the older woman slung over his broad shoulders.

'Good-bye my child' Zalkine hugged his daughter, the Zalks gesturing their own sort of embrace, but behind their headman's back.

'Say my great word of friendship to Joruck, and kiss the lady God of the desert in my name.

Chapter Nine
*** Joruck ***

Zalkina turned and set off at a slow trot and Luke followed, weighed down with his encumbrances, whilst the Zalks jumped up and down, reciting their ritual of travel to the fast receding figures. Zalkina took a different forest trail to the one they had taken the previous evening and Luke again felt he had met his match as he followed the strangely attired, yet energetic girl.

Soon the forest thinned and the shade of the morning sun was interspersed by bright patches of sunlight, their ribbons of light slashing across the trail as it wound through the undergrowth between the sparse acacia and sandalwood trees. In front of him Luke saw the white-yellow gleam of the desert. Zalkina slowed, then stopped and Luke caught up with her.

'Take water' she said, looking into Luke's eyes, her breasts heaving slightly and a thin veil of perspiration evident on her flushed face. Luke brought up the goatskin and they took it in turns to swig the sweet-tasting water. Zalkina took the flapping leaves of the plantain or banana wrapping from around her collar and tied them across her face, gesturing to Luke to do the same. She walked slowly out from the residue of the forest shade and onto the desert, and Luke felt the heat from it flush his face as if someone has opened an oven door.

'Slow,' Zalkina commanded, 'walk slow.' They started their ascent up the steep sand incline and the heat invaded them like a Devil's cauldron. Luke squinted up to the desert slope, the camel-thorn bushes tearing at his legs and he saw a vast sand driven waste ahead, the escarpment shimmering in the white heat high above them. Gradually, they ascended the slope of sand and wind-eroded rock until they gained a natural cave, overhung by a cornice of yellow limestone. They rested in the shade offered by this geomorphologic parasol and shared the water flagon, looking down on the view below.

'That is the forest,' Luke pointed to the dark speck whence they had set off, 'and that is the great plain and the city of Aiyu.' It was now just a speck on the far ridges of blue mountains which receded into the heat haze, yet the jewels of its minarets and domes were still discernable, even from this great distance, glinting in pin pricks of diamond light.

'It is like a city of dreams... greatly pretty.' Zalkina observed in her limited, yet growing knowledge of the strange one's language. 'Come,' she urged, 'let us go onwards and look for Joruck!' They set off again and the blinding white light of the overhead sun burned into Luke's brain as they climbed the remainder of the vast sand escarpment. Finally, they were at the top, and a patchwork of light and shade lay before them, the sun smiting the wilderness of sand and rock in deep patterns of light and shade.

They trekked along the edge of the plateau and Luke saw a temple-like structure shimmering in the heat haze. Nearing the peculiar building, a deep gong-like sound reverberated from the weather-beaten complex and they collapsed into the shade of the small pro-style temple and emptied their water carriers, gulping down the last of the liquid.

Luke studied the scene and noticed a sunken courtyard carved out of the limestone plateau that yet retained some of the strange natural rock formations gracing this forbidding desert stronghold. Dotted around the perimeter of the courtyard were caves carved into the walls, whilst other curious structures towered up behind the flat space to the desert side. The portico of the temple under which they were sitting was raised, thus affording a view of the vast plain below them. Now more distant than ever, the glint from the domes and minarets of Aiyu were barely visible.

'So where is he?' Luke asked, looking at Zalkina

'He will come, he knows we here...he knows everything.'

Presently, the gong sounded again and a very curious man indeed emerged from the largest of the several caves. His head was completely bald and a white goatee beard graced his sun tanned, though sunken and wrinkled face. He wore a large robe of coloured pieces of Camel skin stitched in an open weave to allow the refreshing breeze from the ridge to blow through it, no doubt.

'Welcome, welcome.' the wizened little man said. 'What brings you to my humble abode?' he smiled somewhere in between Luke and Zalkina, and Luke realised that he was cross-eyed as he went to shake his hand, yet looked at the girl. ' I am the one called Joruck...alow me to offer you some refreshment.'

'Thank you' Luke said, and may I congratulate you on your command of the English language...but, where are the refreshments?'

'Oh' please forgive me.' The strange little man stroked thin air as a table of woven palm appeared, supporting various bowls of fruit and sweet meats.

'That's handy' Luke said, trying not to sound too impressed by the magician's conjuring trick.

'Oh that, yes, it is rather useful.' Joruck stood there looking pleased with himself. 'Oh did I forget the chairs,' he waved his hands and three wicker chairs materialised around the table. They sat down and Luke and Zalkina tucked into the food. Just as he thought about something nice to drink, a goblet of red wine appeared in Luke's hand and a gourd of lemon juice suddenly came into existence in front of Zalkina who drank from it unquestioningly.

'You are a man of great magic,' Luke said deferentially as he savoured the heady fruit of the grape.

'May I enquire who you are and whence you originate? 'Joruck asked of Luke.

Luke told the old man his implausible story and there ensued a silence, Joruck scratching his head.

'And you.' Luke asked. 'You seem to be endowed with far more sophisticated powers than the little men of the forest.'

'The tribesmen know me as the great patriarch.' Joruck replied. 'And yet I am not of this time...and I do not believe that I am a tellurian.' He scratched his bald and shiny pate as a look of perplexity overtook his wizened face. 'Truth is,' he continued, 'I cannot really remember what I was sent here for. I know it was for some great purpose, yet that purpose escapes me' he looked at Luke as if he may have the answer.

'And you have no way of enhancing your memory?' Luke asked.

'Ah!' Joruck's eyes lit up. 'Enhance my memory, hum, what an original idea....now how would one go about doing that?'

'Well,' Luke suggested, somehow not too impressed with this little man's grasp of practicalities. 'What if you were to regress... that is.... go back to your childhood...if you ever had one?' He was grasping at straws here.

'Hum,' Joruck conjectured, 'interesting question....childhood....now let me see,' He waved his hand and the small portico was thrown into darkness and a wall of blackness seemed to suddenly descend around the temple. Luke blinked in the extreme change from the glaring sun to almost total darkness and felt Zalkina's hand slip into his, unnerved as she was by the change which this little man had wrought so deftly and without any apparent means... as if by magic!

'Good idea of yours...enhance my memory...now, I need to project...' Joruck said as he concentrated his mind. 'I need to project my memories and take them right back to the beginning. Please bear with me...it may take some while...and don't forget... it was your idea!'

Zalkina gripped Luke's hand as she sat there in the black cube; she was not at home with any sort of magic, for she associated it with the slave-masters and the land of prisons across the valley.

In front of them, a suffused image appeared in the darkness. It was a hologram of themselves as they sat there at the table; a copy of their present time. As Joruck cast his mind backwards through time, a rapid succession of images rolled by in holographic clarity as he rewound his own mind and Luke marvelled at the weird peregrinations of this man from another time; but Zalkina started whimpering as she clutched Luke's hand.

Luke sat entranced, marvelling at the pictorial history of Joruck's association with this region that was paraded in three-dimensional 'solidity' before his incredulous eyes. The fabled city of Aiyu featured prominently in these recent events and he gathered that there had been battles fought and many struggles for dominance over the paradoxical land of the Ancients. Obelisks came and went and Luke braced himself as he saw the re-enacting of the coming of the Obelisk of Time on the plains of Thebes, seeing briefly an image of his Father making drawings of it, surrounded by erudite looking men – Rachid and Labachi were amongst them.

He was about to interrupt, to question these strange images of the Obelisk of Time and its momentous import, yet his lips were sealed and his mind was stayed as the power of Joruck's image-bank swept all other matters aside and he regressed to a world which Luke could not comprehend.

Then there was the sound. As Luke looked into the totally real depiction of an alien world, a strange sound like the rushing of a great wind flowed through his ears, his hair stirring in the transport of this holographic image as he was plunged into its proximity, feeling a chill sweep the marrow of his spine.

For it was not one single viewpoint which was imported into his mind but a fragmentation of many, juxtaposed, one with the other to form not a picture, but an impression - as if the experience was seen from many angles - all with their information collated simultaneously.

He was aware of Zalkina's nails biting into his own flesh as he watched transfixed by this mental exchange and saw, felt, heard, and smelt, the sensory compounds of Joruck's earliest memories as the matrix of manifold experiences engulfed his consciousness.

The hologram was of a very strange and unknown planet of some sort, for the apogee and perigee of the orbits of its twin moons circling it at frightening speeds, seemed to be out of sync: too wildly elliptic; too fast and totally unsustainable. Their mad twirling against the black sky seemed impossible, whilst meteors hatched the circumscribed vault of black sky in a violent assault. As Luke grew dizzy with all this motion, he saw a landscape of black craters and sand-driven wastes, interspersed with emerald outcrops of crystalline structures, which rose up into the void. Amidst this alien landscape he saw figures which bore some resemblance to humanoid parallels (yet not quite), who were feverishly engaged on tasks of an urgent nature that Luke could not quite grasp - except they seemed to be building something; whilst all the time the whine of a million maelstroms of wind and sound shrieked inside his head.

Then a fireball exploded and Luke heard Zalkina scream. But he was inexorably locked into this retelling of history and continued to watch the hologram in mesmerised concentration as he saw a strange bell-shaped structure lift off from the stark alien landscape and arc up into the blue-black heavens as its antennae of strobing lights fractured the sky in a plethora of multi-coloured beams.

'*The Star People!*' The words escaped from Luke's lips and he tore his eyes from the hologram to look at Joruck, who was lying rigid in mid-air over the table, his face contorted in the violent distortions of a human body in the act of escaping huge gravitational forces ... and then Zalkina's shrieks of utter terror tore through his own state of total shock.

Gradually the projected vision dimmed and the sound decreased as Joruck resumed his seat, his eyeballs were up in his eyelids with only the whites of a blind man evident as he projected his next memory, and Luke's shaking hands cradled the supine form of Zalkina who had passed out.

Within the black cube of the Star man's projection, Luke saw the pristine landscape of earth as seen from space. The difference between the harsh, forbidding landscape of the planet he had just seen and his own was starkly apparent. It was as if he were the pilot of some alien spacecraft as it swooped over the planet and the view of fair earth zoomed in to show the vast territories of the Sahara desert, though the Nile valley was vastly wide - far wider than in present times. Then as the projection over flew the desert, he saw them: obelisks - scattered randomly and grouped together. They lit up one after the other as pinpricks of light appeared beside his own 'craft' and a convergent course was steered towards the illuminated landing beacons, the glowing obelisks. The pinpricks grew larger as they joined the convoy and the formation of bell-shaped craft slowed their descent to land in the arid, yellow sands of planet earth.

The scene changed again, as the projected hologram depicted ancient monuments that arose from the naked land as pyramids and temples abounded. The landscape became fertile as the seeds of an ancient star-born civilisation were implanted into the minds of a neolithic people. There was order, harmony and progress as the empires of Ancient Egypt, Mesopotamia, Sumaria and many more flourished in the Genesis of this new era of human kind.

Joruck's eyes rolled back into their sockets as he coughed, the black cube dissipated and the sunlight once again shone into the shady bower of the portico.

'Forgive me' he said, looking bewildered, 'I did not realise it would be such a painful experience.' He looked at the slumped figure of Zalkina and clicked his tongue. 'Oh dear, oh dear,' does she need some water.' He leant over and felt her temples as she stirred in Luke's arms and gradually opened her eyes.

'So' Luke said, 'you are of the star people...you came from the stars?'

'I think that is possible' Joruck agreed, 'it has been so long now that I have forgotten. But yes I must be, mustn't I...why else would I have these memories, these strange powers?'

'Can you tell me about the obelisks?' Luke asked, 'why did your people erect them.... what are they for? Are they simply landing beacons for your spacecraft?'

'The obelisks?' Joruck looked vacant for a while. 'Err yes, the obelisks. Well when we first arrived here on this fair planet, after we decided for complex reasons to leave our own, we were all optimistic. We thought that we could help the indigenous and if you don't mind me saying...the rather primitive people of planet earth as you so fondly call it... to live in peaceful union and to form statehood; and then to establish agriculture. Well it's a damn sight better to grow your crops and rear your animals were you can get to them, than go gallivanting around the countryside trying to chase them, wouldn't you agree?' Luke nodded.

'And we had a little success to start with' Joruck continued, 'but we didn't allow for the sort of tribalism that pervaded this little patch in the vast cosmos. No, as I recall, my ancestors found it very difficult to keep the peace with the warring tribal factions. So they erected the obelisks. Yes, I think, though, don't quote me, they were set up at first for our landing, but later to try to contain different factions...like territorial markers if you will...'

'Did they illuminate... when their inscriptions were incanted,' Luke's voice was a mystery of conjecture.

'Yes,' Joruck rejoined, 'they did do that. But that was just a kind of quasi-magic sort of affect... you know... scare tactics with a bit of mumbo jumbo... Keep 'em in their place sort of thing.

'Until the high priests tumbled it' Luke was guessing.

'Well yes, I suppose you've hit it on the head.' Jouck looked reflective. 'You see my people soon gave up. They did try to impart their superior knowledge to the people of, let us say, lesser intelligence, but when they realised that there was not much else they could do...well, they left!'

'And you were left as a sort of guardian?' Luke conjectured.

'Yes... myself and others. Though I am not sure what happened to the others.'

'They usurped your power,' Luke said emphatically. 'They subverted the power of the obelisks for their own purposes...did they not? Except for one... Neb – Ankh.' Luke was taking an outside guess.

'Neb – Ankh?' Joruck scratched his domed pate as if trying to excavate some distant memory. 'Yes...of course... Neb – Ankh, keeper of the bestiary...my old friend. When did you see him last?'

'At the mock funeral of my father,' Luke replied, 'or slightly after. He tried to stop Labachi and the cult from erasing the inscription on Father's tomb...the inscription from the Obelisk of Time...'

'How do you know this?' Joruck focussed upon Luke and the youth felt a mighty intelligence, albeit rather rusty, boring into his brain.

'I come from the world of the future,' Luke stated flatly. 'It is a world, which I do not think you have seen. Vast progress has been made since your days trying to teach the ancients the rudiments of human cohabitation. There has not been a major war for fifty years, though as old empires have broken up, there have been internecine struggles.'

'Hum' Joruck stroked his long goatee, 'sounds very familiar.'

'Yes,' Luke continued, 'maybe, but out there are the beginnings of a new world order and prosperity for the many – not just the few. You, if you will forgive my familiarity, have been time-locked here as an observer, whilst the real world has been struggling towards freedom.'

'Ah,' Joruck sighed, 'such a word! It has gilded the lips of many a miscreant and dictator to boot...'

'Maybe so.' Luke persisted. 'And it is these miscreants and petty dictators who pose the real threat, for they have subverted and have been misusing the powers of the obelisks it seems for a very long time, whilst you, as guardian of the legacy left by your own people have been either unaware, or unprepared to take action...'

Joruck rose and paced the small shaded portico as Luke flagged; had he gone too far in his criticism of this amnesic alien? He hoped not, for in spite of the spaceman's terrifying excursion into his ancestral memory banks and its vivid projection, Luke quite liked the old boy, alien or not.

After a while the small wizened old man came up to him and looked searchingly into his eyes, and Zalkina gripped his arm again, her eyes like black grapes about to burst, and Luke vacillated between listening to the alien or soothing the native girl. He did both, caressing Zalkina's brow whilst nodding towards the star man.

'Such recriminations from one so young' Joruck rebuked, 'and yet your argument may have some tenure...Tell me about your fears and theories as to this Order of The One dimension again.' Luke gave the non-terrestrial a summarised account of what he had told him before, but included his suspicions as to the true motives of the cult.

'Interesting' Joruck got up and paced again. 'Most interesting...so, the Esoteric Oracle has established his cult at Aiyu... destroyed, driven out, or subverted its inhabitants... but not yet conquered The Temple of the Eon, so the Emperor of the Eon is still in control. 'Hum...and this you say is the future...what is your time calibration?'

'Date you mean,' Luke corrected. 'It is the year of our Lord, two thousand and two... What do you mean the Emperor of Eon?'

'Oh' Joruck looked perplexed. 'The Emperor of Eon is the, err... Curator of Time, I think we shall call him. He is the grand arbiter of the dimensions, and is a just and righteous man.... I use the word loosely, you understand. And your mother has been inducted by these cultist upstarts, the so called "Order of the one Dimension" to travel here to Aiyu to join the subversives, the Esoteric Oracle, whoever he may be...'

'Yes' Luke urged trying to speed up the process a bit.

'So' Joruck finally had it. 'As the Oracle, we shall call him thus, has not yet succeeded in overthrowing the Emperor; we should assume that your mother must have been sent with some vital information.

'Yes!' Luke was getting frustrated, wasn't this alien supposed to have superior powers? So where were his powers of deduction?

'Yes, *she has the incantation!*' Luke almost shouted. 'She knows the correct pronunciation to the message on the Obelisk of Time!'

'Ah ha' Joruck finally had it. 'That's it. She is the catalyst to the overthrow of the Emperor of the Eon, projected here via the astral travelling method, which let me say *we* perfected.... So we must stop her...'

'*It's too late you stupid being!*' Luke shouted now, 'she is already in the city of Aiyu and will no doubt be coerced or drugged to import her knowledge to the Oracle.... and perhaps by now he has already used this vital secret to resurrect the Obelisk of Time and topple the Emperor of the Eon!'

'Tranquillity descend upon thine brow' Joruck raised his hand, not unlike a Pope's benediction, as Luke felt an inner peace pervade his overheated mind, 'not so... all is not lost...for I can reverse time!' The little man smiled as he reassured the beleaguered youth.

'Will you help in the forthcoming struggle between good and evil?' the star man asked, looking into Luke's clear blue eyes. 'Will you help avert the rising of this grotesque cult?'

'I will' Luke replied.' 'But on two conditions!'

'Name them?' Joruck's voice was serious.

'One, you guarantee the safety of my mother?' And two, 'you reveal to me the whereabouts of my father... and after we are repatriated, you help us all get back to our own time...?'

'That is three conditions' Joruck's numeracy was in the ascendant. But yes, I will endeavour to do what you ask. First I must scan you father's records to know where he is...'

'His records?' Luke interjected, 'he is not a felon!'

'Forgive me' Joruck placated. 'I mean the records of his Ka, for no human can be in this domain unless they travel in the name of their Ka! The alien being brought down the black canopy of darkness once more as Luke stroked Zalkina's brow, whispering to her. 'Please stay a moment longer with me. It is important! It is the ghost for my father that will be revealed. Do not be frightened my little sister.' she looked up into his eyes and her fear was dispelled as he held her damp forehead.

Joruck''s eyes rolled back once more into his sockets as he searched for some conceivable connection with Luke's father and they watched a series of images projected onto the far wall. A fussy picture materialised, Luke's heart pounding in recognition of his father as a young man in a strange landscape as the seer connected with Jock Slater's Ka.

He saw a giant black man and a black woman of incredible beauty accompanying his youthful father in adventures in this strange land. Then a white ephemeral being who seemed like a Goddess emerged into the scene to aid the trio in various campaigns against evil forces. Incredulity was put on hold as Luke watched an old lady resurrect into a beautiful Ancient Egyptian Queen by the aid of one of Jock's paintings. But Luke gasped out loud with astonishment to see the artist astral travel back to Bridget via another of his paintings - and then Luke understood the unique gift that his father had in the manipulation of time and space through his artwork – a gift, it appeared from a very old life-force indeed!

Now in a different projection, Luke saw himself as a babe in arms as Bridget and Jock brought him up. Cherished baby scenes from in and around Park house, encapsulated in his father's memory banks were projected in dazzling clarity causing Zalkina to cry out in admiration of the blond haired baby as she clutched her new-found brother to her.

Then this scene of tranquillity was shattered by the image of a barren plain, fallen monuments of Ancient Egyptian statuary and temples, leaving no doubt as to its whereabouts: the west bank of the Nile, near to the Valley of the Kings. And then, searing the eyes of the observers, a sudden golden light reflected around the harsh desert crags, heralding the apparition: the unearthly appearance of the Obelisk of Time.

Luke gulped in a deep breath to see his father, sitting on an eroded column base, casually making a copy of the inscription on the glowing phantom obelisk and then to witness its subsequent destruction as described by Rachid so vividly in Jock's old studio at Park House.

'History.' Luke muttered, becoming impatient again in spite of his amazement of these crystal clrear scenes from the past. 'It is all history...so where is he now?'

The brows of the reader of time frowned as he concentrated his otherworldly mind to dwell in the regions of the present. As Luke looked onto the projected scene, holding Zalkina's head cradled in his lap, he saw a complex structure, the likes of which was so outside of the modern concepts of architecture that it is impossible to describe - except to say that it was like a series of towering pyramids, one heaped upon the other, and diminishing in size as it penetrated the orange and violet afterglow of the desert sunset.

'The Temple of the Emperor of the Eon' Joruck assisted, as Luke's mind boggled. 'And this is where I am going to project you!' I am going to scroll back time slightly so that you arrive at the Temple of the Eon *before* your mother arrives in Aiyu, thus giving you time to locate your father. He has got to be somewhere in the vicinity, or the images of the temple would not show up in his present memory banks.

But it is imperative that you stop your mother from communicating with the Oracle... for he must not gain access to the incantation! 'Do you follow?' Luke nodded. 'Neb – Ankh will help you to find your father, who incidentally may not remember you. However, he, like you, is in great danger from the Esoteric Oracle, whom I remember now, for he has great powers of persuasion... I know this as a fact, for past dealings with him have left my memory impaired. Once you have located your father, you must tell him of our plan to intercept your mother before she reaches Aiyu... are you ready to be projected through time once more?'

Zalkina clutched Luke, sensing empirically that they were to be imminently parted.

'One more condition,' Luke asserted, patting Zalkina's shoulder, 'that I take this beautiful child, who has become my tribal sister, with me!'

'It will be so' Joruck decreed. 'But I will first robe you in attire befitting your destination! With a wave of his hand Joruck replaced the palm-fronds of the unlikely couple with robes of flowing silver. 'Are you ready?'

'We are' Luke replied, speaking for them both, as the alien converter of time hit some cosmological lever in his arsenal of time's gadgetry. 'Hold on!' Joruck intoned 'Hold on to each other...this will not be an easy journey. He raised a complex network of inter-divisional lines criss-crossed in a miasmic three–dimensional maze.

'Look for Neb – Ankh in the garden of the Eon-Beasts'. Joruck's words faded as Luke and Zalkina, clutching each other tightly, were suffused with light as the green grids converged on them - then the small portico, and the wizened little star being dematerialised to become a swirling evanescent mist.

Chapter Ten
*** The Artist Of Time ***

Jock Slater was sitting in the magical Garden of the Eon-Beasts in front of a large canvas, his cornflower-blue eyes squinting in a weather-beaten face as he ran a muscular hand through his grey-flecked beard; his long grey hair blowing in the wind. His brush flew over the surface of the half-finished painting like an angry wasp as he endowed colour and form to the mythological landscape, deftly adding a fabled beast here and there so that they gelled into the composition.

Familiar terrestrial animals: Lions, Tigers, Elephants, Giraffe and an abundance of God's creatures walked together or grazed in harmony with strange mythological beasts: Unicorns, winged Zebras, Chimeras and others unknown, without any semblance of animosity towards each other, or indeed the seated recorder of their sublime state.

From a nearby crag, tiny rills and waterfalls cascaded down into natural pools overhung with large flowering trees and framed by tall bulrushes. In the distance, at the end of this double-ended valley, stood a structure of towering pyramids, one precariously balanced upon the other and the whole aglomeration was imbued with a milky-pink iridescence. Various paths meandered through this Arcadian vale and along one of them walked a man, his long white hair billowing in the breeze. He was draped in a long blue robe and held a staff crowned by a golden Ankh; the sunlight glinted from this arcane symbol as it did from his winged sandals of similar material.

Neb Ankh looked down from the higher path, watching the artist at work on the large canvas and smiled, a benign smile, which softened his gaunt features. He was comforted by the fact that this gifted human could work with such endeavour as to create wondrous paintings of his bestiary. Soon the Temple of the Eon would be complete and these magnificent works of art, which adorned the Temple for the most part, would become the embodiment of his own creation - The gardens of the Eon Beasts, rivalled only by the gardens of Paradise in the adjacent city of Aiyu, across the ridge - it would soon be a time for rejoicing.

The prophet of time sat down on a small carved stone, watching captivated as the artist's brush flew over the canvas, articulating details here and there as the magic of the scene became alive with form and colour.

Breaking into his thoughts, the sage was disturbed by a trumpeting. A group of elephants at the far end of the valley were making a commotion and he looked towards this unusual occurrence. Near to the excited animals he saw a vague glimmer of star-like particles evaporating into the misty air as two figures materialised. He looked at the artist, who had either not heard the sounds or was choosing to ignore it - but it did seem like the artist was just starting his painting – and Neb-Ankh was certain that moments ago, the large canvas was almost completed. The puzzled sage lifted off from the ground and his winged sandals carried him towards the two figures, who were ecstatic as they stood holding hands, transfixed by the wonder of his creation – the garden of the Eon-beasts.

'Neb-ankh?' he heard the taller figure exclaim across the now quiet valley as he sped towards them; the elephant group had returned to their former tranquil pursuit of tearing off leaves from the overhanging tamarisk trees, oblivious now of the presence of their new arrivals.

'What do you here?' Neb-ankh asked as he touched ground and walked towards them. 'How can you be here?' A frown of bewilderment crossed his hitherto placid features as he recognised the youth from the primitive Kingdom of the Three Dimensions.

'It is I, Luke' Luke said, offering his outstretched hand, 'and this is Zalkina.' We come from Joruck who sends his cosmic blessing. He has set back time slightly for us to intercede....'

'Set back time!' Neb-Ankh erupted. 'What knows he about time?' He is not empowered to meddle with time!'

'Hear me out...please!' Luke retorted. 'I come with urgent news.' 'My mother is under the power of the Order of the One Dimension!

'She will soon arrive in Aiyu, where she has vital knowledge which will assist the Esoteric Oracle in his rise to power... Joruck has sent me here to try to intercept her before she makes contact with the Oracle.' Luke persisted with his account in spite of the old prophet's obvious irritation at being upstaged in his own domain.

'Joruck has also agreed to help me find my father, whom he believes is here, here in the garden of the Eon-beasts. He has confidence that father will know how best to rescue mother from the cult and to work out a strategy for defeating this Power of Darkness...do you understand?'

Neb-Ankh's brow boiled with fury as a mere mortal made him privy to such vital news. With great difficulty he controlled his anger, and let the irritation at having his morning stroll in this, his magnificent creation of a garden, ruined by the implications of this youth's story. Yet it must be so and he had to accept the tall youth's account, so forceful was it. He looked at the silver - robed native girl who stood beside the young giant.

'You are from the Zalk's?' he asked in her own language, and she nodded, the fear of her recent journey and the presence of this flying God assuaged somewhat by his now affable manner. After he had listened to her account, voiced rapidly in her own language, Neb-Ankh turned back to Luke.

'If what you say is true, then I must assist you,' Neb-Ankh said.

'Is he here...my father?' Luke's voice was an expectant whisper.

'Yes' Neb-Ankh answered' I will take you to him, although I must warn you that he is engaged on a task of great magnitude...the rendering

of this veritable Garden of Eden into a series of inimitable masterpieces.'
Neb-Ankh hid his pride in the description of his own work of genius with
obvious difficulty.

'And besides, he has been away from your family home for some
time...he may not remember you.'

'He will!' Luke asserted. 'He will remember his own son. Yet I have
bad news for him. Park House is no more. Burnt to the ground by
mindless imbeciles...and now mother, abducted by the cult and brainwashed, mesmerised...'

Luke told Neb-Ankh all that had passed since his abortive attempts to
stop Ishtar's defacement of his father's tomb, as Neb-ankh nodded
seriously.

Zalkina, oblivious to the portentous events which Luke was conveying
to the flying God, was entranced by the magical garden which boasted a
profusion of mythical animals, many of which she had never seen before.

Neb-ankh gestured for them to follow him as he hovered just above
the ground and set off down the valley whence he had come.

'Look,' the winged prophet said, 'there is your father...please do not
interrupt him...wait for him to finish his magnum opus.'

Luke could not contain his excitement as he recognized the stocky
build of Jock Slater - artist extraordinaire, Egyptologist and time-traveller,
alias Sir James Merebrook, his father - who with his long greying hair and
similar beard tugged slightly by the light wind was in front of a giant
canvas, the colours of which were echoed in the paint daubs that adorned
his ragged denim smock. The massive canvas depicted the scene of the
receding valley including an atmospheric rendering of the pearly pink
Temple of the Eon, whilst a group of mythical animals in the foreground,
formed a focal point to the realistic yet imaginative painting.

They approached the solitary painter, who, undeterred that his work
of the last few days had suddenly been reversed back to its starting point,
though now having restored it to its previous state, was working like a
mad man to finish it. Luke watched in wonder as he beheld the dexterity
and commitment of this 'peintre maudit' whose work had been so vilified
in his own lifetime - no wonder he chose to paint in this unworldly place
where his genius was finally recognised.

'Let him finish,' Neb-Ankh entreated 'This is his last canvas and is
almost complete.'

Luke nodded and they watched in awe as the last careful detail was
added to the complex composition and the mad artist threw down his
brushes and stepped back to admire his work.

'Magnificent,' Neb-ankh applauded as Jock Slater turned to look at
the three figures standing on the path slightly above him.

'Bravo' Luke added, as he stepped down to the lush carpet of flower-
bestrewn grass and walked up to his father, who stood there dumbstruck,
a frown of confusion puckering his weathered brow.

'*My son?*' The artist's face slowly registered recognition and incredulity.

'My son...Luke...is that you... How can this be?' Jock stepped forward and embraced him as the tears cascaded from his tired eyes and they held each other for an eternity. They sat down on the lush sward as Luke recounted the events of the recent past and Jock laughed at his son's account of his father's very own funeral, slapping him on the back, unable to contain his joy.

'No,' he said, his face wreathed in smiles. 'It certainly wasn't my body that was found in that tomb shaft near the Valley of the Kings. And I am relieved that you didn't believe it was.' Jock's face turned more serious as he learned of Rachid and Labachi's betrayal.

'So whilst I tried to copy the inscription of the mysterious Obelisk for the sake of science, believing Rachid and Labachi to be my friends....all the while they wanted it for the sake of their diabolical cult.'

But as Luke described how Bridget had been taken over by the cult, Jock's mood turned to wrath as he strode up and down the grassy meadow, tugging at his paint-stained beard; his long greying hair swept backwards by the wind.

'Those duplicitous bastards have a lot to answer for!' Jock shouted at the heavens, then calming a little, added: 'yet from what you say, the one factor on our side is that Bridget is here, somewhere in this dimension and hopefully as you say, maybe is in that not too distant city of Aiyu.' He looked towards the west.

'We must act now!' Jock had turned his around and Luke didn't have the heart to tell his dad about the fate of Park House and his lifetime's work; now was not the time.

'I left you defenceless' Jock castigated himself. 'Whilst I was away, thinking I would create the first masterpieces of another dimension ever seen by man or beast, I was neglecting my duty...and now...now it has all come to this...' Jock stopped and looked at Luke. 'Forgive me,' he said clutching his son to his chest. 'Forgive me...I have been a self-indulgent fool, blinded by my own sense of worth.' Jock's shoulders shook as he exorcised the demons of his unbridled ambition.

'It is time to put matters straight!' He released Luke and took up a large pallet knife, standing in front of his latest painting.

'How much do you value work of art?' He shouted at Neb-Ankh

'Value, value?' Neb-Ankh looked startled. 'Why it is invaluable!'

'Very well then' Jock continued. 'Accord me this privilege in forfeit of my fee. Take us to the Emperor of the Eon. Empower us with what special powers you can...and recall my friends, Smirtin, Ogadile and Errol, for I have great need of them now...and so do you have great need of them.... if you would forestall the overthrow of Aiyu. For the next port of call of this self-appointed Oracle fellow will be here, right here in the Temple of the Eon...and imagine what he and his pretty circus troupe would turn your precious little garden into then!'

Neb-Ankh's face, during such an ungrateful tirade by this petulant mortal, had gradually been turning purple, as his pride wrestled with his incontrovertible desire to have the painting. He could have disposed of this ingrate, reconstituted his atoms, but his overriding desire to see his own handiwork pass into the Halls of Eternity stopped him. Finally he agreed to the barbarian's demands and Jock put the pallet knife down.

Throughout this interchange, Zalkina, who had been left a little on the sidelines, had crept away and was talking quietly to a nearby grazing Zebra, which reminded her of Kina, her own pet - the only difference being, that this one had wings. She had won its confidence and as the three men turned, they now saw her astride the magical beast, patting its head.

'Please' Neb-Ankh cried 'Please dismount.' 'This is not an ordinary Zebra. He is a mythical beast, an Eon-Beast, and is endowed with magical properties...he could hurt you!' Zalkina smiled defiantly and whispered into the Zebra's ear. It whinnied and snorted, shaking its head.

'Let her ride him' Luke said, 'we may have need of a bit of magic...she will come with us? Neb-Ankh talked rapidly in the language of the Zalk's so Luke could not follow.

'Very well' Neb-Ankh reluctantly agreed, looking from the reasonable youth to his obdurate father. 'She wants to accompany you.' I will lend you the Eon-Beast name Skychild... but please do not let any harm come to him. The girl nodded and they set off along the path to the Temple of the Eon, father and son, arm in arm, as Zalkina rode proudly on the back of her new found friend, the winged zebra called Skychild.

They came to the edge of the valley, leaving the mythical animals behind as the series of giant pyramid structures, impossibly inverted and stacked one upon another, loomed over them, scintillating with a milky-rose hue in the sunlight. Up the translucent crystal steps they climbed as long robed people stared in wonder at the lithe girl astride the fabled Eon-Beast, the winged Zebra, marvelling at her control as she urged the animal up the slippery steps.

A man in a flowing golden robe and a dazzling silver turban walked from the interior of the marbled hall towards them, accompanied by a retinue of priests carrying the stuff of their station: books, great tomes, incense burners and others unknown. He addressed Neb-Ankh in an alien though cultured- sounding voice and bowed briefly to Jock, who acknowledged the courtesy in the a similar fashion. The pace of Neb-Ankh's voiced increased, as did the tone until it sounded like some comic strip character played at the wrong speed. As he imparted the latest news to the Emperor of the Eon, Luke had to suppress a laugh as he listened to the high-pitched whine.

The Emperor raised his hand and Neb-Ankh's patter ceased abruptly as he bowed again.

'My friends...welcome,' the Emperor intoned in a soft yet authoritative voice.

I am distressed to hear of this recent news. You shall be accorded all that you ask in order to forestall this unfortunate occurrence. I will straight away send messengers into Nethertime to recall your companions, Smirtin, Ogadile and the eponymous Errol. The Emperor swept his hand to the side, his white sleeves billowing as he gave sharp orders in his own tongue and several men - at - arms bowed and gestured for Jock and his party to follow. Zalkina dismounted and they walked through the rosy, marbled hall to a side room, which was dimly lit. Jock Slater was shown a soft upholstered chair, whilst Luke and Zalkina where accorded similar though smaller chairs either side. 'Nothing like pulling a bit of rank' Jock whispered to Luke as his son stifled a laugh. Neb-Ankh stood on a sort of podium in the centre of the room, holding his Ankh - headed staff; he cleared his throat.

'I would like to present the Guardian of Aiyu' he said indicating some sort of command to the nearby priests, who operated an array of strange machinery at the back of the room, as interconnecting vectors of green light shone down from the pyramidal ceiling.

A translucent white shimmering form trembled on the podium next to Neb-Ankh, and the figure of a woman appeared, clothed in a scintillating white gown. Her black hair fell in tresses about her shoulders, retained by a golden band which encompassed the crown of her head and from which a finely wrought Ureus, the hooded cobre, motif rose; her lustrous black eyes reflected the network of interconnecting green lines which had facilitated her transportation to the Temple of the Eon.

'*Isis*' Jock Slater's voice was a whisper whilst Luke gasped out loud at the beauty of this ephemeral being from the Ancient Egyptian pantheon.

'Blessings of the Cosmos.' Neb-Ankh greeted Isis, 'may I introduce the Artist who has brought his talents from the world of the Three Dimensions to the employ of the recording of our grand garden of...'

'*Strange one!*' Isis's eyes glowed warmly in recognition as she stepped down from the podium to kiss Jock on the cheek and Neb-Ankh looked slightly ruffled at being upstaged. 'I heard you were here and that you have created magnificent paintings of this Garden of Eden, yet why did you forsake your wife and child?'

'Isis' Jock Slater held the Goddess by the shoulders and kissed her gently on the cheek. 'Isis...as you are my guiding star, I say to you that I do not know why. I was urged by some force stronger than myself to venture yet again back here. I was pulled away from my family by the deceit of my own world...by the lure and promise of eternal recognition...which I have earned here in this place of beauty...'

'*This is your son?*' Isis cut though the Artist's rhetoric as she turned to look at Luke. 'Yes...I can see it.... you live in his face...'

'Forgive me,' Jock wiped a tear from his eye, 'this is my beloved son Luke whom I abandoned.' Luke rose, and took the Goddess's outstretched hand, awed into silence by her beauty; for here was the personification of truth and he felt the flow of a strange empowering energy permeate his being that flowed from her firm grasp as he held her hand and looked into her pristine dark eyes. For in this woman of exquisite beauty dwelt all the opposites of Ishtar and he felt awed and humbled in her presence.

'I forgive him,' Luke said to her as he placed his arm around his father.' 'I forgive him, for he was led along a path which was stronger than himself... as has been my mother.... But,' Luke continued 'I want father to show us these paintings of Eternity...before we embark on this mission to thwart the Order of Darkness. Let us leave here with his gift to humanity before our eyes.'

'What nobility of thought' Isis replied and turned to the humbled Artist and said, 'show us, strange one... show us your works before we leave to do battle once more with the forces of evil.'

'Come' Neb-ankh, who had been following this last interchange of emotions closely, and now seeing a chance to reassert his authority, gestured for them to follow. 'I will show you the almost finished Grand Gallery. ' He said.

The proud prophet stamped with his ankh-topped staff on the rose tinted marble floor and the priests prized their eyes from the divine figure of Isis and ushered them into the hall. Isis looked up at the native girl seated so placidly on the mythical Zebra and asked: 'and who are you my child?' Neb-Ankh gave Isis the background on the young woman as Zalkina had lost her voice in the presence of this embodiment of femininity; her own tribe had no gods or goddesses.

They stood in the Grand Gallery of the Temple of the Eon as Neb-ankh explained, pointing to the large murals with his staff and enunciating in glowing terms the gelling of the artist's genius and his own in the magnificent portrayals of the fabled Eon-Beasts from his mythical gardens outside.

'They are superb!' Isis addressed nodded to herself, and with other superlatives from the admiring priests they made their way to the end of the gallery.

'It is bewildering to me,' the Emperor of the Eon was at the end of the gallery, resplendent in his flowing, golden robe, 'that a mere mortal and a tellurian could accomplish such a task.' The art-lovers stopped at the final painting, bowing in acknowledgement to the Curator of Time.

'That this artist from another time, and our great patriarch of the natural world could so endow this shrine with such great beauty,' The Emperor raised his hand as the priests knelt; in his hand was a purple ribbon.

'I bestow upon you, strange one, master of the brush, the coveted title of Brother of the Twelve Dimensions, if thou would'st kneel before me.' Jock Slater knelt at the feet of the Emperor as he placed the ribbon around the paint- stained smock of the prostrate man. From the ribbon hung a highly polished stone, which gleamed in refracted colours of the spectrum as the Emperor lowered it around the Artist's neck.

'Stand now,' the Emperor commanded, and let all who see this emblem know that you are cherished and are one of the Brotherhood of the Twelve Dimensions, so that those who seek to do harm against our just order will turn away in fear...It is your mandate, and to a lesser degree it is your ticket ...for it is a tektite and can be used only once to defeat the limitations of time and space and to travel where your heart desires...and to return!

The Order of the Twelve Dimensions were hushed and even Neb-ankh knelt at the significance of this honour; then The Emperor of the Eon stood back, and in a serous voice spoke thus:

'You have before you an onerous task in the struggle to wrest your wife from the clutches of that vile cult, the so called Order of the One Dimension. And I have sent messengers out to make contact with your old comrades from Nethertime, but, let our enemies know that you carry this talisman of our Brotherhood and that you are cherished by such, so that no man, being, or force for evil will stand in your way.'

Tears of gratitude flowed from Jock Slater's eyes as he held Luke close to him and the jubilant cheers of the faithful filled the Grand Gallery.

Chapter Eleven
*** Genies Unstoppered ***

A nine-foot (three meters) giant of ebony hue was playing boule in the sand with a group of Cutthroats. As the Genie threw the stone towards the marker, the honed muscles of his lattisimus dorsi bulged out from his leather waistcoat and his deltoids and pectorals quivered in schools of hard black sinew. The colossal Genie's shaven head glistened like wet basalt and the long, jet black scalp-lock that graced the nape of his neck flapped upwards as he tossed the heavy rock effortlessly, the desert glare gleaming from his large golden earring.

A young woman of shapely stature, dressed in a flowing black tob, brought another pitcher of Zabeeb, (a local distillate of the date palm) and refreshed the earthenware cups of the players as she retorted to their unseemly suggestions of how to share the winnings of the game with a rustic banter of her own and a sharp slap to opportunist's hands – though a half smile hovered about her face.

However, when she came to the black endomorph waiting his turn to throw, she lingered, leaning forward to present her well-endowed attributes of the Gods as she slowly replenished his cup, her eyes bright and a smile which verged on a leer, gracing her brown, youthful face.

'Come over to me Bethshima.' One of the raggedy group shouted, 'and stop lusting over that oversized good-for-nothing...why he's old enough to be your Great Granddad.' Bethshima turned her attentions to the brigand, topping up his drink, as with a callused hand he tried to grope her backside, but she knocked it away before it found its target and moved on to the others, goaded by the obscene taunts of the group.

'*Silence!*' the black Genie shouted, on making his next throw, and the large limestone rock arced through the air and covered the red granite marker, crushing it into the sand. 'My game!' he declared as dissent and oaths ensued from the disgruntled troupe of vagabonds. He rose from the squatting circle of men and picked up the saffron veil holding a pile of golden dirhams and weighing it, tied the loose ends into a knot as the money clinked and the other players muttered amongst themselves.

'I am out.' The winner announced curtly, striding from the circle of men and up to the well which was the focal point of this remote oasis in the wilderness deserts of Nethertime. He reached for the leather bucket and swung it in from the shadouf's gantry, dousing his shining scalp with the cool water and drinking in many a gulp from the receptacle. The Zabeeb had dimmed his senses and he did not like the mood of his fellow game- players, who were not his fellows in any case and were bad losers.

Bethshima came up to his side and knelt in the sand.

115

'May I wash your feet, my Lord' she said, easing off the gargantuan leather and rope sandals and, pouring cold water over the hard sinewy flesh as the giant unbuckled his enormous scimitar in its leather scabbard and laid it on the lip of the well. He watched the woman's supple hands as they anointed his cleansed feet with date-palm oil and the declining sunlight dappled her ample breasts with barely enough light left for the overhanging clusters of palm trees.

He was in an unfamiliar domain, having travelled far from his home beneath the mountains of Kaf, and the desert had taken its toll. In spite of his mighty bulk, he felt fatigued, and the attentions of this buxom wench were unexpected, and to a degree enticing; yet he had no real inclination for a romantic dalliance.

Only this morning he had received word via a Jinni of the air, that his presence was required at the mythical city of Aiyu, to help forestall the overthrow of the city, which he knew was the bastion of ancient time and hidden to the rest of the world. He was not certain exactly where it was located, but the messenger had said for him to proceed to the Oasis of Dahl, which he was now at, and that a guide would make himself known. So he had flown on the ether for the better part of a day, until his powers had waned as he grew distant from the regions of his magic. Then he had walked, finally to hobble into the welcome shade of the oasis; yet it seemed he had been drawn into a game of boule as soon as he had arrived. His only excuse was that it afforded him the cover of normality, for he surely looked as desperate as these cut- purses that frequented this place; and he could be certain that there were spies abroad.

'Drink this my Lord' Bethshima's languorous tones cut through his reverie as she proffered a goblet of rich ruby wine, 'it will revive you and wipe away the taint of the desert.'

Her words were at once persuasive and plaintive and he imbibed the dark red liquor, feeling his fatigue assuaged for a moment. But then his eyelids started to press heavily on his bloodshot eyes and he felt himself succumbing to a potent drug. Yet the narcotic was not quite sufficient for a man of such dimensions, and as he hung his head in a mock stupor he saw the cutthroats from the group with which he had played boule approach. Encircling the well, their eyes glinted with malice on seeing the saffron scarf containing the giant's winnings that hung from the narrow rope ties of his black culottes.

'There, there my Lord,' Bethshima's coaxing voice whispered in his ear, 'are you feeling a little drowsy?' From the corner of his eye he saw her hand moving towards the leather scabbard that rested beside him on the lip of the well - her intention clear: to push it over the ledge. His bloodshot eyes opened and he crushed the traitor's hand against the mud brick wall of the well and retrieved the scabbard and the blade before it dropped down over the lip.

'And I thought it was my body that aroused your interest, my beauty' he muttered as she cried out and ran back to the arms of one of the approaching men. He saw now that he was encircled and outnumbered by about ten-to-one, but not out manoeuvred as he jumped up onto the flat top of the circular well wall and drew the gigantic scimitar from its sheath, glimpsing as he did a strange camel caravan drawing in from the desert and up to the caravanserai.

'I urge you to come no further' the ebony giant shouted at the approaching ruffians, 'draw back now with your heads, or leave later without them.'

'But you are outnumbered,' the ringleader laughed, adjusting the leather patch over his eye, his arm around Bethshima. 'Ten of us, against one of you...we only wish to have our gold back!'

'Ten against two!' a voice cut in from the recently arrived caravan as a tall, slim, athletic looking man jumped down from one of the kneeling camels, his white satin shirt blowing in the breeze and a scimitar held on high.

'Errol...you son of a gun' the ebony giant shouted as he recognised his old comrade, 'what took you so long...couldn't steer your ship of the desert...'

'Smirtin my friend,' the buccaneer retorted, adjusting the black silk bandanna that graced his head and checking that his long brown pigtail wasn't looped, 'that is a fine welcome for one who comes to help you out of a sticky situation.' As the two men bandied ribald greetings at each other, the band of brigands were caught in the verbal crossfire and a look of confusion swept across their faces.

'Skewer that big black bollard' Bethshima elbowed her man into action as he hesitated, intrigued by the dubious relationship between these two strangers.

'Hold your position' Errol shouted to Smirtin across the heads of the advancing ruffians, 'I'll sever a few calf tendons from the rear ...they do not know what they are up against....'

Seven men closed on Smirtin and the first took a low swing along the top of the well, aiming at the giant's sandaled feet. But the slow-moving blade was no match for the Genie, who revived from his torpor, jumped effortlessly into the air and the ill-conceived sword-swipe from the cutthroat hacked the head of the man next to him clean off.

'One down, nine to go' Errol shouted jubilantly, his scimitar slashing across the legs of the rear guard before they could realise the threat, so that three more brigands rolled down into the sand.

'Stand down' Smirtin bellowed, 'or you shall rue this day!' But his entreaty went unheard and the man with the eye-patch urged the rest of the villains to storm the well as they changed tactics and lunged up at the black man's groin. The clash of steel rang around the oasis as Smirtin knocked two swords out of his assailant's hands and then stepped nimbly aside, avoiding the other's lunges to his manhood and with a great careening sweep of his flashing scimitar, decapitated the remaining three assailants. As their dismembered bodies slumped to the ground, the ebony hulk continuing with his circular momentum around the well top and aimed a side kick into the face of the last cutthroat who was propelled backwards into a nearby palm tree as a bone-shattering sound of his pulverised skull rang around the caravanserai.

The three ruffians who had been slightly wounded by Errol and had hung back at the edge of the oasis to see which way the fight would go, now retreated in horror, fear knotting their loins, as they limped out into the desert sands with Bethshima following. Errol sheathed his scimitar and strode up to the black giant who jumped down from the well and walked to embrace his old comrade.

'Of all the fights in all the oases in all the dimensions,' Errol paraphrased, 'and I just had to walk into this one' he slapped Smirtin on the back.

'Just as well, master capitaine sir,' the black giant rapped back, 'for dis 'ere black boy, he be rattlin' in a cage o' fear 'afor you arrived!' Though Smirtin had never seen a movie in his entire life, he had an encyclopaedic knowledge of the comic stereotyping employed in that genre from his long acquaintanceship with this actor maudit, the failed legend of the silver screen. As he clowned about, playing the part of the underdog, they both knew that this massive Genie could have dispatched twice as many of his recent assailants without breaking a fingernail.

'So did you get recalled from your perennial vacation as well?' Errol cut the black giant's capering short, and looked seriously at his compatriot.

'Yes,' Smirtin replied,' his voice returning to its deep timbre, 'it seems as if our old friend, the Artist is back on the scene, and that he needs a little help.'

'What of Ogadile?' Errol asked, 'did she also get the message to come to Aiyu?'

'I imagine she would have' Smirtin replied, 'if only to keep your philandering in check...yet I have heard no word from her for a while. She spends most of her time with her people at Coral Cove.'

'That is many leagues distant, is it not?' Errol ventured, 'perhaps we will see her at Aiyu. Are you ready to continue, or do you need a rest?'

'We'll have plenty of time to rest in the saddle,' Smirtin answered, 'let's get these scurvy beasts watered and then saddle up.' He gestured at the camels.

As the sky became a jigsaw of purple, pink and grey and the afterglow faded behind the clouds of the western desert, the strange pair swung up onto their snorting camels and headed south on the final leg of their journey to Aiyu. The caravanserai faded into a smudge on the distant horizon and Smirtin clinked the bag of golden coins as a wry smile transfigured his predatory face. 'Payment in advance hey... this renascent caper is not going to be as boring as I thought.' He muttered to himself as Errol looked at him non-plussed.

A ghostly yellow moon rose over the desert plain, picking out the camel train of four (two with riders and two carrying supplies), that plodded on in single file, making its way as if by automatic pilot whilst the two men dosed in the saddle. The blue-black sky blazed with a million stars and a comet, the messenger of the Gods, tipped its white tail and landed beyond the visible horizon.

The yellow moon was nearly at Zenith as the lead camel stopped and snorted, kneeling in front of a strange figure who whispered to it and gently pulled its bit so that it rolled over sideways. The giant bulk of the sleeping cameleer rolled off the saddle and onto the sand. With an oath he went for his scimitar, but a booted foot was across it as he looked up at the leopard-skin tunic of his assassin and saw the very feminine shape of a woman as she bid him be silent.

Her long black frizzy hair was held back by a golden clasp to tumble onto her broad shoulders from which hung a leopard-skin pelt, the tail of which trailed almost in the sand. Her ebony face was finely etched in the moonlight and glowed with exquisite beauty. She unsheathed a thinly curved Arabic blade from her girdle and brought it up to the withers of the second camel, slicing the saddle straps as the slumped, somnambulant figure of Errol gradually inclined until gravity took hold and he fell, as if in slow motion, from the standing camel and thumped onto the sand beneath.

'Have at you, you scurvy knave...' Errol went for his scimitar, but he saw a long, shapely leg clad in a knee-length, alligator-skin boot, hook under the curved hilt, to send it shimmering up in the air and away; then he felt cold steel at his throat.

'So,' a familiar voice spoke, 'outmatched, outwitted, outclassed and outmoded, you prisoners of Morpheus...what comfort can a poor damsel take from this?'

'*Damsel*!' Errol exploded 'Damsel my sweet backside,' you're about as near to a damsel as a toad is to a princess...' he stopped abruptly, feeling the well-soled alligator-skin boot at his throat.

'Well now' she said 'fine words for one at such a disadvantage. ' If you want to keep your brainless head with its garrulous tongue on your body, I suggest you reign in your language, since you cannot keep a reign on your steed... a little pleasantry would do for a start.' Errol felt the boot press into his jugular and he looked desperately across to Smirtin who was lying close by in the sand, his hands over his mouth trying to suppress a deep chuckle.

'Down, down we come,' Errol choked, 'like a glistening Phaeton, wanting the manage of unruly Jades.' A hangover from his acting days, Errol had a lamentable habit of misquoting literature in the pathetic belief that it would confound his opponent; that it generally did - by reducing them to tears of laughter

'Down you came alright' Ogadile mimicked the fake voice of the one time actor to a tee. 'But not to manage Jades. For it a primeval predator

wrapped around my lovely leg that has the manage of thee!' She let up
the alligator-skin boot as Errol struggled to his feet and he saw his
tormentor break into a hearty laugh as she and Smirtin embraced and
their mirth rose up from the desert into the star-spangled night.

'Brother,' Ogadile exclaimed, 'it is good to see you after all this
time...and you Errol, you old reprobate... Tell me, what have you been up
to of late?'

The three old friends - or to be more precise: the Genie brother and
sister, Smirtin and Ogadile, and Errol, a discredited actor who had been
sent down to Nethertime for bad acting and moral turpitude – swapped
their stories; it was as if time had stood still for the three as they laughed
and joked about their respective exploits - and as there *was* no time in the
lost dimension, in a way it had.

'Come' Ogadile said presently, 'give those poor beasts a rest. Let us
walk up to the next rise, for there you will see the fabled city of Aiyu. While
they walked, Ogadile related her story: of how she had flown on the ether
from Coral Cove, her beloved home, after also receiving an urgent
summons to help the Artist.

They walked up the incline and topping the rise, looked out onto the
mystical, Ancient Egyptian citadel of Paradise, Aiyu.

From the barren plain ahead, a wonderland of fragmented limestone
cliffs towered up, overgrown in parts with trailing bushes and dotted here
and there by the dark silhouettes of acacia and tamarisk trees. Amidst this
jumble of overgrown cliffs could be seen a maze of rock-cut tombs and
temples, high gates and pylons, which reflected the waning moonlight in
slivers of yellow.

'That such beauty could ever be threatened' Ogadile murmured as she
signalled for them to return to their camels, noting the desert gate in the
high walls which cradled this jewel of Ancients.

'Our rendezvous is at the northern high gate, the desert gate of the
great boundary wall,' she whispered as they made their way silently down
the stony, sand-strewn escarpment back towards the camels.

Saddled again and proceeding in the direction which Ogadile had
mapped out, they were approaching their destination, with the high gates
of the fabled city starting to tower up into the sky above them. Suddenly
they halted abruptly as an array of flashing green lights arced across the
heavens and touched down in front of the colossal structure ahead. Three
figures, two on foot and one astride some demon-like beast suddenly
appeared at the base of the high gate.

Smirtin went for his scimitar, but Ogadile's hand stayed him.

'Wait,' she cautioned, 'don't you recognize him...it is the strange
one...the Artist!' They closed the remainder of the distance, staring in
wonder at the youthful woman astride the striped beast and then seeing
the flashing grin on the face of the Artist as he made visual contact with
his old comrades from a distant era.

'*You motley crew!*' Jock hailed them as they drew nigh. 'Why you haven't changed a bit, but look at me,' he tugged at his mottled beard, bespeckled with grey. 'I am your father now!' He ran to embrace Ogadile who whooped loud jubilant cheers at seeing the one with whom she had adventured so long ago.

'You son of the brush!' she exclaimed excitedly. 'You are now the *father* of the brush...but who is he?' her tone turned from the jocular to the reverent as she looked up at the tall slim figure of Luke whose long blond hair was as if spun from gold in the remnants of the waning moon.

'This young man is my son!' Jock announced proudly. 'He has travelled from a civilised dimension in order to drag me back from a life of wanton debauchery... back to the cold fogs and mists of my homeland... God bless him.'

'Indeed' Ogadile rejoined 'He will have a hard task ahead'

'Son of the Artist.' Errol bowed 'It is my great honour to make your acquaintance...do you have news of the Old World? Perhaps you recognise me' he held his profile to the light. 'Tell me, are they still doing re-runs of my films?'

'*You posturing pillock!*' Ogadile snapped. 'You are long gone, long forgotten... and pickled in your own oblivion of fanciful fame and glory, you...'

'No' Luke interrupted, and even Jock stopped bantering with his old comrade, Smirtin. 'No sir, you are not forgotten' Luke's tone was serious - all eyes were upon him. 'I have recently seen your movies, they are now available to people to show in their own homes...video, it is called. Why only before I left to come to this land of great mysteries, I chanced to watch one...'

'Really?' Errol strutted, tweaking his over-trimmed moustache, 'pray tell me young man, how did I look?'

'Very fair sir.' Luke continued in similar vein 'you and your two accomplices aroused much mirth in the household.'

'Mirth...my two accomplices!' Errol spluttered, 'what do you mean accomplices, I am a singular actor!'

'Not so, great idol of the silver screen,' Luke was feeling his way into the part. 'When you landed in the barrel of lard which went over Niagara Falls...it was an act of comic brilliance.'

'Barrel of lard...comic brilliance...what mean you sire?' Errol came up to the youth, his face bristling with rage as Jock started to understand the joke and with difficulty stopped himself from shaking with laughter.

'That's right sir, the Three Stooges in which you played...brilliant'

'*The Three Stooges!*' Errol exploded as Jock let go and his whole body creased up in a deep belly laugh and Luke joined him.

'You little sac of shrunken scrotum!' Errol spat and reached for his scimitar, whilst the others stood back, sobering and eying up the stand off.

'Steady Errol...the lad is unarmed.' Smirtim made as if to move, but Jock stayed him.

'I meant no harm...it was in jest.' Luke offered.

'Jest...you jest at me...then jest with my steel!' Errol postured.

'I think not old chap.' Luke was getting rather irritated by this buffoon of a failed actor who was trying to intimidate him. Taking measure of the man, Luke spun suddenly in an arc and delivered a swinging kick to Errol's wrist that sent the scimitar spinning out of his hands, to land in the desert sand some way off.

'Whoops.' Smirtin muttered, and then broke out into a deep guffaw. 'Second time in as many hours, old thing...must try and keep a grip on things...particularly scimitars.'

'It seems we have more than a chip off the old block here' Ogadile observed as she and Smirtin looked at Luke in a new light; what sort of combat was this that the handsome youth brought from afar?

Nursing a near-broken wrist and his hurt pride, Errol retrieved his scimitar and sulkily rejoined the group, his eyes alighting on the slim profile of Zalkina astride the Zebra, who had neither smiled, nor moved since this exchange of pleasantries. In fact she was feeling isolated and left out of it a bit since her golden haired hero had been reunited with his father. And now, after all those strange people she had met at the Temple of the Eon, there were even stranger ones to contend with and the young native girl looked in trepidation at this old man in a fancy dress costume who now approached her.

'My dear,' Errol said ingratiatingly, turning his back on the others, 'allow me to assist you from your mount.' He held out his hand and Zalkina swung gracefully down from the stationary beast. 'These are such a foul crew you are saddled with...Let me tell you about myself.' Errol proceeded to bore the white robe off Zalkina and her winged mount, whilst Ogadile rolled her eyes Heavenwards.

After the initial enthusiasm at their long due reunion had subsided, all eyes focussed on Luke Slater as he described how the cult of the One Dimension had established a hold of unknown magnitude on the outside world. How the Order had infiltrated people of power such as Labachi and Rachid. He told the story of his Mother's abduction by the cult and how he had followed her here to Nethertime, or Ancient time, to be precise. Luke appraised them of the importance of the inscription and how his mother had been sent to convey the exact pronunciation of it.

'And so,' Jock interjected 'the Emperor of the Eon has stopped time, reversed it momentarily...what we must do know is devise a plan, some sort of strategy...I mean it is Bridget, my wife we are talking about, and she will be astral travelling to Aiyu, *even as we speak!*'

'Or she may have already arrived' Luke added not too helpfully.

'There is something you should know.' Ogadile said 'The messenger who flew to Coral Cove to summon me here gave me a map.' She reached into the leopard – skin pelt and brought out a piece of tattered parchment.

'I haven't had time to look at it closely, but it seems to indicate that the main temples are on the other side of that cliff.' Ogadile looked up at the towering moonlit massif.

'May I see it,' Jock said as he looked over Ogadile's shoulder. In this close proximity to the beautiful Genie, Jock felt some overpowering connection between the exotic perfume that Ogadile wore and a map, which sent his senses into overdrive. Try as he may he couldn't recall the memory, and with a great effort of willpower he focussed again on the map.

'But Father,' Luke cut into the artist's thoughts as he posed a new conundrum. 'You don't need to look at a map, do you? Is your memory so short?'

'How do you mean Son?' Jock asked

'You have *been* here, you must have been... you did that wonderful painting of Aiyu...the one that Rachid and Labachi stole, the one they use as a fix when they astral travel.

'*My God!*' Jock's face was a mask of bewilderment, 'You are right,my son... how could I forget that...I have been so long working in the Garden of Eon-Beasts that I have forgotten. It was at the request of Isis, that's right.... Before the cult came...before...'

'It's alright Father,' Luke said gently, seeing the agonised expression on his father's face. 'You have travelled in so many dimensions, seen so many sights...*no wonder you are confused.*'

'I remember now and Ogadile is right. The city of Aiyu proper is located on the far side of those cliffs.' Jock was recovering somewhat from his memory slip.

'Our best ploy is to get up to the top, up there,' Jock pointed to the serrated cliffs which towered into the blue-black night, 'and see if we can locate the headquarters of the Order, which will be, without a doubt, on the other side. It will also give us a good vantage point to keep the activities of the marauding cult under surveillance and to spot when and where Bridget materialises.

'It will be a long climb,' Smirtin said, looking at the looming cliffs.'

'I can fly up' Ogadile said, 'I still have my powers.'

'And Zalkina can accompany you' Luke added

'She is empowered?' Ogadile asked incredulously

'No, but Starchild, her mythical steed is.'

'Wonderful' Ogadile enthused, looking in a new light on Zalkina and her stationary mount 'let us away then.'

The last limb of the waning moon dipped behind the brooding cliffs and cast dark shadows from the high gate as the flying Genie and the native girl on her mythological steed rose up and soared into the star-strewn night, the white wings of the Zebra a sharp contrast against the purple-black rocks.

'All very well for some' Errol grumbled as the four men started their arduous trek up the steep rock face. The black cliffs up which they climbed would have turned a deep shade of Crimson had they had ears, as Errol applied his greatest weapon, his tongue, into the difficult and dangerous ascent. The air thick with blasphemies, Errol climbed and complained in unequal amounts, whilst the others stoppered their ears, the repetition of his maritime invective growing tiresome.

Finally they reached the top of the massif and were greeted once again by the reassuring rays of the moon, which had not yet set over the distant desert plain on the other side of the mountain.

'What kept you?' Ogadile was sitting on a jutting cornice of rock that overhung the valley of Aiyu, whilst Zalkina sat nearby, nuzzling her cherished Zebra, Starchild.

'Any activity?' Jock asked breathlessly

'Nothing.' Ogadile replied, smirking at the breathless and cursing Errol, his face a mottled red. After a while the others got their breath and joined the Genie and the native girl on the cornice of rock, looking down into the mythical wonderland of Aiyu. The resurrected yellow moon bathed this side of the mountain in its amber glow and Jock placed his arm around his long-lost son.

'Isn't it magnificent?' he whispered, 'This birds-eye view of Aiyu is absolutely superb. How could I ever forget that I have been here?'

For it was true; the array of descending plinths of natural rock, overhung with Jasmine, convolvulus, bougainvillaea and many other flowering shrubs and trailers, were home to a variety of dwellings and temples of all manner of styles. These clung in gravity defying profusion to the step ravine at the base of which was formed a semi-circular amphitheatre of natural stone. Upon this was built a singular temple of grand proportions. Beyond lay the great plain of the desert, crowned in the infinite distance by a series of serrated, blue mountain peaks.

From the centre of this vast labyrinth of natural and man-made structures rose the giant Obelisk, which winked at them in the gilded light of the declining moon.

'What is it Dad?' Luke asked as they sat together on the horizontal needle of rock that jutted out into the infinite space below. 'What is the significance of this ancient monolith?' He looked earnestly into his father's face, at the beard and long wavy hair streaked with grey of the peripatetic artist who had dared travel through time itself to further his own obsession.

'I know not, my own son!' he grasped Luke around the shoulder, hugging him tight. 'I only know that those long years ago, when I forsook you and your mother, I was blessed with the task of recording a phenomenon which no modern mortal eye had ever witnessed...I was there to record the inscription before it crumbled into dust.'

'Yet it is here, in Aiyu.' Luke stated the obvious. 'It is the same Obelisk and this is the same scene which, you painted two years ago at the university's head quarters in Luxor and which Rachid brought back to Park House, only to steal and reinstate it at the London head quarters of the cult.' Luke's voice trembled as he mentioned Jock's beloved 'retreat' Park House.

'Luke, my son' Jock Slater looked into the eyes of the handsome youth. 'There is something which you hide from me, is there not?'

'Park House is no more Father,' Luke could put it off no longer, 'it was burned to the ground!'

Jock frose, his expression a testament to the sense of loss that he now felt.

'I sensed there was something else...as if your Mother's abduction into the cult is not enough...who was it, Labachi, Rachid?'

'No,' Luke replied quietly, 'by mindless vandals who thought there was a witch's coven at the house...they saw something, they were intent on malice...they used petrol and burned it to the ground.' Luke was starting to break up as he remembered that time not so far back in the real world when his youth has been suddenly forged into manhood.

'So' Jock's voice was flat. 'All my work of a lifetime gone up in smoke – apart from the Obelisk picture - and that is now in the clutches of this infernal cult. 'Tis divine retribution dear boy...my punishment for being an errant father' Luke saw his father's eyes brimming with tears, 'And your mother abducted by the very two people whom I counted as trusted friends...betrayal son...*we have been betrayed*! 'Jock's voice shook with rage.

'And for what? 'He continued. 'So that some fanatical megalomaniac can attest to his demonic power in this great shrine to beauty and trust' Jock gestured expansively to the lush magical scenery stretched below them. 'For this is the enshrined mythical paradise of the Ancient Egyptians, the protégé of the star people...' Jock looked around at the others who were trying to hide their concern for the poor man as they picked up on the story of his double tragedy.

'But there is a glimpse of hope Father,' Luke added, brightening somewhat. 'And that is that the insurance of half a million pounds has been paid into your account, gathering interest until your return, even as we speak.'

'What relief my son' Jock hugged Luke, 'and well done.' He pulled himself up, shaking off his gloom and turned to the others who though registering concern, had out of respect, left father and son to their own company as they scoured the labyrinth of the temples and rocks down below for any sign of the cult.

'What news comrades?' Jock addressed the silent group casting aside the grief he felt.

'Nothing moving' Smirtin replied, 'whoever is down there, if they are down there are either invisible, very quiet, or asleep...as we should be if we were in our right minds.'

'Wait!' Ogadile exclaimed. 'There is something down there, look!'

As they peered into the distant valley, a faint flurry of movement could be seen.

Errol raised a leather bound sighting-glass to his eyes and announced in the swaggering tones of one who is sole possession of some important knowledge. 'A line of priests, exiting from the large temple down yonder ravine... they are clad in orange robes...they are forming into a circle'

'Ancient mariner,' Jock retorted, mustering his old self back from the brink of morbidity, 'might you be so good as to give us a running report on their activities, as I would be loathe to ask you lend me your eye-piece.

'Aye, Captain.' Errol responded in like tone, the camaraderie of his old alliance with comrades of previous voyages through space and time reappearing as naturally as if they had never been apart, and Luke marvelled at the familiarity which his father summoned up to address this odd man of a million walk-on parts. He also marvelled at the indomitable will that which Jock brought to bear as he disguised his deep sorrow at hearing of the loss of his work.

Smirtin winked broadly at Jock and Ogadile's gesture of ridicule behind Errol's back almost had Luke in fits until he checked himself in the realisation of the seriousness of the imminent event heralded by the formation of the cult way down in the valley below.

'A man enters the circle' Errol pronounced in his clipped, anglicised voice! He has long white flowing hair'

'What another one!' Jock cut in sarcastically. He must be the leader...the so called Esoteric Oracle...What's his costume then?'

'Red' Errol affirmed.

'Bloody communists...I knew it!' Jock slapped Luke on the shoulder, his jocularity was pretty transparent, Luke thought. He was trying to play the joker, yet Luke detected an undertone of deep concern in his Father's voice.

'A comet in the sky' Ogadile exclaimed. 'We have a messenger, an arrival is imminent.'

They looked into the blue-black vault above. A white flame was descending in a trajectory that had to coincide with the temple below. As the last limb of the finally waning moon slipped its yellow crescent behind the rim of the distant mountains, all eyes were on Errol as he gasped aloud seeing the apparition from another world 'land' into the circle of the orange-clad cultists.

'My God' he oathed, '*she* is a beauty!'

'*Hand me that glass sir!*' Jock snatched the telescope from the ancient mariner - cum actor, sighting it on the circle below, his breast heaving in consternation.

'Bridget, my love' he gasped as he saw the arrival of his estranged wife who stood bemused and encircled by the ring of orange-robed cultists, as the white haired Master of the Order of the One Dimension approached and embraced her.

'It is time, my friends, for action!' Jock snapped the small telescope shut and handed is back to Errol, turning to Ogadile.

'Can you fly with Zalkina, down to the group of devil worshippers, and distract them.' Jock's eyes were bright as he pointed to the distant ring of cult members, 'I do not think that they have any weapons, or would hurt you. But if you can engage their attention for a while, until we climb down...the hard way... and then see what we are up against. The important thing is to prevent Bridget from handing them the incantation, either by fair means or foul.'

'We will!' Ogadile turned, summoning Zalkina, who mounted her mythical Zebra and together they launched off from the rock cornice and into the blue void, flying like creatures from another world, to descend rapidly towards the temple below.

Smirtin had already secured the grappling hooks and payed out the rope over the edge of the precipice, and the four men abseiled down from the overhang. Smirtin was somewhere below them, his hardened hands more accustomed to the friction of the rope when Jock looked down, noting with concern that the rope down which they climbed stopped some distance short of the cliff base. Smirtin had reached this point and was swinging uncertainly in space, wishing he were better at measuring lengths of rope.

But their fears of a shortfall in the rope's length were eclipsed and rendered meaningless as a bright orange beam of light cut through the shadowy blue haze, causing the giant obelisk to tremor. Then a bolt of liquid fire infiladed the rock above them, searing through the fragile ropes as one by one they dropped down from their tenuous perches into the sickening void below, enveloped by pulverised rock fragments blasted from the towering cliffs.

It was the bushes and willowy trees clinging to the lower sections of the rock-face that were to be their salvation. For before any of them had scarce time to cry out, they had crashed down into the trees below, relieved to feel the springy branches break their headlong fall. Rolling down the steep incline, their senses left them in a tumble of twigs, bark and fragments of rock.

✳✳✳

Ogadile and Zalkina were gliding above the glade, aware that they had had been spotted by the cultists below, when a bright orange beam shot out from the temple, blinding them. They turned to follow the direction of the light and saw to their horror the rope severed and their four compatriots plunge down into the canopy of trees below; then they took stock of their own imminent plight.

The Artist's assessment of the order of the One Dimension as being unarmed or pacific could not be further from the mark as the orange beam swung inexorably towards the two women and they felt the heat from the lethal bolt scald the air close over their heads.

'Dive!' Ogadile commanded 'head for the ground' and the black supernatural being took hold of the bit in the whinnying Zebra's mouth and forced steed and rider into a dizzying crash-dive as they plummeted down into the trees below.

Suddenly the orange light was extinguished, its targets gone to the ground, and an eerie silence hung over the labyrinth of trees, rocks and temples and the valley fell hushed, as if in waiting for the next move.

✳✳✳

Smirtin was the first to recover and after disengaging himself from a snagging branch by breaking it in half, looked around to assess the fate of his three colleagues. Jock and Luke had fallen through the trees and landed on a slope of soft sand; they signalled that they were all right, and raised themselves gingerly out of the fine yellow sand, standing silently trying to get their bearings.

'I spoke a little too soon, didn't I?' Jock said, dusting himself down. 'Are you all right?' Luke nodded. 'Nothing broken, except a little pride...but what the ruddy hell was that weapon...it's got to be a laser gun.'

'Yeah.' Jock shook his tangle of greying hair, like a dog exiting a pond and spraying Luke with sand. 'These cultists...or whoever they are down here, appear to have unearthed the star people's old weaponry.' 'But what is more scary is that they know how to use it...I just wonder what more little surprises they have in store for us.'

Luke was about to ask how his father knew about the star people and was about to recount his experiences with Joruck, but the sound of breaking branches startled him.

'Liquid fire' Smirtin stumbled out of the undergrowth and stood towering over them, his black eyes were showing a lot of their whites as he looked in apprehension down to the temple resting in the shady bower of the wooded slope.

'Big magic' he articulated carefully, trying to suppress his fear of the unknown.' 'Demon magic down there...'

'Will you numskulls stop twittering on about bloody magic, and cut me loose!' Errol's high-pitched voice spoke out into the darkness from somewhere over their heads. They looked up and saw the flim-flam artist dangling by his white silk scarf from an overhanging tree; his face was a misery of outrage and helplessness.

'Perhaps it would be a good idea to remember your manners.' Jock taunted, looking up at the hapless fellow who flailed in mid-air. 'You have a sword...why don't you cut yourself free'

'This is me best and only silk scarf' Errol bickered, 'you don't think I'm going to sacrifice that do you?'

'Well old chum' Jock retorted, 'you could wait until they vaporise you with their laser cannon, I suppose.' They watched the various stages of compromise cavort across the actor's face as he wrestled with the two choices, and finally cut himself free, falling close by in the soft sand and preceeded by a litany of verbal abuse.

'I mean' Jock added, clasping his old friend around the shoulders as he staggered to join them. 'Half a scarf is better than non!'

He took the end of the severed, though prized garment and tied it in a Windsor knot around the red-faced Errol.

'There!' Jock exclaimed' 'you've got a nice silk cravat now.'

'Enough of this' Smirtin counted. 'We have to find the other two...they could be in danger...did anyone see where they landed?'

'I saw them come down on the other side of the temple' Luke replied, which means we are separated from them...and we will be picked off by the laser if we walk around to them'

'Unless we silence their guns' Jock mused as he took the small telescope, miraculously undamaged in Errol's recent fall, from around the actor's neck.

'There is no sign of anyone.' Jock said gruffly, as he levelled the glass on the temple below. 'There must be some sort of bunker or refuge below the temple floor, because the deck of the temple is completely devoid of human presence...where have the cult of the One Dimension gone?'

'Where have they taken my wife?'

'Phantom-time' Smirtin intoned, his deep voice dirge-like. 'I have seen this before. They are still there, yet they are not...they are changed'

'Is this one of your mumbo jumbo stories?' Errol asked sarcastically.

'Quiet, you baffoon!' Jock turned upon Errol and his eyes did not countenance any rebuff, 'let the man speak!' he swung back to the towering black supernatural, sensing his unworldly knowledge of such events and how they impacted upon their present predicament.

'I have seen this' Smirtin continued. 'There are some who hold their presence, yet in a changed state...they are the ones of supreme magic who will disappear from human view, and yet are still there...they have the power to turn themselves into phantoms'

'So we would walk into a trap if we descended towards the temple?' Jock summarised.

'Yes,' Smirtin's teeth were starting to chatter and his eyes were playing ping-pong, 'or the other option is that you would join them... you would enter their phantom world, and be in their power'

'Hum,' Jock's mind was in overdrive as he struggled with the possibilities of a new strategy, 'but what if we *knew* we were to be phantomised....what if we were prepared and entered willingly into that changed state...yet hold onto our mortal identities, disguised as they...*pretending* to be changed. Then we could infiltrate...we could find Bridget, rescue her from their powers.'

'Only if you are of the one will, the one great strength.' Smirtin countered. 'Can you hold onto that which you are, and resist their temptations?' The black afreet's face was fractured in the lines of one who contemplates the impossible.

'*Yes we can!*' It was Luke who spoke. 'If we rehearse our bond now, and hold it in our mind's eye at all times, we can resist this evil of the cult of Satan. Then we can outwit them at their own game... once we find out what that game is; for we have that with which to barter, *the incantation!*'

'Aye' Jock took up the challenge. 'Well spoken my lad.' He clasped the others to him and in a tight circle they pledged their bond of fealty to the cause of the overthrow of the cult of the One Dimension.

'Let us descend' my friends, but can we get a message to Ogadile and Zalkina?'

'I will send a message.' Smirtin replied, and busied himself in the making of a bow from the multitude of branches that lay scattered around; a result of the recent bombardment. Pulling out a menacing looking curved knife he sliced off another section of Errol's white scarf.

The former matinee idol said not one word, his eyes focussed on the lethal blade. Smirtin plucked a juniper berry from one of the overhanging bushes and crushing it in his anvil of a fist, wrote a cryptic message with it onto the scarf. Then He wrapped this around a straight stick and winged the arrow across the grove, high over the temple to land somewhere on the other side.

'They will find it' he said. 'They will understand...and wait for our return.'

'Come on then!' Jock led the other three down the slope of sand which formed a passage through the arboreal canopy above. In his hand he carried a stick with the remnants of Eroll's white scarf tied to it, whilst the disrobed theatrical fellow muttered obscenities under his breath as he followed behind them.

Emerging from the trees, the ground levelled out somewhat and they strode onward with baited breath, expecting any minute to be picked off by the laser-weapon. But an eerie silence hung over the grove as they reached the courtyard in front of the temple and felt the hard echoes of the sandstone floor under their feet. The massive pylon, its winged serpent insignia glowing dimly in burnished gold above the door threw shivers of fear along their backs, but the surrounds of the temple were as empty as a beggar's purse and the massive obelisk towered silently above them.

Jock halted in the centre of the main court and waving his flag, he called out loudly in the louring gloom.

'We come to barter, we come unarmed,' although it was not strictly true. 'We offer you the incantation in return for your hostage, the red-haired Bridget.'

The silence was palpable and hung heavy on the airless space of rock-hewn columns and towering masonry. Jock heard Smirtin's giant teeth began to chatter as the whites of his eyes darted this way and that - for all his physical power, he was reduced to quivering jelly in the presence of this invisible, phantasmagoric enemy.

'Show your hand!' An effeminate, yet authoritative voice commanded from nearby. 'Convince us of your claim, for we already have the orator of the incantation in our midst...even though she may need a little coaxing.'

'There is no need!' It was Luke who spoke. 'Release her and take us, *we* will deliver you the incantation, I promise!'

'Ah!' the effeminate voice exclaimed, slightly nearer now, as Smirtin started to shake visibly, his giant black frame trembling in a mass of muscular contortions, his eyes wild. 'It is the seed of our newest convert...an interesting equation. And you purport to know the incantation.... From whom, may I ask, did you learn it?'

'From Ishtar' Luke half-shouted into the blue-grey gloom of the nocturnal temple complex, 'my sometime mentor....'

'Ishtar!' the slimy voice rose a pitch into a steely rasp, and then seemed to rise up over the temple structure as if coming from the overhanging amphitheatre of trees and rock. It was accompanied by the sound of a slithering, scaly dissonance that echoed around the hung valley as Smirtin collapsed to the ground, blubbering like a baby.

'I forbid you to speak that name....' the voice rose to a crescendo and subsided somewhat, almost as if its orator struggled to control conflicting emotions - finally it levelled out into the slick, whining tones of the enchanter.

'No Matter...she is of little import.... now you say you have the incantation in its true form, for which you wish to exchange the freedom of your mother... but can you deliver to me proof?'

'I can' Luke said firmly. He faced the place where the unearthly voice seemed to be positioned and spoke clearly - the long days of committing the incantation to memory were engraved upon his mind. He carefully articulated every slight inflection of the strange, arcane language; even as he did, the memory of his liaison with Ishtar swam before him.

'Neb – Ankh – Sar - Eff....'

'*Enough!*' the sibilant form of the ever-changing voice rasped out from above.

'It is enough! You will not complete the incantation until we are ready! But know you, seed of my convert, yet still seed of my enemy, that I believe you. You *have* the inflection, you *have* the tongue.... And *you will* deliver to us, the power!'

As the faucal sound of this terrifying voice faded, Luke felt himself struck down by an arrow of thought, or some powerful hypnotic intelligence, which burned into his brain so that his mind became awash with all manner of horrors and obscenities that caused him to cry out in rejection; to try to hold on to his inner resolve to repel this powerful force of pure evil that used his own mind against himself. But the satanic mind-cast was overpowering and Luke felt his resistance ebbing away and his consciousness begin to fade. No use now their oath of mutual loyalty to their cause as Luke saw his father, and the other two comrades similarly despatched, as they were forced to their knees in the onslaught of some irredeemable, mid-numbing power - and all he could think was they had been *tricked*!

***

Ogadile and Zalkina had landed on a slope of limestone rubble and sand as they dove down to avoid the searing ray of the heat-weapon. Starchild had kicked and whinnied as he rolled down the slope, toppling his rider and finally had come to rest at the bottom of the hill, thrashing and moaning in fear.

Ogadile had run down the slope to tend to Zalkina, who was half-buried in the debris after being thrown from her beloved mount and was whimpering like a baby, her body shaking in utter dread of the unknown force that was beyond her native imagination. Now she embraced the ebony beauty who gently lifted her out of the morass and checked her for broken bones. Then she released herself from the motherly grasp and teetered down the slope to tend to Starchild who was similarly whimpering and shaking.

'There, there' Zalkina cooed as she stroked the mythical Zebra's head, and tried her best to comfort him.

'Is he hurt?' Ogadile asked, concernedly, bending over the two of them.

'He all right...big big light...what was that? Zalkina asked, tears in her eyes, 'it like liquid fire....'

'It was a weapon of great power. A weapon of the future I think....' Ogadile was trying to hide her fear.

'*Star people!*' Zalkina's voice was hysterical, 'It come from star people!'

'What?' Ogadile was not quite sure of her ground here.

'Star people! They make city below earth. They leave machines, leave things of big power...'

'How do you know this?' Ogadile asked, perplexed.

'I been there' Zalkina's eyes were brightening. 'I been to city below the earth. I take beautiful boy...show him.

'Luke?' Ogadile guessed in amazement, '*you took Luke*?'

'Yes' Zalkina pointed to the east. 'I take Luke down below water to old city, forgotten city of Star people. Much machine of great power...old power...'

'Shush' Ogadile put her hand on the hot temple of the lovely native girl; she was burning up. 'Quiet now...' yet an idea was forming in her mind.

'Come' she said after a while. Let us climb up to the rim of the slope and see what is going on. Leave Starchild here, we will return for him later. Zalkina kissed the Zebra's forelock and took the black Afarita's hand and they climbed silently up the slope of limestone rock and sand.

132

'Look' Zalkina said, pointing to an arrow sticking out of the sand at the top of the slope. Ogadile snatched it from the ground and read the message written on the remnant of Errol's scarf.

'They are alright... the others,' she looked relieved. 'They are going to descend to the temple and pretend to surrender themselves to the men of evil. They bid us to wait and watch...we must be cautious!'

She shredded the message with her cat-like talons of fingernails, and buried the remains in the sand. Then, taking Zalkina's hand again she edged her way up to a vantage point and looked out onto the level amphitheatre that housed the temple complex.

What she saw or rather didn't see made Ogadile's flesh crawl. The four men had descended the slope on the other side and were advancing steadily; Jock was waving a flag. Suddenly their progress was impeded as they entered into a dialogue with non-people - there was nobody there, and yet they were talking to them, and the strange conversation came to her in snippets; carried on the light breeze. She heard the falsetto voice of the non-entity, the phantom, rise up in a shrill hissing sound as she saw her brother, Smirtin, buckle and fold, gripped by a superstitious fear that rendered him into a little boy in the presence of ghouls. She knew him too well, for even with such physical might, he was but a child when faced with the supernatural or black magic – and this in front of her now was wizardry of the Devil himself!

Ogadile saw Luke freeze like a statue, as if all the living essence had been sucked out of him, and she shivered to see the others similarly un-empowered and held static in the enchanter's thrall. Then, as she looked around the temple complex of arched portal's and giant pylons, which formed the mythical city of Aiyu, she saw a small shrine to the side, and within its dull alabaster pillars gleamed a machine, its metallic form reflecting the starlight. Gradually Ogadile made a tenuous connection between this strange, futuristic object, which was outside the realm of her medieval upbringing, and the fusillade of orange fire that had nearly rendered them to ashes; *it had to be the light-gun!*

Squeezing Zalkina's arm and bidding her to follow silently, the two women edged their way around the slope, careful not to break cover as they made their way to the small separate enclosure housing the gun. Though there were no visible cultists to be seen didn't mean they weren't there – for they were invisible - and they advanced cautiously; even so - the big lightning and fire machine did seemed to be unmanned.

Zalkina gave one last backward glance at Starchild who seemed recovered enough and stood pawing the ground nervously below them.

The emplacement of the frightening fire-stick of the star people glinted, a dull gunmetal colour in the suffused dimness as Ogadile steadily approached it. Its barrel was pointing up to the towering cliffs that stood sentinel to the obelisk standing higher even than they. The raking fire across the cliffs was where it had last been used and the black supernatural felt a frisson of excitement course through her veins as she approached this awesome weapon of mass destruction. Yet she was uncertain what she should do with it as there was no enemy, no visible targets - except for her comrades who seemed still rooted to the spot.

Though the whole mechanism was foreign to her and Ogadile was technically inept, her superior intelligence argued within her as she stroked the various buttons and levers, trying to access the functions of each one as Zalkina crouched, trembling at her side. She sighted the barrel down and onto the broad base of the temple's structure, trying out the azimuth inclination system, which displayed red and green grids on the sighting readout panel. Her finger crossed the lever which, she figured was the trigger though she whispered for Zalkina not to nudge her; she was fairly confident that she could use the weapon and direct it when and if the right time came. They watched and waited.

Suddenly and without warning, it was show time. On some arcane command from the cult-master, the grisly array of ghouls entered their phantom-time forms. The amphitheatre was alive with sentient transparent beings that manifested themselves in a grotesque carnival of serpentine, bovine, piscine, and other lurid, hybrid forms as they were released from their sojourn of invisibility and danced in a frenzied unworldly dance on the stage between the towering temple walls and the columns. The leader of the jig appeared as a giant four-headed snake, which rose up over the blue-grey grotto and urged the cultists to engage their atavistic attributes in an orgy of nocturnal metamorphosis.

Zalkina Gripped Ogadile's arm, drawing blood, and she sobbed in total terror at the sight of the mutants of the un-dead who cavorted in squalid passion as their release into their former states empowered them on to new and more perverted measures. Above it all, and besmirching the holy temples of Aiyu, arose the din of bedlam: the chanting of the acolytes, the mewing of the neophytes, jangling, nerve-gratering dissonance like a cacophony from Hell!

As Ogadile and Zalkina watched dumfounded, the cult-master, the polymorphic creature of many guises and dimensions, reared up over the demonic throng in his serpentine form, a huge four-headed, then six-headed cobra that hissed in an abomination of sibilant, rasping sound.

'Homage, homage to your master. I command now you pay homage to me...The Esoteric Oracle. The Grand Master of the One Dimension...'

As the reptilian tones of the apparition reverberated around the courtyard and labyrinth of temples, the cultists stopped in mid orgy and obeyed, kneeling in a sickening display of fealty to their mutant Lord and Master.

The serpentine phantom reared over them whilst its followers returned to their human form of orange-clad cultists, who now looked upwards at their Oracle in a grovelling show of allegiance. On a gutteral command, the cultists seized the defenceless, hypnotised, and terror-stricken bodies of her four comrades as Ogadile stared in total fascination.

Their bodies limp and powerless, the four men were dragged across the courtyard to an alter in the centre and were laid out on it unceremoniously whilst the snake metamorph writhed in grotesque, luminescent, half- presence over his children of the Devil.

Then, as Ogadile watched in continuing horror, she saw a woman of handsome stature; yet pale as ashes, escorted from the largest temple and across the courtyard by two orange robed acolytes. Her fine, auburn hair was tugged slightly by the light breeze, as she was half-carried, half-led, towards the alter; it was obvious that she was drugged or hypnotised, for she offered no resistance to the two cultists.

Bridget was ushered to the alter where she stood obediently, showing no recognition of the prostrate figures of Jock or Luke; with eyes glazed, she swayed, transfixed, her white gown stirring in the light breeze, its colour mirroring her ashen face.

'What a miracle this day, my children,' The mutant rasped, his voice filling the dim grove. 'What a sight for sore eyes.... for here we have the three exponents of the incantation, and all together in the same place.'

'For surely this night, we will drive out the good and the blessed from their un-rightly sanctuary of Aiyu. We will take over.... convert this holy place and subsume it to its rightful owners; those of the inexorable will – the Order of the One Dimension.'

'Aye Lord' the cry of the demented rose up in the night air as the hissing voice pervaded the dark grove and echoed around the silent temples and the giant obelisk, which towered up from the end of the amphitheatre, dominating the hanging valley.

'We will command them with our will to recite the incantation, together, in its correct form...it will be strong, and incontestable!'

'Tis so master...'tis the collective will...' the cultists shouted.

Ogadile's hand was getting trigger-happy, but she resisted the impulse to let off a barrage of fire, for she was herself captivated by the authoritative tones and cajoling rhetoric of the cult-master and her eyelids were starting to feel like lead.

The illusionist serpent which fluctuated from being visible and then not, craned its four heads towards the alter on which rested the comatose bodies of the four men, whilst Bridget, her eyes unseeing, leaned limply and forlorn against the two acolytes. A dirge like intonation filled the grove:

'I command you now to recite together the incantation, so that I and my brethren shall inherit the Eternal Shrine, The Aiyu of the Ancients...' a deathly hush fell over the cult members as they watched in fascination for the fulfilment of their prophecy - the inheritance of their being into the eternal world of Paradise; the ultimate goal of their perverted devotions. Their eyes gazed upwards towards the mutant, the unspeakable abomination of the living, as they swooned in obedience to its all-embracing will. The satanic polymorph uttered its faucal command once more:

'So that we shall render the apocalyptic power of the Obelisk of Time into the hands of The Order of the One Dimension, I command you three of mortal flesh and blood to now to recite the incantation...'

The silence hanging over the amphitheatre was palpable and crawled with the sentience of a changed order; a nascent awakening of a new scourge yet to come.

Neb – Ankh – Sar – Eff – Rheckit – Djed

The voices of Jock, Bridget and Luke, the three masters of the incantation began to recite the dread command, in perfect unison. Their wills were rendered null and void as the power of the apocryphal inheritor of Paradise burned into their sub conscious minds.

The incantation, recited to perfection by its three proponents invaded the hushed silence of the eerie vale and the great Obelisk, standing high up on the towering cliffs and dominating the temple bestrewn valley began to glow in a spectral light, its hieroglyphs standing out in a golden radiance, illuminating the grove as the incantation of all time and space was spoken. An awed cooing arose from the assembled group of arcane cultists as they were silhouetted in the golden light from the Obelisk of Time, their outstretched arms cradled in their orange robes.

Ogadile felt the surge of blood run down her arm as Zalkina's nails dug into her flesh, shattering her entranced state of bewitchment, so mesmerised was she by flickering vision of the serpent, the would-be King of Paradise who tortured her mind into an hypnotic trance.

The pain of the girl's terrified grip shocked her into action, so that with her mind clearing, her powers returned and she depressed the firing trigger on the star people's weapon. Suddenly the blue-black grove was lit up with an orange light as a random burst of laser fire filled the air and the screams of the cultists rang around the chaotic courtyard. With an accuracy that was governed more by intuition than practice, Ogadile swept the courtyard with a death dealing infilade of fire, pausing momentarily to release the trigger when she got to the alter in the centre with its precious cargo, and then continuing to swing the mounted cannon in an arc of destruction.

Ranging the line of fire upwards, Ogadile cut the writhing, semi-transparent serpent form of the Esoteric Oracle to pieces as its unearthly shrieks rose above the staccato sound of the laser cannon and the cries for mercy from its own cultists.

Still the giant Obelisk continued to glow as Ogadile panned upwards, bombarding the massif of towering cliffs whilst trying to aim for the base of the colossus as she felt the heat from the laser bolts singe her hair. Yet she held her aim   steady at the base of the Obelisk as the illuminated inscription was pulverised into a maelstrom of cascading incendiaries that rained down onto the courtyard below.

'**Eieou...Nilleantiam...Infinitatum...!**' A crescendo of sound like the seven Devils of Hell issued from the mangled torso of the cult-master that was morphing into grotesque permutations of unspeakable beasts as he vented his demonic wrath towards the destroyer of his cosmic ambition. Feeling a satanic force hurled in desperation against her very soul Ogadile repeated inwardly the sacred beliefs of her tribe, deriving strength against this manifestation of Satan, and continued to bombard the towering monolith with orange light bolts, seeing the subverted testament of space and time smashed into a million smithereens as she strafed the ancient bastion of power. Only then did she release her grip on the trigger, as the sky turned vermilion and the cusp of the morning sun rose suddenly from above the eastern heights, capturing the turrets and towers of Aiyu in a feast of light!

✳✳✳

Luke awoke as if from a nightmare – yet stepped from the tormented dreams of the bewitched into another nightmare, one of reality! As his senses flailed, desperately trying to bring his mind back from a tortured sleep, his eyes flickered open and rejected what they saw.

From the top of the alter on which he lay, along with the corpse-like bodies of his father and compatriots, the scene which greeted his waking eyes was one of carnage. All around lay the bodies of the cult of the One Dimension; their orange or purple remnants stained a deep crimson with the blood, which floated like a sea upon the stony courtyard.

Interspersed between the corpses and in some places, over them, lay the remains of the former temple and its obelisk, its masonry fallen in fractured pieces; its columns smashed and contorted into jagged limestone fragments that littered the ground like a battlefield.

The cries of the wounded floated on the morning air as the bright light of sunrise raked across the gory space; not one square metre of the court was free of the bloody shambles as the youth gagged on the smell of putrefaction. Luke's blue eyes, all the more blue in their contrast to the red rims of his eyelids, beheld in utter disbelief the horror of this massacre; then he felt a hand grope upwards to touch his inner arm.

Looking down from the stone alter, he saw his mother, her eyes beseeching as she knelt in abject numbness at the base of the edifice.

'Forgive me my child' she choked, her voice a whisper; 'I was lead astray...I was lead into idolatry...I forsook you.' Bridget collapsed, her grip on her son's arm slackened as her nails clung in one last desperate attempt to reach out to him, drawing blood across his wrists as she slumped to the floor. Disengaging himself from the other corpse-like bodies, Luke levered himself up and slithered down over the cold stone capping, dropping onto the base of the alter and cradling his beloved mother in his arms.

'Never say that,' he spoke hoarsely into his Bridget's ear, 'never say forsook...it was not you...not you ...you were taken over by the Devil's own.

It was not your doing!' He held his mother in a vice- like grip as she lapsed in and out of consciousness, her tears falling in warm rivulets upon his cheeks.

'I came here Mother, to find you. To bring you back...and I have wonderful news... I have also found *Father!*'

'*What!*' Bridget's eyes opened and narrowed in disbelief as Luke turned to look backwards towards the slumped shapes atop the alter. Bridget gasped in amazement as she followed the direction of Luke's eyes and saw a shadowy figure silhouetted against the bright sunlight lever himself up on the capping stone of the alter, as Jock, an expression of utter incredulity in his eyes, heaved himself from the great slab of stone and staggered to join them, his arms enfolding them both in a strong embrace.

'*My love!*' his eyes searched Bridget's face. 'You are here... I cannot tell you... words fail me...'The sight of his wife, alive and rescued from the clutches of that infernal cult were too much for Jock as his gaze wandered from his beloved to the indescribable carnage which surrounded them.

The sun's rays struck the edge of the court, its cradle of light moving across the carnage, and the dismembered and bloodied corpses of the former Order of the One Dimension, as well as those still living were rendered into an eerie vapour. Their unclean souls were garnered in the sweeping scythe of the true light, as the inexorable march of sunlight seared the courtyard, sweeping clean the putrefaction of the Devil's deciples until not one remained. The triad who stood locked in an embrace, watched in awed silence as they witnessed this apocalyptic cleansing that left only themselves and the two prostrate figures of Smirtin and Errol untouched.

'*My God!*' Jock's voice was a whisper. 'This is not something for mortal eye to behold...and yet it happens. This is the work of the one true God!' His voice faltered and was quiet.

A black giant struggled upright on the alter top and looked in disbelief at the celestial wiping of the slate, his massive frame trembling in fear as he witnessed the last throes of the miracle which was enacted before them. He pulled up a dazed Errol, who looked also in bewilderment, his mouth opening as if to speak, yet no words issuing from the white pallor of his lips.

'Welcome to the land of the living!' Jock voiced everyone's thoughts as he extended his hand to the other two. It seems my friends, as if we have come out of a very sticky situation, victorious.'

From the edge of the courtyard a deep sobbing could be heard, and Smirtin's senses focussed on it.

'Ogadile' he whispered, his deep voice cracked, as he slid down from the alter and staggered towards the small shrine which housed the awesome weapon of a thousand deaths. He knelt over his sister and cradled her to his bosom as she sobbed against his chest, whilst Zalkina's wide, frightened eyes looked helplessly on.

'What have I done?' she whispered, 'what have I done to destroy an entire community...it was not my intention to slaughter...'

'Grieve not my sister.' Smirtin whispered into his distraught sibling's ear, as he held her shaking body in a tight embrace.

'This was no community, but the spawn of Satan who would have subjugated the entire world to their will if they had been granted the power of eternal life. Remember what our remit was. To assist in the overthrown of that cult of Demons! That we have done, and this strange land is well rid of such pestilence...'

'Where did you learn to talk like that?' Ogadile looked up at her towering brother, the light of admiration and astonishment burning in her tearful dark eyes, framed by the truss of frizzled black hair.

'From me!' the vision of Isis materialised beside them, her pleated white tunic fluttering in the breeze and her golden Ureus emblem catching the sparkling rays of the morning sun. 'Smirtin speaks eloquently, and though guided by my thoughts, he tells the truth... You Ogadile, by your bravery, have saved us all; saved Aiyu, our ancestral home from annexation by that wicked cult.'

'My Lady,' Ogadile rose, as the others walked towards her, her radiance a focus of purity upon the devastated space of splintered rock and masonry, though devoid now of ensanguined corpses.

'Come, my old friends from the Nethertime,' Isis embraced Smirtin and Ogadile. 'Be not sad, for your bravery has won the day. The ephemeral Goddess turned to Errol; his sober face was out of character. 'Are you not happy to see the strange one again, the Artist?' her gaze accommodated the others who drew close, 'and to meet his wife and son.'

'It is well met, my lady.' Errol took Isis's hand and kissed it. 'It is like the old times...'

'But what of the cult master, the Oracle?' Jock said prudently. 'Is he destroyed for all time...and your people's temple...can it be rebuilt?

'Your second question, I shall answer first' Isis's eyes were bright as she looked at the assembly of the victorious. 'I shall rebuild it even as you watch,'

The shimmering Goddess pointed her slim index finger towards the fragments of masonry littering the courtyard that now moved to her will, rendering the sandstone columns with their lotus capitals to be raised up. The porticoes and the roof blocks trembled on her majestic command until in front of their eyes the entire temple structure stood resplendent; glinting newly in the morning light as gasps of admiration hung on the thin crystalline air.

'But if you have that power' Luke broke the hushed silence as he looked at the mythical beauty who shimmered before him, clad in a silvery radiance, 'why could you not destroy the cult ?'

'I am the Mother Goddess' Isis answered simply, her vision of purity humbling all those who looked upon her, 'I cannot take life...only intercede in the events of the human soul.'

'But...' Luke's question hung unanswered on this magical morn.

'No more,' Isis forbade, 'you are the splinter from the block,' her eyes sparkled with humour which was lost on the youth as she looked at Jock, who put his arm around his son; now abashed, and somewhat crestfallen.

'Now for your first question' Isis resumed, looking at Jock. 'The power of the cult is not quashed; it is only removed. The laws of temporal time and space do not apply here. We must be vigilant at all times for they have infiltrated the matrix of our universe and learned the secrets of the ancients, our mentors, the star people. That is why they are the most dangerous threat to the order of stability ever to be seeded upon our fair planet!'

'And I fear' Isis's expression turned to one of great sadness, 'that we have a long way to go before they are rendered extinct.' Isis placed her hand on the transfixed Ogadile.

'But the bravery of this woman.... Ogadile, a Djinn of air and supernatural being... this great morning, will set them back and impede their progress...yet I fear we will see them again, and other battles will be fought!'

An awed and reverential quiet pervaded the restored temple complex of Aiyu as the compatriots listened as if mesmerised to Isis's dulcet voice; her beauty not lost on any one of them.

'One task remains' she spoke evenly, yet with resolve, 'we must restore the Obelisk of Time, for it is pivotal to our continued existence, as it maintains equilibrium between truth and falsehood!' She seemed to disintegrate, and then re-emerge at the base of the portico that housed the laser-weapon. She bid Ogadile to join her.

'Will you fire this weapon of our ancestral mentors, the star people one more time?' she bad Ogadile. 'Aim it like you did before but only at the place where the Obelisk stood,' Ogadile shuddered and moved tentatively to the star-people's fire-stick and with shaking hands redirected it at the site of the vaporised Obelisk high upon the towering cliffs. Her finger trembled on the trigger as she unleashed a succession of bolts. And as orange laser-light issued from the weapon, fragments of pulverised granite flew up from the base of the cliffs to reform into a patchwork of particles, until the whole gelled together and the Obelisk stood once more intact, its electrum- capped point catching the rays of the morning sun.

'Thank you my child' Isis helped Ogadile down from the small portico to the group of friends whose faces were a collective mask of disbelief. She described a sweeping arc with her right hand as her white gown of incandescent gossamer flew in the sunlight and the laser gun, that metallic monstrosity of the destruction, melted away and was swallowed up into the marbled floor of the shrine.

'There will be no more blood spilt on this holy shrine... and now my people can return' Isis's hand performed a benedictum and the courtyard of the restored temple was filled with the white-clad followers of the true light who went about their business as if they had never been absent, whilst Jock and the others were bathed in their own stupefaction.

CHAPTER TWELVE
*** ISAAK ***

Molly paced about her small flat; her mind was in a state of confusion. Stopping to look out of the window, her fingers tapping nervously on the sill, her mind went back to those long days ago when Luke and herself had talked late into the night. It seemed an age away now, and yet she still cherished the memory of their all too short union. In fact, hardly a day went by when she didn't dream of him or try to visualise what he was doing and where he was; in truth, she missed him deeply.

She had stopped waiting for the phone to ring. When the first few days went by, then weeks, Molly began to realise that wherever Luke had travelled to – to find his mum and dad - as he had told her was his mission, that it would not be some overnight trip - and she believed him now. Even though Molly had found it difficult to swallow his far-fetched story, she knew now that he was for real; or more, she felt it, intuitively.

A lot had happened in the weeks since Luke had gone back to Elgin Crescent in an attempt to travel back to that alternative world, Nethertime, or some such place that sounded like something out of a fantasy novel. That he had achieved the cross over to another dimension, she remained sceptical of, but not knowing for sure how he was or where, was causing her a great deal of heart break.

What if, for instance, he had been captured by one of the cult? What if Labachi or Rachid had either physically detained him, or worst, indoctrinated him into the cult - for he knew the incantation!' What if they had coerced him into revealing it? But Molly's worst nightmare was that Ishtar had somehow got to him! For in her irrational mind, which was the casualty of love, Molly imagined Luke in the seductive clutches of the beautiful Egyptian woman. Her most far-fetched scenario was of Luke chained up in some sort of dungeon in which the scantily dressed temptress did a dance of the seven veils before having her wicked way with him.

She laughed in the cold light of morning that her imagination could conjure up such stereotypical images of jealously, yet the after taste stayed with her all the following day. Added to that the fact that she had still to work with those two detestable men, whose manners were becoming even more unbearable, made Molly wish at times she had never met the handsome youth with his far fetched stories. But events had moved on since then, for she was now out of a job.

It was Saturday and as Molly looked out of the window of her small flat, her patience broke and she catapulted herself into action. She dressed and walked out towards the tube. She was not sure what she was doing, but as she took the underground train to Notting Hill Gate and re-enacted their walk down the market those many days ago, her mind was set on determining some sort of clue, some break- through which would lead her to Luke; at least to divine some knowledge of his whereabouts.

Portobello Road was alive with the smells, sounds and sights of the Saturday market as Molly picked her way through the jostling crowd, aware only that she was alone and lonely. Her mission was to reconnect with her one true love, Luke, and every recollection of those days so distant, jarred her memory to relive the all too short time she had spent with him. Poignant thoughts jostled at the outer reaches of her mind as she relived that sunny day they had walked arm in arm down this very street with never, it seemed, a care in the world. Then the grim reality of her predicament set in as she recalled the hostility of her boss, Doctor Labachi, and how he had quizzed her about what she knew as she carried out her menial duties in the department of the British Museum.

He had looked right through her, demanding to know what her relationship with a certain Master Luke Slater was, and when she refused to speak about him, she had found her papers of dismissal on the table the day after. No point in trying to fight bureaucracy – she was on a temporary assignment, which had been terminated out of hand - so now she was not only without a partner, but jobless because of it!

This injustice however gave new impetus to her dilemma and now Molly strode down Portobello Road with not just her desire to find her lover pressing at the back of her mind, but also another more powerful motive, revenge! For was she not after all, of good Irish stock - and she was not to be trampled upon!

As Molly passed the Duke of Wellington pub where Luke and herself had sat on the patio those long weeks ago, she couldn't resist the impulse to go in and relive a little bit of the past as her memories of those previous days of them together came flooding back.

'Sorry' she said as the throng of jostling people pressed against her and a man carrying a pint of Guinness had it reduced to a half as her shoulder caught his arm in the melee. The man, who was dressed in a baggy pair of chequered trousers and a green pullover, his long mousy hair flowing down over his shoulders and mingling indistinguishably with his curly beard, locked eyes upon her. 'Steady my girl,' he muttered in a highly accented tongue, 'you'll reduce me to a ruin yet...'

'I am sorry' Molly apologised, 'Please let me top up your drink...it's the least I could do'

'Chivalry,' the old man retorted, 'is not dead...'His cultured, though thick Irish accent was distinctive.

He winked at her and fought his way across the pub to a table, which was just being vacated as Molly pressed on to the bar. She ordered a glass of port for herself, and a half-pint of Guinness, pressing past the fresh influx of in-comers who stormed their way towards the bar; then she set the half-pint solidly on the table in front of the old man.

'Goodness, gracious me!' The old man exclaimed and with a side motion of his foot which seemed slightly too adept for a man of his years, slewed a chair around from the adjacent table just before a staggering youth sat down on it.

'Please be seated' the old man said, his eyes a cornucopia of gratitude, as Molly quickly sat dowm on the requisitioned chair.

'What der yer think yer doin!' the shaven headed youth came up to the table 'Ah was yest ganta sit down on that bleedin' chair!'

His unsteady gait and threatening posture as he lurched over them made Molly cringe and she was about to get up and relinquish the chair when the bearded old man intervened.

'Finders keepers, loser weepers.' he muttered laconically at the skinhead teetering uncertainly above them.

'Like 'ell mate!' The youth took hold of the back of Molly's chair and was about to wrench it from her when, the old man rose, and in a movement which was too quick for human sight, placed his thumb on the carotid artery of the lout, who recoiled in total shock to join his mates on the adjacent table.

'And I thought you were a gentleman.' the bearded man said in the general direction of the louts and then, resuming his seat he fastened his eyes on Molly.' 'Thank you for this', he said as he poured the half-pint into his near empty pint glass and took a sip, 'Allow me to introduce myself, my name is Isaak...'

But the youths at the adjacent table were not satisfied and rose up in number, all four of them as they hovered over Isaak and Molly.

'Chair', one of them said, 'give us back our bleedin' chair!' their threatening posture caused a pulse of fear to cavort down Molly's spine as they stood leering down at them.

'Gentlemen.' Isaak rose, and threw back his long, nondescript locks as he stared at them with disconsolate green eyes, 'we don't want any shenanigans here, now do we?'

'Stand aside old fella,' the tallest youth said, 'all we want is our chair back.' he made a move towards Molly's chair as the old man blocked his way.

'Haven't learned then, have we?' Isaak stood his ground and Molly's hand started to tremble as she held her glass of red wine. The last thing she needed now was trouble.

'Very well then my good men,' the old crone said as he lifted his own chair high above himself with one hand, 'here is your chair' he made a figure of eight movement with the chair, swiping the heads of his would-be attackers to render them into a sprawling mass on the floor of the saloon. Isaak quickly brought back his chair over the table and was seated and ensconced in polite conversation as the landlord and his minders elbowed their way to the commotion.

'Out!' the landlord shouted at the gang of youths who, daggers drawn, eyed the old man with a look of unfinished business as they were ushered from the pub and into the thronging street.

'Why oh why?' Isaak shook his head, 'why do some people think they can rule the roost, when actually they are not even in the pecking order?' Isaak sipped the glass of black liquor as he looked at Molly.

'Come my dear... I have something very important to show you...follow me and do not be afraid.' Isaak rose from the table and before Molly could protest, he took her arm he led her from the pub and down past the stalls of antique dealers and bric-a-brac, then off into a side road which was quieter. His gait was athletic and somewhat hurried for an old man and Molly saw that he carried a stick, a strange walking cane of carved wood inlaid with lapis-lazuli and other precious stones; curious, she had not noticed it before. Puzzled at why she had not questioned this strange man as to his intentions, Molly followed after Isaak, who leaped up the stairs to a small terraced house and pushed the door with his stick – it opened.

'Please...don't mind the shabbiness of my humble abode.' he gestured for her to enter and Molly walked into the dark hallway as the door closed behind her; still she followed unquestioning. The noise from the nearby market faded as she climbed up dingy stairs after Isaak, then into a room so small that she gasped in a fit of disgust at the chaotic jumble of old clothing, unwashed pots and pans and general cheap and shoddy items which filled the small space. An unmade bed with other heaps of junk piled onto it was secreted in the corner of the grubby room and Molly's tidy eye was in shock that such an intelligent and courteous man could live in this tiny slum.

Isaak drew open the faded curtains and a shaft of grey afternoon light illuminated the tiny room as dust motes flew everywhere.

'Fear not, young lady' Isaak said seeing the revulsion on Molly's face, this is only my temporal residence and there is nothing here that you can catch.' He made a poor attempt at a laugh, and then continued.

'I am only a humble physicist, retired, but I have learned the secrets of the Ancients...I have learned to travel...!'

'Astral travel you mean?' Molly eyed the old rogue cautiously.

'Aye that', Isaak rejoined, his eyes lighting up with a green fire, 'but also time travel!' He moved over to a corner of the nauseous room, and pulled an old blanket away from the only table as more dust motes flew. Isaak turned to the unearthed array of gadgetry and depressed a switch and a computer monitor flickering into life, its screen saver displaying a moving set of hexagrams, which oscillated in a hypnotic spiral.

'My remote laser pen' Isaak said proudly as he pointed to the screen with an elongated black instrument from which infra red light was emitted and the screen displayed a menu.

'Now where shall we go today?' the old man scrolled down the menu on which were a complex set of symbols, 'Your day out?' He looked at Molly and winked.

In spite of his squalid life style, Molly could not help but be intrigued as Isaak brought up images of familiar scenes, scenes which she had seen that day, and she stared in disbelief for she seemed to be reliving her morning walking down Portobello Road. As the images on the screen retold her recent experiences, she saw herself walk into the pub and bump into Isaak.

'How can you do that?' she asked incredulously.

'By accessing your memory' Isaak stated simply.

'But how?' Molly asked flatly.

Isaak drew aside another curtain, which was hung across an alcove in the wall. On various shelves was an array of devices that likes of which Molly had never seen in her life. Some were like antennae; others were what looked like crystal cones which glowed with a subdued irradiation of wonderful, yet indescribable colours.

'They are beautiful' Molly pronounced 'they should be in some sort of museum...no, they should be in the Tate Modern!'

'Thank you Isaak replied humbly, the makings of a bow forming in his athletic posture, 'but these are not modern ... In fact, these little beauties are older than our planet! They are are tektites, you know, of meteoric origin, but they have unique powers.'

'Go on' Molly urged, her interest piqued and a strange feeling forming in her breast that this old man knew something, and was about to reveal some information about Luke.

'I appropriated them' Isaak confessed, 'I led an expedition once, a long time ago, to install ultra-sound equipment in the great pyramid at Giza, you know, to measure cosmic rays to see if there were any undiscovered chambers in the pyramid of Cheops. Well we didn't find any... at least none that were disclosed... but I did find these little pearls in a secret chamber, so secret in fact that no-one apart from myself got to know about it...until that is, I published my findings.'

'You stole them!' Molly accused.

'Well, yes and no' Isaak demurred. 'I mean they were defunct... and it had to take a genius like me to determine their function, their purpose....'

'Which was?' Molly persisted.

'That is a disputed point,' Isaak scratched his tangled mane of mousy hair, 'I did try and explain them to the scientific community. But all of my papers were thrown out... and my reputation discredited by the various societies... though I *did* try and share my findings with all the archaeological departments in Universities worldwide. It's not that they just threw out my research, but they demanded I return the artefacts to Egypt... I couldn't of course, or wouldn't, so I was on the run for years. You are the first person I have allowed to see them.'

'Why me?' Molly ventured.

'Because I have been following your activities...in particular your relationship with a certain Dr Labachi, who is a very dangerous man!'

Isaak scrolled the image of the monitor at an incredible speed and brought up a scene of Molly walking into the British Museum and then a subsequent scene of her meeting with Luke.

'So that is all from my memory banks' Molly said astounded, 'but how can you store all these things....'

'This little beauty,' Isaak pointed to one of the cones which was flickering, 'is storing as we speak,' He pointed then at an antennae affair. 'And this little gismo is receiving...from your projected brain waves... your memory.'

The discredited physicist saw the look of perplexity on Molly's face as he continued.

'Your mind stores every single waking second doesn't it?' Isaak stated, 'and a lot of unconscious thoughts as well, even though it retrieves only a fragment of that vast reservoir at a time'. Molly nodded.

'So if the human mind has the capacity to store all that information, it follows that an advanced civilisation would have developed even greater facilities.... which is what these little gismos are... a vast repository of stored brainwaves!' Isaak was pointing to the other cones which were dullish green, obviously inactive. 'These are storage jars, full of heavens knows what'.

'You mean you don't know?' Molly asked bemused.

'No, and neither does anyone else. Because no one has had, or could ever have, the time in their own lifetime to look at everything in them, only brief glimpses'.

'So that is what you do?' Molly asked, turning back to the monitor which showed erratic quick moving images of her and Luke in the canteen of the British Museum. 'You record people's memories...Isn't that a little suspect, sad, I mean a touch of big brother?' she asked ingenuously enough.

'It would be if I were a despot. Certainly it would be if this equipment were to fall into the wrong hands. Just think what an espionage agent or rogue government could do with it; not to mention the military'.

'So what do *you* do with it?' Molly demanded.

'As I said' Isaak ran his fingers through his long wavy hair 'I do what any genius of conscience would do...I record, I store, I edit, and I use them, hopefully, for the betterment of mankind....'

'All on your own?' Molly was starting to trust this strange man.

'Yes' Isaak conceded. 'It is not a welcome task, working in solitary confinement, not knowing who one can trust.... and yet I believe there may be a purpose, some undisclosed reason for me finding this equipment of an advanced civilisation.' He coughed to clear his throat.

'I don't think that I am God...and yet I have been awarded the trappings of one. It is an onerous responsibility.'

The light coming from the grimy windows was beginning to fade as the old man stood looking at Molly. In his weather-beaten face, wrinkled and scoured by lines of concentration, Molly sensed a deep loneliness and she felt a strange maternal surge of feeling towards this walking contradiction, whose fitness belied his advanced years and who held in his powers the secrets of the ancients, or purported to.

'You were saying about Doctor Labachi, and Luke' Molly continued as the room faded into darkness, with only the monitor playing its images of her received memory, similar to scenes from an old movie, whilst the cone in the dark alcove fluoresced.

'I have accessed the cult' Isaak stated flatly, 'I have recorded their brainwaves though I would be loath to play them to you....'

'Please,' Molly insisted 'I am not of faint heart. I just want you to tell me what you know...so I can try to help Luke!'

'Very well.' Isaak said 'Allow me a minute to install a new cone, a very special cone... if you are quite certain.'

Isaak went to the alcove and bending down twirled the knob on a small safe, half hidden by junk. He opened the heavy door and very carefully took out another cone.

'If you're sure you have the stomach for it.' He enquired as he fiddled with some equipment and the monitor showed a blur of movement. The images became clearer as the speed of the scrolling decreased and Molly recoiled in horror as she witnessed the secret rites of the cult of the One Dimension, who were engaged in their ritual of perverted sexual acts as they cavorted in grotesque debauchery.

'It is obscene...what they are doing is beyond perversion!' Molly exclaimed as she turned away from the sickening sight of the naked orgies of beast-worship and worse. 'What...who are these people...'

'People...err, possibly. These images I recorded from the strong brain pulses of the cult at Elgin Avenue.' Isaak stated categorically. 'And yes I agree, these cultists are entranced and are enacting a very perverted ritual indeed, yet it is not of their making. They are the modern-day ancestors of a bizarre cult, which existed possibly millions of years ago. They have been indoctrinated by the telepathic power of an alien or extra terrestrial civilisation, who were expelled from their own tribe... driven out by their own people.

'The origination of these lewd practices, which seems to suggest some sort of purge had taken place, happened on a distant planet, perhaps millions of years ago. Some entity, some life force infiltrated the minds of our own civilisation, say at the dawn of human consciousness some millions of years ago, and it has held sway in the manifestation of various secret societies and cults up to own time!'

'I don't understand.' Molly collapsed onto the debris-strewn bed and covered her eyes against the scenes of debauchery that wracked her senses, 'stop it, she cried as she sobbed in tear-stricken dementia, '*stop it!*'

'I am sorry' Isaak killed the screen with the remote and looked disparagingly at Molly's shaking frame. 'But you did ask to see it.'

He waited until Molly had composed herself as he retrieved another cone from the safe and brought the monitor back to life.

'But I must show you' Isaak persisted. 'Where these cult rituals originate,' he scrolled down the time-line menu on the monitor until thousands, then millions of years rolled by in the twinkling of an eye.

'This cone is the prized one,' Izaak stated proudly, 'For it is without a doubt a record of a very old and very confused society, if you can call them that.' Isaak slowed down the scrolling images. 'This is where the grotesque goings on of your Elgin Crescent lot get their little ideas from....and I mean that quite literally'

On the monitor was a furry, out of focus image, which showed similar contortions of bodies in a multitude of nefarious acts of lust and carnality, but the perpetrators were not human! They were some sort of alien creatures which cavorted in carnal delights against a backdrop of a distant planet; a frightening, hostile place of jagged rocks and barren wastes, where the sky was jet black but seared by two luminous moons which revolved at impossible speed around the heavens. And above it all was a noise, a noise that penetrated the abject room with a sound; a sound so unworldly that it made the flesh creep.

'This is the origination of those unspeakable practices of the cult. This is the source of their indoctrination...from a non mortal, alien species from some distant galaxy where they had their being, and from where I believe they were expelled...thus to land on our fair planet and continue with their diabolical rituals. For, my good lady,' Isaak turned to look at the distraught woman, 'these images which you see now are very very old. They come from one of the cones I appropriated from a secret chamber in the pyramid of Cheops! And that begs the question that has rattled my brains ever since I found them...*who left them there...and why*?'

'*It is too much!*' Molly screamed at the old man. '*Turn it off, Now*!

Issak described a figure of eight movement with the remote and the screen of the console went blank. 'I am sorry' he said lamely.

Molly was convulsed in a fit of violent sobs as she lay on the dirty mattress, her head buried in the unwashed pillows of the old man's bed. Isaak knelt at the bedside and cradled the red tresses of the distraught woman as a tear ran down his time-ravished cheek, the fluorescing cone which now afforded the only light in the room etched his face in harrowing lines of remorse.

'Forgive me' he said gently, as he tried to comfort the sobbing young lady.' I only wished for you to see the true nature of what we are up against.'

'We?' Molly managed weakly as she pulled herself together with enormous effort, wiping her cheeks and rearranging her hair. 'So you see us as...accomplices...?

'Well.' Isaak looked thoughtful. 'Put it like this.' I have spent a lot of time gathering this information, and yet no one believes me... they think I'm a basket case. So when I came across you and realised your involvement or concern in Luke Slater's great mission to find his parents ...I think, well, why don't we share our information...work together to overthrow the cult...'

'So our meeting was no accident?' Molly asked, sniffing a little.

'No, I'm sorry' Isaak looked sheepish, 'I set you up. But I hope you believe everything I have shown you here today.'

'Yes...though what you have shown me is distressing in its perversity... I believe you.' Molly straightened, throwing back her red hair in the near-dark room. 'So what can *we* do now to help Luke and destroy the cult?' Molly questioned; stated so simply, it belied the complexity of the issue.

'I have some good news' Isaak spoke swiftly, a hint of excitement in his voice. 'I've been keeping it until the last...' He changed the cone and turned the screen back on.

'By wizardry and a great deal of luck, I have broken through to Ancient time, which is a parallel dimension to Nethertime.' The old man stated, it as though it happened every day. 'It's a bit tricky cos you have to make sure the dimensions are well separated... otherwise you could create an alterative universe, and what would yer do with that? I mean, we've enough problems with one, don't yer think?' Isaak cleared his throat, as Molly didn't laugh.

'Like I say, with this futuristic junk you see before you, I have got through to the city of Aiyu, the ancient Egyptian paradise that had been conquered by the Esoteric Oracle and his cult...yet there is good news. I have set up a listening network and eavesdropped on this secret dimension. It wasn't easy! This new transmission is a bit garbled.'

'But what is the good news?' Molly asked, her mind awhirl.

Isaak fine-tuned his array of hardware and blurred images flickered on the screen. 'Ah yes...the good news. You have been wondering about the whaereabouts of Luke, have you not? Well I have found him. He and his group appear to have fought a battle for Aiyu, and from what I can pick up, though there is a lot of stactic, they have defeated the Esoteric Oracle and his time-travelling cult of the One Dimension. One of Luke's group, a female Genie, found a weapon of the star people, a laser cannon of sorts, and used it to render the satanic master and his followers into oblivion.

Isaak slowed down the picture and Molly gasped as she saw a hail of orange fire strafe across an ancient temple courtyard, and then cut to pieces a giant Obelisk, which stood sentinel over a valley of woods and temples.

Then the image was one of Luke and an older man and woman – his parents?'

'*Luke*!' Molly exclaimed, her eyes brightening to see the image of her distant love flash across the screen. 'So Luke has been successful,' she asked breathlessly, 'he has found his father, rescued his mother, and destroyed the cult?'

'It would seem that way' Isaak turned to the young woman whose eyes were bright in recognition of her distant love as his image flashed briefly across the jumble of other jigsaw pictures on the screen.

'But one cannot be sure. We don't know what other little tricks they have up their sleeves, for the Esoteric Oracle has transcended death and destruction many times before by regenerating himself on this planet and perhaps others. We can never be certain that he is extint for he seeds his evil genus into other creature's minds...that is how he proliferates. Also, we have the other little problem of the Ladbroke Grove cult. They are nearing migration, and this new breed is armed with science. My listening stations have detected some very worrying trends. But here is is my idea?' Isaak paused the monitor and ran a hand through his tumbled locks.

'If the cult members here in Elgin Avenue, Rachid and Labachi and not forgetting the delectable Ishtar are beyond accountability - that is, the law can't touch them... then *we* send them somewhere they *can* be dealt with.

'Where?' Molly asked.

'Back.' Isaak replied, the hint of a gleam in his eyes.

'What, back to the galaxy which spawned them?' Molly asked

'Oh, If only,' Isaak sighed 'Not even *I* can do that!'

'So where then?' Molly looked puzzled.

'Back to their precious Oracle,' Isaak replied. 'Back to Ancient Time, were Luke and his compatriots can deal with them!

'But the Oracle is dead.' Molly argued.

'Technically yes...but they don't know that, not yet.' Isaak countered.

'How?' Molly's face was a wonder of perplexity.

By getting them to defect.' Isaak's green eyes roamed around the miniscule room as he developed the idea. 'Well not so much defect, but relocate... Yes, an urgent summons from their beloved Furer, the Esoteric Oracle, to the effect that Aiyu is secured, the Obelisk of Oblivion has been activated by the correct incantation... and that their place in Paradise is secure. All they have to do is astral travel!'

'Brilliant!' Molly exclaimed, getting carried away by the force of the old man's argument, though she hadn't a clue what he was going on about.

'I have edited a little screenplay for them' Isaak continued, his eyes wrinkled with humour, 'from some of the old footage you saw, and some of the new - but I've doctored the dialogue so it reads like an invitation to join their cult leader. Hopefully they will buy it, and transfer themselves en mass to Ancient Time where they will be dealt with accordingly.'

'But Isaak's tone was more sober now, 'there is one little problem! He reached into a drawer and carefully drew out an oblong box; opening it, he picked up one of the cones from cotton-wool padding.

'We need to get this into their meeting room at the Elgin Avenue. I've encrypted the message on this little beauty.' He said gingerly replacing the cone. 'I can't do it. They know me too well, and I am on their hit list...enemy number one. In fact I'm surprised they haven't raided this little slum yet...that would spell disaster.'

'So you want *me* to do it?' Molly guessed

'You could disguise yourself.' Isaak suggested. 'Different hair, makeup etc. Claim you were a new cleaner from the agency that they use. I will delay the real cleaning woman before she arrives.'

'When?' Molly asked.

'Monday, ten am.' Isaak replied 'I know that's when the cleaner goes in, I've watched the house enough...Keeping well out of sight of course.'

'I thought they needed the correct pronunciation of the Inscription of the Obelisk of Time' Molly said suddenly, 'that's what Luke was always going on about...you know, so they could all travel back and join their leader...the...'

'Esoteric Oracle' Isaak finished her sentence 'Don't worry, I've given it to them in the message, it's the original incantation I gleaned from one of the cones, it should be word perfect!'

'Alright' Molly agreed after a long pause, I'll do it'

'Good girl!' Isaak's voice was jubilant as he squeezed her shoulders. 'I'll see you here at nine am, Monday morning.'

Molly left the strange man in his miniscule room, not too sure of her feelings as she groped her way down the dark, dingy stairs. She vacillated between pity for the old physicist, left to live out the remainder of his lonely days in such abject squalor, joy in establishing that Luke was alive and well, and hope that her own unspoken dreams of a meaningful relationship with him could still be on the cards.

Sunday was spent doing menial tasks around her own flat, and then radically altering her appearance with a pair of scissors, a bottle of hair-dye and some pretty serious makeup. Her thoughts however were focussed on the coming event of the morn. As much as she abhorred the cult and what it stood for, and loathed Labachi and Rachid, did she really have the nerve to send them to their doom?

After a sleepless night, she rose early and worked on her disguise. A pair of rubbishy earrings and a red leather coat, which she hadn't worn for years, completed the picture as she took the tube to her assignation.

Isaac was at his door, handing her the box containing the encrypted cone and giving her precise instructions as Molly nodded and they walked down Portobello Road towards Elgin Avenue and to the house of her former boss.

Molly watched at the corner of Ladbrook Grove and Elgin Avenue where she had waited for Luke those long days ago, seeing Isaak who was standing outside the tube station engage a woman in conversation. As she watched, the woman, a shocked look on her face, turned and hurried down the steps back to the underground as Isaak signalled. Molly set off down Elgin Avenue, rehearsing the lines she had made up as she checked her watch: ten to ten.

At one o'clock, Molly walked into the Duke of Wellington, and sat down at the table opposite Isaak.

'How did it go' he whispered, pushing her drink towards her.

'I need this' she said, gulping down half the glass. 'I did it,' Molly whispered jubilantly. 'I did most of the housework and then slipped into the forbidden room on the first floor... the one with that strange carved chair. I hid the cone behind some books on the book shelf...I don't think they suspected, they didn't recognise me.'

'I'm hardly surprised' Isaak winced at Molly's changed appearance. 'How long will it take to grow back?' he asked frowning at her short blonde hair.

'Oh I might keep it' she joked. 'Quite suits my new image of covert operations don't you think.

Isaak looked serious and whispered. 'When the cult meet, I will activate the cone remotely from outside the house and pray it will do the business...send them all back to Ancient Time and hope Jock, Luke and his forces are still in the vicinity. Isaak rose and hugged Molly. 'Thank you,' he said, 'thank you...but I shouldn't show your face around here until you've changed your appearance again. Oh and I did prefer your original colour by the way. I'll contact you when I have further news. Be careful.'

He escorted Molly to the door and they walked their separate ways in opposite directions along the comparatively quiet Portobello Road.

Chapter Thirteen
*** Prophecy In Paradise ***

Jock, Bridget, and Luke were stretched out on the reconstructed terrace of the upper level of the great temple complex of Aiyu. Their ostrich-feathered pillows felt languorous and soft as they rested, holding each other's hands, and lapping up the warmth of the golden sun, which suffused their bodies with a convalescent heat.

The restored gardens of paradise assuaged their ears as the palm fronds and acacia trees dipped gently into the twinkling rills of the irrigation system and blue lotus gleamed from the shady pools, resurrected magically by the followers of Isis, the Goddess of Childhood, and the protector of nurture. It had been like the witnessing of the dawn of creation, as the pantheon of Ancient Egyptian Gods had returned to their own world, the mythical Land of the West. Jock had told Luke and Bridget many stories of his first journeys to this ancient abode of tranquillity; his first wanderings, before Luke was born and whilst he as a young man had learnt the secrets of Time Travel through the False Doors of Time, those long years ago

'Those were the days my beloved ones.' Jock sighed in nostalgia as they took in the fragrance of the Paradise gardens and listened to the murmur of the small waterfalls that tinkled over beds of granite boulders to feed the numerous pools which reflected the pristine sunlight.

'So it was an old lady, Sinitrew, who captured your mind' Bridget enquired, 'Not some lovely Egyptian temptress who captured your body.'

'Aye lass' Jock replied, his eyes closed as the light dappled his recuperating body. 'I never left you in my heart of hearts, yet it was a mission I was compelled to take. The Old Lady did seduce me, but only with her imagination and her stories... and what a storyteller she was. I thought she was crazy...I certainly didn't believe her nonsense about reincarnation and how she was really Ankh Essen Amen. But by golly she was, and I didn't half do some crackers of paintings on her say so!

'But I told you all this when I returned didn't I... I should have known then that you found my story implausible... that you didn't believe me. That was what caused you to drift away from me wasn't it?' Jock looked keenly at Bridget.'

'Will we meet her...Sitinetrew, the Old Lady?' Luke asked, 'is she here in the Paradise of the Ancient Egyptians.

'Perhaps, lad' Jock answered nonchalantly, 'perhaps. But only Isis can tell us that, for she is now in command, back in her own domain of restored Ancient Time.' He opened one eye and looked at the beauty of the place. The sun had just passed Zenith and crept steadily across the bright blue sky. The resurrected monolith of the Obelisk of Time towered over the valley, the gilt-edged tangle of profuse vegetation tumbling down from the distant crags amidst which were nestled temples and shrines of varying design. Cascading waterfalls made cadent and reassuring music whilst Kingfisher and aigret skimmed the water in their darting flight and giant dragonflies glided over the brimming pools encircled by high banks of papyrus reeds.

'She was the architect' Jock murmured. 'Sinitrew, or woman of the river was the designer of these gardens, for she was the first lady of the waters and the one who brought peace and beauty to the land of Ancient Egypt, the Land of the West...'

'There now,' Bridget squeezed Jock's hand, 'lets hear no more of it for a while. Let us lie and give thanks, particularly to you two, for my release from the clutches of that abomination, the cult of the One Order...'

'Yes my love' Jock replied, his eyes, half-closed, yet devouring the spectacular beauty of the landscape stretched out before them with the eye of avarice, the eye of the painter of the sublime.

On the lower level of the terraced courtyards, Smirtin, Ogadile and Errol lay on similar cushions, imbibing the rays of Ra, the restorer, whilst Zalkina rested against Starchild, cradling him like a newborn babe.

'You did well my brave little sister,' Smirtin said to Ogadile, his huge mass depressing the ostrich-down cushion flat against the flagging stones, his eyes closed, 'you did a brave and masterly thing...'

'I saved your skin, you knuckle head...' Ogadile spoke lazily, her leopard-skin pelt thrown aside, stretching out her lithe body in unladylike fashion to soak up the healing balm of the Ra, the Sun God.

'You saved all our skins' Errol added, his tanned chest exposed from the confines of his crumpled white shirt. 'In fact, if you had not found that lethal weapon, I would have had to hack them all to pieces on my own.'

'You Jack 'o Napes' Ogadile spat in fake rancour, 'you couldn't hack a decent line of rhetoric, never mind an entire army.'

'Thank you me lady,' Errol returned the gibe, 'I'll remember that remark when you're feeling the pinch of steel about your throat.'

'Shut it!' Smirtin cast his remark into the sunlight, 'lets get some down-time, some shut eye...' No more was heard for a while apart from some pretty serious snoring.

The scene of this primeval place, held magically in the dimension of Ancient Time seemed to radiate a sense of security and tranquillity and its original inhabitants moved about their pursuits, smiling, their white kilts scintillating in the strong sunlight as they gathered flowers and fruit and cultivated their beloved celestial garden.

Isis, her pleated white gown flowing, walked amongst the gleaming tiered pools redolent with jumping golden carp, touching the waist high papyrus with her outstretched hands. As she spoke to the gatherers and the cultivators in an Ancient, arcane tongue, greeting everyone by name, they bowed to her, importing their thanks for the return of their lives and domain whilst she blessed each one in a heavenly benediction.

She stepped up onto the terraces, passing the somnambulant bodies of the three cavaliers from Nethertime and the sleeping child-waif who cradled the resting mythical Zebra, Starchild. Her benediction was bestowed on the four figures though unbeknown to them as she approached the next terrace and walked towards the others.

'You have pressing business to discuss,' she said to Jock and Bridget and bid them to rise and follow her, leaving the exhausted and sleeping Luke on the cushion of ostrich-down. Isis guided them into the temple complex and up to a room over the high gate of the ancient building. The floor of the small chamber was bestrewn with reed mats and cushions whilst the walls were richly decorated with ancient, brightly coloured Egyptian paintings depicting the King and Queen and their son in various pursuits including several riding in a chariot. In the corner were scenes of two princesses who cavorted in jade pools of lustration, each holding giant blue lotus flowers; the similarity in their features might leave one to conclude that they were twins!

'But this is magnificent' Jock exclaimed. 'This is like a scene I copied for the University... a scene over the High Gate at Medina Habu...I need my sketchbook...'

'No!' Isis interjected, her tone somewhat vexed. 'You need to address the more urgent needs of your long lost wife, and to show her your gratitude for those years of waiting...not knowing if you were alive or dead!' Isis gestured towards the soft cushions below the scene of the princesses.

The Goddess lit incense sticks and closed the papyrus blinds so that the room was suffused with an amber golden light as the afternoon sun glimmered through the reedy fabric.

'I will leave you now,' Isis said, 'for there is an omen of the outcome of your repatriation which augurs well, and is written in the stars.'

She made a sign of benediction over the painting of the princesses and the two figures looked in awe at her. Then she left, leaving the aroma of Musk and Sandalwood as Jock turned to his wife, holding her gently and kissing the nape of her neck.

'Come my love' he said. 'We have unfinished business, delayed so long that I scarce can contain myself.' He laid Bridget down on the soft ostrich-feather pillows and they kissed a deep passionate kiss of a thousand years of separation.

Much later, the patterns on the papyrus blinds twinkled as the sun declined in its western orbit and the tall acacia and palm trees dappled their gilded branches in faint silhouettes and the light wind brought a fragrance of blue-lotus, the opiate of the Gods, into the small high - turreted bower of love.

'I am sorry my love' Bridget whispered into Jock's ear. 'Sorry that I forsook your memory and fell under the spell of Labachi. It was he and the memories he unleashed in my lonely heart, those memories of Cairo

155

when he first seduced me...it was his doing that mesmerised me for the second time and persuaded me to join the cult; I think he drugged me...'

'My dearest love' Jock put a finger to his wife's mouth, stopping the self-reproach, which bubbled up inside her. 'Twas not you, it was I, in my errant ways those long years ago when I was taken over by the heady notion of Egypt. It was I who missed the arrival of your flight at Cairo airport and it was I who remained a stranger to our bed. Chide yourself not, and let us banish these thoughts from our minds, because we have found each other again... though time and space have separated our two souls and we have both strayed from our first commitment, it matters not...for we have found each other once more! And we shall renew our first bond of marriage, and it shall be everlasting; it will not break again this time!'

Jock took his wife in his arms and they lay for a long time, watching the flickering patterns on the flapping blinds and listening to the evensong of the multitude of birds that warbled in the tall palms outside as they settled into their nests for the oncoming night.

'What did she mean?' Bridget asked, looking into her husband's eyes. 'What did Isis mean, "there is an omen that augers well for the future which is written in the stars..."'

'I think she means,' Jock replied softly, looking up to the fresco of the twin Princesses which were portrayed joyously on the walls above them, 'That there will be an outcome from our union, so long thwarted.'

'You mean...' Bridget's voice was a mystery if imagination, 'you mean a child?'

'Children my darling...twins, if I am interpreting her meaning correctly. Two Princesses which will thrill our later years when we return to our own time...' Jock's face darkened as a shadow moved across it.

'What my love' Bridget read the signal 'what are you thinking?'

Jock then told Bridget of the news Luke had given him, and that their beloved mansion, Park House in Kirkcudbright had been burned to the ground by drunken vandals. But then his face brightened as he recounted Luke's pursuance of the insurance and how it was invested under their names.

'There is hope my dear' he said, kissing her cheek, 'we will return and find us a new home, for ourselves, Luke, and our coming family.' They held each other in an eternity of embrace as Jock felt his wife's heart beat steadily once more against his naked breast.

Luke stirred from his reveries in which memories of Molly and the brief time they had shared together plagued his fitful rest. He looked around the terraces and saw his compatriots shaking themselves from their stupor as the light from the western sun dappled the courtyard with long strands of gold. Though he was no artist like his father, he could not help but wonder at the beauty of the scene as the tiered waterfalls tinkled in unison to the evensong of the twittering birds.

A white lotus seemed to twinkle in the pool below, then detach itself and float up towards him, growing in size until it stood hovering over him. He watched transfixed as the white lotus dematerialised to reveal a woman of ivory hue, incandescent in her flowing white gown as Isis floated in front him.

'Awake' she bad, 'Wake up your mortal remains, or those remains of you Djinns of the lesser order...if you want to eat that is!'

'Eat' Smirtin rose up suddenly like one from the grave. 'Did someone say eat?'

'Your feast awaits you' Isis pointed to the upper courtyard, where a series of tables were laid out with a sumptuous banquet of great demijohns of red wine, flasks of arak and a smorgasbord of fowl, fish, sweetmeats and sun-baked bread. 'Our custodians of Aiyu have not been idle and want now to show you their gratitude.

'Awake Sir Knight!' Smirtin kicked the still snoring Errol, 'your fix of alcohol and young maidens awaits you...'

'Maidens?' Errol sat up with a snort, 'did someone say young maidens,' he rose to his feet unsteadily, smoothing down his rumpled shirt and leather breaches as he felt his jowl. 'But I need a shave, he said dejectedly...'

'A shave you will have,' Ogadile interjected as she stood up, her leopard skin in need of some rearrangement, 'a close shave, with my boot if you don't stop preening and pooping.' She shook her frizzy black locks, pinning them back with the golden clasp and strode up to the top terrace.

The afterglow of the sunset incarnadined the gilt-edged banks of clouds hanging over the western horizon and the long shadows from the high-gate of the Temple of Aiyu melted into the golden gloom. The voices of the liberators of the Paradise gardens were raised in high jest as they toasted each other, ate and drank, swapping tales of bragardly daring-do whilst their hosts waited upon them hand and foot, bowing at every conceivable opportunity.

'To the mistress of the cannon!' Errol toasted Ogadile, who bowed in ceremonious camp before she tweaked the ends of the actor's moustache, and various cheers resounded from guests and hosts alike. Jock and Bridget had joined the party and Luke could not help but look at the flush of warmth suffusing his mother's cheeks, his heart rejoicing to see them reunited once more after so many years of separation and loneliness.

The Obelisk of Time captured the last rays of the declining sun high up on the ruddy limestone cliffs and beamed its reflected light down onto the U-shaped valley whose tumbling wooded slopes were fast turning into a blue-grey of shadow.

'To the restorer of the Obelisk...the restorer of Ancient Time.' Ogadile raised her cup in a toast to Isis who, flitting in a white luminous omnipresence, bowed, her benign smile embracing all on the terraces, except one.

Then Luke, his cup raised, became aware that there was one of their party absent from the celebrations. He turned and looked down into the gathering murk of the lower terraces and saw Zalkina, her arm around Starchild's nuzzle; she seemed to be fretting and looked dejected and alone, excluded as she felt herself to be, from the raucous goings-on. Luke stepped down to the lower level and approached her.

'Why do you not join us?' he asked in his stilted Zalk-talk.

'I am not one of you' Zalkina replied, her voice teetering on the edge of tears. 'I am not your kind. I miss my own kind...I miss my father...'

Luke put his arm around the woman-child and comforted her as she started to sob.

'I am sorry Zalkina' Luke said. 'I have neglected you. In meeting these old friends of my father, and in finding my family again, I have not considered you.'

'I want to go back' Zalkina cried. 'I want to return now to my own kind. I do not understand all that has happened, or what these people are...where they are from...I wish to go back to the Zalks.'

'Yes' Luke agreed as he squeezed Zalkina's shoulder. 'You are right...It is time for you to return...'

'But I not want to leave Starchild' Zalkina sobbed.

'No,' Luke reassured her, 'and you shall not. I will speak to Isis. You shall keep Starchild. Ride her back to your own people...it is only fair.'

'Wait here!' Luke ordered as he leaped back up to the higher terrace and engaged Isis in animated conversation. Then, leaping the terraced levels in a series of jumps, he came back to her side.

'Isis will talk to Neb-Ankh. She says you can keep Starchild. He is yours forever!' He saw the tears of joy well up in the waif's dark eyes as she held the mythical Zebra's head to her own.

'Go now' Luke said 'Do you know the way?

'He will guide me' Zalkina said; Starchild whinnied and nodded his head.

'We will watch you' Luke's voice was terse as he kissed the beautiful child-woman on the cheek. 'Farewell my lovely girl. I will see you soon again I know.'

Luke choked back a tear and slowly stepped up the terraces to join the disorderly throng on the top level as they sobered somewhat to watch the lithe body of the native girl muster her mount, jumping bare-back over its high flank, her white tunic floating around her, and then came the sound of a pounding of hooves upon the stone flagged terrace.

'Farewell' the well wishers shouted, watching the magical beast rise up into the air, then describing an arc with its whirring wings to cut a feathery swathe across the primrose-white full moon, newly risen behind the dark silhouette of the Obelisk of Time.

***

It was some little time later; the ghostly full moon had risen over the wooded crags of Aiyu, gilding the hanging valley in a yellow-white light and smiting the lone sentinel of the Obelisk of Time.

The party had subsided somewhat as the revellers had eaten and drunken their fill. Jock, Luke and Bridget were sitting on the upper level of the terrace, taking in the rapture of the ox-bow valley as the yellow moonlight lit up the carpet of trees and trailing creepers that hung from the limestone crags ; the pools cascaded in a cadence of silvery sparkling light whilst a light zephyr brought with it the scent of jasmine, myrtle and lotus.

'This is the most sublime, magical sight we will ever bear witness to in our short temporal lives' Jock whispered in subdued tones, awed by the beauty of the scene. He put his arms around Luke and Bridget as they breathed in the aesthetic experience of a lifetime. Let us cherish this vision, no matter where life takes us in the future.'

'Look' Bridget interjected, their own tranquil thoughts broken by her startled voice. 'Isn't that the young girl Zalkina? She is returning on the winged Zebra...'

Luke broke away from his parents and peered into the bright moonlight, picking out steed and rider arcing across the heavens to head straight towards them. Moments later Starchild landed, his hoofs clattering on the stone flagged terrace, as Zalkina jumped from his back and ran up to where they now stood; she was trembling with fear.

'*My people gone!*' she shouted hysterically, '*my people dead!*'

'What?' Luke put his arms around the shaking girl as her black eyes brimmed over with tears that cascaded down her gaunt face, 'What say you Zalkina' Luke spoke in her own language.

'Strange people come from the sky, white people like you. They kill Zalks, they take them away...'

'What people?' Luke asked as Jock and Bridget joined the distraught child. 'Where they take them?'

'Come from strange world...your world' Zalkina took a hold of herself. 'Kill the elders, take woman and child to...'

'To where?' Luke prompted as Zalkina broke down again, weeping,

'Take to swamp. Take to lost city...Where I take you...'

'To the city under the water ' Luke clarified 'To the city of the star people...*Ancient lost city!*'

'Yes' Zalkina collapsed into Luke's arms as Jock and Bridget looked to Luke for some explanation.

'It must be the cult.' Luke fumbled to find an explanation, glancing back at the incredulous faces of his parents. 'It must be those of the One Order...'

'But we wiped them out!' Jock replied heavily. 'Ogadile and the laser cannon took care of them...'

'No,' Luke interjected, 'don't you see...it is the cultists from our own dimension, our own time, Labachi and his lot. They must have some how got word of our purge here in Ancient Time. They have astral travelled here to infiltrate, to try to conquer this dimension again! At least that could be one explanation!'

'My god!' Jock oathed as his face became a mask of incomprehension.

'You talk,' Luke turned to Zalkina as he held her in his arms, 'you talk to some of your people...'

'Some escaped,' the young woman said, 'some tell me what happened, they hide in jungle, they watch while the white devils take our people under great river...to Lost City...'

'Wait,' Luke shook the swooning girl, 'was one of them a lady, a woman of great beauty...'

'Yes,' Zalkina whispered tremulously, 'a Goddess who led them, how you know this...'

'Ishtar!' Luke stated emphatically, turning back to face Jock. 'Ishtar, Labachi and Rachid, they have travelled, and they have brought with them the Chapter of the One Dimension...they have superior knowledge and they will resurrect the weapons of the star people. This dimension is doomed unless we can stop them!"'

'By all that is holy!' Jock exclaimed

'By all that is unholy!' Luke retorted, his jaw set hard as he grappled with an import of such magnitude. 'We have to intervene...wake up Ogadile, Smirtin, Errol ...and summon Isis! We need some council of war now, *like we have never needed it before!*'

'Aye lad' Jock looked at his own seed, seeing with welling pride that he had fathered not just a son, but a leader of men.

'I foresaw this.' Isis was standing on the upper level as the other's looked anxiously up to her.

'This transmigration of one more chapter of iniquity has been well prophesied. This new cult, which has travelled on the ether, sought to join their Grand Master, the so- called Esoteric Oracle. But their plans have gone awry because they were not counting on your brave efforts and thought that Aiyu had been conquered.

'But when I restored the great Obelisk of Time, it formed an impenetrable shield once more around the Eternal Kingdom of Ancient Time. So that on their arrival into this domain, this new cult slipped sideways, were deflected from their landing target... and in similar fashion to Luke's astral journey, they landed in the Zalk's territory.

'And so, I am afraid, through their powers of subversion, they have learned from the Zalks the location of the lost city, which must seem to them to be their second best choice for the diabolical relocation of their chapter.

'If, my friends, you are prepared to do battle once more with this enemy of humanity, I will help you.' Isis addressed them as she looked upon the gathering of the four men, two women and a native girl who clutched her fretting winged Zebra close.

'I will take you in the blinking of an eye back to Joruck. From there you can descend upon the territory of the Zalks and as you will come unannounced and unexpected from the heights of the plateau, though you will have to travel the cruel desert path, you will surprise their guard.' The assembled company nodded their answer in a tense silence.

The waning full moon was in decline as it descended towards the higher crags of the ox-bow valley of the domain of Aiyu, as the group of mortals and supernaturals stood ready, waiting anxiously for the Goddess's divine intervention.

'Once you are across the time-line, and are outside the influence of Ancient Time, I will not be able to help you' Isis stood, her white gown of gossamer silhouetted against the declining full moon as its light struck her golden Ureus hair band.

'You have all shown great courage and bravery here in Ancient Time,' She continued, 'but I cannot help you in the shedding of blood. 'Yet there is not one man, woman or child who will not rejoice once you have defeated this vile cult, and their thoughts and prayers will strengthen your resolve.'

Smirtin, his giant frame of ebony steel cradled Ogadile, her black locks flowing in the light breeze as they looked in awe at the goddess whilst Errol his aged, yet handsome features were set in an earnest resolve as he stood alone. Luke stood tall between his parents as he primed himself for the challenge of a lifetime.

'May the Gods of my domain, and your own God be with you.' Isis swept her delicate hand in a benediction, then she flew up slowly to the alter in the centre of the higher terrace, now enveloped in the shadow of the high gate of the Temple complex of Aiyu.

'Close your eyes' she whispered and the subjects of her commands did so. As she recited the arcane spell, her white clad form glowed in a silvery incandescence, silhouetted against the shadowy cliffs and her high priests, silent in this magical ritual, swung burners of incense.

'You will not remember your passage, for it will be a rite of passage, and yet we will meet again.'

Seven human figures and one mythical animal hovered on the brink of being, then their evanescent corporeal forms were swept away and the terrace of Aiyu was empty and void.

Chapter Fourteen
*** Mission From Mars ***

Joruck was in his chambers and thinking about going to bed when his astrological wall panel displayed some aberration. His domed pate contorted into a maze of wrinkles and he pulled violently at his goatee beard – he was not expecting, nor did he relish visitors!

'Project this forthcoming event!' he muttered angrily to his communications panel. 'Am I not master of time and space transport? I should know of a new arrival, or I should have been informed...too long in this out post, old man.' he soliloquised as he threw on his long robe of patch-work camel-skin over his crumpled tunic.

'Image!' he commanded as the maze of interdivisional lines projected onto the back of the small temple, and Joruck scratched his denuded head as he saw several green dots converging on his own outpost.

'Visitors?' he asked himself, at this time of night! I must establish identity...' He strapped on some very strange headgear that sported an array of antennae. 'Request Emperor' he shouted into the dark space of his small temple abode and the image of the Emperor of the Eon appeared as a three dimensional hologram in the centre of the room.

'Are you sending someone?' he spoke to the hologram.

'Not to my knowledge.' the disembodied face replied as the image faded, then reasserted itself.

'Vectors of time and space predict I will have visitors' Joruck stated, trying to hide his irritation, 'and I was about to rest...'

'Keep me informed.' The Emperor of the Eon retorted. 'This is not a good time for your communiqué...over and out' and with those ominous words ringing in his head, the hologram went dead. End of transmission, an abbreviated sign said and then the image was gone.

Joruck looked at the time/space vectors as they converged on his cluttered and untidy outpost and shaking his head, he went outside into the courtyard, seeing the phenomenon of a fast approaching time travel cluster, their green tails lighting up the star spangled night.

Before he had time to check his appearance, seven humanoid figures and one large beast materialised in the rock-hewn courtyard outside and Joruck, smoothing back his hairless head nervously, prepared to meet the intruders.

'Joruck!' It was Luke, who recovered from the futuristic means of transport first, stepping forward and greeting the dishevelled old man, 'We come on urgent business...did you get the message from Isis...have you heard from the Temple of Eon?'

'I have heard nothing!' Joruck replied angrily. 'Nobody keeps me informed. They all seem to think I know everything as, or before it

162

happens...well I don't and I am pretty upset by the shoddy treatment I have had of late in this cosmos-forsaken wilderness!'

Luke nodded his acknowledgment of the extra terrestrial's complaint and then brought the disgruntled old star-man up to speed with the recent course of events.

'I see,' Joruck said, massaging his furrowed brow, 'so you are going to evict this new chapter of the cult from the lost city, save the Zalks and get a medal of honour from Isis...very nice, very good.' His face looked dejected. 'So how can I help you? I mean nobody bothers to keep me informed...I am the last to know what is going on. But, oh yes, when somebody wants help, oh then, lets turn to Joruck...he will sort it out...well its not good enough!'

'My friend' Jock intervened, 'I know the feeling well. I for years have suffered the same torment...'

'You have?' Joruck eyes the grey bearded man up and down 'of course, yes, it is you. The mad artist who started all of this hullabaloo, you and your drawing of the Obelisk...'

'Yes my friend' Jock took the old man in tow and in a gentle patter of words, commiserated with his plight as the lonely old crone began to look more amenable and his sour expression lifted somewhat, as Jock winked at Luke.

'Well,' Joruck announced finally, 'that is different. Yes I will be your commander, if that is what you all have suggested. I will devise a strategy and help you implement it...action at last, after all these millennia!'

'Well done!' Jock turned to the others as they took up his cue and applauded the sad old man. After all, he only needed a little encouragement.

'Are you sure this is the right man for the job?' Luke whispered to his father as Joruck paced up and down the small forecourt in front of the pro-style temple and then turned on his heel and strode into his inner chamber.

'Humour him' Jock whispered back, 'he may be slightly senile, yet from what you told me, he has powers and info. that we lack. Let's give him a shot...' he winked at the others who stood uneasily and not too sure if they were still in one piece, disorientated after their recent astral transfer from the temple of Aiyu.

'Come,' Luke said to the others, 'let me show you the view.' He led the way up from the little courtyard onto the lip of the escarpment and pointed out into the vast distant valley where two minuscule cities could be descried.

'There is the Temple of Eon' Luke stated proudly, for he had been here before, and over yonder distant crags lies the city of Aiyu from whence we have travelled.

'It is beautiful' Bridget took Luke's arm and they gazed out into the star-lit desert landscape. The full moon had set, but the two strongholds of Ancient Time twinkled in bejewelled dots as their respective stacked pyramids and the cap of the obelisk of time, just visible behind the further mountain range, glittered in the white starlight.

'We travelled a long way, but so quickly' Bridget said.

'Do you feel alright' Jock took her arm and squeezed it.

'I feel a little queasy' she admitted, 'that was some trip'

'It was indeed my angel, and if you are not up to the next little episode, then it is best if you stay here with this doddering old alien, until we win the day.'

'I'll be fine' Bridget said stoically 'I don't want to leave you two now...'

'I have it!' Joruck burst out from his temple shrine, his corrugated pate glistening in the star strung night, 'where is everybody?'

The seven of them filed down again into the small courtyard and Starchild strutted nervously at the empowered genius.

'This is the plan' Joruck projected a holographic map in the middle of the courtyard as Starchild bucked and retreated. Joruck turned to the mythical steed, whilst Zalkina held his traces. The ancient star man whispered something into the beast's ear and the winged Zebra fell instantly quiet, whilst Zalkina looked at the strange man in awe

'Right!' Joruck reasserted his position, 'this is the current situation. My thermal imaging drones that are now in place show a hive of activity in and close-by the Lost City. The Lost City is so called because our people founded it, but unfortunately it sank...a tidal wave, deluge or some such thing; anyway we lost it...thousands or make that millions of years ago.' Joruck rubbed his outrageous, white eyebrows as if the thought of having to have to recall dates irritated him.

'So based on what you have told me from Isis's account, it would seem that her predictions are correct...not that I have many dealings with goddess's out here. So the London chapter of the Order of The One Dimension have transmigrated to this dimension with, it would seem, the intention of setting up a colony in the Lost City. I cannot be sure of their numbers, but the danger is if they have advanced technological skills that Luke has indicated in his description of your so-called 'modern' world, then they may be able to resurrect and harness our now defunct, but formerly awesome machines.

'The Zalks have taken to the woods, and though there were some slaughtered, and some captured, there are enough of them to harness into a fighting force.' Joruck's eyes were bright as he savoured his new position of commander.

'As your appointed commander, what I propose is that we infiltrate the territory around the Lost City. We contact and recruit as many of the tribesmen as we can, and form a resistance movement, closing quarters in unison...mopping up stragglers of the cult as we go, then focus on one attack point.'

Joruck spoke rapidly and animatedly as he jabbed at the holographic map with a light pen, encircling the area of the Lost City in red. His voice was animated and his manner rejuvenated; it was as if he had just won his first badge in the boy scouts.

'You say this new cult may be able to resurrect your people's space-age weapons?' Luke interjected as Joruck frowned at him. He did not welcome interruptions.

'The answer is yes they may be able to, if they have the right commands...'

'The recital of the inscription?' Luke guessed.

'Correct.' Joruck nodded. 'But,' he added, 'this incantation can be rendered obsolete.'

'How?' Luke asked

'Ah, yes, how...now let me see' Joruck brought down a menu onto the hologram scrolling through the fast-moving options.

'By rendering it in reverse' Bridget spoke as all looked at her

'Why, Madame, I believe you are right' Joruck eyes lit up, how did you know that?'

'Well,' Bridget said nonchalantly, 'it works in black magic, which I suppose your people invented as well...'

'Uhem.' Joruck coughed in sarcastic politeness. 'Please, my good lady, do not hold us responsible for the oppression of your race's middle ages ... but you are, I believe, correct. The point is, can any of you commit it to memory, never mind administer the correct utterance when required.'

'We can try' Bridget retorted defiantly. 'After all, it is we in our own world who have struggled to rid ourselves of this time-travelling cult's scourge.'

'I will translate it, and print it phonetically' Joruck beamed as he realised he had just had a brain wave. 'I will give you each a copy to memorise...is that not a brilliant idea?'

'Brilliant' the reply came back sarcastically from the few who were still following the conversation.

'Wouldn't it be easier to give us some kick-ass weapons of the future?' Smirtin interjected as Ogadile looked at him agog, astonished that her brother had been following the argument.'

'That is also a good idea' Joruck agreed as Smirtin beamed in the acknowledgement of his more than obvious request. 'I will see what I can dust down from my own personal arsenal...though I cannot vouch for their safely after so long in storage.'

'Now we are getting somewhere!' Luke slapped the grinning Smirtin on the shoulder, only to encounter rock-hard muscle.

'Any fancy cutlasses in your personal arsenal, Mr Joruck.' Errol chimed in from the back row 'something a little classy...'

The request went unacknowledged as Joruck dove back into the dark confines of his little bolthole and the others heard the sounds of clanking metal and what sounded like oaths issuing from the rock niche. Presently the wizened space-age veteran staggered out from the carved doorway, dragging a large heavy box of some unidentifiable metal.

'There should be something of interest in here' Joruck said dragging it to the centre of the small courtyard. He pointed his remote device at the lock and an infrared beam shot from it but nothing happened.

'Corroded contacts?' Joruck muttered, looking defiantly at the box, 'electronic circuitry discharge? How am I supposed to...'

'Allow me' Smirtin walked up to the box and delivered a mighty kick to it and the lid flew open 'old tricks are the best tricks,' he said to himself, his grin turning to a grimace of delight as his eyes lit up at the sight of star-people's weaponry. The black giant picked up a weird and dangerous looking weapon that resembled an old Gatlin gun, except for the sophisticated laser sights and other refinements beyond any terrestrial's ken. Heavy as it was, he waved it around casually and Joruck and the others froze,

'Careful!' Luke strode quickly to Smirtin's side and gingerly relieved him of the weapon, 'this looks pretty lethal, big fellow! Shall we get some handling lessons from Joruck?'

'Good idea.' Smirtin said as they turned to the old man

'Don't look at me' Joruck exclaimed, 'I don't know how to work any of this apparatus...I am an administrator of time...a professor of dimensional interactive cellular physics, if my translation is correct...not a ruddy heathen!'

'Yeah,' Smirtin grimaced, 'we get yer drift. Yer just invent em, design an' make em, but you ain't got the stomach to use em!'

'Alright, big guy' Luke stepped in. 'We'll take these dubious old artefacts anyway and learn to use them the hard way, in the field of battle...but God help you if they are useless...' he glowered at the cringing academic.

'God,' Joruck retorted soberly, 'has not helped any of my people left here to perish on this forlorn and doomed minor planet...I hope, however, you can persuade him to come over to your side...it would be a distinct advantage!'

'Don't worry.' Luke retorted. 'He *is* on our side, and our planet is *far from doomed!*'

'Come on.' Smirtin placed the dubious weapon back in the box and slammed the lid down with his enormous foot, then slung the box up onto his shoulder. 'Let's leave this self-pitying old prune to his miseries. 'Let's make a move on the Zalk village and the lost city before the sun gets up. This desert ridge will get pretty hot when it does.'

'Tell me about it, Luke added, 'I've done this little trip before.'

Smirtin stepped down onto the desert ridge and carrying the case of futuristic junk easily on his massive frame, strode into the sand, followed by the others.

'Stay in touch' Joruck called to the descending party, 'you will find a head-set I've included in the case for brain-wave contact...I will be here, listening for it should you need help or advice...Your commander will be here...'

'Oh Yeah,' Smirtin muttered under his breath, 'he will be there listening to our brain-waves, from some derelict piece of space junk that don't probably work...some Commander!'

The seven figures and one subdued animal walked down the star-lit dunes towards the forest far below, starlight glinting off a very weird looking piece of equipment.

As they gained the fastness of the dark woods, the endless sand dunes gave way to a firmer footing of bark, pinecones and bracken. Smirtin, still in the lead became aware of eyes watching from the eerie blackness as he wound his way through the maze of tall pines and stilted trees which formed a dense canopy overhead, hardly penetrated by the starry firmament above.

Soon the pines became interlaced with the dense foliage of acacia and sandalwood trees that were covered in trailing lianas and vines, whilst gigantic orchids bloomed from the rotting trees fallen across their path. The chatter of baboons encouraged their progress as they came finally to the swamp and Zalkina pointed to the submerged lotus pool with the overgrown pylon standing mutely at the far end, as if sentinel to its secret. The ground was boggy here and there as Smirtin struggled often, cursing the great weight of the box he carried.

As they reached the side of the lotus pool, Smirtin suddenly stopped and laid down the heavy box, flexing his huge shoulders to exercise them.

'Did you see any eyes?' he whispered to Luke, his own eyes looking around ominously, their whites large against the darkness of the forest; Smirtin didn't take too kindly to spirits. He opened the box and fingered one of the defunct weapons as the others looked questioningly.

'Wait!' Zalkina said stroking Starchild's spooked brow,' it is the Zalks, I can sense them, and Starchild can smell them.' Zalkina called out in her own language, a soft low call. There was a silence as the group of seven waited, and then an answer came, another low call, then another as several of the tribesmen emerged from the undergrowth and Smirtin laid the space-age weapon back down in the box.

'An animated and rapid exchange of conversation took place, too quick for Luke to grasp as Zalkina jabbered to her own tribesmen in her native tongue. Finally she raised her hand and the small band of natives fell quiet; she had some mean power over them - she was, after all, their chief's eldest daughter.

'These men escape!' Zalkina summarised their conversation, turning to Luke and hugging him. 'Me happy! Father alive! These men say my father and Medicine man have been taken hostage by bad ones... devil worshipers...like I tell you before.'

'Okay' Luke nodded, 'what else has happened?'

'The bad ones have taken Zalks to Lost City.' They say they will be sacrificed to their big God... S...Satan if anyone attacks!'

'Right' Luke thought for a moment. 'Is there another entrance to the Lost City?' Zalkina's face was thoughtful and then became overwrought with fear. 'Yes,' she said 'but it means going down through Fire Mountain...'

'What mean you?' Luke struggled to divine the native girl's meaning.

'Big-Mountain...breathes fire!'

'Volcano?' Luke translated incredulously as the other's heard his words and flinched in unison. 'You mean we can go down through fire-mountain and come to Lost City? Much danger?' he looked at the trembling girl

'Big danger...but I know a way.' Zalkina reassured, her eyes brightening somewhat, 'I will show you'

'Very well' Luke nodded, clasping Zalkina's hand. 'Will your people come with us?' Zalkina spoke rapidly and the Zalks started to shake and roll over on the ground in terror.

'No!' Zalkina stated somberly. 'They are too much frightened.'

'Right,' Luke decided, 'you show us way to fire-mountain. Tell your people here to stand guard at the entrance by Underground River. Tell them to kill any devil-men who come out...' 'We will go in...we seven.'

'My man,' Smirtin exclaimed, catching the drift of the discourse, 'I ain't carrying no friggin' box this weight down no volcano!'

'Okay my friend,' Luke handled the black giant like a knife through butter as Jock beheld his son in admiration. 'Chose your best weapon, gunnery sergeant...we will leave the rest of the munitions; such as they may be, with the Zalks.'

Smirtin rummaged through the box that he had carried so far, and vacillated between two pieces of lethal looking, yet probably ineffective firepower. 'This'll do' he said strapping on a very curious bit of equipment around his shoulders. 'But I surely wish that old wizard would check out his equipment once in a while...like every million years or so!'

'Zalks, stay guard here... look after big gun,' Luke ordered, pointing to the box, and the tribesmen jabbered amongst themselves before finally nodding reluctantly.

'Blind leading the blind' Smirtin grumbled as he headed the vanguard that veered off with Zalkina's directions towards the Fire-Mountain, whilst the tribesmen were left gibbering amongst themselves in gleeful tones as to who was in charge of the Star-people's arsenal.

'Talk about cutting out the slack' Jock whispered to Bridget, looking at his son as they walked through the tangle of undergrowth, trying to keep up with the black giant's massive strides. 'Who does he remind you of?'

'You,' Bridget managed, breathlessly...'he is the spitting image of you when you were a youth...'

'Can you manage this journey my love?' Jock turned to his hyperventilating wife as he suddenly became aware of the dangers that may lie ahead.

'I am fit,' Bridget stated categorically, 'and I am dammed if I am going to lose you again!' Jock put his arm around his wife as they tracked through the endless trails of dark woods.

'You will never loose me again.' Jock reassured her as he also began to feel the toll of their arduous trek.

Gradually the ground changed from the soft cone-strewn terrain of the forest and the path they followed started to incline as they marched unmercifully upwards, feeling the hardness of basalt cinders under foot, whilst the trees thinned noticeably. Soon the star spangled night emerged in front of them as the seven climbed more slowly up the tortuous ridge of a mountain whose summit could be seen as a the distant outline against the velvet sky.

'I need to rest!' Bridget exclaimed, her breath exhaling as white vapour on the cold air. 'I must rest.'

Luke called a halt as they rested and looked back from their high vantage point. The dark forest, from which they had emerged, was a vast jigsaw shape far below them.

'We have climbed far' Luke exclaimed, turning to Zalkina 'How far to the mountain of fire?'

'It is there!' Zalkina answered, pointing with her finger to the summit. A forbidding orange glow seemed to emerge from its apex as she whispered to her beloved Starchild not to be frightened, his snorting breath condensing on the cold air.

'Ow much bweedin' further' a voice rasped breathlessly from the panting figure who joined them. Errol was devoid of his R.A.D.A. accent and stripped of his persona as he caught up, breathless. 'This kinda physical high jinks was not in der bweedin' program!'

'Come on you old stage-hand,' Ogadile jibed, slapping him on his weary-worn shoulder. 'You used to eat this sort of stuff up for breakfast...or so you told us.'

'When 'ah was a young man in me prime.' Errol retorted

'Yer still in yer prime me lad, ain't yer?' Ogadile mimicked

'Alright for you...you ruddy supernatural. I'm just a bleedin' 'uman...they didn't give me any extra powers when they sent me down 'ere.'

'Grog time!' Smirtin shouted, seeing the old conflict between his sister and the ancient prisoner of Nethertime about to re-emerge.

'Grog?' Errol smartened up at the mention of the word. 'Did someone mention grog?'

'Ere yer ah me duck.' Smirtin reached into his leather jerkin and produced a sealed bottle of arak, no one thinking to question where the levianthan had appropriated it from. With a deftness of hand he threw it through the air and Errol caught it equally deftly - strange for someone in his perceived state of collapse. He uncorked it and took a long swig. 'Manna of 'eaven' he muttered. 'Manna of 'eaven.'

'Alright folks,' Jock spoke, 'the question is, are we all up to this? He took a swig of the white fermented liquor, and looked around him. 'Where is the entrance my dear?' he looked quizzically at Zalkina.

'We go down tunnel, go down underground' she replied, not quite sure of herself.

'We're not going down that tunnel!' Errol stated emphatically, pointing to a dark aperture in the basalt outcrop from which a mist of red-hot gas effulged, testament to the ever-nearer semi-dormant volcano atop the mountain.

'No' Zalkina said, 'Too hot down there, Tunnel further up.'

'I'm glad to 'ere it,' Errol retorted, blessing his lips on the bottle that had come his way again.

'Are we ready?' Luke rose from the lump of basalt on which he had been resting. 'Mother...do you feel up to pressing on?'

'Yes Luke, I'm rested now. Let us proceed.' Bridget smiled

'So show us the way' Luke continued, looking expectantly at Zalkina.

Smirtin shouldered the alien gadget of warfare once more as they proceeded up the narrow track, none of them aware of the strangeness and potential danger of the terrain into which they now walked. The cinder path led upwards between gigantic nodules of black basalt from which the remains of trees, scorched and distorted, overhung their tenuous track. The valley to the east of them seemed to be hung with a white, phosphorescent mist which became periodically tinged with orange as the so-called dormant volcano spewed its wrath not too far above them.

'This is the place' Zalkina stopped, quieting starchild who was in a state of deep fear. 'This is where Medicine man take Father and me to get powerful magic.' She walked off the track and down to a glistening lime-green pool, which bubbled in a turbulent display of froth and foam. 'But it has changed' she exclaimed excitedly, yet confused.

'This is where you used to go underground...to the Lost City?' Luke asked, looking in horror at the frothing pool of green liquid.

'Yes' Zalkina replied 'this was the stairway down to path below mountain...path to Lost City...'

'But it's filled up with burning acid' Luke conjectured

'It means the volcano is getting ready to blow!' Jock stated emphatically. 'It means we cannot access the underground tunnel, but it also means we should get the hell out of here!'

'Are you sure this was the entrance' Luke asked a puzzled Zalkina who nodded dubiously, as if unsure of herself.

Smirtin had put down the large cannon and was playing with the controls.

'Let's blast it with this little green mother' he whispered, his eyes bright, as having erected the tripod and directed the space weapon at the seething pool of bubbling green acid, his fingers roamed the control console as a red light started to flash

'*For heaven's sake No!*' Jock shouted, 'Smirtin...are you out of your mind...you will burn us all to death...stop him Luke!'

Even if Luke had been able to stop the black giant, which would have been very unlikely, it was to late, for a high-pitched sound was emitted from the cannon. A bolt of orange light shot out of the machine, though not down into the acid pool but up into the star-lit sky, singeing Ogadile's afro hairstyle. Smirtin had directed the awesome weapon back to front.

'*You imbecile!*' Ogadile shouted as she jumped sideways, holding her treasured mane and pointing a long fingernail at her brother who cowered in anticipation of his sister's wrath.

'Which one do you want, you gung-ho gorilla' Ogadile spat, 'the toad-newt hybrids or the groin-seeking tarantula...*or both?*'

'No' Smirtin croaked, his giant frame lurching from side to side as he covered his head in his arms, rocking on his bended knees like a baby, 'no please, not that curse, you know I can't stand those creepy crawlies...'

The company switched their attention from the desperate giant to his comparatively minuscule tormentor, astonished to see her wink at them, whilst Luke diplomatically took possession of the lethal weapon.

'Okay' Jock intervened 'Let's just cool it a bit...we are all lucky to still be here you know...if Smirtin hadn't mistakenly reversed that cannon, he would certainly have turned that pool of acid into an inferno...ugh... ' He shivered at the thought, but his rebuke was interrupted by a shout from Zalkina.

'Wait' Zalkina's voice was strident. 'This is not right place! I do mistake...entrance over here!' She pointed to the other side of the track where a dark hole could vaguely be discerned.

'Thank god for that!' Jock breathed a sigh of relief as he wiped a bead of sweat from his brow, then looking in despair at Smirtin, said: 'Our over-sized gunnery sergeant needs a few lessons in how to point his weapon...I will have to take this dangerous bit of space junk away from him until he understands which is the hot end.' He looked at Smirtin's disappointed face and suppressed a chuckle; it was indeed like the face of a child who had had his favourite toy confiscated.

'Come on big fella.' Jock slapped the disconsolate Genie on the back, and raised him up off his haunches where he had been squatting in a sulk. He looked up towards the flaring volcano with apprehension as they left the pool of acid and made towards the correct entrance.

Zalkina was also in a mood. She was having a hard time saying goodbye to starchild.

'I not want to leave him here' she started sobbing 'Fire-god too angry...'

'We can't take him down the tunnel, that's for sure' Luke stated the obvious

'She's shown us the correct entrance' Ogadile reasoned, putting her arm around the poor girl, 'can't she go back to her own people?' 'Wait for our return...'

'That's the best sense I've heard for a long time.' Bridget nodded and Luke agreed. They watched Zalkina leap up onto her beloved winged mount and circle around the angry red sky, then zoom off back towards the forest far, far below.

Having accessed the dark entrance to the subterranean shaft, they stopped suddenly; it was pitch black in the vent hole, and none of them had a torch.

'Wait a minute.' Luke bent over the cannon and depressed a switch that more by luck than judgement turned on the laser sighting device, to the relief of the others. Now they could see, and they walked in silence along the tunnel for a long while, Luke up front with the cannon, leading the party down a steep slope by the light of the green sighting laser. Jock held Bridget's arm, helping her over rocky outcrops of black basalt with which the floor was bestrewn. Ogadile walked on her own and Smirtin and Errol brought up the rear, Errol breaking the silence now and again to whisper some stupid joke to Smirtin, trying to bring the black giant out of his sulks.

'Fantastic!' They all heard Luke cry out involuntarily as they followed him from the dark black winding passage into a vast cavern of twinkling green crystal. Luke set the heaviest flashlight conceivable down in the centre, whilst the others just stood looking up in astonishment.

'It's like a crystal chandelier, only inside out,' Bridget exclaimed. 'It's spectacular.' Jock agreed, enchanted by the myriad gems of green crystal, themselves illuminated and magnified in brilliance by the green laser light.

'What is it?' Jock threw the question to the others, in his mind was a ploy to get Smirtin out of his mood.

'It's chrysolite!' Smirtin spoke, a note of pride in his voice. The giant had not done so well at Genie school, and was dyslexic to boot. Not only did he mispronounce spells – creating mayhem for himself and all around him – but his vocabulary was somewhat limited. Ogadile had often chided him about his lack of scholarship and it had been something of a hang up for him. But by persistence, he had mastered this difficult word and now, with Jock's baiting, he was feeling fine...he had said the word correctly. But it was to get better.

''Chrysolite?' Jock sounded puzzled, 'what the ruddy hell is that...?' all eyes turned to Smirtin.

'It is a naturally occurring green crystal which fluoresces, emitting its own light.' a hushed silence ensued and the others noted the changed mood of the monstrous man as he paraded his hard-learned knowledge.

'Well done...excellent description...' and other accolades were heaped upon the academically disadvantaged Genie, who revelled in it, a scimitar of a smile splitting his dark face in half.

'And to demonstarate this phenomenon...would you be so kind as to turn off the laser gun, Master Luke.' Smirtin was working the crowd.

'Ignominy is banished' Jock whispered, seeing the inverted icing cake of the cavern glisten in a green rapture of sparkling light. Ogadile clutched her brother around his massive shoulders, bending him into a stoop. 'I am so proud of you,' she whispered, tickling the big man's chin, so that he broke out in a fit of giggles, big baby that he was.

'What's the next move, big fella?' Errol looked up at his old buddy.

Smirtin picked up the heavy cannon cum flashlight and Luke drew a sigh of relief.

'Let us proceed,' Smirtin, proud to have been praised by his sister for his hard-won oratory skills, continued in like vein, 'let us smoke-out this vile cult, and rid us of this pestilence from our shores once and for all'

'Not bad,' Errol had to admit. He was going to ask Smirtin about any ambitions he may have for treading the boards, but thought that may be a little beyond the big man's grasp; better to leave it on a positive note.

Smirtin switched on the laser-sights, leeding the way out of the crystal grotto toward the continuing tunnel on the other side and the others followed, their spirits noticeably lightened. As they proceeded down the volcano corridor towards the Lost City, a thought was nagging at Luke's mind! Let us smoke out this vile cult, was what Smirtin had said...could that be a viable possibility? As they wound their way around the chock-stones and lumps of basalt set in their way, Luke hung onto one thought; Zalkina had made this trip before, as if she had, then so could they.

'Wow up!' The unmistakable deep voice of Smirtin came from the vanguard of the group 'Hang back people.' Luke pushed his way forward to stand next to the giant supernatural, balancing on a ledge of black basalt as Smirtin clutched him in his giant hand and Luke's ears were filled with the overwhelming sounds of rushing water.

'We have a little problem my straw-haired friend.' Smirtin whispered, holding onto Luke who had nearly stepped into oblivion.

As he looked down into the object of his near demise, Luke's blood froze and he stared in horror at the scene in front. From the black chasm above, a turbulent cascade of water descended into a deep chasm, its thundering roar battering his eardrums; it was like a cataract from hell.

How did Zalkina cross this?' Luke shouted, but his question was lost on the almighty din. Meanwhile Smirtin was busy with spikes and rope as he relieved his leather jerkin of most of his assault gear, slamming the steel pitons into the black rock with his bare hands. He soon had a cradle of ropes, which he slung across his broad shoulders and climbed up the glassy rock before he poised himself on an overhang and leapt into the torrent, catapulting himself across to the other side.

Luke gasped at the man's strength and agility as he clung to the far wall, and with one death-like strike, embedded a piton into the hard pumice of the precipitous rock face. Luke paid out the cats-cradle of line and soon a rope-bridge of sorts started to materialise, whilst the others stood on the small ledge, looking on in some trepidation.

But Smirtin's expertise in the realm of confronting the impossible was to be proven beyond compare and one by one, the group edged their way across the watery chasm to be gripped by the steadying arm of the Genie.

Onward and downward they went, following the miasmic green laser-light as the passage of black basalt gave way to less igneous rock, and the floor and ceilings were adorned with stalagmites and stalactites until they exited into a vast chasm, so immense that the furthest reaches were lost to view amidst a grey, greenish mist.

'This is it!' Luke exclaimed, 'This is the enormous cavern... and,' Luke shaded his eyes, looking into the veiled distance, 'there is the Lost City! We have approached it from the opposite side to the underwater entrance!'

The others joined him, peering into the distance as they saw, far, far out in the centre of the cavern, the incandescent silhouette of the Lost City which seemed to   float in the centre of this vast cavern, bathed in its own eerie light.

'The light is kinda weird.' Smirtin observed laconically, switching off the laser-sight and laying down the heavy weapon, then shading his eyes against the fluorescent grey-green haze that seemed to hang heavily over the vast underground cavern.

'Any sign of life... any defences?' Jock asked.

'Can't see anyone, nor even hear anything...Smirtin said' 'It's not gonna be them spirit-fellas again is it... please tell me it ain't!'

'I wonder,' Luke was thinking, 'if that monstrosity of a cannon has a telescopic sight... give us a heand with it Smirtin.' They lifted the heavy space-weapon up onto a flat outcrop of basalt nearby, and Luke looked through a complex array of tubes, adjusting levers here and there.

'Voila!' he exclaimed finally as he brought up an image, then gasped 'Wow...some magnification!' 'I can see the city clearly, but' Luke frowned 'what is that strange aura around it?'

'Let's have a shufty' Jock said. Then looking through the eyepiece he let out a long, low whistle. 'It looks like something out of a science-fiction novel,' he added sucking in his breath, 'like some sort of tubular shield, domed at the top'

'But what a size' Luke exclaimed, 'it wasn't here last time I was down here with Zalkina... mind you, that was on the other side of the cavern. Though if it *is* a shield, then by what is it powered? I mean I thought this Lost City had been deserted thousands of years ago when the star-people got fed up and left. And then it sank or something, the whole region was flooded and it sank...that's what Joruck said, wasn't it?'

'Ah!' Jock retorted, 'The lost city of Atlantis'

'Your next project, Dad?' Luke smiled, noting the element of sarcasm in Jock's voice.

The others took it in turn to look through the scope but all were as mystified as Luke and Jock.

'Well I suppose it proves that the cultists *are* in residence,' Luke advanced his observation, 'as I don't suppose the star-people have come back.'

'Unlikely.' Jock replied. 'And I fear it is as Joruck predicted. This new cult, my old friends as I once thought of them, Labachi, Rachid and company, seem to know a lot more than the last lot we just got through demolishing...Like how did they rig up that monstrous shield, and will it keep us out?'

'I am afraid it will.' It was Bridget who spoke. 'It *is* as Joruck warned...this new cult has in its membership, eminent physicists. Before I was projected to Aiyu, whilst I was in the clutches of the cult in Ladbrook Grove, I remember them talking about how they had unlocked the secrets of the ancients, the star-people. They had several scientists in the cult who were working towards perfecting the star- people's technology... they were intent on creating their own super race... they ...they.' Bridget's voice broke off as she regressed to the memory of those days spent imprisoned in that satanic house in Elgin Avenue.

'So they have started up the star-people's machines.' Jock put his arm around his distraught wife. 'And how, I wonder do they power that shield?'

'It is a shield of anti-matter...' Bridget whispered, 'and it is powered by a *nuclear reactor*!'

CHAPTER FIFTEEN
*** LOST CITY OF THE DAMNED ***

Labachi, Rachid and Ishtar watched the sliver of green light that issued momentarily from the cave, identifying their enemies, yet unworried by their dramatic reappearance. They had made their transition from the house in Elgin Avenue in the old world with the entire compliment of the cult via the mass incantation of the inscription. This they had believed to be a message from their founder, the Esoteric Oracle who had bid them migrate to Aiyu and start a new life. They had no inkling that this message had originated from one of Isaak's cones, and was a fake, so clearly had their Master's words been indoctrinated into their subconscious minds.

But convinced as they were that the message to migrate had come from the Esoteric Oracle, they could do nothing to avert the shield that Isis had thrown up around her re empowered city of Aiyu. So, on realising they were short of their landfall they had interrogated the Zalks who had revealed to them the secret of the lost city of the star-people, and taking them hostage, they had gained access to it through the underwater caves, though some of their number had perished.

Their scientists had got to work in resurrecting this ruined futuristic city and so successful had they been that the leaders of this chapter of the cult, Rachid, Labachi, and Ishtar had convened a plan to make this Lost City their own Aiyu; to evolve from the Order of the One Dimension, and creat a new order, their own chapter, in which they would reign supreme; for all time!

To this end they had instructed their scientists to fire up the nuclear reactor that had been located below ground, and to imbue themselves with the trappings of Gods in their facility to deliver big magic. These eggheads could be disposed of at a later time when they had got everything running smoothly, as could be the diminutive natives with even smaller brains - and whoever it was that was training a laser light on them from the perimeter of this immense cavern, then they had better watch out – for with the re-activated shield of the star people, they were untouchable!

'Gather, my children' Labachi moved into the centre of the vast arena, his golden gown flowing as he imbibed the scent of the blue lotus flower from the bouquets his neophytes carried, themselves attired in gowns of gilded gossamer.

'We are here, we have arrived at our final destination.' His white-streaked hair was longer and ranged over his shoulders as he worked himself up into his part as "Inscriber of the ways"; though he looked like a mad prophet.

'Come, my chosen ones,' he entreated with a grace and dignity belying his base motive, 'let us give thanks this day for our deliverance.'

'We have left our former selves, left the ones we cherish, who did not, could not see the sanctity of our ways...no matter. We have followed the interdict of our master, the Esoteric Oracle, who bid us make this last leap for mankind into the cherished domain of our ancestors... and yet we need him not!.' Labachi raised up his hands in some sort of votive offering.

'Let mine hands be full,' he intoned, 'let our ancestors from the stars show us a sign...'

The empty hands of the "inscriber of the ways" were suddenly laden with bouquets of lotus flowers, their incense pungent and promulgating the entire throng before him as he spoke in a cajoling, almost pleading tone.

'Thanks, our Lord of the Universe. Thanks Oh Oracle...for your disciples, though migrating to a higher plane, are with you now!'

The silence in the great open space before the toppled ruins of the lost city was palpable as Labachi stepped into the midst of his followers, scattering the fragrant blossoms amongst them.

'We have made the great journey, oh ye of the faith, we have mastered the science of dimensional travel, thanks to that most gracious message from the stars, from our ancient brethren. And though this was not our first choice of location, it shall be our last. For the Cosmic fates have decreed we walk a separate path...a path to rival even the Grand Master, the Esoteric Oracle. We are invincible here as we have resurrected and harnessed the greatest power of the universe, thanks to our physicist brothers...who have constructed a shield around us, which no one can breech...'

Labachi accorded acknowledgement with a deferential sweep of his hands to the awestruck followers, then extended it to include the barely visible shield.

'And you shall be rewarded!' his voice rose to a note which edged on hysteria as the occultists shouted their assent.

'Our path is clear now.' Labachi personally seemed to change, along with his voice as his heretical eyes, drunk with power swallowed up the gaze of his adulating following; this expression was mirrored in the expressions of Rachid and Ishtar, who stood either side of their leader.

'Our way is clear.' Labachi continued. 'We will construct Paradise on Earth here in this world within a world. It shall stand for all time as we keep the faith of our own cult, and it shall be a place of staggering beauty, rivalling and even surpassing that of Aiyu, the conquered city of our patriarch, the Esoteric Oracle!' A sudden cooing of wonder issued across the barren expanse of the sandy floor of the Lost City as acolyte and neophyte alike gave sway to their reverential awe.

(Labachi of course, was not aware of the fate of the Esoteric Oracle or the other cultists, nor of the battle that had ensued in the rescuing of Aiyu from them)

'My friends, are you ready?' Labachi raised his hands, his eyes glazed in the thrall of his power. 'Our scientist have prepared the blueprint...watch now as I render this ancient ruin into one that will be the eighth wonder of the world...only it is *we alone who will know it*'

The group of scientists left the main gathering and walked to a flight of steps which led down to the labyrinth of caves below, in which was secreted the nuclear fusion reactor. There was an expectant silence, which hung over the assembly as the walls of the towering elongated dome which housed their sad, encapsulated world scintillated briefly as the physicists below worked the controls. Then from the crumbled ruins of the Lost City came a rumbling sound as the eroded fragments quaked and trembled and then started to be superseded by other structures, faint, transparent outlines at first, which grew more substantial until the complex array of strange un-earthly buildings emerged solid and substantial, eclipsing the evanescent tumbling ruins.

All around the central space where Labachi, Rachid and Ishtar stood, surrounded by their devotees, strange structures materialised - organic and cellular, with never a geometric form anywhere to be seen. And encompassing these crystalline formations grew strange crystal-like trees and flowers, some as large as the buildings themselves as they scintillated in the grey-green light that fluoresced from high above this sanctuary of artificiality.

A raised dais was circumscribed by the cradle of rock which was still forming in pinnacles of crystal, its natural buttresses reaching up halfway to the top of the dome, glittering and sparkling in the unnatural light.

Ishtar, her white gown flowing about her lustrous form, stepped up the crystalline stairs to the silvery plinth as Labachi and Rachid followed.

'My people,' Ishtar addressed the re-grouped obscurants, her voice tremulous yet only a shade away from shrill. 'See what we have given you. From the ruins of black basalt, we have rendered a fairy-tale kingdom. A kingdom fit for a king!' she gestured to her father, as Labachi acknowledged this accolade in a solemn bow

'Crown him, crown him...' the shouts wafted up to the three figures on the plinth who breathed in the sweet scent of power. Ishtar raised her hands.

'In good time, my chosen ones, in good time.' She turned to a group of neophytes of the lower order who carried a variety of hampers and flagons up from the level below and laid the manufactured food and drink out on long crystal tables - perhaps the only geometric shape to be seen in this reconstructed, weird grotto of a city.

'Let us break bread and give thanks,' Ishtar trilled, 'let us eat and drink.' she raised her hands to the applause of the throng below as they headed for the laden tables.

'They are like sheep.' Ishatar whispered to Labachi as they stood watching their followers begin their revels.

'The promise of the pleasures of the flesh, my dear' Labachi smiled at his daughter.

178

'What of the intruders' Rachid's curt voice cut through the smugness of father and daughter. 'What of our little contingent with its puny weapons! Are we not invulnerable here, and yet we have to dispose of them...their presence is irksome...and yet what is their mission?'

'You are right Harun,' Labachi's voice was appeasement personified, 'we should be curious about our former friends...it's just that in the glory of our transition to this empire, in our hasty departure from the temporal world into this universal dimension of Paradise, we neglected to ask ourselves about our enemies.' Labachi put his arm around his more cautious comrade, and led him down the crystal steps.

'Let us join the festivities dear friend.' platitudes dripped like slime from the un-crowned King as he attempted to address Rachid's discontent of being marginalized on the podium; we will discuss this matter at length as we eat, drink and partake of the pleasures of the flesh.

They had eaten their fill, sitting at the head of the long crystal tables, and were imbibing the manufactured nectar of heaven, which their scientists below in the vast underground laboratory of the star people had prepared so meticulously that it tasted almost like the real thing. The dancers, in their brief transparent costumes of gold and silver swirled around the decadent disciples of the former One Order, their gyrations and the obscene figures of their erotic choreography bringing a sudden change to the onlookers, transfixed by the libidinous gestures of their imagined ancestors from another world.

'They have a weapon,' Rachid persisted with his previous argument, 'the group which we observed as they came into our domain are armed with a weapon of the star people... how did they come by it, and how do they know we are here?'

Let us consider for a moment what we know,' Labachi murmured, 'We ourselves sent Bridget to join the Esoteric Oracle...to offer him the inscription. That she is here now must mean she has escaped. Jock was here already in this dimension... and Luke, whom my own daughter taught to travel, must have honed his skills in that arcane art somewhat. He has, however found his parents... a touching end.'

'It is our worst nightmare,' Rachid interrupted, 'that they are reunited has got to be our worst nightmare!' Rachid looked at the growing tide of carnality as it disported itself against the backdrop of the reconstituted Lost City

'And what of their friends,' Rachid voiced his fears, 'that black giant and his cronies...who are they?'

'I don't know,' Labachi answered, 'but I will tell you this... it doesn't matter... because we are invulnerable, behind this shield of manner, no man nor beast can get to us!'

'Luke!' It was Ishtar who spoke, 'Did you say Luke is amongst them?'

'Yes my dear,' Labachi answered his daughter, 'it would seem as if that little cuckoo has flown the nest once more, but how?'

'I taught him, remember?' Ishtar replied harshly, 'it was I who taught him...we should have disposed of him totally when we threw him out of the house...' A look of disbelief crossed Ishtar's face. 'I wonder...could he have broken in again...used the throne of the Oracle...resurrected the incantation...'

'It matters not,' Rachid retorted, 'How they got here is a matter for conjecture only...how we dispose of them is a more urgent practicality!'

'They cannot access our New Kingdom,' Labachi repeated his unshakable conviction, 'for the shield is impenetrable, is it not?'

'Of course.' Rachid replied with less conviction. 'Let us observe them though, for I do not trust them and I want to know how the woman escaped from the powers of the Oracle!'

'You are right my friend,' Labachi acknowledged, 'let us send in the drones!'

Ishtar watched the semi-naked dancers whirl around below them, smiling down on the indoctrinated followers of this new cult of the One Dimension, her eyes smouldering to see them despoiled in a carnal lust. Turning to the others, her eyes now alight with a new kind of evil, she intoned: 'Yes.... send in the drones...they will access their minds and impale them upon the horrors of their unconscious... for they will be the *devourers of their souls!*'

***

'They are rebuilding the Lost City!' Luke exclaimed, taking his tired eyes from the telescope of the laser-cannon, 'they are restoring the ancient Lost City...'

'Let me see!' Jock insisted, placing his face close up to the eyepiece. 'Well I never. You're right my old son, now how can they be doing that?'

'They have resurrected the old powers of the banished ones.' Luke replied 'By restoring the reactor, they have been able to unlock the long-buried secrets of the ancients...It is as mother feared, this new chapter of evil comes armed with superior know how.'

'All this talk!' Smirtin bellowed, his nerves near to snapping, 'why don't we just blast them with the fire stick, before they become to powerful.'

'This time' Jock reached as far as he could to place a hand on the black giant's massive shoulder, 'this time old pal, I think you are right...*let's do it!*'

'About bloody time' Errol chimed in from the rear of the group, but I think the ladies should take cover...back in the tunnel.'

'How courteous.' Ogadile pulled a face at Errol, taking Bridget by the arm and they walked back into the tunnel whence they had entered this God-forsaken arena; this loathsome cavern with its unnatural light and morbid sense of foreboding.

The four men lifted the laser weapon onto a high outcrop of basalt, and piled blocks of stone around it to cushion the recoil. Luke put it into what he guessed was manual mode, reluctant to deploy the laser-sighting device until all were happy with the rough alignment.

'We don't have to worry about elevation or azimuth calculations as there will be no drop,' Jock said with a certainty not backed up with any particular knowledge; just a hunch, 'because it is a weapon of pure light, therefore it will fire straight.' He qualified.

The others nodded in baffled agreement, for they had no other theory to offer, nor did they understand the original.

'Are we ready?' Jock asked as they fell silent. 'Very well old friend, he said tapping Smirtin on the back, 'it's your shooting party.'

A gleam of white teeth accorded acquiescence as the great hulk of a man crouched down behind the cannon, his eyes bright and focussed as he stroked the controls, and then depressed the trigger mechanism. A single bolt of green light blasted from the gun and instantly found its target at the base of the towering dome as an incandescent fury of light erupted from the distant globe and the deep boom of energy hitting energy, reverberated around the eerie cavern in a deafening roar.

The four men watched as a giant cloud of dust and debris rose up from the basalt strewn sand at the base of the shield and then the sound of the impact came back to them, piercing their ears with the rumble of blasted rock. Luke looked through the telescopic sight.

'Not a dent' he muttered dejectedly, his voice withered with disbelief. 'Give them the full Monty!' he shouted and Smirtin released a round of laser-light at the city-shield, the others plugging their ears against the brutal noise.

'Still nothing' Luke could not hide his dismay. 'Whatever they have constructed there is beyond belief!'

'Look' Jock said as he peered into the storm clouds of swirling dust and rock debris, 'there is something coming...'

They saw a dozen or so of strange glider-like contraptions that zigzagged towards them, bucking up and down on the turbulent air of the recent bombardment.

'Bring 'em down!' Jock shouted in Smirtin's ear as the giant picked up the cannon, handholding it in an impossible display of strength and enfiladed the flying drones with a fury of green laser beams.

Two or more he hit, and they were sent to oblivion, but the others seemed to evade the raking stream of cannon-fire, still gliding towards them. As Smirtin walked towards the drones, spraying the air of the cavern with sporadic bursts of fire, his aim became more erratic and the tracers went all over the place, exploding in a dull, yet audible sound on the distant ceiling of the cavern, hardly discernible to human eye. Great chunks of basalt rained down onto the sandy floor of the cavern until the whole of their section of the gigantic underground vault was filled with a choking dust.

'*Stop it!*' Jock yelled, as Smirtin walked towards the evasive drones. 'Cease fire you great bullock, or you will destroy us all!' The ebony hulk eased his talon-like finger from the trigger and laid the weapon down on the floor, his face a mask of dust clinging to his sweating skin; his expression of failure was beyond consolation.

Smirtin dropped to his knees as a drone hovered above his head and released its cargo; a plethora of phantoms who writhed in front of him, tapping into his worst nightmares as they shape-shifted and convulsed in a hallucination of abhorrent and grotesque half-human, half-animal horrors, many in arachnid form.

'They are trying to psyche us out!' Jock shouted, 'beware and be brave...they are playing on our subconscious minds, but it all a trick...'

His words fell on empty ears as the metamorphisms descended from the group of drones which now hung close above them, unleashing their mutatiing spectres onto the ground in front of their victims.

Primordial anthropomorphic demons berated the four men as Smirtin drew his great scimitar and slashed through the nearest one. Its lizard-like, fluted- winged body was severed by a lethal sweep of the silvered steel, yet it mutated into a pig-headed armadillo, only to attack again, its wild-boar tusks and curved fangs protruding from the green bile -lined cave of its gaping jaws. Then it shape-shifted into something far more terrifying: a towering pregnant spider, its obscene belly pulsating in a million contortions, its open maw slavering green vomit, only to give birth before the stricken giant and spew out its cargo of the devil onto his massive form. As the thousand-legged spawn of Satan ran amok over the defenceless body of the Genie, Smirtin cowered, rolling over in the sand, his arms and legs thrashing at this, his worst nightmare, blubbering and then wailing like a baby!

Witnessing the devastating effect of these monsters from the unconscious on the colossus, and on hearing Smirtin's regression to terrified babyhood, Luke shuddered, realising that his own personal demons were upon him.

As the sounds and sights of his immediate surroundings faded, he was aware only of the divine form of Ishtar who walked slowly towards him, her pleated white cape and kilt swishing, her slim waist and curving hips visible through the transparent fabric.

'Luke,' Ishtar held out her hands, 'why do you seek to destroy us?' she murmured, her musky perfume of sandalwood and oil of lotus inflaming his nostrils. 'Why do you destroy yourself?' her voice, sultry and persuasive seduced his ears.

'For you know,' Ishtar continued in her sultry voice, pressing her excited bosom against his chest, 'that you are one of us...you know that you want me...and I am yours, if you come now and join us...come...come now.'

Luke felt his feet float up from the ground, Ishtar gripping him in a passionate embrace; his immediate environs seemed to dissipate in the illusion the temptress created, drawing him from the ground up to the cavern's roof. His friends and family were mere specks now, although they still seemed to be entreating him to return. But the odd thing was that he didn't want to; his loins were on fire at the proximity of Ishtar's flesh and her passion dragged them upwards, forever upwards. He could see the others below and the crystal city as they flew towards the roof of the cavern and then in a supernatural passage, cleaved right through it into the bright blue sky of the heavens; now, unable to restist her satanic spell, he embraced her and kissed her sensuous mouth whilst she locked him in a demon grip and their bodies flew up to the ether.

Luke felt the heat of her loin burning into his groin as she caressed his flowing blond hair and he felt her heart pounding against his own, seeing the continents fly by far below, whilst high above them they consummated their passion in a climax of celestial ecstasy.

Aware of the first fruit of his perverted longing coursing out of his body, Luke felt the maniacal grip of his demon lover loosen, all too belatedly conscious of a feeling of deja vue. Shocked into hyper-reality, an aborted scream of terror froze on Luke's blue lips on seeing his astral lover re-inhabit her real state, her face aged beyond the norm, her mouth like the cavern of a toothless hag, laughing in his face; then she released him from her witch's grasp to wing her way back to her cult, and Luke plummeted downwards towards the barren desert below.

'Neb-Ankh...Sar-Eff...'

Luke uttered the incantation for astral-travelling, which was still embedded in his mind and he watched in desperation to see the rock-strewn desert wastes rise up to meet him. He had thought that these aerial drones, these apparitions were just that, and that soon he would be back in the cavern with the others, but this little horror of an hallucination was for *real!* '...**Jded-Rhechit**' He completed the inscription and felt a slowing of his descent, trying to direct his falling body towards a giant slope of sand. Luke's speed reduced a little more though he realised he was going to crash, and angled his flight into a curve as he collided into the massive sand dune and ploughed into it. The whole slope avalanched down and he was carried in a breathless tumbling heap along the tube of sand, feeling with total relief his descent cushioned by the sliding impact, until he finally came to rest.

Still thinking that this nightmare would evaporate and he would once more be with his family and friends, albeit themselves in a difficult quandary, his hopes were dashed when he felt the weight of sand, real and palpable about him, as he pushed himself up to the surface of the dune. A gasp of astonishment issued from Luke's bruised lips when he realised that he was at the same place of his trial flight with Ishtar those long months ago; there was something more than déjà vu here; more so, there was some grave deception of miasmic proportions: *the deception of the Devil!*

✳✳✳

Jock, Smirtin and Errol watched in bewilderment as they saw Ishtar locked in a demonic embrace with Luke rising up from the floor of the cavern into the grey-green fluorescent vapours above. Even their own phantoms seemed to pause and watch for a moment, and then they were all over the three men again, and they backed into the cave where Ogadile and Bridget were secreted, the latter screaming '*Luke, where is Luke!*' for she saw only three men being pushed back towards them.

'He has been taken off by Ishtar' Jock shouted back, fighting off an avenging angel who was dressed in shimmering white, but with black wings and from whose elfin face shone strange green eyes which were too wide- spaced to be human. Errols' scimitar cut through a group of nubile maidens whose libidinous, gyrating bodies belied their true nature, for each one had the head of a toad and as they attempted to lick his face with their bulbous slimy yellow tongues, their eyes popping out of their rime-rimmed sockets; his efforts at slaughter were to no avail as the blade hissed through thin air. Suddenly Errol dived for the shelter of the cave and was joined by Jock and Smirtin, the demons of their own sub-conscious minds snarling and slavering at the entrance.

'Luke...' Bridget shuddered, 'Luke where have you gone now...'

'Try not to think the worst' Jock reassured her, 'remember that he is able too astral travel.' 'He will beat her, his personal demon. He will conquer his own fear and return...we shall see him again...*I promise!*' Jock comforted the near-hysterical Bridget as they peered out from the cave, seeing the drones fly aimlessly around, releasing more and more monsters of the grotesque.

'I've had enough of this!' Smirtin shouted, sheathing his scimitar. 'I'm going out there to get that cannon!' The black giant bent down and crawled through the cave exit, and ducking and dodging the talons and slime-infested maws of the phantoms, he retrieved the weapon, and was about to fire it again from the mouth of the cave when Jock stayed him, shouting to him: 'Bring it in here, bring it here!' An idea was forming in his mind. Smirtin hesitated, his mind a whirlpool of conflicting emotions; finally he shuddered and dragged the cannon back into the small cave.

'We want to destroy the cult, don't we?' Jock threw the question to the group.

'Yes' the others acknowledged 'that is our mandate. That is what Isis sent us to do.'

'Right' Jock continued 'We cannot penetrate their shield ... but what if we could *seal them up for all time!*'

'Huh?' Smirtin's bemused expression elicited a wry grin from the grizzled artist as Bridget looked at her husband; she had seen this expression on his face before; he meant business.

'Come on,' Jock was out of explanations, 'grab this device. We want to carry it back to the stream we crossed back there...'

184

'*What about Luke!*' Bridget's voice was shrill 'we can't leave him down here!'

'My love,' Jock took his wife by the shoulders, 'you don't seem to grasp it...he isn't *down here*! He has travelled again...with Ishtar. But he has the knowledge to do a reciprocal, a reverse course...he will find us again, *believe me!*'

Bridget, not too reassured, followed the others with just one last backward glance to the cave entrance still alive with the preternatural flickering of the spectres of the unconscious. After a while, climbing back up the sloping cave, they heard the sound of rushing water. Soon they were standing on the lip of the chasm, the laser-sight on the weapon illuminating the sparkle of tumbling water and casting an eerie green flickering onto the cauldron that boiled in tumultuous spate, its watery flume raging down into the blackness below; a shiver went down Bridget's spine.

'Set up the cannon' Jock commanded, pointing to the tunnel on the far side of the cascade 'align it with the mouth of the tunnel!'

'What!' Ogadile exclaimed in dismay 'It's our only way back...surely you're not gonna blast it...'

'This is not an arbitrary choice... it's not our *only* way back' Jock retorted, looking into Ogadile's dark eyes, the green light reflecting from them reminding him of a doe in front of the hunter's gun and he saw her start to tremble, peering in doleful apprehension down into the black abyss below.

'No' she whispered 'No, man, you can't mean down there not into that...it would be certain destruction!'

'Be brave!' Jock put one arm around the terrifiedGenie and the other around his wife, 'It's our only way...don't you see...to rid us and humanity of this vile cult...by blasting the tunnel!'

'How, why?' Errol chimed in 'It's going in the wrong direction from the Lost City...how will that destroy them?' 'It will not in itself' Jock replied 'but the laser beam will deflect off the walls of the tunnel until it travels past where we entered it, and up to the volcano, through these old lava flow tunnels...it will trigger the eruption, don't you see?'

The others looked at Jock, then at each other as the comprehension of his strategy registered, slowly, then as the idea dawned on them, it was replaced with a look of total disbelief and terror.

'My god' Bridget spoke at last 'you would sacrifice us all for some crazy scheme which, may or may not work. And what if the eruption overtakes us...'

'It won't!' Jock stated emphatically. 'Look at the pace of water. This cascade will sweep us quickly down to the base of the mountain, where it must rise into an aquifer, a spring perhaps. We can make it!' Don't you see, it's our only chance to seal up the cavern below, and with it the city of the new cult of the One Dimension!'

'You had better be right, my friend,' Errol's voice was weighty, 'or you will have a pretty price to pay...'

'I'll take that risk' Jock retorted, 'now let's set up the cannon!'

The three men placed the laser-weapon on the floor of the cavern, near to the gushing cascade and trimmed it with basalt rocks, pinning it heavily whilst leaving just the controls showing. Jock trued the sighting manually and searched for the remote continuous-fire mode which, he had noticed previously.

'Are we ready?' The question was ridiculous, and Smirtin's eyes rolled up in horror as he looked from the mad artist and back down to the racing torrent. 'Smirtin and Errol.' Jock ordered. 'Lock your arms around the ladies, and keep them locked until you exit the underground river...and keep your heads tucked in! May god be with you' he whispered as his finger trembled on the trigger mechanism.

'*Now go!*' He shouted, seeing as in slow motion the four terrified figures poised momentarily on the black basalt edge of the abyss; then they were gone. Jock pulled back the trigger and locked the continuous fire mode as a hail of laser bolts blasted across the lip of the waterfall, turning it into a liquid green. As the cannon kept firing he heard the ricochets heading deep up into the opposite tunnel, their echoes filling the chasm with ear-splitting noise. He paused, genuflected, then leapt into the roaring green- flecked water and felt the terrifying cold of oblivion knot his bowels as he was gripped by the tumultuous surge of the underground river.

✱✱✱

Zalkina was back in the dark woods of the swamp with her countrymen, the Zalks, who were encamped by the bubbling springs that welled up from the ground. As steam rose slowly from the pool into the blue haze above, the natives chattered to each other, now and again cautiously touching the controls of the assortment of space-weapons that now lay strewn haphazardly among the pine cones, recipients of the native's fervent but short-lived curiosity.

The pylon stood sentinel over the clear lotus pool and the light filtered through the pines and acacia from which hung liana's and vines tangled into a mesh of dark interlaced silhouettes. Baboons, the domestic pets of the Zalks ran around unchecked, stealing whatever they could, whether it be edible or just decorative, and running up the high overhanging trees with their find, to either eat or wear.

It had been awhile since Zalkina had arrived back at the camp and after feeding Starchild, she had enquired from her countrymen the whereabouts of her father. The only information that she could gather was that he had been taken by the cult to the Lost City through the underground river. But she was puzzled; for she knew her father couldn't swim - yet she was certain he was still alive. Also nagging at her native, though intelligent mind was how the bad men, the devil worshipers knew of her Lost City, as she thought of it. She was aware that it was an ancient abandoned city, left by the star-people, and Joruk had endorsed that view, but how could they know how to find it?

She sat at the campfire discussing it with the remainder of the Zalks, as the blue smoke rose lazily into the pine grove, its scent mingling with the aroma of pine needles that littered the ground. But they did not understand the implications of her conversation, and soon turned to cooking the fish they had speared that afternoon, skewering them with a spit of wood and twirling them over the hot embers of the fire and chatting in their incomprehensible tongue amongst themselves. The young girl was left to her own thoughts, talking now and again to Starchild, the group of tribesmen throwing her strange looks periodically – they didn't really trust her, for though she was their former chief's daughter, she was different, more knowledgeable than themselves; and she talked to animals... big, big magic!

As Starchild nuzzled her shoulder, Zalkina saw a baboon that had been around in the clearing quite a lot. It seemed to be interested in the host of abandoned space-weaponry strewn across the encampment - now totally ignored by the tribesmen - their interest in them quickly having warned when, after fiddling with them, nothing happened. (They did not of course realise how close to their own destruction they had been).

The baboon climbed down the tree at the back of them and went and sat by the spring of clear bubbling water and as Zalkina watched, the animal appeared to be distressed, sobbing almost. The Zalks ignore these animals in the main, and only resorted to killing them for food when they were desperate. There were a number of their ancestors who had been killed by these primates and their folklore and common sense told them to leave them be.

Zalkina turned to Starchild and asked him in simple animal tongue, which she had picked up instinctively after their first bonding at the Garden of the Eon-Beasts, if he knew why the baboon was sad.

'She Mother, sick Mother, sick with sadness' Starchild told her 'She wait for little ones...loose little ones in water...'

'She loose babies'Zalkina queried 'babies fall in water...go down...'

'She tell me' Starchild continued 'she tell me men who came take babies with them...'

'Through water?' Zalkina asked 'like they take Zalks, like they take my father...'

'Yes' the winged zebra nodded his head as the Zalks, busy with their meal, shifted uncomfortably. They didn't trust human's who could talk to animals...too big magic!

'Ask her to come and join us' Zalkina said quietly. The mythological beast raised his head and whinnied softly; the baboon's ears picked up and she turned around to look at the origin of the voice. Then she bounded around the campfire and came to join them, and Zalkina groomed her, looking at her swollen teats still full of milk and her sad eyes. The native girl told her via Starchild how the bad men had taken her father. But she added, there was hope, and that is why she was sitting here waiting.

The baboon listened quietly as Zalkina spoke, and then put her arm around the girl.

'I will call you Mimi' Zalkina said quietly. 'We will wait here together until our family returns!' The other baboons up in the trees stopped their chattering and looked at the strange group of three whilst the native's turned from their icy stares to devour their meal. After a while, one of the Zalks came hesitantly and offered some baked fish to Zalkina, who thanked him readily, devouring it ravenously.

The Zalks were settling down for their night, grunting in contentment at the great heaps of fish they had crammed down their gullets. An occasional passing of wind echoed around the encampment, rebounding in increased volume from the towering pylon, and the tribesmen laughed, goading one another to produce a more resonant fart, which brought little amusement to Zalkina; they are just children, she thought.

As the quiet of the blue twilight of the jungle descended on the camp and the last embers of the fire rose up in a crackle of sparks to the canopy above, Mimi and Starchild lay on the soft bed of moss and pine needles with Zalkina resting her head on the Zebra's withers, feeling the slow steady pulse of his breathing and smelling the reassuring scent of his body. Her thoughts went back to her first meeting with the beautiful boy with the golden hair and how she had shown him the way down to the Lost City through this lotus pool in front of her. She imagined how it would have been in ancient times, and dreamed she was there, bathing with the handsome youth, yet in her dreams she was older, a real woman - able, even willing to show her love for him.

Starchild stirred, and she was nudged into consciousness again as her memories of them diving from the pylon brought back memories of those long days ago into vivid focus. She had shown him the way as they swam though the three siphons and her heart beat faster at the recollection of his white naked body, wishing only that she were older.

Zalkina wondered where he was now and though not understanding the nature of love, she knew that there was a great sadness in her soul for she craved his caress, his voice; to feel the warmth of his divine body pressing against her own. She dosed off into a fitful sleep, wondering why her thighs felt so damp, as visions of herself and the beautiful boy paraded themselves in front of her disturbed mind.

Mimi stirred and sat up on her haunches. There was a sound - not the sound of the forest or the jungle but a strange alien sound. Starchild heard it also and snorted in a subdued way; Zalkina felt his body tense and saw his large dark eyes open as he looked around the glade. The Zalks were in the torrid lock of Morpheus, snoring in harmony into the dark night and huddled together in a circle of male bonding, letting an occasional passage of wind exit into each other's face; anaesthetised by each other's odours, they were like the dead.

Yet as Zalkina's ears pricked up in a semi-human, semi-animal state, she focussed on the direction of the noise and realised it was coming from the discarded spaceman equipment, which the black man of muscle had dumped in the clearing before she took them up to the fire mountain. Mimi, now fully wakened, leapt across the clearing and started pawing the device from which the sound emanated. Cocking her head from side to side, she picked up the set of headphones, listening to the cracking voice, and feeling a pulse of communication, which sounded quite pleasant.

'This is your commander.' The voice said as Mimi jumped up and down, listening to the curious sound talking to her from the communicator.

'Have you anything to report...have you established contact...'

Mimi jabbered into the mouthpiece, a high- pitched cackle of baboon – talk as the headset fell silent. She banged it with her paw, then bashed it on the ground, cacklng and squealing into it once more.

'There is static...I am not receiving,' the voice sounded irate, 'can you give me your location...'

'Jabber, jabber, jabber' Mimi mimicked down the sender and Zalkina got to her feet. Picking her way through the somnambulant and disgusting tribesmen, she came up to where Mimi was engaged in a pointless conversation, but obviously enjoying every minute of it.

'Joruck?' she questioned, taking the headset from the disgruntled Mimi, 'Is that you Joruck...?'

'This is your commander.' Joruck's voice replied in an exasperated sort of tone 'please give me a report...what are your co-ordinates?'

'We OK Joruck' Zalkina was trying her best, though she didn't like the tone of the little wizened up Star-man, 'we wait here at jungle entrance...I take other's to fire mountain'

'Fire-mountain...what do you mean fire-mountain. Give me a report, this is your commander.' 'What are your co-ordinates...?'

Zalkina frowned at the headset. She was not accustomed to being shouted at like this. Mimi crouched, looking expectantly at the headset as Zalkina handed it to her. 'Jabber, jabber, jabber' Mimi shouted excitedly into the headset

'*Clarify your position!*' Joruck's voice erupted in a shouted angry command as Mimi got spooked and jumped up and down, squealing and banging the headset on the ground until it was smashed to pieces.

'Well done.' Zalkina said, steadying the distraught baboon. 'Nobody likes being shouted at... now, can we get some sleep!' A silence ensued over the glade as they settled down again for the long night; even the Zalks were silent now, their gastronomic problems having been expelled into the dark night.

189

CHAPTER SIXTEEN
*** LOST IN TIME ***

Luke's consciousness gradually returned as he clawed his way up out of the sand and sat upright, his eyes burning in the bright glare of the desert sun. He looked back whence he had fallen, and saw the zigzagging crest of the sand dune down which he had made his hasty descent. It was gouged by the trail of the avalanche he had made, that had, by its cushioning effect, saved his life. He swore there and then, but not for the first time, never ever to trust a woman again.

His first assumption had been correct. As he had hurtled downwards from the ether, just managing to utter the incantation in time to avert certain destruction, he realised that he had landed nearly in the identical place where first he had fallen on his ill-fated flight of astral travel with that arch temptress, Ishtar, so long ago. A frisson of foreboding ran down his spine at this strange coincidence. Was it deja vu, or had he been hurtled back in time to before Park House had been torched?

His mind ranged over the numerous possibilities as to where he was and in which dimension, but he could not come to any logical answer. The only certainty was that he had been duped once again by his nemesis: his one fatal weakness for that damnable woman. And what was her agenda? Was she even now back with the new cult? For there was no sign of her here; as his eyes ranged the overhead blue of the sky, he could but assume that she had winged her preternatural way back to the Lost City to join those who had wrought so much havoc on himself and his family.

Redirecting his glance earthwards, Luke recognized the distant structures, seen in his previous, though short visit to this place; they looked like temples, shimmering in the mirage of the desert Wadi below, and shrugging at the banality of the situation, he decided that he had no option now but to walk towards them; for he knew from experience that he would not last long in this cauldron of burning sun.

One thing he didn't want to risk was trying to return to the Lost City via the incantation - not until he had established where he was now, for a prescient thought was emerging, and one that he was trying to suppress: that Ishtar had some sinister reason for dumping him off here – an accident it wasn't!

Luke checked out his body for broken bones, reassured that he had only minor abrasions caused by sand burns. Pulling up his shirt over his head, as he had done that long time ago, he set off with anger; this girded his loins with resolution, for walk out of this crucible of heat, he had to. Imperative in his cofused mind was the need for water, and down there in the distance was the glint of a river.

Many times, as he trod the vast stretch of stony ground, which led slowly down towards the cluster of the temples and tumbled mud brick dwellings, he felt that there was an element of predestination about this strange journey he had elected to make in search of his father. Surely it was no coincidence that Ishtar had tricked him a second time into landing in this God-forsaken wilderness, So his heavy steps were lightened somewhat by curiosity as Luke walked out of the desert and onto the harder, more rocky terrain of the vast wadi.

The windswept sand dunes were behind him and his feet felt blistered and raw; his whole body was crying out for water. He closed the gap on the temple structures and clusters of mud brick dwellings as the scene began to swim in a sea of hallucination and he recalled the strange and mysterious events of the recent past though they were all a jumble in his delirious mind.

He reached a crumbled wall and walked up to the entrance to a ruined mud brick house that afforded shelter from the blistering sun and collapsed into its dark welcomed respite as his senses left him.

Some time later - he knew not how long - he became aware of voices and felt a cool sensation of liquid cascading down his chin and onto his chest – water, it was water! His eyes were open yet he could not see, only feel the indescribable beauty of water as it sloshed over his face and he imbibed it, swallowed it down as if it were the last drop in the world.

After many gulps of the staff of life, his eyesight partially returned, and he saw through thick, sand-encrusted lids, a woman bending over him, framed in the entrance of the hovel. She was pouring water into his parched mouth from an earthenware jar. He tried to rise but could not, and the woman quietened him in a soft, motherly voice - coaxing him - as one would to a child - bidding him be still and urging him to drink from the jar that she held.

Luke felt nauseous as his senses returned to his dehydrated body, whilst the woman knelt over him, gently mopping his feverish brow. He relapsed into unconsciousness and after a while, came too, aware of a feeling of well-being as his body became rehydrated and he propped himself up on one arm - his sight was back.

The woman was still there, bending over him and holding a cold compress of some sort of herbs to his sweat-stricken forehead, though he felt his fever dissipating and looking around, he tried to take stock of his immediate surroundings. He was in a rustic mud brick dwelling with an open hole for a window and a larger aperture for a door. Over the window and flapping in the hot breeze, was tacked a ragged piece of sackcloth that alleviated the glare from the desert outside. The hovel was devoid of any ornament or furniture, and Luke saw that he was propped up on a low leewan, or rustic low bed of stuffed striped hessian.

The woman who tended him had a kind face and seemed of Egyptian origin. She wore a dark tob, which enveloped her large build and her black hair was oiled into long ringlets that fell over her shoulders. Her oval eyes looked down on him and he saw the tenderness of her concern as she wiped the sweat from his face and pushed back his mop of blond hair.

'Enter quiese del-wahti?' she asked; he could just make out the meaning of her local dialect, 'are you better now?' Luke was grateful for the rudiments of his Arabic, acquired from conversations with his father on his returns from his stints of work in Egypt. 'Escot, Escot' the woman quietened him as she cradled his head in her bosom. 'Quiet, quiet now.'

'This is Egypt?' he asked in his unschooled Arabic

'You speak, you speak my language?' The woman exclaimed, astonishment gracing her lovely face. 'You are khouwager... foreigner...tourist?'

'No' Luke replied 'Not tourist...just traveller...'

'From where?' The woman asked incredulously 'this all desert here...no travellers...no foreigners...'

Luke struggled to get up and the woman helped him; he sat bemused, looking around him at the mud brick hovel and the woman in antiquated Egyptian garb who looked like something from one of his father's books on the Egypt of the nineteenth century.

'Es-mak-ie...What's your name?' Luke asked

'Es-ma Yasmine' the woman replied.

'Senna-cam...what year is it?' Luke asked, with baited breath.

Luke translated it fromYasmeen's local date. 'Nineteen Sixty-eight' he spoke aloud, 'no...it is not possible...I am here in Egypt before I was ever born!'

Luke relapsed into a fearful delirium again, his body wracked with cramps, for he had sweated out all the liquid he had been given to drink by Yasmine, who now tendered to him again, once more pouring copious amounts of water into his damaged system. Finally the fever broke and Luke staggered to his feet; his hallucinations had stopped and he felt his strength return. Walking gingerly around the small mud brick hovel Yasmine eyed him anxiously.

'You better now?' she asked; Luke took her hand and kissed it.

'Thank you, kind lady...thank you for saving my life. I will never forget your kindness,' he replied, but Luke's mind was in turmoil. How could his trip of the light fantastic with that devil-woman from the Lost City have ended up with him travelling into a time in which he was not even born! He thought of confiding his anxiety to the woman but then countered it by realising that even if he could explain the concept of astral travel to her in his pigeon Arabic, she would never understand.

Yasmine moved to the entrance of the hovel, the westering sun, declining across the western range of mountains silhouetted her figure to reveal a prominent bulge standing out from her abdomen - she was heavily pregnant; not just fat as Luke had previously thought.

'Come,' she said, 'I will give you food.'

Luke followed, blinking in the late afternoon sunlight. Though the heat of the day had moved off the anvil of the plain, the golden light stung his eyes and brought back the nausea of his midday desert sojourn.

Yasmine took Luke's hand, like a mother leading a child, and they walked from the mud brick dwelling across the sandy floor of the plain. Dotted here and there were ruins of temples and mud-brick houses and rouged by the setting sun, clusters of swaying palms and the occasional column leaning melancholy in the sand that added an air of gilded neglect. So these were the 'temples' that Luke had thought he had seen from a distance as he started his long trek towards what might barely be described as civilisation.

Climbing some badly worn steps they entered the small courtyard of a portico or small shrine from where the glinting river, now quite near, scintillated in the last of the sun. The walls of the shrine were adorned with carved and painted scenes, though the paint had been eroded in the most part. A small circle of stones was situated at the back of the shaded portico, and on the embers of the fire within it were the grilling carcasses of rabbit and pigeon, skewered by slivers of hardened palm.

Yasmine picked one of the delicacies up from the coals and proffered it to Luke.

'Eat' she said simply, and Luke did not hesitate as he devoured the tasty, if stringy meat of the desert; Yasmine did likewise. After they had demolished the game and poultry between them, Luke leaned back and took in the surroundings of his new abode whilst Yasmine eyed him quizzically. The scenes on the walls of the shrine were familiar from the numerous drawings Jock had done for the University in Egypt and which Luke had pored over in his illicit entry into his dad's studio- come library at the former Park House

'Isis' he said at length, 'this is a shrine to Isis?'

'No' Yasmine replied 'this is a shrine to *Ishtar*!'

'*What*?' Luke felt a rivet of shock shoot through his brain, He sat up from his sprawled position, his mind awhirl as he spoke:

'But Ishtar was the Mesopotamian equivalent to Isis...how can this be?'

A frown of incomprehension spread across Yasmine's face. He did not want to recount his recent experiences with the resurrected Ishtar - not yet - as he didn't want to say anything to this kind lady that would lead her to think he was 'magnoon,' crazy.

'This is a shrine to Ishtar!' Yasmine reiterated emphatically, and Luke nodded in acquiescence...so be it!

'Tell me about yourself' Luke said, changing this contentious issue into something more ordinary, as he grappled with his rudimentary Arabic, 'where is your family?'

'My family leave me' Yasmine replied, a tear welling in her large dark eyes.

'Why...how?' Luke asked ingenuously enough, 'you here in desert all alone?'

'It is a long story' Yasmine said dolefully. 'I do wrong... I go with man...not my husband...my husband and his family leave...leave me here

193

alone' A large tear brimmed in the woman's dark eye as Luke moved uncomfortably. Did he not have his own problems - separated once more from his own family and transported back in time to a date before he was even born! Yet as he looked at the distraught face of the woman who had saved him from the desert, the milk of human kindness flowed through his veins as he put his arm around the weeping woman.

'There, there come now' he said as well as he could muster in his clumsy Arabic. Yasmine clutched him and buried her face in his breast, weeping, her body shaking, and he felt the dejection of her loneliness sweep through his being. He smelt the strange fragrance of her long, oiled hair and the odour of her body as he hugged her to him - then a curious sensation of deja vu overtook his senses and he embraced the pregnant cast out and kissed her tear-stained cheek. No! He wrestled with the conflicting feelings, which welled up inside him. No, I should not be feeling this! It is just the loneliness and anxiety of my own life of recent times, which compels me to feel drawn to this woman, he whispered to himself.

Luke broke away from the incestuous motherly smell of Yasmine and waited until his heart had stopped beating. He put it down to his delirium and fever he had suffered from just recently in his hard trek from the desert. Yet he could not explain the extreme emotional impact this woman had upon him.

'The sun is going down' he was trying desperately to distract himself from this unwholesome feeling. Yasmine composed herself and wiped her face with the black sleeve of her capacious tob. The western sun glinted from the distant hills as the last limb of the orange orb sank below the blue-grey horizon. The violet afterglow seared the sky in an iridescent light as Venus appeared low on the horizon, followed by a myriad of other celestial bodies; then the stars shone bright in the blue-black velvet night.

'So who is the father of your child to be?' Luke asked, a feeling of inexplicable foreboding tugging at his subconscious as he looked at the sad face of the pregnant woman.

'He great man.' Yasmine seemed reluctant to talk about her lover who it seemed had abandoned her, as had the rest of her family. Then encouraged somewhat by the affable expression on the handsome stranger's face, she gathered confidence.

'He great man... man of great knowledge... understand much about Ancient people, Ancient Gods.'

'An Egyptologist?' Luke exclaimed, that anxious feeling of déjà vu asserting itself once more in the back of his mind, 'What is his name?' He asked breathlessly, although he already knew the answer.

His name is Labachi... Dr. Labachi.' Jasmine replied proudly, 'He great Egyptologist, man of much knowledge. He give me this job, guardian of this shrine. When husband and family go and leave me here alone... he give me this job as gaffier, custodian of shrine to Isis...'

'And what will you call your child...your child to come?' Luke asked, a frisson of fear like a presage of the future crawled along his spine, bidding him not to think, not to ask as he willed away the answer he knew was to come.

'If boy,' Yasmine replied, sensing the tension in the youth yet not comprehending the reason. 'I call him *Wabib* ...like father...if girl, I call her *Ishtar*!'

Luke stood up and staggered down the stairs to the rock-strewn desert below; clutching a palm tree, he convulsed in a fit of paralytic fear and disgust, spewing up his spleen onto the outer wall of the shrine. He had known it all along. This is where Ishtar had dropped him: at the very place of her birth! Out of his time, before he, or even she was born; the very place where she had brought him on their first disastrous flight! And this is why he felt such a fatal attraction to this pregnant woman...her smell; it was the same smell as the enchantress, the demon woman, the irresistible Ishtar.

Luke collapsed in a pitiful heap, his mind reeling, groping desperately for answers; some sort of explanation. Why? Why had she brought him here, perverse and inhuman as she was? How could this black witch be so contemptuous of human feelings, human life, that she could cynically exploit, not just his own weakness - his inexorable desire for her - but embroil her own mother in whatever witchcraft she was cooking up now. Was she trying to make him loose his mind; she was contempti, but this was beyond the laws of humankind!

Try as he may to find a reason for this gross act of duplicity, Luke could not help but think that she must have a reason, some master plan. Though Ishtar was toying with his mind, making him suffer, Luke was certain that she had planed this little excursion back in time to involve him in some portentous outcome; but what? He had no way of knowing, but of one thing he was sure – and that was Jasmine, the woman who had shown him kindness, even maternal nurture, was as much a dupe in this cosmic game as he was; for he was certain that she was not in on the plan!

As his senses rallied, two thoughts were uppermost in Luke's mind. One was that Yasmine, the mother to be, was not responsible for the daughter to whom she would soon give birth. Second, that he could possibly intercede in her giving birth, thus saving humanity and himself from the clutches of this demon-woman yet to be born. Perhaps he could persuade Yasmine to abort her phantom child to be; but Luke cast this option aside. He could not do this. Yasmine was a pawn in the game, and he could never bring any harm to come to her. No, as he wrestled with the diminishing range of his choices, it was clear...he could do nothing! And so he must await the outcome of this fatidic journey, this trip back beyond his own birth, to see what future plot these consanguineous wizards of time had dreamt up.

Dejected and weary, Luke climbed back up the steps to the shrine, to face the woman who would bear the daughter who would destroy him. He placed his arms around her and she responded to his touch. 'I hope you have a little boy,' he whispered, 'he will be a great man like his father.' They went to sleep in each other's arms as the moon rose over the eastern mountains and bathed them in a white light; the light of a new era.

✳✳✳

Embraced by the icy cold water of the underground river, Bridget and Ogadile, cocooned by the mighty grasp of Smirtin and Errol, were swept onwards and downwards. Their lungs were on fire, panic beating at their breasts as they waited, in moments which hung like an eternity, to draw breath again. They were knocked senseless by the cruel grasp of the plunging cascade that smashed them against rocky protrusions in the chasm, the torrent threatening to rip them apart.

Smirtin, broke surface and gulped air, heaving the others up into the pitch-black cavern where they were twirled around for a brief respite before the icy waters transported them once again into a sliding, white-knuckle ride of watery terror.

On the verge of oblivion, their bodies bloodied and battered, they sensed a change: a lessening in the flow of the current and a warmth; a warming of the water invaded their immobilised senses; they were approaching a siphon.

Deep breath now!' Smirtin shouted, sensing an impending overhang, and they were sucked down once more into the watery grave to feel a surge of whirling current bearing them upwards; they were through the siphon and swirling upwards as the torrent exited in a deep aquifer, a cave of sorts.

'I can see light.' Errol exclaimed as they avoided the overhanging rocky protrusions and were carried along and up to a pool where gleamed the star spangled night. Aware only that they had exited the underground river alive, and each of them blessing the bounties of nature as they looked at the starlit sky, vignetted by tall trees, they groped for the bank, feeling reassuring rock under their feet.

'We made it!' Ogadile cried. She held Bridget tight in an embrace of victory and relief, but no sign of life seemed to emanate from the grey features of the slumped woman.

'Quick' Ogadile shouted, 'get Bridget to the bank. Get her out of the water!'

Smirtin and Errol stumbled for a footing on the slimy rocks and mud of the spring and lifted the rigid body of Bridget up and out of the warm, bubbling water, and onto the soft reedy bank of the pool. Ogadile bent over the comatose form of the still woman and breathed the breath of life into her as she kneaded her lungs, holding her spine for a second in an elevated position and then blowing into her mouth again. The black supernatural put her hand across Bridget's still chest and felt the faintest murmur of a pulse as she continued her revival technique.

Smirtin and Errol heaved themselves onto the bank and looked in concern at Bridget, who was a ghastly shade of white, and refusing to breathe.

'Press' Ogadile commanded her brother, 'press here, hard!' The giants hand pressed on the water-laden lungs of the corpse and with a splutter, Bridget vomited up a stream of water from her ashen mouth and Ogadile turned her onto her side. Bridget coughed and choked and muttered strange sayings as she miraculously was brought back to life.

Jock surfaced moments later, drawing deep breaths of the sacred air above the pool and pulled himself up to join them as Ogadile massaged Bridget's abdomen.

'She is alive' Ogadile said victoriously, 'but she is different?'

'Thank god!' Jock exclaimed embracing Ogadile as he looked down at his recovering wife, the faint glimmer of colouring apparent on her cheek in the dim light. .

'But what do you mean, she is changed?'

'She is with child' Ogadile said quietly, 'to be more exact, she is with two children...'

'Twins!' Jock exclaimed... it is as I thought... but we didn't want to tell anyone... not until it was certain.' For had he himself not prophesied the miraculous gift from Isis, in the Tower of the Princesses at the City of Aiyu?

✱✱✱

The laser cannon, which had been sighted securely so it would not move from the blocks of basalt which weighted it to the sill of the cascade, continued firing in its mode of continuous fire into the facing tunnel across the rushing waters.

As the bolts of light ricocheted off the walls of the opposite cave, they penetrated high into the upper reaches of the volcano, dormant, yet, though on a razor wire of instability.

The unstoppable laser bolts hit a rock of hard gneiss and were deflected downwards into a labyrinth of volcanic chambers. The energy of the rapid-fire fusillade ruptured the softer pumice between the interlinking tunnels, and the light bolts were directed downwards towards the nascent mount of larva crust, which had so far been restrained from erupting by the cooling effects of the vents as they drew air in from the surface.

As the cascade of undiminished firepower ripped open the hot mantle, the larva, looking for a release from its accumulated pressure, exploded upwards into the higher vents, gathering momentum as it ascended. The fury of an active volcano spewed out from the crater and the blue-black night was turned into day.

✱✱✱

Jock turned, feeling the ground beneath his knees tremble and looked upwards to the high crest of the crater to see the volcano surge upwards in a magnificent spume of molten, larva. The birds and the beasts of the forest glade took fright, squawking and jabbering and making their frantic exit from the doomed mountain.

'It has happened.' Jock whispered, not wanting to scare Bridget, and the others followed the direction of his gaze. 'We have set it off...we have started the eruption ...we are witnessing the destruction of the cavern of the Lost City...and with it, the cult!'

'You had better be right,' Errol spoke curtly, 'and you had better pray that it doesn't come this way...because you have a burden of care to cope with now!' He looked down to the recovering and distraught Bridget.

'Come,' Ogadile said, ever practical, 'let us mover out of here. If we follow the stream we must come to the camp of the Zalks further down the glades...there we will find Zalkina, and we can report back to Joruck with that strange equipment he gave us. We can get help for Bridget through him from Isis ...she will know what to do.'

'That is if that antiquated collection of junk still works!' Smirtin added. They lifted the prone woman up and carried her carefully along the swampy turf of the glades, their interconnecting pools beginning to bubble in a spume of excitement and the acrid smell of sulphur permeated the dark woods.

✳✳✳

Ishtar rose up into the ether. She had discharged her pathetic cargo at the shrine of her own conception and birth, and her sensuous lips were disfigured by a malevolent smile as she winged her way back to the cavern and the resurrected city of her cult.   She had no misgivings about the treachery she had played or the evil of her intentions, as she leered in a brutal grimace of one who has sown deceit and destruction and yet revels in it.

Her powers were at a new high and she mentally rehearsed the plan she had made, the trap she had set to ensnare that trusting blond haired Jack'o napes, if he were ever to survive the heat of the desert and be fortunate enough to stagger down to her shrine...her own shrine...for she was Immortal now!   She had honed her powers at the Lost City in the installation of this new chapter of the One Dimension, and she had visions, dreams of further power – power that would eclipse even those of the Esoteric Oracle!

She was glad that she had made the transition, along with her father and Rachid and of course the expendable members of the cult, from that time-locked, pathetic little enclave at Elgin Crescent. For here, in this world of multi-dimensional space and time, she was free, powerful and invulnerable. She had the knowledge and the experience to travel at   will through the ether and to descend wherever she chose.

Her white tunic and flowing braids of black hair floated out behind her as she swept across the outer reaches of the either.

She was supreme, an entity of power who would go where she chose and be beholden to no man, ideology, or religion. Her humble origins that she had over flown and the sight of her lonely mother meant nothing to her now; she was Incarnate...a Being of the Ether! As she directed her flight path back to the dimension whence she had come and saw the forest and smoking dormant volcano come up far on the eastern horizon, she fantasised about her new command: the Goddess Incarnate that she would become to the new members of the cult. Yes, she would be worshipped, and poems written about her prowess, her magic, her beauty...she would oust Rachid, even her father, to become a legend in the annals of time!

A flurry of air feathered her trim and she saw far in the east a spume of red ascending into the lower atmosphere. The column of fire was accompanied by a gigantic cloud of grey ash that poured out of the summit of the mountain and she realised in some trepidation that the volcano above the cavern of the resurrected Lost City was in eruption.

Two choices collided simultaneously in her crazed mind: should she go back and warm her father, Rachid and the cult of their imminent danger, or should she save her own skin. It didn't take long for Ishtar to decide on which course to take and she glided down to a pinnacle of fractured rock, thrusting upwards from the desert sand, and landed, shielding her eyes to watch the steady but fearful progress of the volcano.

As the infernoes of Armageddon glowered in her satanic eyes, Ishtar watched the night turn to day as the ribbon of the red dawn in the greying eastern sky was eclipsed by a plume of fiery spray which shot out of the distant crater. Rivers of larva ran down the outer slopes of the volcano as similar streams of molten magma coursed through the subterranean passages to vent their wrath in blowholes further down the slope. The top margins of the forest, dry already from surviving on the rocky altitude of the tree line, caught fire and the inferno raged down the mountain, heading for the denser pine forest and jungle below.

∗∗∗

Then the crater blew, and the air was filled with molten rock, the explosion reverberating deep underground to the cavern of the Lost City. A violent tremor surged across the underground cavern; the rebuilt city of crystal shook and trembled, and its inhabitants looked upwards to see yawning cracks appear in the roof of the cavern high above them; then they ran amok. Labachi turned from the sight of mass hysteria to address his scientists.

'Gentlemen, it seems we are in the middle of an earthquake. Will the shield withstand a total collapse of the ceiling?' .

'It may do, protector of the ways.' one of them ventured, as the shouts and screams of the terrified cult who ran here and there in total panic, filled the dome. 'But this is not an earthquake, oh prophet. From the sulphurous fumes that seep even through our shield, I fear we are in the middle of a volcanic eruption!'

'But the shield man... will it hold?'

'Rock, yes....but I am not sure about the molten larva...it would generate too much heat...and even if it holds, we will all fry...'

'Come' Labachi said to Rachid. 'Get those natives from the cells, but don't make it obvious. We will make our escape via the underground stream!'

Rachid nodded as the two men rushed past the scientists and Labachi called out to the cult: 'Fear not, my children, the shield will protect us, even from this inferno.'

'Ishtar!' Rachid shouted to Labachi as they made their way underground to the cells. 'Where is she?'

'She was playing a little game with the artist's spawn, Luke.' Labachi replied, 'but she will return when she sees our pridicament...she would not desert us.'

They opened the cells and hurried the group of Zalks out of their rock-cut prison, prodding them down the tunnel and finally into the dark waters of the first pool of the series of siphons, which was now bubbling; a pungent smell of sulphur hanging in the air.

'Quick, dive!' Rachid ordered as he poked the reluctant Zalks with an instrument, which one could only describe as a cattle prod. 'You will show us the way out of here...or you will perish!' He commanded them.

Zalkine shouted something at his tribesmen and they all took a deep breath, plunging into the bubbling water, and dived deep, lost to sight.

'Let's get after them' Rachid shouted and the two men inhaled deeply themselves, plunging into the sulphurous water.

At that moment the cracks that had appeared in the roof of the vast underground cavern opened, and molten larva oozed out of the fractured rock, dripping down in ruddy stalactites from the high ceiling above. Simultaneously, the mouth of the small cave ran red with a moving wall of smoking fire as the magma spewed out onto the floor of the cavern and flowed in rivers towards the Lost City.

The obscurants of the One Dimension watched in fearful fascination to see the tide of smoking red larva push its inexorable way towards the base of the shield. As it made contact, it stopped, solidifying a little and cooling, until the next wave pushed it up the force field a bit higher.

Similarly the larva descending from the ruptured ceiling, cooled and solidified, dropping down onto the apex of the giant shield.

'It works!' one cultist shouted. 'It's working...it is holding back the larva...we are the chosen ones...we have been saved!' They crowded up on the podium and watched the cooling level of larva abate slightly, dancing their licentious dance and coupling in bestial fashion one with another. Then one of them saw something, his screams aborting the depraved aberrations of the cult members who looked in the direction of his pointing finger.

'It is coming up from the lower levels' one of them shouted in a blood curdling cry of horror, 'the larva is coming up from the caverns below...we will all die!'

The red magma bubbled up from the control room; its legacy of heat in the former workshops of the scientists where was located the nuclear fusion reactor, soon to be evident. The futuristic generator of the star people was melted and the shield, dependant on this awesome power, flickered transparently on the brink of being and non-being, then disintegrated as the larva flowed in from without and upwards from within and the crystalline reconstructed city cracked and exploded into a million shimmering fragments.

The decadents, the naked sect of Satan who thought they were beyond the wrath of God were burnt on the stake of their own depravity, their abortive shrieks rising up into the sulphur-laden, swirling, red air of the cavern. Then only larva and flames and the stench of burning flesh remained as the roof of the cavern dropped down onto the remains of the Lost City to bury it for all time.

***

It was Mimi who sensed there was something not right. As Zalkina slept, nestling like an infant against the warmth of star-child, the baboon rose to a crouch, then a standing position as she sniffed the air.

There was a strange smell in the glade. It was not the smell of the man-beast's red burning thing, (the campfire) which she had learned not to touch...too much pain.

No, it was some other alien smell that hurt her nostrils and made her want to cough. Then she looked up beyond the towering man-thing of the pylon, and saw a strange orange flame in the blue-black sky. She stamped her feet on the soft earth and started chattering. There was danger in the foggy air, a threat to be feared...to run from...she must warn the kind mother-girl, who slept with the strange animal...she must alert the camp!

As the Zalks snorted, their faces buried in each other's bodies, Zalkina sat upright. Though still half asleep, she sensed there was danger and seeing Mimi jumping up and down and screeching, she focussed her somnambulant mind on the immediate situation.

A pungent smell invaded her nostrils; the pool in the glade bubbled, and in the sky, through the trees was an orange glow. It was the fire-mountain...the fire-god had woken! But where were her friends – the beautiful boy?

The grey light of dawn was suffusing through the overhead canopy of tangled trees. Zalkina stood rubbing her eyes; she was just about to wake the Zalks when she saw a group of figures emerge from the jungle to the side of the overgrown and flooded lotus pool. She took Mimi's hand and walked down to the bubbling water; the smell of the nauseous gas was stronger now and she watched three men carrying a still-lying woman, the light from the distant volcano glinting on the hair-band of the second woman.

'My friends' she shouted, running to the edge of the pool and assisting her comrades who carried the mother of the beautiful boy.

'Lady, not well...' she asked as Bridget lay breathing heavily, yet with her eyes closed. Mimi jumped up and down in an excited frenzy. 'Quiet!' Zalkina ordered the baboon and Mimi stood still.

Smirtin lifted his giant wet frame onto the bank and pulled up Ogadile, Jock and Errol and Zalkina looked around, expecting to see the youth of her former dreams; her awakening of womanhood, but the pool was empty.

'Luke!' she exclaimed, trying to stop her heart from beating so fast, 'where is golden- haired boy?'

Jock put his hand on Zalkina's shoulder. 'He is all right my child...he will come later. Do not be troubled...we have to look after Bridget...she not well!

Zalkina fell quiet, a tear welling in her dark eyes as she helped them cut and collect branches to form a sledge, placing the semi-conscious Bridget onto it and covering her with animal pelts that she raided from the still snoring Zalks: her tribesmen liked to sleep.

The travois was completed in record time and Jock addressed Smirtin: 'My friend, can you use your strength now to drag Bridget away from this place...these waters are turning to poison...' he gestured to the bubbling sulphur which was now belching from the black waters

'I will my friend.' Smirtin avowed solemnly, taking up the end of the triangular sledge and pulling the inert body of Bridget away from the pool and onto one of the many paths leading out of the glades.

'Come' Jock said to Zalkina, 'you must get away from this place...not good air...do you understand?' Zalkina nodded, then a large tear welled up from her dark globes of eyes. 'My father' she sobbed, looking at the pylon.' He no come back?'

'I am sorry.' Jock put his arm around the distraught native girl. She had lost the two people she loved. 'But we have to leave this place now...'Stir your people.' Jock gestured to the sleeping Zalks, 'before they end their life in internal sleep!'

Zalkina wiped the tears from her face and went over to the tribesmen, kicking them with her foot as Mimi jumped up and down in glee...the loss of her babies almost forgotten.

Ogadile and Errol were about to join Smirtin and Jock as they pulled the travois holding Bridget away from the doomed spring, the orange light of the volcano reflecting in its black waters - then they espied some figures emerging from the siphon under the pylon at the far end of the lotus pool.

'Wait' Ogadile stayed Errol with a firm arm, 'who are they?' They watched and waited as a group of men spluttering and cursing, took their bearings and swam unsteadily towards them.

The baboons jabbered excitedly and the Zalks stirred to the guttural oaths of Zalk-talk that sounded as if its orators were hurling every abuse under the sun at their countrymen.

'Father!' Zalkina shouted 'Father is that you?' she peered into the pool, seeing the unmistakable face of her father, supported by the medicine man and the other Zalks as they paddled towards them.

A cry rose up from the half conscious tribesmen who had so rudely been awakened and they jumped up and down, shouting their delight and encouragement to the "non swimmers," whilst Mimi joined in with the other baboons that swung from the trees, chattering and squealing in their delight.

The Zalks grabbed their chief and the others and hauled them up onto the slippery banks, venting their glee in a cacophony of incomprehensible mumbo jumbo, whilst Zalkina, tears of joy replacing tears of sorrow, bent down to embrace her sodden and shivering father.

The medicine man was the next to be helped up and he gestured wildly, shouting orders for them to be careful. The other natives pulled themselves out of the water and the medicine man reached into his waterlogged, tiger-skin cloak, carefully taking out a bundle of pelts. Amidst a spray of water, the animal pelts suddenly came to life, wriggling violently and squealing in delight, and the shaman handed the large pouch to Zalkina.

'I save them' he said breathlessly. 'I save them from the demon men'

Zalkina opened up the bundle of kicking, squealing cargo and revealed the babies that Mimi had lost to the cult.

Mimi's joy new no bounds as she yelled her delight and then took to the trees, doing a very good Tarzan impression, swinging from one liana to another, finally to land next to her precious offspring who locked onto her teats and jostled for the pleasure of her attention. All the others were silent for a while as mother and babies were reunited, and then Mimi, her brood clinging to her and suckling at the same time, approached the apprehensive medicine man and kissed him on the cheek, much to the delight of the Zalks who applauded and shouted their approval. They chaired Zalkine, and the shaman, back from the glade and onto the track through the jungle as the Zalks formed a column of victory and started to exit in single file from the fire water.

Just as they did, two figures emerged from the siphon under the pylon, one of the tribesmen spotting them and shouting a signal of danger. Mimi looked back at the two men and her brow furrowed in instant recognition...they were the abductors of her babies! She cuffed the little ones away from her body, and the tribesmen picked them up to watch in disbelief as Mimi bounded across the glade to the assortment of weapons, still lying strewn on the grass.

The she-baboon fingered and fidgeted with various switches on one of the laser cannon until a red light glowed. Then, as all who watched marvelled in total disbelief, she unleashed a maelstrom of liquid green laser-bolts at the men who trod water below the pylon. The rapid-fire, one-second burst that the baboon had selected, more by luck than judgement blasted the pylon to Smithereens as great chunks of limestone hurtled down on the men in the water and Labachi and Rachid, the little tin prophets who would be Gods, met their end at the hands of a baboon, to sink down into a watery oblivion, and be buried for all time amidst the rubble of the ancient pylon of the Star-people.

As the sulphur spewed from the doomed lotus pool, the column filed out - Mimi taking back onboard her babies and following - and an ululating cheer rose up from the tribesmen, echoing around the fiery woods.

CHAPTER SEVENTEEN
*** THE DEVIL WITHIN ***

Luke woke in the cold light of pre-dawn as the grey band of firmament spread its tentacles across the blue-black vault of night. His arms still around the sleeping Yasmine; he felt her warmth and inhaled the smell of her womanhood as a prescient fear chilled his spine.

What was he to do - the woman who had saved his life lay in his arms, and yet she was destined to bear the girl-child who, as a woman would bring about his own destruction. As he watched the Lord of Light illuminate the Heavens with a brush of silver and gold, he struggled with the dilemma that raged deep within his heart.

Yasmine, the pregnant bearer of the Ishtar to be, was not culpable. She was unaware of the portentous new life, which she carried and was as innocent as the encroaching dawn. She had been seduced be a man as faithless to his friends as he was fickle and a great anger and sadness welled up in Luke's breast as he held the sleeping woman.

She could not be blamed for falling for the charms of a seducer of women. Had not his own mother fallen for the same fatal attraction of a man who led innocent lives into a slavery of occult beliefs, a man who would dispose of them at the merest convenience - and this satanic legacy would be handed on to his daughter to be!

Luke's heart was filled with remorse as he untangled himself from the sleeping Yasmine. She had lost everything: her husband, her family; they had all deserted her, leaving her to fend for herself in this remote outpost, a shrine to an ancient civilisation. Yet what could he do? He could not intercede on what was ordained. He had to leave, and let what was written, happen. He had to think about his own plight, and find a way back to his own time, and rejoin his family: And what of them? Were they still battling with the demons of their unconscious minds in the cavern of the Lost City, or had some other hand of fate taken over, turning fortune onto their side once more?

As Luke sat dejected and alone, looking at the still sleeping Yasmine whom he had wrapped in a covering of jute-sacks, whilst trying the quell the anger he had felt for the betrayer of this woman and his own mother, the sun rose over the eastern mountains and its finger of light struck the wall of the shrine across from him in a blinding angled beam.

The energy from the cosmos decorated the painted relief of the temple shrine in vibrant shining light, and the figurative motifs and inscriptions were thrown into   vivid contrast. The central scene was of some unknown Pharaoh being suckled as an infant by the goddess Isis, whom, Yasmine had declared, was Ishtar. Yet the symbolism was unsure and Luke craned his neck to read the hieroglyphic text.

The carved relief read: " **Neb Ankh Sar Eff**..." Luke sat bolt upright as he suddenly recognised the inscription for astral travelling, so cherished by the immortals – the star-people, and so sought after by the dissidents, the cult, for their immeasurable purpose of evil. Yet why here? In this furthest outermost marker of the Ancient Egyptians, why would they record their most arcane and secret message at such a place; right in the middle of the desert?

Typically, this precious inscription had been carved onto an Obelisk, which Luke now realised was the key to time/space travel. Could this have been a cache left by the star people, a memory bank, or a note left to remind stragglers who had strayed from the main pack into the desert, to assist them in returning to their tribe.

Luke read the inscription again, rehearsing it in his mind with the specific articulation needed to invoke the magic, and as he did so, the inscription illuminated in a golden glow.

'You are a traveller?' Yasmine asked sleepily as she yawned and sat up, her hands stroking her distended belly; she had been woken by the light.

'I am a traveller, yes.' Luke replied, bending his rudimentary grasp of Arabic into the local accent, as he tried to disguise his shock at the import of her question.

Why you come here?' Yasmine asked 'Why you here?

Luke vacillated between a lie and the truth as Yasmine turned to look at him, her eyes like dark coals with a glimmer of apprehension blowing on the forge.

'Your daughter, Ishtar brought me here.' Luke blurted, all pretence of a cover-up, gone. Yasmine's eyes lit up; the coals were hot.

'So,' Yasmine said in an ambivalent tone, 'You come here to give me non-birth!' Her body, pregnant as it was, suddenly erected into a standing form, yet there was no apparent sense of movement; she had shape-shifted!

'I see,' Luke said quietly, though his heart was pounding. 'You are more than you said you were...'

'I am the union of Geb and Seth' Yasmine spat venom at Luke's face. The youth, horror written all over his face, quickly side-stepped the green bile, seeing as in a trance, the thing that Jasmine had become gradually shape-shift, rearing up over him, her pregnant belly hanging down below her waist as she convulsed in a multitude of grotesque anthropomorphic forms.

'You come to steal my child!' Yasmine rasped as she hovered above him, her matrix of fluorescing forms changing from one hybrid animal to another: all variations of the Ancient Egyptian Goddess Taueris, the flail - bearing pregnant crocodile.

'No' Luke stuttered, abject terror knotting his bowels. 'I ... I do not come here to *abort* your child...I am *in love with your child*!' Though the youth did not have the luxury of rational, so petrified with dread at this apparition was he, he instinctively said what in effect was true.

'Love' the towering hybrid exclaimed, 'What know you of love?'

'I feel love for you, poor lady,' Luke's voice shook with fear, but he stood his ground as the monsters that possessed the poor woman's body convulsed in a struggle for dominance and she wrestled with the demons that had taken over her psyche.

'You have been misled.' Luke stated flatly, trying to muster all the strength he could as he looked up at the writhing metamorph. 'You have been seduced by a demon, and yet you are not one, are you?'

The gargantuan shape of the pregnant hybrid, controlled by a power far greater and demonic than she, subsided and Yasmine regained her own form, cascades of tears pouring down her cheeks as she looked at the defenceless youth.

'Yes.' she said, softly at last. 'I have been taken over, possessed. My body has been invaded by demons and the seed has been planted. And yet I will fight for that seed, evil as it is, I will kill anyone or anything who tries to take this baby from me!'

'So be it.' Luke said quietly as he embraced the distraught woman who trembled in the memory of her recent metamorphosis and whose tears made runnels of black eye khol course down her smooth cheeks and onto the sandy floor of the ancient shrine.

'I will not intercede.' Luke assured Yasmine. 'You shall have your Ishtar, and the course of our lives will be as written...I cannot, nor will not hurt you anymore my poor woman.' Luke held Yasmine close, her odour of salt-water mingled with kohl and the scent of her natural musk, once more inflamed his senses as he was reminded of his demon lover; slowly he released her.

'You must help me go now.' he stated. 'You must help me return to the future so that I may continue in the struggle between the forces of good and evil in which it was preordained I participate, so what is written shall be so.'

'Come' Yasmine said after a long silence, 'I will show you something'

She took Luke by the hand and led him to the back of the shrine, which was built up against a limestone cliff. In the yellow cliff, half illuminated by the bright morning sunlight was an arched door carved into the rock. The low angle of the morning sun moved across the inner wall in a blinding brilliance; the rest was in a shadow, a diagonal of light and shade across the doorway.

Yasmine led the way down some steps, the sunlight extinguished abruptly, and Luke almost stumbled in the sudden contrast from light to dark. Yasmine stopped and pointed to a niche in the far wall of the tomb, whose chamber was at right angles to its main axis, unusual for an Ancient Egyptian funerary chamber.

As Luke's eyes became accustomed to the gloom, he saw that the niche was decorated around its side and top with hieroglyphics and almost before he started reading them, he recognised that it was the inscription Neb Anhk Sar Eff...

'This is a false door' he stated rather than asked Yasmine.

'It is a door for going far... travelling' Yasmine replied

'You have used it?' Luke asked

'No' Yasmine said. 'Not use it, me. But my lover, Dr Labachi, he use it...'

'Dr Labachi?' Luke muttered, though his astonishment was muted into a logical acceptance, 'of course! Your lover, your tormentor and destroyer of your faith used it to come and visit you...'

'He used it' Yasmine concurred, 'but he spoke the lines of magic...'

'The inscription!' Luke clarified in English. 'Will it take me back to my own time?' He added, looking at the dewy-eyed woman.

'I think it will' Yasmine brightened, trying to dismiss the memory of the man who had seduced her, impregnating her with demons, and lost her the right of a family and friends in this barren place, so far from civilisation. 'But you need these'

Yasmine reached down into the capacious pockets of her tob, and withdrew a string of green faience mummy beads. She pulled the cotton cord as the small beads poured into her hand as she retained two larger items. Handing them to Luke, he saw they were amulets, Ancient Egyptian in origin, and in the form of the Coptic cross or Ankh sign. (the sandal strap equivalent of the word 'Ankh,' the symbol for eternal life).

'You must hold these, one in each hand,' Yasmine said as he offered them to Luke, 'Dr Labachi used them to fly around the Heavens...they will help you return to your family...though you must form a picture in your mind of where you want t go.'

'Yasmine,' Luke whispered, brushing aside his blond curls matted around his sunburnt face as he bent down and kissed the poor woman on her cheek, 'thank you...thank you for helping me return!'

Yasmine clasped the youth around his slim, muscular body as a tear trickled from her dark eyes, 'I am thankful that I met you.' she said awkwardly. 'I am thankful that I save you...you are a beautiful boy, and not deserve to die out here...I hope you find your family...I hope you find love... Forgive me the darker side which lives within...it is not of me...'

'I know it is not you,' Lake said gently, 'and I wish it were different. Thank you for giving me sanctuary.' He watched her as she walked back from the funerary sanctuary into the bright light of the shrine to await the birth of her daughter, alone and isolated, and felt a bitter tear well up.

Luke seated himself on the low stone-carved step within the niche of the sacred tomb to Ishtar, which he knew was a false door. This door would permit the spiritual body of the deceased to embark on the solar voyage of Ra the Sun God in his barque of a million years.

Though the tomb was devoid of a sarcophagus, he knew that Labachi had created this escape route for his daughter to be - all the funerary cones embedded in the walls bore her name. It was as if this decadent mystic had planned for his own daughter's life to continue into the future, using his own arcane knowledge of the powers of the ancients to ensure it; the thought of a resurrected Ishtar made Luke's flesh creep.

It was also painfully obvious that Labachi had no intention of putting similar care in place towards the poor woman Jasmine – the bearer of his child to be – as she was patently just a vehicle for him to further his own satanic seed.

If Luke had known at this time the fate of Labachi and the cult, he would perhaps have saved his anger, but he was unaware of all that had transpired at the cavern of the Lost City. He now directed his attention to travelling back, visualising the place of his destination, whilst rehearsing the incantation. Then at the last minute he changed his mind - it was Ishtar that filled his search waves. For it was Ishtar he would find first and exact his revenge as his own personal demons intervened beyond his power to control them. He adopted the folded arms posture of the Astral Traveller, clutching the sacred eye amulets, one in each hand, and speaking out loud the incantation:

'Neb Ankh Sar Eff Djed Rheckit'

...Let the heavens be open to me, a traveller on the either. Let my Ka be guided into which ever place I desire...'

The hieroglyphics around the false door ignited in a glow, a molten shining of golden light and Luke felt the false door grow faint as his body was propelled once more up into the either. Luke clutched the blue faience amulets in each hand, looking down onto the shrine, searching for the pathetic figure of Yasmine who was shading her eyes, tracking his ascent. Then the oblivion of the vast matrix of space and time descended upon his hurtling mind.

***

Smirtin was in the lead, his black muscles rippling as he dragged the travois containing the motionless body of Bridget away from the glades that were now filled with nauseous gases of sulphur and burning as the volcanic flow descended into the jungle and the trees caught fire, flames leaping from one tangle of branches to another.

The others were not far behind and the Zalks were audible as they bought up the rear, their victorious chants giving way to whoops of fear as the flames leapt high above in front of them.

'Come on' Jock encouraged his old comrade as he took the branch of the makeshift sledge and helped Smirtin haul it along the jungle.

'Is is going to blow again old son?' Errol asked as he pulled on the large branch of the travois, whilst looking back at the orange tongues of flames that roared up ominously into the dawn sky.

'I don't know' Jock muttered putting his whole body weight into helping Smirtin, so that the three of them broke into a trot, the two branches of the rear of the makeshift structure dragging great furrows through the soft ground of the swamp.

Ogadile was not far behind helping Zalkina with the terror-striken Starchild, who snorted and kicked his heels, cloying the air, his nostrils distended and belching out the foul air of the swamp. Zalkine, the medicine man and the Zalks ran after them, though non-of them got near to the mythical, demon animal with its strange silvery wings, of which they were in mortal fear.

Soon the terrain changed and they were out of the swampy jungle and into the pine groves again. Even so, they were beset by leaping firebombs, like phosphorous candles that rained down on them as they tried to out pace the forest inferno.

'New team!' Jock shouted down the line as he felt Bridget's forehead, Zalks take up your station!' Zalkina translated and Zalkine backed it up, ordering the lagging tribesmen to take up the reigns of the travois. They didn't argue with the chief, who had been resurrected from the demon men, and a group of them threw themselves into the harness and the sled was transported at speed out of the burning forest. Smirtin rubbed his tired shoulder, a broad grin spreading across his angular face as he trotted easily behind the trundling travois.

Soon they were out of the burning debris that had cascaded down upon their unprotected heads, and Ogadile stopped to snuff out an ember, which threatened to do serious damage to her afro hair style.

The lower level of the desert escarpment was in front of them and the Zalks, undiminished in their mission to escape the wrath of the fire-demon, climbed steadily up the sand dunes.

After a long trek, they arrived at the top of the sand escarpment to deliver their cargo to a confused old man who ran out to greet them.

'Welcome' Joruck exclaimed. 'Welcome, my warriors...'Tis your commander at arms who speaks!'

'Get this woman into your fort!' Smirtin shouted at the bemused star-man, and get her the best of help your pathetic worn-out command is able to offer...or I will decorate this little temple with your head!'

Joruck coughed and withered at such an outrage and yet hurried to obey and Bridget was carefully lifted from the travois by the Zalks and carried onto a sort of bed in Joruck's cramped apartment.

'I want the best of your medicine!' Smirtin ordered as he fingered his enormous scimitar in its sheath and Joruck protested no further. He brought down some sort of ultra-sound scanning device from the junk of equipment that was crammed into his diminutive abode and placing a strange visor over his head, he kicked the machine, which grumbled into life as he bent over the prostrate woman.

'She is with child!' he exclaimed after a while.

'We know that!' Ogadile took over, 'now tell us what is wrong, why is she unconscious?'

Joruck looked at an imaging system, which was secreted amidst a pile of other space junk, turning some controls that actually did work. A deep sigh issued from his mouth as his brow furrowed into lines of concern.

'What!' Ogadile exploded impatiently, 'what do you see!'

'This young lady, or not so young lady, is pregnant with twins!' Joruck stated finally, grasping his thin goatee with two spindly fingers.

'We know this old man,' Jock restrained his impatience, 'but do you know what is wrong with the mother?'

'Two girls...I am certain' Joruck said, looking at the father, whose concern registered on his face, 'but there is a problem...'

'What?' Jock pushed closer to the imaging screen as he saw two minuscule figures, foetuses, who were moving in unison.

'They are conjoined' Joruck articulated carefully. They are joined at the head. This does not allow them space or freedom to move in the womb. They are also pressing on Bridget's spinal cord, causing her much pain and unconscious lapses.'

'Is there anything we can do?' Jock asked, his face a mask of total shock as he wavered unsteadily on his feet and the strong arms of Smirtin held him upright.

'I am not a surgeon,' Joruck stated flatly, 'but if they are not separated at this early stage, then they will become joined twins...'

'Siamese twins!' Jock uttered, his voice betraying his anxiety.

'They will be born as one' Joruck stated simply.

'Can you do anything?' Smirtin reiterated Jock's request, looming ominously over the alien.

'I can enter a programme into the computer, which will identify the correct procedure and carry out the task via remote micro laser surgery.

'But will it be safe?' Jock's voice faltered as he leaned against Smirtin.

'If my equipment still works,' Joruck said, a knot of uncertainty in his voice, 'then it will be safe...though I do not think you have an option. I will program the computer to be as efficient as it is able...but,' Joruck looked up at Jock and the others as they held their breath, 'because of their shared brain, which the remote surgeon will separate and make whole, they will probably still be able to access each other's brainwaves...'

'You mean,' Jock whispered, wrestling with this prognosis, 'that they will be telepathic...'

'Yes,' Joruck replied, 'that is the word...*telepathic*!'

'So be it then,' Jock confirmed, pulling himself together. 'There is no other option. But please Mr Joruck, do it as skilfully as you can. Please make sure that *they and my wife live!*'

'I will ensure that it is done to the best that I can do,' Joruck said, looking with not a little concern at Smirtin, who played with the bejewelled handle of his scimitar.

'Go now,' Joruck commanded as fresh white sheets appeared magically out of nowhere and the clutter of an elderly batchelor's pad was transformed into an operating theatre, albeit a small one. Bidget was lifted off the bed by some telekinetic force and set down gently on the newly made bed, whilst an array of futuristic gadgetry, hovered in gravity defying strangeness over the body of the unconscious woman.

'I give you my bond that I will, with the help of the computer and the remote surgeon, do all that is to be done.' Joruck mopped the sweat from his wrinkled brow, 'but I need solitude to do this...*please leave me now!*'

'Come' Jock said as he took one last look at his wife, kissing her gently on her forehead. 'Let us go outside and pray to God that this Star-man can save Bridget and the twins!'

The four exited onto the small courtyard, where the Zalks where encamped, Zalkine and the medicine man turned, their eyes bright, looking for any news of the woman whom they had help save from the fire demon and Mimi and her brood jabbered in a hushed expectancy, also fixing their eyes on them.

'We have to wait' Jock said quietly. Zalkina bid her tribesmen to be quiet and the band of natives followed the bearded man, whose woman was not well. They walked up to the top level of the balcony, looking down into the distant forest that had been their home but was now a smouldering, blackened scar. Above this the volcano raged, its anger vented by a succession of spectacular fireballs and a plume of thick grey smoke that rose up endlessly into the blue sky.

'Luke,' Jock muttered under his breath as he looked out on to the scene of destruction, ' *Luke, my boy...where are you...?*'

CHAPTER EIGHTEEN
*** SAVING BRIDGET ***

In the run-down house just off Portobello Road, in his lonely little room, Izaak was locked in front of his monitor. The remaining cones that graced the cheap bookshelf in the alcove of his hovel had been glowing in a florid orange light as they detected faint signals (brain waves perhaps), from one of their ancient outposts – for there was still a faint link with the outer world; the so called "spirit world", which they, the star-people had invented, primarily as a means of communication before they had aborted their mission on earth several millennia since.

The flickering set oscillated in a confusion of wavelengths, occasionally granting its sole viewer a tantalising glimpse into another world. That other world was the arcane dimension of Ancient time that was adjacent to the lost dimension of Nethertime.

Isaak had kept abreast of the many developments caused by his little trick with the cone Molly had planted, putting together the picture from his intermitant signals.

Now, however, there came an urgent message from the star man whom Isaak thought he may have had some dealings with in the past as he scanned the airwaves like a sort od dimensional hacker.

'Isaak!' Joruck's voice brought the old man sitting up to attention. Isaak...I need your help!'

Joruck was in some sort of dwelling, small and cluttered, not dissimilar to his own as Isaak replied 'I copy...Isaak here...' even as he spoke he saw a woman, whom he identified as Jock's wife, Bridget, laid out on what could only be described as a bed, surrounded by a variety of futuristic equipment.

'I need help, Joruck spoke solemnly, 'I am going to separate the heads of two joined foetuses by laser surgery, but I need a map of the human genome, the whole genetic blueprint of mankind...So that I can effect a healing program...'

'But the genome hasn't been mapped yet,' Isaak said breathlessly...scientists are still trying to puzzle it out...'

'Well,' Joruck scratched his bald head, then said, 'you will have to scroll through into the future...I see you have the cones. Link up four of them in parallel and you should be able to download from future databases. You have an hour...I won't need the map until then...Can you do it? A life here depends on it...no three lives!'

'It sounds impossible' Isaak replied 'So little time to ...'

'Just try!' Joruck snapped as he bent over Bridget, his brow creased up in a deep furrow of concentration as the picture faded.

Isaak did as he was bid, repositioning the cones so that the monitor showed images of future events that were happening in the lost dimension of Nethertime. They were too quick to watch, but he recorded them and would play them later. Now though, he had to find the map, the blueprint of life that had only recently been discovered, never mind decoded. It would have been useful of Joruck could have given him a date!

Isaak came out of the Nethertime / Ancient time programme and shifted back to his own time as the cones scrolled through the future. Endless images of events, some good, some bad, like a rapid-action news bulletin flashed across the monitor until Isaak's eyes grew weary and the beginning of a migraine started to cloud his vision. Something flashed before the screen that could be promising. Isaak stopped the scroller and replayed the video in reverse pausing it on a diagram.

'The map of Life' the title read, it was from a book or some newspaper. Isaak didn't bother to find out. 'The key of the genome, unlocked' it was subtitled. Under it was the most complex diagram Isaak had even seen. There was no doubt this was it, and though it meant nothing to him, Isaak's migraine increased and his fingers trembled on the keypad as he held the image on pause and repositioned the cones to how he remembered them, in order to reconnect with Joruck.

At last a tenuous connection was established.

'Joruck' Isaak spoke into the microphone, 'I am sending you the map now. I am sending you the diagram of the human genome...If I do not hear from you, I will assume you have got it...I must go now...I have to lie down...I'm not well. Good luck with the operation. I pray it will be a success!' Isaak switched the set to receive only, and keyed in the screen saver that was of slow moving geometric shapes - a lot more soothing for his aching eyes.

As the migraine attack pursued it course, Isaak's restless mind went through the plethora of tumbling images of the future, the future of Nethertime, which he had been privy to recently via his futuristic paraphernalia. There was one image in particular, which had stuck in his mind. It was of two girls endowed with beautiful blonde hair. They were involved in some sort of power struggle in the future, some sort of battle, and they were flying through the air, communicating to each without speaking - *they were telepathic!*

Chapter Nineteen
*** Descent Into Hell ***

Luke's consciousness returned as he travelled on the ether, feeling a sense of exhilaration, for he was sure that he had locked onto Ishtar; he could sense her presence growing stronger as the matrix of time/space flew by and he returned to Nethertime.

The miasmic swirling of bright silvery particles that enveloped him as he travelled through space and time, fixed his landfall by some means borne of instinct, like the instinct of a mariner in a strange sea navigating in the fog, unseeing, yet all knowing. Frozen to the marrow, Luke made a dead reckoning calculation, and then gripping the amulets between his white knuckles, kicked, and dived down out of the ether as a vast desert plain became apparent below him.

'Target at twelve O'clock' he muttered to himself as he accelerated down from the upper air and saw the minuscule figure of Ishtar astride a jagged rock, which protruded from the sweep of the endless desert dunes below. He was getting the mastery of this arcane art, and beginning to like it!

As he descended, he glimpsed the seething inferno of the burning forest, capped by the spectacular explosions from the crater of the volcano as large rocks and flames belched up into the distant sky.

Ishtar saw his imminent arrival and rose, her white gown and long black hair flowing out in the disturbed air that swept up in flurries of heat waves from the crucified valley below.

'Oh...behold the time traveller of all time!' she shouted up into the morning air, her taunts blow away on the thermals as Luke slowed his descent until he trod air, getting the hang of the blue faience Ankh amulets which repelled, or controlled, time/space. 'Have we finally learned to travel...well done my courtesan of the narrow ways...but you have a way to go before you can match me...'

Luke had controlled his descent and his confidence had gathered as he approached the rock on which his baiter, the temptress of his body and duplicitous monger of souls, stood. As he watched, transfixed in a moment of time, he saw Ishtar's eyes dilate, then crackle with an inner fire of hatred which seethed in intertwining convulsions of green light to envelope his body and smash the amulets which he held into smithereens. His flight path was in ruins and he fell helplessly into the sand dune below the jagged rock, hearing the inhuman cackle of the enchantress's laughter as a black void of powerlessness overtook his senses.

Struggling to reassert his will over this mocking trickster, Luke struggled in the shifting loose sand but he lost his footing and was carried down to the base of the sand dune as it avalanched, whilst he tried to claw his way to the surface.

As the sand fall stopped and his senses slowly returned, Luke looked up into the bright blue sky of the morning and the grim realisation dawned on him...it was only his head that projected from the slope; the rest of his body was buried in the sand and rendered inert, ineffective; he was trapped!

Luke looked up to the jagged rock atop the massive dune, but it was a silent witness to his arrogance only; Ishtar was gone. Then from the other side he smelt the aroma of her perfume, she was behind him, her breathing punctuating the eerie silence of the desert.

'So Master Luke,' Ishtar whispered as she approached, 'we have learned to astral travel...yet we have not learnt to be cautious...or to be clever enough not to lock horns with a Goddess.'

'Goddess!' Luke spat, 'You are no Goddess...you are the trumped up little bastard of a seducer of women...you are phlegm in the mouths of the Gods!'

'Oh,' Ishtar clicked her tongue, 'it would appear that we have been practising our invective as well.' Her body loomed over Luke, casting a shadow across his face as he looked up at her divine form, her tunic and cloak revealing tantalising glimpses of her beautiful body; could this enrapturing female really be his executrix?

'Lust, my little child,' Ishtar splayed out her legs so that all he could see was the dementing cradle of her womanhood, the thrusting curve of her mound of Venus with its central cleft, now thrown into high contrast by the angled morning sunlight. 'For even buried up to your neck in the sand, you still feel lust for me, do you not? Ishtar taunted.

'I hate you!' Luke shouted. 'I hate and despise you for your feminine wiles, and I will see you dead, and rot in hell...'

'Now, now,' Ishtar played with her victim, as a cat plays with a mouse, and as she bent over him, the seat of her femininity so close to his face that the stench of her inner perfume caused him to hyperventilate, and - although cursing himself for it - he felt his desire for her rise, buried as he was in this unyielding prison of the sand.

'Come with me!' Ishtar urged, 'be my lover, be my Prince...and together we shall be Rulers of the Cosmos! We shall resurrect the cult and we shall be infinite!

Her madness was palpable as Ishtar bent over him and gradually an idea formed in Luke's mind. She had the power to smash him, kill him now, any satanic way she chose - yet she still thought that her powers of womanhood could enchant him – and perhaps she was right. Luke decided to play a very dangerous game; really he had no other option.

'You want *me*?' he asked incredulously, and it was not entirely a subterfuge.

'I have always wanted you.' Ishtar whispered as she squatted in front of his face and Luke smelt the heady odour of her passion.

'Take me then!' Luke whispered 'take me up into your body, you Goddess of eternal night, and let us fly through the ether like we did before, let us consummate our love in the four corners of the universe so that our beings are one...'

'Luke,' Ishtar's lips were upon his, 'Luke my darling child, do you *mean* it...do you *love* me?'

'I love you like I have never loved another woman!' Luke said, and that much was true, as he wrestled with reality and deception. 'Let us fly up into the ether again my Goddess and then we will rule over whatever or whosoever falls to our domain!' (this latter was a total lie)

'Come.' Ishtar lifted Luke out of the sand as a mother picks up a child, and held him in her demon grip as their corporeal bodied left the ground and soared up back onto the ethereal plane; their raiment was cast asunder and their bodies became locked in the wildest, most spectacular display of carnal lust that it is possible, yet not permitted to describe!

Worlds went by, planets spun around their orbits and asteroids and shooting stars crashed to earth as they travelled in the glittering white milk of the ether. Their respective passions were assuaged and gelled into one as the cosmos shook to this unholy engagement.

'*Forever!*' Ishtar shouted in satanic hysteria as she climaxed again and again, '*for eternity!*'

'For eternity.' Luke whispered into her burning ear, yet eternity for him meant one thing...the damnation of her craven soul!

Their respective passions were finally assuaged and the entwined lovers fell to earth as Ishtar guided them down into a lush oasis. Gently she lay down the body of her phantom lover in a pool of tepid green water as Luke determined to resurrect his mind towards the downfall of this passionate devil, who played so well, the part of an angel.

'This is a good place to recover' Ishtar murmured as she nibbled Luke's ear. 'It is called the Oasis of Ishtar and was dedicated to me when I was a child. It is isolated, secret and above all, empowered to do my bidding...welcome home!

Luke lay in the lustrous waters, hearing the song of the hoopoe in the enveloping branches of the jacaranda tree, whilst the fronds of the palms and acacia gently swished, enveloping the secret pool of the oasis in a cool shade. Ishtar came to him after a while, a smile of sweet serenity about her lovely face as she fed her new conquest dates and orange segments, holding a wooden gourd to his lips as he imbibed the sensuous- tasting arak and he felt the press of her distended breasts against his chest.

'Did you ever think it could be so good?' Ishtar whispered, her fragrance overwhelming him as his emotions vacillated between love and hate. 'Could you ever envisage a more perfect, pleasurable act?'

Luke lay back in the warm waters, eating and drinking the proffered food and drink as Ishtar caressed his body with her own and he looked into those dark fathomless eyes and saw a longing, a love which she, arch-devil that she was, needed above anything else.

'This is your weakness, my good lady,' he whispered so low that Ishtar frowned slightly, not catching the hidden menace which was secreted in his voice; for Luke was good at playing games, and this game, the ultimate game of deceit, in which life and death were the stakes, he was going to play to the bitter end.

'I want you again' Ishtar whispered, pouring arak into Luke's mouth, setting down the platter and cup on the lush grass of the oasis bank. Squatting in a primitive posture and squeezing herself down onto his ever-aroused manhood, she gripped his responsive flesh and transfixed herself in an ecstasy of fulfilment, pushing his long blond locks away from his forehead. The hoopoe called out from the high jacaranda tree and the palms swished across the jade green waters of the pool as they made love, again and again. Luke felt his body being taken over, in absolute subservience to this beautiful demon-incarnate, until their passion culminated and was carried up to the surface of the oasis pool, there to disperse in a silvery stream of rivulets as they lay in each other's arms until the sun started its decline towards the impending night.

They slept there, locked together in the warm torrid waters of the pool and Luke dreamt of how he could have done things differently: how he could have resisted the charms of the exotic creature who consumed him with a passion beyond his control as she cradled him like a mother. He could have finished her right here, killed her whilst she slept - as he could have prevented her from ever being born in the disturbed tangle of emotions he had endured as he wrestled with conflicting feelings for her mother, Yasmine. Yet would he have ever have known such bliss like this?

But the realisation was never far from his waking mind that he had no choice. He had been buried in the sand dune, an easy target. She could have killed him easily, yet she chose to reveal her love, her passion for him, and had instead of slaughtering him, shown him an exquisite ecstasy that he felt even now as he moved inside her; the smell of the heady spice of her flesh even now inflaming his loins, forced him to realise that he was not just her prisoner, but more alarmingly, that he was her prisoner of *love...and a willing one*!

All the trauma, worry and feelings of loyalty towards his parents were rendered as naught, even though he tried unconsciously to resurrect them. They were nothing and of no value as he held this devil-woman tight, and relapsed into a long sickness of lust where only the moment of his union into her flesh mattered.

Though Ishtar slept, Luke's body moved inside her as one possessed as he flagellated himself with the guilt of his failed mission - to kill this otherworldly being – until his spent passion told him (and he could not now deny it), that he was taken over; whatever she wanted from him, he would do her bidding, and wherever she went, he would follow – he was a man possessed!

The sky was incarnadined in a rosy glow as the clouds, low on the horizon, reflected the volcano's last belch of fire and Luke's passion, like the fiery phenomenon taking place just below their horizon told him that he was null and void, his cherished dreams of revenge, damned for eternity; he had sold out!

The ensuing night was a lost slot in time as Ishar and Luke rode on the chariot of Eros and the oasis was awash with the sound and the smell of passion - even the nightingale in the jacaranda tree was hushed into silence; no one was listening.

'Come.' Ishtar said, stepping out of the warm murky waters of the oasis. 'Let me show you our kingdom!'

The eye of the dawn had broken through the membrane of night, and the last stars extinguished by the light encircling the heavens. Ishtar rose up like the Goddess Nut from the waters of creation and donned her costume, replacing the emblem of the silver crescent moon on her tousled lustrous black hair; then she reached out a hand and drew up the bemused youth from the limpid waters. Luke stepped naked onto the bank, his body was bruised and aching; his mind was awhirl, remembering, though only in fragments, the long evening and night of their lovemaking.

'You will need some new clothes, my Emperor' Ishtar jested in a way that the exhausted youth found strange. But, yes, of course, this little temptress was well satisfied, and even had a glint in her eye and a smile on her face.

'I am all right as I am, aren't I?' Luke asked.

'No' Ishtar retorted. 'I do not want anybody else looking at your lovely body...it belongs to me!'

'Very well' Luke agreed, his voice docile; he did not feel disposed to argue, though a memory of some previous commitment hammered on his brain.

Ishtar uttered a guttural command and a nearby fallen palm was graced suddenly with various garments. The enchantress selected a black and white striped tunic and a pair of yellow trousers, a pair of sandals and a rope belt. 'Try these on,' she said affably enough.

'How do you do that?' Luke asked as he dressed 'are you a conjuror as well as an astral traveller.

'I am a supreme being' Ishtar corrected, 'I can do anything, in any dimension I want...but don't forget this is my oasis and near to where I was born...It holds for me, big magic!'

'But you are the daughter of Labachi and that poor woman, Yasmine' Luke stated flatly; there was a hidden dimension here, though he smiled at the pun as he thought of it.

'I am not the daughter of Labachi, as you so impolitely put it, and Yasmine!' Ishtar rose to her full height as she levelled Luke with those dark, satanic eyes that flashed their menace, so mercurially transformed from the eyes of love - eyes that mesmerised him as much as her perfumed body - to dark liquid pools of hate.

'What?' Luke exclaimed, bewildered now,

'No!' Ishtar fixed him with a stare similar to that of a praying mantis about to devour its mate after copulation.

'I am the daughter of the *Esoteric Oracle* and Yasmine!'

'What?' Luke repeated himself ineffectually. 'What do you mean...?'

A blind panic was beginning to burn into his brain. Hypnotised, taken over by the spell of the enchantress, the seducer, as she was now, Luke's mind recoiled in shock at this grotesque revelation.

'Labachi was a pawn,' Ishtar fixed Luke with her eyes, bright as black diamonds in the ascent of the morning sun. 'He was only the vehicle, the illusion in human form of the Esoteric Oracle. His seed was implanted in my dear mother, Yasmine as it was in many around this region and in other parts...'

'You mean there are *more!*' Luke dropped to his knees as the terrifying light of day blinded his reason. 'You mean that the Oracle has planted his seed across the globe...'

'Don't be so tearful, my love,' Ishtar knelt at the distraught youth's side, 'it is not something to regret, but something to nurture...for it means we have a Kingdom, you and I. We have a flock of followers who await our call...and together, we shall rule!'

'We shall rule!' Luke arose in Ishtar's arms, embracing the prospects of dominion over the children of a satanic clan, as he played his role as dupe. For this recent catastrophic revelation had shocked Luke out of the enchantress' spell - his mind was back and his original plans were regrouping. That the Oracle's seed had proliferated the planet was a nightmare beyond comprehension and Luke struggled to keep from vomiting so as to pursue his disguise of the bewitched.

'We shall unite the others' Ishtar murmured into his ear, as Luke fought her smell, the smell that was the key to her enchantment, with every ounce of will he could muster.

'Yes my love!' he replied, faking his fawning obedience. His will was back!

'You look, much better my Prince' Ishtar cooed, brushing his unruly hair with her long fingernail, yet unaware of Luke's resurgence of will.

'Thank you, my beloved' Luke smile at her, his confidence now in the ascendant as he steeled himself to keep up this act.

'So, you are the descendant of the Oracle.' Luke mused nonchalently, impressed at his ability to carry off this bluff.

'I am his principal daughter,' Ishtar shook her lustrous dark hair, as if to reinforce the point, 'Ishtar...Daughter of the stars!'

'Daughter of the decadent star people!' Luke was remembering Joruck's revelations, but he was also blowing his cover.

'What?' Ishtar spun around to face Luke, her pleated tunic and skirts a dazzle of whiteness belying her black purpose.

'Didn't they tell you,' Luke, though wanting to play dead, couldn't help himself, 'Labachi, or is it the Oracle now...didn't they tell you how they came into being...that the cult is no more than the dregs of a perfidious and decadent sect who were abandoned here by the star people when they left this planet, having given up on their attempts at civilising the human race.'

'How can you say *that*!' Ishtar faced Luke, her breasts heaving and an ugly flush stealing across her face. 'How dare you say *that*! You know nothing of the true story of the One Dimension...of its aims and beliefs....But you will learn!...By the inverted ankh of the spectral void, you will learn it, as will *your children*!' Ishtar's venom spat out across Luke's face as she transfixed him with her fathomless, obsidian eyes.

'*My what*?' Luke spluttered, '*Did you say my children*!'

'Your seed is within me and has taken root' Ishtar seized Luke's hand and pressed it to her belly. 'Do you feel them grow? your seed in me, I who art of the Oracle, ergo, *the Oracle lives in me*!' Ishtar's eyes looked straight through her lover as he slumped to the ground, retching onto the sand, his lips performing a litany of self-contempt.

'What have I done...what have I done...forgive me...forgive me...'

***

Joruck emerged from his quarters; his hair was straggly and damp with sweat. Ringing his hands in a strange gesture of remorse, he climbed up the rock-hewn stairs to join Jock and the others as they looked onto the volcanic onslaught in its last throws of mesmerising activity.

'What news?' Jock turned to face the wisened little man who held the power of life and death in his alien hands. 'Tell me now, tell me the worst...'

'There is no worst' Joruck replied evenly, his face lightening into what could be described as a smile 'there is no bad news' I have performed the surgical task and separated the foetuses, and the mother is recovering. It will take time, a little time, but mother and babies are out of risk...'

'Praise be to God!' Jock stepped away from the parapet and embraced the exhausted-looking surgeon. 'Thank the Lord, and thank you, my friend' Jock seized the star-man by the head and kissed him repeatedly on both cheeks, if I live one hundred years, I will not stop thanking you enough...'

'You will live until you are ninety three' Joruck replied, detaching himself from the strong grasp of the human, 'and you will see your daughters born, and their children...you will in fact be a grandfather!'

'What?' Jock released the little old man recoiling in horror. 'You can see that...me, a Grandfather?' Jock's countenance resembled that of a man reprieved from a life sentence. 'I hope you are right, dear friend' Jock exclaimed, 'now can I see the proud mother, my wife!'

'No' Joruck raised his hands, 'she needs to rest. I have put her and her twins on a resuscitation program and she and they will be healed internally in a matter of hours, but she needs quiet...please leave her to recuperate for now!'

'Very well maestro.' Jock agreed, his eyes over-brimming with relief.

'There is one thing I must say to you.' Joruck spoke solemnly

'What is that?' Jock asked anxiously,

'The twins which will be born to you will be very special. Because they have accessed shared brain waves in the formation of their minds and bodies, they will be of the one will.'

The one will?' Jock reiterated 'Ah yes...telepathic, you have said as much.'

'Telepathic and more.' Joruck added mysteriously.

'So be it' Jock replied, 'and I thought you were going to give me bad news.' He hurried back to the others who were looking anxiously on at the recent interchange and told them the good news, and a cheer broke out from those on the overlook; even Mimi with her babies seemed to understand as she whooped for joy.

'Master Joruck,' Jock called down to the tired old man who was about to turn in for the night, although it was day, 'could I just have a word?'

The star-man walked back heavily up the stairs to join the gathering on the overlook, his eyes were creased with fatigue, and lines of rigour moved across his furrowed forehead, 'what is it?' he asked.

'The Zalks have lost their homeland, and I feel it is I who am partially to blame.'Jock stated the obvious

'I wonder if you would have any ideas as to how to relocate them.' Jock added lamely, his voice tailing off as he looked at the exhausted star-man.

'You do have a habit of asking my people to solve your problems, don't you!' Joruck replied, though his voice was absent of malice.

'Do they wish to return to the stars?' he asked ingenuously enough. Zalkina interpreted, as the Zalks went into a frenzy of horror and Mimi jumped up and down clutching her brood.

'I will take that as a no,' Joruck deduced, a spasm of knotted muscles moving across his bald pate, 'very well, let me devise a location.'

He moved up to the overlook and looked down onto the smouldering remnants of the forest.

'Do you wish to go to another domain or were you happy where you were?' he asked Zalkina, who put it to the Zalks.

'Where you were.' Joruck got the answer. 'Very well, let me see what I can do!' his tired body almost creaked as he walked wearily down the steps to his habitat and emerged presently carrying a dish-like antennae. Positioning it on the overlook, the other's looking on in interest, he spun the dish and checked its polarity.

'The web of reconstruction.' he muttered to himself, as he plotted the direction and tapped a dial.

'First,' he said, 'we need to seal up the volcano.'

'Smirtin, my muscular friend, would you be so good as to cap that geo-thermal monstrosity, I think it has done its job rather well.'

'Yes Sir, Master Joruck Sir!' Smirtin stood to attention, 'I will seal it up sir, but how?'

'Ah' Joruck said. 'Sorry, but I cannot carry the damn thing, its in my little quarters down there; Orange contraption, you can't miss it...'

'Get it Sir, at the double Sir!' Smirtin leaped down the dozen or so stairs in one giant leap and was in and out the star-man's headquarters in less time than it takes to tell, carrying the sister of the laser-cannon cylinder as if it were a babe in arms up to the overlook.

'Tripod out sir' Smirtin did in without orders, such was his enthusiasm with the star-people's arsenal as he positioned and sighted the weapon; Joruck pushed back a wisp of white hair, stunned by the efficiency of this legendary Genie.

'Ready to fire on your command, General!' Smirtin stood to attention, his massive hand at a salute (this he had learned from the actor fellow), as a smile spread across the faces of Jock, Ogadile and Errol; the Zalks, however, backed away, a certain reverence towards this enormous man never far from their minds - they didn't realise it was just a campy act.

'Take aim...and fire' Joruck ordered, disguising a self satisfied grin at being called General when in fact he was only a technician of the lower order; he didn't realise he was being sent up. On the command 'Fire' Smirtin depressed the lock override and the trigger fired, releasing a hail of light bolts that hissed out of the rotary laser cannon and headed straight towards the volcano.

As they found their target, the phazar-beams melted the remaining crust of the rim, and the rock was pulverised into liquid molten flux that collapsed inwards and then upwards. Spewing larva was congealed; the ventilation shafts of fuelling air sealed under a million tons of semi-liquid rock that fused into a core, thus plugging the main vent.

As the pressure built up inside the volcano, a few small peripheral shafts vented upwards, but Smirtin damned these with a precise small burst of fire and the volcano grumbled underground as if in constipation, emitting groans of dissent and a few non-threatening tremors that raged around the base of the fire mountain. Yet the terrain held, and in a few minutes the monstrous fire-spirit was subdued, returning whence it had been awakened, possibly to find a new vent many miles away.

A cry rang around the overlook as the Zalks cheered Smirtin who could not but hide a massive grin at his new found skills as an artillery officer.

'Gunner of the ranks! Well done my old friend' Jock congratulated the beaming Genie.

'Good aim.' Joruck appropriated an over-large flagon of Zabib from mid air, and poured drinks into rapidly appearing goblets. Those on the terrace took mighty swigs of the firewater, the Zalks chattering animatedly and looking up at Smirtin in some sort of totem worship.

'My work is done for the day, and I bid you goodnight,' Joruck said wearily, though not before taking a long swig of the date distillate liquor.

'Hang on a minute,' Jock caught the patchwork leather sleeve of the star-man, 'didn't you mention something about restoration...the ruddy forest down there is still burning!'

'Ah.' Joruck sighed, returning yet again to the overlook. 'I'm sorry, yes I did promise, didn't I?' He turned to the dish antennae and directed it at the lower slopes of the now dormant volcano.

'Smirtin?' The exhausted old man asked, and the giant leapt to his side 'this little job is not so spectacular...Could you keep rotating this dish to cover the slope of the former forest. It should work, but if it gives you any trouble, kick it! Joruck turned once more to the steps; his eyelids were like an avalanche ready to happen, his voice as from another planet, so to speak, as he declared: 'Comrades, I bid you goodnight, once more...'

As the weary alien retired to his quarters at long last, Smirtin directed the antennae projecting the web of reconstruction with one hand, and putting a great deal of damage into the large flagon of zabibe with the other, Errol coughing periodically and signalling for his goblet to be recharged.

'Swinging this little gismo backwards and forwards is not quite as interesting as knocking great holes into that fire-breathing mountain.' The giant Genie observed, grabbing Errol's hand as he upped the flagon of drink into his cup for the fourth time, 'now it is your turn to do something useful for humanity, for once in your miserably little life.'

Errol felt the crush of Smirtin's hand on his and did not argue, swinging the dish diligently. The large flagon of Zabib was being depleated at a rate of knots, the tribesmen helping in no mean degree and quickly becoming inebriated as they watched their little kingdom becoming refoliated almost on the embers of the recently cooled larva flow. New shoots sprung up from the charred ground and from their distant vantage point they saw the base of the mountain become once more clothed in green.

'Big Magic!' Zalkine stated the obvious, dicing with death as his puny hand sort to redirected Smirtin's pouring of the firewater into his own flagon.

'I hope you will be able to explain this to your wife and daughters in the morning' Smirtin cautioned the old chief as he topped him up.

'This is morning' Zalkine stated as Zalkina frowned in disapproval.

Soon the forest and the jungle below had become as of old, and Smirtin switched off the dish, though a frown of puzzlement crossed his brow.

'I wonder,' he said, pointing the dish at Errol, 'if it can do that to nature, what can it do to old friends...do you fancy losing a few of those facial lines and removing the bags under your eyes?'

'Stop it, you ape,' Errol covered his face, 'these lines are fine lines...they add character...a certain look of one in command...'

'The only command you will ever get,' Ogadile chirped in, 'would be as master of ceremonies to a troupe of geriatric camels.' A peel of laughter echoed around the overlook and Mimi and her clinging brood jumped up and down screeching applause; then they realised, she was holding an empty goblet - how many more had she emptied?

A certain expression came over the face of the baboon as she looked up at Errol, hiccuping profusely. Then she cantered along the ground, her babies clinging to her fur as she leapt up from the ground and seized the failed actor around the neck, planting a series of kisses on the bemused man's mouth.

'Errol!' Ogadile exclaimed, 'after many wanderings and false starts, you have finally found your ideal woman!'

Smirtin slapped his thigh sending the Zalks into retreat again and collapsed onto the ground as his peels of deep laughter vibrated around the overlook. Errol reached for his scimitar intent of striking of the head of the man who showed him so much contempt. But Mimi was not about to be upstaged and she covered the actor's face in great salivating kisses; then Errol looked into her ardent eyes and saw only undying love...perhaps Ogadile *was* right!

CHAPTER TWENTY
*** SATAN'S LOSS ***

Luke lay cradled in the arms of Ishtar. The sun had passed its zenith and was declining into the western sky as the shady bower of palms, acacia and the giant jacaranda tree threw a web of shadow over the desert glade and the beasts and birds of the oasis habitat were quiet; all was siesta.

Luke woke, and disengaged himself from his lover, looking in disgust at his new set of clothes, cast off in a moment of passion and now lying in a crumpled heap – the Emperor's new clothes! The long night and early morning of passion hung like a limp memory as he felt his body ache with the residue of their carnality. As he stood over her, looking at her beautiful form, tears brimmed on his eyes as he remembered her last words.

'The Oracle lives in me...' she had said it as if to beguile him further into her web. Was it not enough that the passion he felt for her and had regaled her with in their all-night lovemaking was to be the precursor of her new Order? For he knew that she was stronger, much stronger than himself. Was it that she had inherited some cursed gene from her father – or was it the Oracle – did it really matter? He knew he was still under her spell as her sleeping body gave off her distinctive aroma that gilded his loins even as he stood over her in hatred.

Luke unsheathed the blade from his discarded clothes and knelt down in the soft sand of the oasis floor, his long blond hair falling across his forehead as he bent over his satanic mistress; he would stop this now, end this madness. Luke's finger caressed the sharp blade, drawing blood as he held it to Ishtar's throat. One cut, one slash, and his seed would be aborted, this abomination of the future would be null and void. His hand trembled as he steeled himself to do the deed, to finish off the last mortal carrier of the scourge that had corrupted this planet for thousands of years.

Then her words came back to him...they were others: carriers of the satanic seed, the rejects of the cosmos, the fruit of the devil in the Oracle's offspring, who awaited Ishtar's call to arms...what of them? He could not hope to find them or to kill them all! As his hand wavered before the life-severing slash across her sleeping throat, he reasoned with himself. Surely he had to continue with the pretence a little longer until she had mustered the other aliens, the cult of the decadent star-people. Once she had gathered them together, as had been done at Aiyu and the Lost City; then would be the time for the cull. Not now, but later...he must await the final denouement!

' My Love.' Ishtar stirred, feeling the wetness of Luke's tears fall onto her face as he hid the knife and bent over her.

'Love of my life.' Luke awoke her with the gentlest kiss he could muster as his body shook in a suppression of hatred for her, which was once more subsumed into the carnal desire for the woman that he could not resist.

'Come,' Ishtar threw off his advances as she rose, resplendent and refreshed, 'we have business to do. We have to call the followers to our cause...we have to forge our empire!'

Ishtar washed in the now clear pool of the oasis and dressed, combing her long lustrous black hair with a lapis lazuli comb, golden sparks flying from the tresses, and clasped it with her silver crescent moon hairband. Her pleated white tunic she slipped over her thrusting bosom, her muscular body performing an anatomical impossibility: to arch backwards in a witchery of abnormal curvature and touch her hands to the sand; then to perform a backwards cartwheel, her long, shapely legs swishing close to the enthralled youth's face. Any slight hopes Luke may have had as to her human origins were dashed by this display of supernatural contortion; there was no disputing it - she was an alien, goddess or not.

Ishtar strode up from the oasis to the rock-strewn crest of the ridge where they had landed and surveyed the surrounding landscape.

Luke joined her, looking out onto this land of conquest: the conquest of the damned. 'Where are we?' He asked, as a child asks its mother.

'We are at the gates of a new dawn' Ishtar replied ambiguously. 'But let us proceed with caution until we find our kind...Are you armed?'

'Only with this.' Luke pulled out the serrated dagger with which only a few moments ago he was contemplating cutting her throat.

'You could file your nails with it, I suppose,' Ishtar mocked; unaware of the deadly use the keen blade had nearly been put to.

They set off down the ridge, the escarpment of sand and stone boulders making difficult walking, Luke lagging behind his athletic and supernaturally empowered mistress, seeing in the distance a cluster of monuments.

'Couldn't we fly' Luke asked, feeling the sharp rocks tear through the fragile sandals he wore as his feet grew warm with the flow of blood.

'No' Ishtar replied 'we cannot fly now...we are only a few miles from our objective and if we astral travelled, we would overshoot by miles, perhaps hundreds of miles...or lose our dimension'

'Is this the right dimension?' Luke asked as he lagged behind his queen and the rocks still tore at his feet.

'It is the only dimension I will countenance' Ishtar threw the words contemptuously over her shoulder, as her high rope sandals avoided the abrasions of the flints that littered the path.

Finally, after coming down from the high escarpment and into the dried up riverbed, a wadi that afforded them hard sand upon which to walk, they gained the sanctuary of a cluster of mud-brick dwellings, grouped around a temple of outstanding magnitude, its pylons thrusting up into the fiery sky of sunset.

'My palace...My people...My flock' Ishtar murmured, and Luke followed like a lapdog, rehearsing his hatred for her whilst trying to repel the aphrodisiac effect of her oil of lotus perfume, his split personality on the brink of regression, once again.

Ishtar strode into the hamlet, the western sun gleaming low over the range of desert hills and glinting on her crescent moon emblem. As the dwellers of this primitive desert enclave rushed out from their hovels, bowing in obeisance to this Goddess who had walked out of the vast wilderness of the eastern desert, they whispered to each other about the day for which they had waited so long: their Queen was amongst them; she had come – a miracle!

Then a silence descended upon the place and Luke felt nodules of fear move up and down his spine; for these lowly peasants were venerating their patriarch, their Queen, but understood nothing about her true purpose: her desire to dominate and subvert them into her own kind: worshippers of the devil!

'Ishtar' her name was recounted in numerous hushed voices as the 'holy' woman walked past them and up to her temple. As Ishtar walked below the high gates of the pylons of the forbidden temple, the villagers congregated at the outermost markers of the avenue of sphinx. They watched in awe as she passed into the forecourt of the temple, followed by the strange tall youth of flaxen hair, and a cry went up from the people; a shrill, ululating, wailing call of recognition as they saw their votive Goddess take charge of her abandoned temple.

'It is Ishtar...It is Ishtar,' the chant rose up into the sky as the sun set below the serrated dunes of the western desert and a yellow full moon rose from the eastern mountains, that becase of the domed house in front of it made it seem like a crescent moon, only inverted; an augury of doom.

'Ishtar is here, Ishtar is amongst us...her mascot rides the skies...it is a sign, a portent!'

The Goddess incarnate walked up to a throne-like chair in the centre of the courtyard, its eroded limestone carvings of strange feline forms catching the last gleam of the afterglow as Ishtar seated herself on the ancient monument sacred to Bastet, the great cat Goddess. Her followers, gathering nerve, proceeded up along the avenue of sphinx to squat or prostrate themselves as they beheld their Mother Goddess, benefactor to their ancient creed, take her rightful seat, whilst the blond haired, blue-eyed devil, her love-slave, stood silently behind her throne.

Luke stood as still as the granite plinth the chair was situated on, awed by the flock of wide-eyed local people who came into the courtyard, kneeling or sitting in hushed reverence as more arrived on camels and donkeys, or on foot from the surrounding hamlets scattered around this ancient temple. Luke looked around the enclosed walls of the courtyard, seeing large carvings thereon: all various representations of the Cat Goddess, Bastet. Many were of her in human form, giving succour to an infant, or the infirm, (the archetypical maternal benefactor of the poor and needy), yet in each portrayal, the Goddess was graced by the cats head.

Luke knew that the cult of Bastet, which emerged in the city of Bubastis in the delta of Ancient Eygpt, was linked to the worship of the cat goddess long before Christianity was formed. Each province or nome, had its own cult, and sometimes these anthropomorphic deities had become very complex, subsuming aspects of the other deities until it appeared, the very people themselves were not sure which one, or ones they were worshipping. This was to the advantage of the high priests of course, who used the ignorance of the local people and their inherent superstition, to subdue them and harness them to their own purposes, which was not always to do with religion but more a battle of survival in the power struggles of the elite hierarchy of the priesthood.

Somehow, perhaps in the minds of these lowly peasants, there was an association between Ishtar and Bastet, though, Luke thought sardonically, that it didn't much matter, for this was not ancient Egypt they were in, but a copy of it. This artificial world was a clever cloning of ancient Egypt, a manufactured dimension existing somewhere in Nethertime with one express purpose in mind: the recruitment of neophytes, new blood to be indoctrinated into the order of the One Dimension or whatever cult the alien polymorth, the Esotric Oracle had dreamt up with his mastery over the souls of men; these new recruits would become slaves of the damned!

Another thought that played uneasily on Luke's mind as he watched the multitude of local people pay their homage and move on to allow others to do the same, was, where were the priests? Surely, if Ishtar's purpose was to resurrect the cult from the scattered seed of the Esoteric Oracle as she had postulated, then these lowly people were only the fodder, not the feeders ...so where were they?

Then Luke remembered a book he had read on the Adamites, the medieval heretics or so-called Brothers of the Free Spirit, who had believed that they could hide their libertine beliefs, which were punishable by death by the Orthodox Church, within the disguise of orthodoxy.

They had encoded their devotional paintings above altarpieces and the like in secret messages pertaining to their libidinous practices, like a cult within a cult. Perhaps their methods might afford some clue to these questions posed in the carvings and the painted scenes that adorned the walls of this vast, gloomy temple; the answer to this would have to wait for a more opportune time through.

That time came after the last pilgrim had left, an old woman who had asked Ishtar's blessing to be called down on her family who were without food and shelter. Ishtar had given it, as she had in a stereotyped monologue, called on the Gods to propitiate in granting health and good fortune. Her tone had become increasingly monotonous and weary as she called repeatedly for the Gods to bless this sick child, that elderly relative. Irritation had replaced monotony as her true nature started to reassert itself - her fake persona was wearing a little thin - and she had called to the people outside that their goddess was tired and must rest.

Then, the gaffier or guardian of the temple, an old man, had closed the bronze gates, which were embellished with finely wrought reliefs of Bastet. The throng had dispersed and Ishtar had sighed a long sigh of relief, taking Luke's hand and leading him from the courtyard, up some steps and under the massive pylon into a vast, though gloomy hypostyle hall. As weak shafts of a fading twilight slanted randomly from the small roof windows to alleviate the murk of the of the interior, an angled ray of light struck a column here and there lending an unreal, foreboding presence to the colonnaded temple.

'It is to much,' Ishtar complained, sweeping up and down the darkened hall, her white tunic illuminated here and there by the glance of angled light emanating from the high roof windows. 'I cannot continue with this act...I am not their Goddess, I am their Ruler, and when I summon up the cult, I will be omnipotent!'

'You should rest.' Luke replied diplomatically, yet he noted that her first person singular had left him out of the equation completely. Dominion, power over others is what she craves for, Luke thought - there could never be a humanitarian word in her vocabulary or an altruistic notion in her mind; she was in effect mad!

As Ishtar stretched out on the granite slab of a giant sarcophagus in the inner sanctuary of the temple, Luke watched her hooded, almond-shaped eyelids close in fatigue as he perambulated around the massive hypostyle hall. He was searching for some clue as to the attributes of the cult goddess, the cat figure, Bastet. What nature of beast was she, and what were her powers?

The murky interior of the vast hall, punctuated here and there by the splashes of faint light, which cut across the columns in a raking, forty-five degree angle, was growing darker as Luke looked up at the walls. On them were ten feet high figures, their anthropomorphic shapes of animal heads on human bodies brought a violent shudder to Luke's spine as he sensed a preternatural presence: an innate sentience in the heiractical pictograms of some strange religion as the waning light dimmed to blackness.

'The phantoms of the unconsciousness mind,' Luke mused to himself as he walked along the walls, peering up at the gargantuan figures that leered out at him from the dark walls, their staring eyes illuminated in a green radiance whilst they tracked him, staring down malevolently so that his flesh crept and a cold sweat ran down his back.

'These are the hierophants' Luke whispered to himself. 'These are the hybrid creatures of the id,' the suppressed images of a fearful superstitious people who would never dare do what he was doing, look them straight in the eyes. So the mysteries of the cult to come where graven here, the priests that he had noticed were so lacking were here upon these forbidding walls, stored for eons in this repository of evil; dormant, waiting until their high priestess came to unlock them from their graven image and resurrect them into the world of mortals; what an ingenious idea!

'Apophis, Nut, Sekmed' Luke rolled off the Ancient Egyptian pantheon as he recognised their respective forms. 'The snake, the great sky goddess, the lion...Tauerus, the pregnant crocodile – yes he had seen the manifestation of her, albeit briefly, in the horror of Yasmine's mutation – and that was enough to convince him that these carved effigies were sentient: capable of coming to life! Horus the hawk-god who was the eyes of the four horizons of time and space, Anubis the God of the underworld in his jackal headed form,' Luke uttered his thoughts in a whisper, yet there were some which were missing!

'Where is Ra, the sun god' Luke muttered 'where is Mut and Khonsu his wife and son; they were not here!' As he searched the walls for the higher orders of the Ancient Egyptian pantheon, he drew a blank.

'Why are the Gods of the heavens, the gods of the light not here?' he intoned to himself as the puzzle began to fit into place. 'Because that is what they are,' he answered his own question, 'they are the gods of light, and here are only the lower gods, the gods of darkness, the devourers of the human soul!'

Then it dawned on him: clear as the last ray of fading light outside this blighted place. Only the lower orders of the hybrid Gods of darkness, the hierophants of an order to be, which dwelled in the lower depths of the human psyche would be portrayed here, for they were the totems of the devil-worshippers. The icons of this vile cult, which the Oracle had spawned after his ejection by the star-people, and which he had carried in his debauched mind from the far-flung regions of outer space in his mission to infiltrate this planet and indoctrinate the minds of humans - only the dark gods were here!

So these obscurant hybrids, which seemed to crawl all over the walls of this dark sinister temple, were the pawns of the Oracle and would descend from their static forms to enact their duties in the ascendancy of the cult yet to come, the spore of the decadent star-people, the banished ones! As Luke completed his tour of the hypostyle hall, his mind was pretty much satisfied that he had some idea of what the future may hold, and in this forewarned, forearmed mode, his confidence increased somewhat. Except for one factor: namely – what was the catalyst; what signal did these prenascent entities in the making require for their release into the world?

Ishtar was still asleep on the granite sarcophagus. Looking at her in this new dawning of his understanding, Luke's mind toyed once more with the idea of slitting her throat, so close, so vulnerable was it as it lay extended in her prone position; but he knew that no sooner would he approach her and inhale her smell that his loathing would turn once more to lust. He was a man torn in two, a captive of both love and hatred, for he knew that no sooner would he approach her that he would once again fall prisoner to her spell. His desire for her, aroused by her natural aroma of the blue lotus, or whatever aphrodisiac it was, was her protection, her shield against his hatred.

Rejecting, and not for the first time, the notion of killing his lover, Luke moved away from his nemesis – he had to think things through. Walking in the stygian gloom of the vast hall, he noticed then a set of spiral stairs in the corner of the hall, which on climbing led up towards the ceiling. There was an opening at the top, which let out onto the roof of the temple. Walking out onto the roof, his mind rejoiced in the purity of fresh air and he tried to shake off the feeling of apprehension that his recent preview of the demonic carvings had caused him. From his high vantage point he could see the surrounding desert and the hovels of the nearby village, quiet now after the excitement of the morning, its inhabitants having taken their siesta. Luke lay on the limestone blocks of the high pylon and smelt the fresh breeze of evening that wafted across his confused senses; then he drifted off into a deep sleep.

The light faded totally over the low sand hills of the desert and the chill of the oncoming night spread around the temple. Luke awoke and raised his body from the sun-warmed slab of the temple roof. He looked down into the stirring village as the sounds and smells of the revitalised community drifted up to him. Eddies of blue smoke rose up through the palm groves and mud-brick houses that nestled together, their occupants starting to prepare the evening meal; it was indeed a timeless scene.

Luke got up and walking along the roof, was tempted to wave at some of the people who had noticed him. But he saw them quickly hurry their children inside and shielding their faces from his gaze, went back into their hovels as he heard the doors barred and a wail like a high pitch chant go up from the women; they were obviously terrified of him.

At first he was puzzled as to why the locals should be in such fear of him until he remembered reading of some of his father's accounts of his travels. In their medieval minds, some of the remote villagers of Upper Egypt who had never seen anything of the modern world, still believed in the old folktales, the stuff of the Arabian nights, with stories of Jinns and Genies, white and black magic -look how readily they had acclaimed Ishtar as their Queen. Yet Luke, with his blond hair and blue eyes represented, not an angelic nature to them as it would in a Christian country, but the reverse. He was the epitome of evil, and it was obvious he could elicit no help from them if the time came - they would just as soon kill him out of fear and ignorance; to their minds he was a blue-eyed demon. With that chilling thought in mind, Luke retraced his footsteps, descending the stairs and looking down into virtual blackness, expecting to see the faint outline of Ishtar's white tunic - the sarcophagus was empty!

As he approached the great capping slab of mottled granite on which she had lain, he was certain he could detect the lingering fragrance of musk and lotus that bound his body - but not his soul - to the enchantress of his loins. Then he heard the sound of a woman's voice, high and clear, floating through the murk from the rear of the temple.

Luke walked slowly from the hypostyle hall, through the ambulatory and into a group of smaller buildings towards the rear – the fatal lotus fragrance getting stronger!

'Ishtar' he called and the singing stopped. 'Where are you?'

Ahead was a faint flickering band of orange light, which issued from one of the stone-built rooms and Luke thought he could hear water. Approaching the door he looked inside and saw Ishtar standing in a circular font that was filled with milk. A young boy, his saffron robe wet with the white fluid was pouring a goatskin bucket of milk over Ishtar as the burning torch in the bronze wall-grille cast an eerie flickering glow across the room, illuminating the would be Goddess's naked body in a contrast of glimmering orange light and deep shadow.

'Where have you been?' Ishtar asked and before Luke could reply she continued, 'no matter, you could not leave the sanctuary of the temple...you would be killed by the locals...It's your colouring...'

'I thought as much.' Luke said flatly

'This is Yacoup,' Ishtar announced, 'he is the grandson of the gaffir, the Guardian...I am getting ready for my people.' She spoke to the boy in a rapid dialect that Luke did not understand, whilst he watched her exquisite beauty accentuated by the guttering wall torch as she craned her head backwards to rinse out her hair from a trickle of water, which dripped from a goats-bladder suspended by a hook in the ceiling.

As she arched her back in that obscene, unnatural way, her firm, upwardly tilted breasts capped by elongated black nipples formed a vivid silhouette, the trickling water rinsing the milk from her body and causing the white froth to descend in patterns to reveal the dark beauty of the brown flesh beneath. The boy and Luke stared at her, both spellbound.

The Gaffir, or custodian of the temple, passed by the doorway carrying a large bronze tray laden with food and drink. He paused, staring, his eye balls as if on stalks as Ishtar turned to face him with not a hint of modesty.

'Shouldn't you cover yourself?' Luke whispered feeling a red flush creeping up into his cheeks as a pang of jealousy seized him. Ishtar raised her finger bidding him to be silent as she delivered a harsh rebuke to the old man, sending him bowing on his way.

'My body belongs to the people,' Ishtar fixed her levelled stare on her lover, 'not just one man...remember that!' she added menacingly. Luke felt contempt and desire for her wrestle within him, his eyes drawn irresistibly towards her, seeing her magnificent curves accentuated by her wet flesh and the guttering orange light.

'Fetch my robes!' she commanded, and Yacoup bowed, though not without one more lingering look at her, then backed out of the doorway.

'You do not know what power you body holds over men.' Luke stated limply, though he knew that she certainly did. Ishtar laughed derisively as she wrung out her thick lustrous hair and stepped out of the font, like a Botticelli "Birth of Venus" - only in negative.

'Help me dress my love' Ishtar took Luke's hand and placed it on her hard nipples and he felt the dark-brown goose flesh stir in a tumescent erection as he fought back the pain in his groin and the dilemma of his divided loyalties.

The boy reappeared with a folded robe of pleated gold thread, so delicate that it seemed to float. Luke held it for her as Ishtar, her arms held upwards, allowed him to robe her - but the transparent gold-thread did little to hide the nudity of her divine body.

'Pass me my hair band.' she whispered. Luke positioned the silver band like a crown on her damp hair, adjusting the crescent moon to the front as Yacoup letched in adolescent wonder.

'A Goddess if there ever was one.' Luke whispered, transfixed by this enchantress of men; inhaling the natural aroma of her skin that set his flesh on fire and caused a tear to run down his cheek; for he was a prisoner without walls, a slave to this creature of dread, this demon of beauty - as was any man or boy who beheld her!

'Come,' Ishtar entreated, 'just one final touch before we dine.' She took Luke's hand and led him like a doting child to an antechamber, spartan and without decoration apart from one large mirror of highly polished copper along one wall. On an oblong table of onyx lay the accoutrements of the enchantress's art; a range of jars, pots, vases and dishes containing sea sponges and large and small pointed brushes with ivory handles.

'My homecoming has been prophesied and my vassals have been diligent... my trappings of Godhead are generous.' The devil's spawn murmured.

Ishtar sat on an onyx stool against the table as she plied her trade of misleader of men and ambidextrously applied a multitude of creams, astringents, rouge, and mascara; then finally with the finest brush, painted the Ancient Egyptian style of eye makeup around her eyes with black kohl. Then she sprayed her distinctive perfume in a fine mist, defused via a leather airbag attached to the lapis-lasuli jar. And as Luke inhaled that fatal perfume, he knew it: it was the opiate, the bender of minds and wills, the all-powerfull Blue Lotus; and now he understood! It was the aphrodisiac of the Ancient Egyptians, the lotus-eaters of legend, the food of the Gods! No wonder he had been under her spell!

Ishtar rose, and Luke recoiled, powerless in the full effect of her witchery; she stared into his enchanted eyes and spoke: 'Come my paramour, my farmer of the seed within...'let us dine while we wait for the full moon to reach its zenith.' She walked from the anti-chamber through into the ambulatory where a low red granite slab, a sarcophagus, was laid with a wealth of food, wine and zebeeb. Two wooden benches had been placed either side of the tomb-table and Ishtar arranged her sheer gown of transparent goldthread around her, being careful not to snag it on the rough-hewn surface and Luke seated himself opposite, feeling definitely inferior.

'What shall you drink?' Ishar asked, gesturing to the wine and date-liquor as Luke pointed the zabeeb and she poured a large measure into a lapis goblet. As Luke sipped the strong distillate his mind was suddenly thrown back to that first time he had seen Ishtar. Then he had been the host calling the shots, asking her the same question. Now however, the shoe was on the other foot; it did seem as if Ishtar had come home.

Luke looked across the low slab of red granite, steeling himself with a long draught of the strong liquor, and focussed on the Egyptian styled eyes of his archenemy-lover. Her hair had dried into a tumble of black curls that descended from the silver crescent moon hairpiece onto the gown of gold thread and did little to hide the upward tilt of her breasts capped by their protuberant dark nipples that thrust through the gossamer fabric. There was a mischievous, insouciant air about her that led him to believe that their liaison was at an end; as if she knew something of great import that she was keeping secret from him – for after all, like the preying mantis, he had done his duty in impregnating her and was now expendable...

'Tell me something' Luke asked, as ingenuously as he could, 'do you love me?'

Ishtar cupped her head in her hands and stared at the youth with her deep black, fathomless eyes. The flambeau in the ancient walls of this temple to Ishtar guttered momentarily, their orange flames making obeisance to their demi-god, their votive mascot whose presence subdued even the nightingale.

'I love you like I have loved no other,' she answered ambiguously, raising the lapsi goblet to her mouth and wetting her painted lustrous lips so that their chiselled perfection became highlighted in the lambent glow from the wall torch.

'But,' she continued, 'we have a gathering to garner. We have a new flock to the fold, and a new cult of the Order of the One Dimension to initiate.' She reached out to touch Luke's hand.

'Could you give it up?' Luke asked softly. 'Could you give up your desire for dominance...give it all up for me?'

'*No!*' Ishtar's voice was ruthless. 'I will not concede my right as the High Priestess in this clan to come. It is my destiny!' She withdrew her hand as if it were from a leper's touch and rose from the table, her body taught with anger, to walk haughtily into the dark temple; Luke bit his tongue - not a good move, he thought.

The full moon had risen some while ago, and now its white disc moved across the velvet black of night, alive with the sparkle of stars scintillating in a silvery abundance – except for one: Mars, the red planet and bringer of war, which seemed to wink as if with some urgent message to convey.

As the moon began to move into zenith and the dogs of the village howled and bayed, a sliver of white light shone down from the round portal in the roof of the temple. The sliver became a crescent as its shaft split the interior blackness of the vast hypostyle hall asunder, its reflected lunettes shimmering on the silent columns. The clamouring white light of the full moon moved along the floor and climbed up a black granite sarcophagus on which lay a figure, her exposed flesh rendered into a milky-white effulgence by the deep contrast between light and dark. She lay prostrate, immobile; then with a sickening snap of her unworldly vertebrae, her back arched in an animalistic curve, her breasts thrusting upwards in anticipation of her own metamorphosis, causing her protuberant brown nipples to tear through the thin fablic of her golden threaded gown.

Luke watched Ishtar, a prescient cramp of foreboding gripping his bowels as he stood in the darkness, rooted to the spot. The crescent of white light climbed up over the lid of the sarcophagus moving between the woman's open legs until its light shone onto the dark pulsating mound of her womanhood and Ishtar chanted.

'Take me, oh Satanic light, fill me with thine inner being...' Luke heard the words but could not believe it came from that divine figure splayed out obscenely on the sarcophagus. Her lips moved yet the sounds that issued from it were faucal, beast-like, and seemed to project up into the temple's murk, echoing malevolently around the walls.

'Light from the uncursal hexagram of Hell, invade me now, take my body and impregnate me with thine light of darkness that the incubus growing within me shall be reborn and the dark Gods resurrected!'

Luke watched spellbound, hearing the guttural un-worldly voice reverberate around the dark temple, and then seeing to his horror the belly of the pregnant High Preistess begin to swell and to vibrate as if gripped by some inner demonic force.

'Come to me... come out into the Satanic light, oh son of mine, oh dark prince... reveal thyself as leader of men, Esoteric Oracle that lives through me!'

Luke clutched the column, his nails tearing clawmarks through the soft plaster as he retched in abject revulsion at the manifestation of evil that writhed on the unholy sepulchre, her distended belly convulsed in imminent delivery; the bride of Satan who had stolen his heart.

He felt warm liquid run across his hands and looking down, saw that the knife he held had cut through his palm, narrowly missing his veins. An involuntary frisson of repugnance sent spasms of icy dread along the entire length of his body, causing him to focuss and nerving him to steel himself for what he knew he must do. Moving as if in a trance, his feet like lead, he walked towards the writhing woman, his hand clutching the knife. After what seemed like an eternity he drew close to Ishtar, seeing her arched body shimmering in a halo of silver and gold, electrified by the crescent of supernatural moonlight that took over her body as she splayed open her legs ready for her Satanic delivery, her divine face ecstatic!

He held the blade to her throat, his hands trembling, damming his mind against the proximity of her skin and her smell of seduction, the fatal perfume of the Blue Lotus, and willing himself to make the cut. For he knew now that this being in front of him was not the woman he had loved; nor was it woman at all, or even flesh and blood: it was something far more sinister!

'Come into our wold...come out of me now!' the beastial voice echoed about his ears as Luke took the knife in both hands and held it high above the hyperventilating chest of the woman, the moonlight catching it in a dazzle of white particles, 'come out...come out into the dark light...'

'*No!*' Luke shouted '*It shall not live!*' Luke's hands shook violently as he resurrected his last vestage of willpower to make the thrust. Whilst he hesitated, Ishtar's beautiful face began to change. Her almond eyes turned from black to green; fur started to sprout from her skin and her face and hands mutated as she metamorphosed into the cat goddess Bastet.

'*No!*' Luke shouted hysterically as he plunged the knife into Ishtar's sternum, her arched body thrusting upwards towards the silvery blade and an unearthly scream echoing around the temple as an evanescent vapour carrying the image of bastet rose ghostly from her body and up into the dark reaches of the temple.

'*Too late, mortal!*' the guttural voice intoned, its rasping inflexion full of menace. Something was happening, something inexplicable as Luke looked down at the still form of his lover, seeing an ooze of bright red blood welling up from the hilt of the knife. As his senses began to leave him he saw Ishtar's face had returned to her former beautiful self and her belly was flat! She had released the forces of evil *before* he had killed her; *he had acted too late*!

His last memory before the blackness descended over him was the eerie crackle of green light as it flickered about the figures on the walls; the dark gods of the Egyptian pantheon, who were no longer immobile, carved reliefs. They were sentient and alive, resurrected through the body of this beauty whose face swam before him, her pallor, *the pallor of death*!

Chapter Twenty-One
*** Joruck Flips ***

Bridget emerged from the star-man's abode and onto the small courtyard, guided by Joruck as Jock jumped down the steps from the overlook to embrace his wife, a labyrinth of conflicting expressions cavorting across his face.

'Is it good news?' he asked of Joruck, 'is all well...'

'The patient is doing fine.' Joruck replied, his temples knotted with fatigue. 'She will need not to exert herself for a few days, but the separation and the gene transfusion...a rapid healing technique the computer has administered, that has also been successful.'

'Thank God!' Jock whispered, extending a hand to the wizened little non-terrestrial, 'and I owe you a great deal...is there someway I can repay you?'

'Your gratitude is enough for now,' Joruck replied, 'though if I can think of anything, I will not hesitate to ask you.'

'Twins eh?' Jock placed his hand on his wife's stomach, 'we must think about getting you home.'

'Aren't you forgetting something?' Bridget looked at Jock; a tear was brimming in her eyes.

'*Luke!*' Jock cursed himself for his insensitivity; his negligence was about to open up old wounds between them, he thought as he berated himself for his crass amnesia, so relieved was he that his wife was well again.

'We will find him' he said resolutely 'we will find out where he is...' Though his face gave him away as he realised that none of them had a clue as to where he had gone, or if he was still alive. Once again, his eyes, imploring in their concern went back to Joruck.

'You want me to find your son' Joruck stated simply. 'Very well, it is a request I cannot refuse for he was here as you know, and I enjoyed his company. I will try to locate his brainwaves here with my monitors, but there is someone I have to make contact with first within your world of three dimensions. His name is Isaak and he is also monitoring the progress here...he is dedicated also to the overthrow of the cult. When I have established contact, I will signal you so you can speak with him. In the meantime, enjoy the company of your lovely wife.'

Jock nodded, for once stumped for words as the little old man volunteered to help them yet again. Joruck returned into his cramped quarters and started to transmit his message.

Jock led Bridget up the steps to the overlook where the others welcomed her profusely; they had been quiet, not wanting to interrupt this reunion of sorts. Now though, they congratulated Bridget on the success

238

of the operation and Errol leaned over to pluck a flower from one of the blooming hyacinth bushes, handing it to her.

'You look radiant, my dear' he said as she accepted it, colouring a little.

'The landscape' Bridget changed the subject, 'it is so beautiful from here...but what happened to the volcano? Did it erupt, did that mad plan work?'

She looked down from the parapet whilst Jock explained the success of the eruption and its literal liquidation of the cult, though he left out the details of Labachi and Rachid's death at the hands of Mimi, not wanting to overburden her with any residual guilt. He explained that she had lapsed into unconsciousness in the underground river and that they had carried her to safety, then Smirtin described his blasting of the volcano and the resurrection of the forest in proud detail.

'So the Zalks can return' Bridget said, looking at the tribesmen gathered quietly in a corner, some of them swaying a bit on their hairy feet, due to their overzealous imbibing of the white-man's fire water.

'And we can return as well my dear,' Jock added, 'as soon as we locate Luke...'

Bridget's face crumpled at the sound of her missing son's name, but before she could pursue the matter further she was interrupted by the sound of a gong and everyone turned to look down into the courtyard. In the centre of the sunken patio, was a large black box that seemed to have no visible surface to it. Joruck walked out of the rock-cut doorway holding an odd array of gadgets.

'This is the first fix I have got of Luke' Joruck spoke from inside the black cube as the others sat on the steps and watched the spectacle unfold. A holographic image of Luke and Zalkina appeared as if in total reality as Bridget clutched Jock's knee, 'my son' she exclaimed, choking back a tear, 'he was here...?'

'Yes' Joruck said 'I had the privilege of his company, and of that good lady.' he gestured to Zalkina, who was trying to hide her fear as she recalled her terrifying experience as Joruck had unleashed his memory banks of them.

'Don't worry, my dear, I won't repeat that little trick... I know it must have been frightening.' Joruck reassured the distressed native girl and the others frowned in puzzlement. 'What I need to do is scroll forward to the present, to see if I can still connect to his brainwave patterns.' The hologram in the black box oscillated in bursts of light as Luke's progress since him last being here at Joruck's temple flashed across the three dimensional space too quickly to tell what was happening.

The star man slowed down the holographic projector and the image of Luke in the cavern of the Lost City became clearer.

'That's it!' Jock shouted, 'that's the last time we saw him!' Joruck slowed down the hologram and they saw Luke being whisked up into the ether by Ishtar, only to be left to perish on a barren desert escarpment.

239

Bridget's face coloured slightly at Luke's attachment to Yasmine, but that was nothing compared to the scenes of passion that followed, for it was obvious that Luke had been brainwashed into becoming Ishtar's lover, just as she had herself been taken over by that Satanic cult. But Bridget's concern for the morality of her son, realising as she did, the delicate nature of obsession from her own painful experience, was totally eclipsed by the scene which followed. Bridget screamed, her hands going up involuntarily to cover her eyes as she saw Luke plunge the knife into Ishtar. But it was not merely this desparate act of killing that caused Bridget to shudder in disbelief, for she now saw the arch-temptress - who was stretched out on some sort of sacrificial alter in a very strange and forbidding temple - saw her thrusting body: it was the body of a pregnant woman, in the act of giving birth! Then the hologram went black and Joruck stopped the projector.

Bridget had slumped onto the floor, unconscious. Smirtin and Jock lifted her up, Smirtin clearing the overlook patio table with one great swipe of his arm and they laid down the limp woman; the healthy glow that had graced her cheeks had turned to a pallid white. Joruck ran up the stairs, stangely athletic for an old man. He did some quick checks, then pronounced: 'She is well, still well...it was the shock of seeing her son kill. But he had to do it to stop that incubus...but I fear he was to late!'

'Incubus?' Jock blasphemed, '*what in God's name is that?*'

'It is about as far from God as you can get,' Joruck's voice was serious, 'did you see that section of the transcript before Luke passed out, he was scanning with his peripheral vision and he was seeing something pretty horrendous...as he was driving the knife into his lover's heart.' Joruck whispered, looking concernedly at the still unconscious Bridget.

'Oh, don't spare me' Jock retorted, but Joruck didn't understand the sarcastic vein, 'so what is an incubus?'

'It is an embryonic life form, developed by us, for use in fast-breeder farms when we were on the verge of starvation.' Joruck stated flatly. 'Once brought to life, the embryo develops rapidly and reproduces itself...'

'Like a virus' Jock rejoined

'Just so' Joruck nodded solemnly, but this plague needs to be incubated – that is kept warm, and free of contamination until it matures...'

'Into what?' Jock asked, a shudder running down his spine.

'Into what ever it chooses.'

'You mean an entity that can assume many forms...a polymorph?' Jock's desparate voice was giving him away as the others looked at him, realising that there was seriously bad news on the way.

'Possibly, but I am afraid my friend, that from the images we have just seen, your son, though doing the only the thing he could in killing the host, Ishtar - but only after she was seeded - has increased the strength of this incubus. And after its 'birth' it has called down the powers from the temple's graven images into its own manifestation.

'What do you mean... that it has grown stronger on mere carvings, mere paintings?'

'Did you not see the flickering green light around those images' Joruck asked. 'That means only one thing. The manifestation, which arose from the coupling of your son and this witch, has released the Esoteric Oracle again. That alien metamorph who is now resurrected and is becoming more and more powerful as he feeds on the negative energy from the dark gods...a creation of the human race, not ours, I do not hesitate to point out?'

'*So where is he now, my son...Luke?*' Jock shouted at the alien, as Ogadile frowned, holding a cold compress to Bridget's brow.

Joruck sighed deeply, the weight of the entire human race borne upon his insubstantial shoulders; he spoke: 'Let us progress our enquiries further...to after his blackout'. The star-man played the recording of Luke's brainwaves and the black cube flickered into life again; except there was not much life. The hologram showed four walls of a dark cellar, a dungeon more like, with a grilled door through which a single, guttering wall torch burned.

'This is what Luke is seeing now.' Joruck spoke solemnly. 'this is calibrated to actual time...the present, here and now...'

'They have cast him into some cell.' Jock choked, 'he is a prisoner...'

'At least he is still alive.' Joruck retorted.

'Where?' Jock's voice was breaking 'where is it...we have to get him out of there...*we have to rescue him!*'

'Let me see what I can do' Joruck manipulated the controls of the star people's futuristic equipment and the hologram appeared to rise up through thick stonewalls. 'Project,' Joruck commanded the machine, 'scan the periphery... project and amplify,' he banged the black box on its top as the hologram shuddered and continued to move up until a strange structure could be seen: an inverted translucent pyramid of rosy light glowed in the centre of the black cube.

'Luke is underneath the Temple of the Eon,' Joruck's voice was strained, 'It looks as if this new manifestation of Esoteric Oracle and his resurrected eidolons have captured or taken over the Temple, for that is certainly a view of one of the pyramids that comprise the Temple of the Eon.

'What!' Jock's voice was incredulous, 'what about all my work, my paintings ...all the murals I did for the grand gallery... they can't do that...'

'I'm afraid they can, and have.' Joruck retorted, 'It is as I have been warned by my predictors ...my scanners of the future...it was always on the cards. Having been literally blasted out of Aiyu, and vulcanised out of the Lost City, this new hybrid cult of the incubus have focussed their newfound powers on the Temple of the Eon, the repository of time...and if these predictions are right, they show that this new strain of Esoteric Oracle will, if they are not stopped, transform the Temple into a fortress called the pyramid of the spectral void which will be impregnable to any natural or cosmic form of energy ....a cocoon of non-matter.'

'*So where is Luke!*' Jock shouted, unable to bear the strain of losing his one and only son – *and* all his work.

'I have told yo this already. He is below the temple of the Eon which will be turned into the Pyramid of the Spectral Void...he is, ipso facto in the dungeons of the Esoteric Oracle!'

'What,' Jock shouted, 'in a dungeon below a pyramid of non-matter...what sort of fate is that!'

'*Do not shout at me!*' Joruck raised his voice as the crescendo of his wrath shook the surrounding structures and echoed like a tornado into the sand dunes below.

'I have had enough of your sponging weakness. I have saved your wife, saved your twins and it seems now I will have to save your son...' Jock stood back in unabashed terror as the aged star-man, driven to distraction, metamorphosed into his own kind, and a sphere of swirling particles hovered about the courtyard. Crystalline shapes of bright iridescent blues, greens and purples transmogrified into a beautiful multi – pointed star that scintillated in oscillating kaleidoscopic colours as the alien assumed his real shape.

'I cannot, nor will not abide your ingratitude!' Joruck's voice penetrated the petrified group of comrades, the Zalks leaping over the parapet into the sand dunes below, to be quickly followed by Zalkine and the medicine man, whilst Zalkina shrieked in a cry of unmitigated terror, leaping onto the spooked Starchild who zoomed up into the sky. Mimi stood transfixed, her brood of babies squealing as she leapt up on Errol's stunned shoulder, planted him with one last kiss and was gone over the low wall, to leap down into the desert below and chase after the Zalks, her chattering brood clinging to her fur and teats.

'Are you happy now, Mr Joruck?' Jock spoke to the hovering transmutation of non-matter, 'have you had your say?' Smirtin cautioned him with his giant hand on the distraught shoulder of his friend, as Ogadile looked concerningly at the comatose form of Bridget who was still lying on the table.

'I am sorry.' A voice of reconciliation spoke from the pulsing stellate structure, which evaporated and Joruck the wizened little man stood there once more. 'I am sorry, but I am at my wit's end.' his voice faltered as Jock sensed a deep sadness in the man.

'I was left here as a rear guard many thousands of years ago. When my own people asked me to stay on I did not know then the enormity of the task, nor the loneliness of it. I have tried to protect, tried to help your race as it has pulled itself out of the darkness of ignorance. I have watched and waited, through all the wars, internecine struggles and torture pursued in the name of religion, trying to remain impartial. Yet the awesome responsibilities of this command have left me depleted, exhausted...even my own instruments do not work any longer!'

'Joruck, my friend.' Jock approached the distraught alien, grasping him around the shoulder. 'You have succeeded, you have helped bring mankind into the dawning of a new era...and you have helped this woman,' he gestured back to Bridget. 'You have done wonders, you have performed a miracle in the saving of her life and our unborn twins to be...'

The withered little man embraced Jock and sobbed in great shaking fits of loneliness and isolation onto his chest as Jock comforted him, patting his back.

'You are our friend.' Jock pushed the sobbing man back from him as he looked into his strange yellow eyes. 'You have helped us here, and you have saved our planet from your race's decadent seed...the cult. Or you will do now, if you show us what to do!'

'Yes' Smirtin and Errol jumped into the act as they lifted the demoralised alien over their heads, carrying him up to the overlook.

'Yes, my main man.' Smirtin grinned as he slapped the little man's hand, 'chill...and be happy...have some zabeeb...join us, cos we, my man, are your fans...we are your friends!'

After a while Joruck had turned into a different person and a few goblets of the liquor had cheered him up no end; the convivial company of the humans after Bridget had recovered, her colour returning to her cheeks, had given him a new lease of life.

'So.' Smirtin summed up the predicament in his off-handed cheery fashion. 'We have a new cult, the Esoc...Rollercal, pardon the zabeeb, has established his new residence at the Temple of the Eon....am I right, or am I right? Okay, not a problem, all we have to do new is blast him out of it!'

'How simple,' Joruck patted Smirtin on his massive deltoids, 'and perhaps you are right. We have the firepower, as you know my muscular friend, but can we be selective?'

'Selective is the word.' Jock added emphatically. 'Don't forget my masterpieces are in that Temple!'

'*Your bloody masterpieces!*' Errol's voice was one of uncharacteristic sobriety as he looked from Jock to Bridget in total disbelief. 'To hell with your so- called masterpieces... it's your *son* whom you should be selective about!'

'My God!' Jock's face dropped a mile as he looked at his wife's expression, which registered incredulity at his insensitivity. 'You are right my friend... and I hope now that all my work *is* destroyed, as it has been at Park House... and I swear here and now, never to pick up a brush again as penance for my confused allegiances.

'That is a heavy penalty,' Joruck stated, looking hard at the beleaguered artist. In him he felt some sort of strange bond, for they both had laboured at impossible tasks with very little thanks.

'It is time to replace brute force with brute intelligence.' The wizened little man's eyes lit up as he looked at Smirtin's doleful face.

'Where will we find that?' Smirtin asked looking hopelessly at the faces of his friends.

'Not from where you are standing.' Errol gibed

'Now, now, gentlemen!' Joruck reprimanded 'Let us keep focussed on the matter in hand. We can't use force, because of endangering Luke and let us not forget the lives of the Emperor, Neb-Ankh and all the others...also it would be sacrilege to destroy such an architectural wonder as the Temple of the Eon...not to mention its undeniably priceless collection of paintings!' Joruck added deferentially, acknowledging Jock's wan smile.

'So we need some ploy in order to infiltrate the Temple.' Joruck conjectured, a decoy perhaps...' he thought for a moment and then announced.

'I have it...Starchild...Zalkina riding Starchild would create a distraction. If she were to ride in as if carrying a message, it may give you time to get into the temple unobserved...but you will have to use your judgment.'

'Wouldn't that make her something of a target?' Jock asked

'Target, yes,' Joruck persisted 'but I can protect her.'

'Anyway,' Jock added non too helpfully, 'she's done a runner...when you went into regression...it blew her mind!'

'I can recall her.' Joruck countered. 'I will bring back Starchild and she will follow. The two are inseparable, aren't they?'

Joruck cupped his hand across his mouth as a strange noise, like the whiney of a horse, yet pitched slightly higher, echoed out across the lower desert and towards the reconstructed forest far below.

A faint answer came back from the depths of the distant forest as they watched, seeing presently a dot soar up out of the woods and into the sky.

'What was that noise you made' Jock asked.

'Mating call of the Eon-beast...a bit cruel I know.' Joruck winced.

Everyone watched the magical animal and its rider approach, then come to a clattering halt as it landed on the balcony, snorting and shaking its head, looking for his mate. Zalkina jumped off Starchild and was greeted by all the group.

'We are going to rescue Luke.' Jock said 'will you help us?' Zalkina nodded her head as a far away look stole in her eye. Joruck was fitting a belt of small black boxes around Starchild withers.

'Press this button here.' he said pointing to the control at the top of the belt. 'Not now...only when you see danger... it will throw up a shield. Then press again to resume...do you understand?' Zalkina nodded.

Joruck turned to Bridget who had recovered and had been sitting up for some time, quietly listening as the plan unfolded.

'How do you feel my love?' he asked. 'Do you feel well enough to go and find your son, or would you rather stay here until they return?'

'I am feeling much better.' Bridget replied, moving towards Jock and placing an arm around his waist. 'I want to go with you,' she looked up at her husband, smiling a brave smile and trying to hide the foreboding she felt.

'Are you sure my dear?' Jock asked, frowning in concern.

'Yes' Bridget reiterated firmly. 'Let us go and find our lad and do what is needed to rid us all of this cult, for once and for all...and then let us go home!'

'I will transport you into the Garden of the Eon-beasts...you will be following in Luke's footsteps, so to speak.' Joruck said, directing them to stand in the lower court. The black cube materialised around them, and Starchild whinnied. 'Watch out for their little tricks...this new strain of the cult will be very cunning, and powerful...Good luck,' he added a little more cheerily... 'I will be following your progress.'

The black cube of non-light trembled as Joruck pressed some invisible remote; then it was illuminated by green vectors. The two mortals, two supernaturals, one condemned actor, one native girl and one mythical zebra were transported through space, but not time to the Garden of Eon-beasts in the twinkling of an eye.

Chapter Twenty-Two
*** Showtime ***

'Everyone alright?' Smirtin was the first to regain his orientation as they found themselves looking out onto the mythical Garden of the Eon-beasts. Starchild was excited, smelling the air and pawing the ground, obviously glad to be reunited with his old friends: the various wild and mythological animals that ranged the long sheltered valley; perhaps this is where his mate would be.

'Let us get into cover.' Smirtin led the way to the margin of trees which cradled the vale with its river winding slowly through it.

'What a magical place.' Bridget whispered.

'Indeed' Jock agreed, 'this is what took me away from you. I could not resist the temptation of a commission to paint all of this...it kept me here longer than I would have wished.'

'Let us not rehearse the past again' Bridget said 'let us look to the future; let us find Luke!'

'There is the spot where Luke found me,' Jock pointed to the place of his last painting, 'and there is the Temple of the Eon!' From their slight elevation as they peered out through the woods, they could see the iridescent pink glow through the veil of blue-grey mist at the end of the valley.

'Let us rest until sundown,' Ogadile suggested, 'we can survey the place from here, and go in under cover of night. They lay in the shelter of the woods, some sleeping, others just drinking in the beauty of the place, their mission put on hold.

The last limb of the sun dappled through the foliage and then was gone, the blue mist darkened and the pearly glow increased as the inverted pyramids threw their suffused rays down along the vale.

'How do you feel' Jock asked, placing his hands on Bridget's tummy and feeling a stir of movement in the small bulge, which was now visible.

'I feel well,' she replied, linking her hands across his, 'and I will feel much better when we release Luke...'

'Are we ready?' Smirtin rose, checking his array of assault gear crammed into his leather jerkin.

'I have a distinct feeling of a deja vu,' Errol replied, tucking his crumpled white buccaneer-style shirt into his broad belt. 'This had better be our last take or I am going to the union.' he slapped his thigh as Smirtin frowned in incomprehension.

'Remember,' Jock cautioned, 'low profile! We are not going in to destroy the cult this time; they are too powerful...that may happen later, I don't know. We are going in with one mission in mind...to get Luke out, and others, if it is practical!'

'Has Starchild quietened down a bit?' Jock asked of Zalkina as they made their way cautiously along the track he was so familiar with.

'His heart glad to see old friends... he good boy now' Zalkina assured Jock, patting the animal on the forelock

'And you know what to do. Press the black box if you see trouble...don't go too close, just make the guards look up at you...wave this, they will think it is a message.' Jock took a crumpled old drawing from his jeans.

'I understand' Zalkina nodded.

The towering agglomeration of the Temple of the Eon with its stack of pearly- pink inverted pyramids rose high above them as they made their stealthy way through the dark blue mist hanging over the riverine valley; there seemed to be not a sound coming from the looming architectural impossibility.

They reached the end of the valley, blessing their good fortune that the mist had intensified, granting them a cloak of invisibility. The translucent steps up to the entrance to the Temple could just be discerned through the swirling fog, and Jock bent down, whispering into Zalkina's ear. 'Fly now... ride up towards the entrance and across the façade of the temple, waving your paper. Use the black button if you are fired upon, and encircle the pyramids, it will distract the guards. When you return back to the entrance, and you do not see us, we will be inside. Ride then on Starchild back to Joruck and rejoin your people. Starchild will guide you back, he will know the way; do you understand?'

'Understand' Zalkina nodded, spurring her magical mount to a gallop through the eerie mist, to soar up and towards the great crystal doors of the Temple of the Eon, the winged zebra snorting, his breath a white tendril behind him and his wings making strange patterns through the ground fog. Just then, an almost full moon rose above the dark woods, its silvery presence coruscating from the swirling banks of mist, and catching mount and rider in an ethereal light as Jock cursed: 'Damn! We do not need this light, it will make us more visible.'

'Advance now' Smirtin ordered as they approached the strange glowing steps of the temple, looking around for the guards, novices, or anyone who moved; the entrance was devoid of human life. They passed through the great crystal doors that stood open and into the translucent pink temple, walking towards a set of steps leading downwards towards a long corridor.

'Wait one minute' Jock held back Smirtin's progress with an arm as he turned to Bridget. 'The Grand Gallery is in front of us, before we descend into the lower regions, would you like to see my exhibition... my work of a lifetime?'

'Quickly then!' Bridget looked alarmed as Smirtin oathed under his breath; this was no time for art shows. Jock led them along the Grand Gallery, whispering little anecdotes about how he had painted this, when he painted that, and Bridget cooed in delight, looking guardedly around her at the same time; the place was too quiet.

'They are marvellous,' she whispered, truly masterpieces...now can we proceed with our search for Luke?'

'*Ah...the Artist himself!*' A guttural voice came from nowhere, accompanied by an orchestra of inarticulate voices and alien sounds like disembodied spirits that appeared to come from various points in the Grand Gallery.

'Where are you?' Jock spoke into the empty gallery, 'who are you...why do you not show yourselves?'

'Unfortunately Mr Artist, your childish pride in these kindergarten scribblings has led to your undoing.' The faucal voice seemed to be everywhere, reverberating around the crystal walls. It continued: 'For in your arrogance and naive ego, your desire to share your lamentable daubings with your friends has, as we had reasoned, led you into our little trap; you are ipso facto, surrounded!'

'We come not to fight...we come for my son Luke.' Jock spoke into the void.

'Ah yes...that murderer of my fair daughter...I am afraid his fate is sealed. He has been tried and found guilty; the sentence shall be executed shortly.'

'*No! No! No!*' It was Bridget who let out a long shrill scream, its attenuated cry ringing around the walls of the pyramid whilst the others drew their weapons.

'Know you that your puny little arsenal is of no import to me. Also your pathetic little bond to your kin would be touching...if it stuck any chords of sympathy. But here, in my new abode that I shall make into a timeless fortress, where my new order shall be forged...it is merely tedious. I do not want to mess up this beautiful temple of mine with the gore of mortals, but you leave me little choice!' The Oracle intoned.

Smirtin had his massive scimitar drawn but his eyes were beginning to show tell-tale signs of his one great weakness: his total dread of the spirit world, particularly invisible ghouls.

'They cannot harm us,' Jock attempted to reassure him. 'Though the Oracle talks tough, his little helpers cannot lift a finger to us until they become solid...as yet, they are only the vapours of our sub-conscious... they are only voices.' Unheading of this naïve advice, Smirtin's eyes were wild and his massive scimitar was starting to shake; experience had led him to have a healthy respect for the invisible foe, particularly dead ones.

Zalkina had encircled the Temple and was about to command Starchild to take off into the night, back to Joruck and her people of the forest, when looking through the open doorway of the Temple, she saw her friends in the long corridor, their weapons drawn and looking around them in dread.

Seizing the rein, she banked suddenly and commanded Starchild to land close to the steps of the pyramid temple. Then having a better idea, she urged the winged zebra to climb the stairs and spurred him on into the interior, the sound of his hooves echoing along the Gallery as he slipped on the shiny surface.

Zalkina guided the mythical beast through the crystal doors, seeing her friends beset by enemies that could not be seen as she patted Starchild's mane and bending over, whispered something into his ear. The zebra whinnied and nodded, pounding the pearly translucent floor with his hard but un-shod hooves. Zalkina drew a deep breath and flipping the reigns, her naked thighs squeezing his withers, urged Starchild into a full gallop down the hall of the grand gallery.

As the striped mustang snorted, he broke from a trot into a canter and then into a full gallop. Zalkina depressed the button on the black box in front of her, and a green shield of brilliant particles enveloped horse and rider, Jock and the others gawping in total disbelief as she bore down on their invisible foe.

Zalkina felt only elation as bare-backed she threw out her arms and flew with the mythical animal as his hooves, scarce touching the slippery floor careened into their un-mortal enemy and crushed them underfoot their cries and wails rising up into the high vaults of the Gallery. The winged zebra snorted, belching fire in his fury and his wings flapped out either side decapitating many of the mutants until Zalkina reigned him up at the far end of the gallery.

She turned her steed's head now and readied him for the reverse charge back towards the entrance. Then the ghouls materialised, their dismembered bodies a carnage of alien gore that slipped and skidded in their own blood, a sea of green bile strewn across the pearly-pink of the crystal floor.

'Our salvation!' she heard Jock cry as she saw Smirtin wade into the now visible carnage and amputate the grotesque limbs of the unspeakable men-beasts, decapitating several at a time with his enormous scimitar.

Zalkina steadied the frightened Starchild and urged him into one last charge, hearing the shouted thanks from her friends, the wind humming in her ears.

'Go now, escape while you can!' Jock shouted up to her as the mythical beast galloped by him. And as the now visible guards, who had been hiding in the dark recesses either side of the entrance aimed their laser guns to fire, Starchild and Zalkina galloped out from the Temple's entrance and up into the moonlit night as the white bolts of the light from the guards futuristic weapons exploded in a miasmic show of spectral light from Zalkina's shield.

'Finish them' Smirtin commanded Ogadile and Errol, who set about the task of slicing to pieces the maimed and crawling metamorphs. The black giant struck off the head of a snake, and with the verso stroke, sliced a crocodile's body endowed with a vulture's head into two pieces, causing green fluid to spray into the air. Their faces testament to their total horror and disgust, the defenders were covered in the bile of the mutants as they decimated the new seed of the Oracle.

But other guards had arrived on the scene and laser bolts raked along the Grand Gallery, hitting more of the alien phantoms than their slayers as the three armed combatants jumped and somersaulted and ducked to avoid the wild, desparate fire.

'My paintings!' Jock pleaded with the guards, looking on in abject horror to see his masterpieces not only blasted to shreds in the enfilade of laser fire, but also desecrated by alien graffiti as great chunks of mutant flesh and slime were splattered over them.

Bridget hauled her sobbing husband back into an alcove as the guards depleted their arsenal. Smirtin, grasped the bemused Errol in his giant's hold, slapping hands in a 'high five' salute with his sister as they ran into the vault at the end of the gallery.

'They are re-charging' Smirtin shouted, 'get to them before they get to us!' The three approached the guards, each selecting a target; then they broke formation and all hell was turned loose as they went on the offensive, Smirtin and Errol employing their scimitars in cuts, thrusts, but mainly slicing, to render death and destruction into the new order of the cult so that the floor ran with vile green plasma that sprayed out of these resurrected ancient incarnations, reborn by what black magic they could onle guess at. Whilst the two men employed their skills in scimitarmanship, Ogadile employed her feet, and many were the recipients of crocodile-skinned boots that seemed to come out of fresh air in an un-choreographed display of standing, turning, wheeling and flying kicks that wrecked bone-shattering havoc amongst the ranks of the beast-headed ghouls. Soon enough there were no more targets left alive, and the three paused, breathing heavily and looking guardedly around them, their guts retching at the rivers of otherworldly 'blood' that ran like green rivers over the crystal floor.

A menacing quiet pervaded the Grand Gallery as Smirtin, Ogadile and Errol looked at each other, their expressions tense.

'You dare destroy my heirohants!' the rasping voice permeated the eerie silence, jangling their nerves. 'You dare come in arms against me...take my priests, and my guards...who are you, you beings of clay...?'

'Who are you?' Smirtin shouted in the direction of the voice. 'Why do you not show yourself, so we can deliver you from your dilemma!'

'You...you intruder from another world...you meddler with dimensions! You who would dare question my domain,' the faucal voice intoned, 'you will be fed to the rats in the dungeons of hell...fed to the devourers of your imperious souls...'

'How so?' Ogadile retorted. 'We have killed all your henchmen, have we not...and if I am not mistaken, I have killed you once before...and I will do so again!'

'Oh it is you.' the voice rasped, reverberating around the crystal gallery. 'You who played the little hero with powers that are beyond your ken...I don't think we have too much to fear from you...for know you that I am indestructible! I have been reborn...resurrected from my own seed and the seed of this so called Artist's spawn...you see, I am not averse to fresh blood...I am democratic, ubiquitous, for I am everywhere!'

'Your humble self-description is good for one thing only...and that is for execration!' It was Jock, who had pulled himself together, and holding Bridget tight, shouted his own abuse at the resurrected Esoteric Oracle.

'Oh my,' the Esoteric Oracle replied, 'The Great Artist of Time...the Old Master of hack...what a way with words we do have, well see how you find words for this next chapter...'

A deep spine-chilling peel of laughter, accompanied by a dissonance of slithering scales, reverberated around the Gallery, moving up into the high vault, whence the voice originated.

'Ishtar's seed' the guttural voice commanded 'Angels of darkness...my little eidolons. It is time. It is your turn to avenge your murdered mother!'

Smirtin and Errol, scimitar's drawn and Ogadile, her guard at the ready stood in a triad, peering up into the darkness of the high vault of the inverted crystal pyramid, whilst Jock and Bridget clung to each other in the alcove, tears welling in Jock's eyes as he looked at the ruins of his finest work.

'Come on me now!' the preternatural voice beseeched, 'Eidolons... angels of the dark...it is your turn for revenge!' Out of the gloom of the high vault descended a score of winged youths, their blond hair flowing as they dropped down on the three defenders, their crenulated swords swishing in the air.

'Avenge thine mother.' the voice exhorted from above as Ogadile, her eyes wide in apprehension shouted: '*It is Luke*, they are all Luke, may the prophet save my soul!'

'No!' Smirtin seized his sister's arm. 'This is a deception, they are not Luke...they are some sort of trick...it is an illusion conjured by this black wizard!'

The first Angel of the dark, his orange robe billowing as he flew down from the high vault, wielded his sword and made a looping sweep at Ogadile but Errol's blade parried it and sparks flew from the clash of steel. 'Defend yourself' Errol shouted, '*this is not Luke!*'

'Oh my bewildered children,' the omnipresent voice echoed, 'it is indeed Luke...it is the essence of his seed, come to avenge his murdered mother.'

'No!' Bridget shrieked from the alcove as Jock held her shaking body. 'You iniquitous monster from the depths of Hell... Luke did not murder anyone... he killed an alien slime-form!' she looked across from the illusions of her son to her three comrades. 'It is but deception, illusion...cast Luke from your mind...kill these imposters,' she shouted to the three, 'kill them all *before they kill you!*'

251

Ogadile, shocked from her state of inertia, arched backwards like a spring and leapt high into the air, seizing one of the clones by his leg as he flew upward, taking her with him. Her long nails tore into his flesh and he screamed an inhuman scream, green bile running down his leg. She clawed her way up his body in mid flight and clutching his sword arm, broke it backwards as the blade somersaulted through the air to clatter onto the slimy floor. Then, grasping his long blond locks and jerking his head back, she broke his neck; his vertebra snapping and the gruesome sound of shattering bone reverberated around the vault. Ogadile jumped off her dead ride to somersault through the air, kicking another Luke lookalike in the face on the way down, to land safely on the slippery crystal floor, skating to the wall on the supernatural floor-covering. The corpse of her defective transport had collapsed dead in mid flight, his body crashing to the ground to explode in a mist of sparkling vapour that sprayed green bile into the air.

'They are phantoms!' Jock shouted, as Smirtin hitched a ride, taking a leaf out of his sister's notebook. Dodging backstabs from behing, Smirtin used the trajectory of his adversary to lop of the heads of most of his cronies, leaving the two on the floor to finish off. His scimitar cleaved the air, swishing across in giant swipes as he cut in half or decapitated these so-called Eidolons, these phantoms of some unborn, unheard of presence; his rage was his revenge!

The air was filled with the clashing of swords and the thump of bodies as they hit the ground, to explode in a silvery mist until the floor was covered in their ghoulish blood; then even that disappeared in a surreal evanescent mist. Only when all the Luke-replicants had been sliced to pieces did Smirtin dispatch his ride, though his superior strength caused him to overkill for he literally tore the creature's head right off and was sent spiralling out of control to crash into the far wall, sliding slowly down it onto the floor.

'Smirtin!' Ogadile cried, 'are you all right?'

'Bit dazed,' The big man replied, picking himself up and quickly tossing away the head that he still held; then smirking foolishly, 'that phantom didn't have no brakes!'

A deafening cacophony of wails, howls and shrieks decended on the ears of the group as the Oracle gave vent to his anger, and metamorphosed into nameless horrors that gave their vocal contribution to the nightmare of noise.

'And the council on low sent me down here for a thousand years for overacting.' Errol tucked in his bile-stained shirt. 'They should just hear this fellow!'

'Now is our chance!' Jock shouted, ignoring the actor-chappy and trying to make himself heard above the unholy racket. 'Whilst the incubus or whatever it is, is still counting its losses.... let's go look for the real Luke... I mean we've killed enough replicas...let's make a run for it down into the dungeons...its got to be this way...though I don't recollect the Emperor mentioning any sort of prison when he gave me this.' Jock pulled out the tektite amulet from under his shirt; he had forgotten all about it until now.

'Blasphemy!' The mad artist pronounced as he took one last look at his totally destroyed paintings, 'works of genius...gone, all gone...all of them g....'

'*Come on!*' Bridget pulled him off his feet, dragging him away from his shrine to self pity and they followed Smirtin through a small door and down some steep stairs, leaving the alien incarnation of the devil to bemoan his loss in a cacophony of cosmic dischord; like an innebriated out of tune orchestra playing God Save the King backwards in a very small bathroom.

'You've got him mad now!' Jock slapped the black giant on his rock-hard shoulder. 'Well done old friend.'

The steps became slippery; wet with water that dripped from the rock cut tunnel as they entered a narrow corridor; flames guttering in rusty wall brackets here and there, showing them the way. The tunnel now was no longer man made but of natural water created limestone, and stalactites and stalagmites impeded their way, Smirtin colliding into one and then another as his stooping massive bulk slowed down their progress. They entered a large cavern; its ceiling lost in the pitchy darkness; from it four passages led off.

'Good place for an ambush,' Errol said helpfully...'a bit like Hausman's rebuilding of Paris, so Napoleon could get his troops in to quell a riot...'

'That had five avenues.' Bridget corrected and Errol made a face.

'This is not a good time for a history lesson.' Jock rebuked his wife, but smiling at her put down. Errol always did seem to get it wrong; he should have been teacher, Jock mused, and then more to the point, added: 'so do we split up, or keep together.'

'Keep together,' Ogadile said, 'we mark one at a time, and if it goes nowhere, we come back and try the next one. Let's try this one first.' With a chunk of stalactite that was nestling in Smirtin's outrageous hair, she carved an X above one of the tunnels and they proceeded down it. After a while it got so low that even the others where almost on hands and knees as Smirtin grumbled from the lead. 'Back,' he said, 'lets try another one.'

This also proved impossible but as they entered the third one it opened up into a long gallery, within which they saw a mass of catacombs, comprised of large and small caves and cells, some with grilles across their arched doorways, the large cavern illuminated by numerous tapers burning in wall niches. 'This has to be it.' Smirtin said staying their progress with his arm 'lets reconnoitre...before we proceed.'

Watching from the shadows, they saw a raised gantry, a sort of catwalk, along which various men clad in leather jerkins and spiked metal helmets were walking; all of them were heavily armed.

'Guards,' Smirtin pronounced, 'this has to be the dungeon.'

It was evident as they looked through the grilles in the rock hewn cells that there were inhabitants within. Dark silhouettes could be discerned, gaunt shapes against the light cast by the wall torches, but none looked familiar.

'I don't see Luke,' Jock said, trying to hide the disappointment in his voice, 'but this is the place...if Joruck read his brain wave memory correctly, he must be here.'

'We cannot wait too long' Ogadile added, a note of urgency creeping into her voice, 'it won't be long before the demon above alerts them of our presence...I know,' she said, her voice brightening, 'let me try a little distraction!' She readjusted her leopard skin to reveal more of her generous cleavage, dropping her weapons-belt to the floor and hitching up her tunic to reveal her shapely legs.

'They can't have seen many women down here, particularly ones of easy virtue.' 'I will play the tramp and divert their minds whilst Smirtin, dear brother...do not be dismayed...and Errol...take your beady eyes off my legs...surprise them!'

'Good ploy' Errol rejoined, admiration and more glinting in his eyes.

'Give me some little time to introduce myself and dally a while' Ogadile added.

'Don't dally to long deary.' Errol jibed and caught her wrist just in time to avert a slap. Ogadile strutted out from the cave and into the cavern as Errol's eyes popped and Smirtin expelled a deep breath; never had he seen his sister looking so much like harem-fodder. Her knee length crocodile-skin boots, more items of footware favoured for delivering beheading kicks , than fashion accessories, were now more devastating in their roll as sexual arousers, as with her hips swinging provocatively she sashayed towards the gantry holding the guards. Errol tweaked his moustache, muttering: 'She reminds me of one of my old flames ...trouble is, I can't remember which one.'

Jock tried not to look, holding onto Bridget for dear life as his senses were inflamed in partial memory of their liaison during his first sojourn in Nethertime. Though long forgotten, his daliance at the festival of Afreets and in Pendulem had come back now and then to haunt him. Now seeing his former paramour strut her stuff was playing havoc with his mind - or was it his body. Yet all of that had been put well in the past, and casting one last lingering glance at the femme fatale, he turned back to his wife.

'She is going to knock 'em dead!' Bridget exclaimed without any inflexion of malice, for there was no doubt Ogadile was a looker, even though she strutted like a hooker.

Ogadile approached the metal ladder leading up to the gantry, as the guards' jaws dropped open and they leaned out on the metal rail drooling in an expression of disbelief.

'Hello boys,' Ogadile grasped the handrails, wiggling her curvaceous derriere, 'would you like me to come up and see you sometime...'

'Where does she get that line from?' Errol muttered, gawping at the electrifying effect the black Genie was having on the guards. Ogadile climbed up the stairs in the most lascivious manner possible, the guards colliding with each other at the stairwell, scrambling over each other to help her up. Whilst they were distracted, Smirtin ran around the cavern wall, quickly followed by Errol who didn't want to miss the scene from below. They crouched in the shadows below the gantry as Ogadile recited some rustic comments about the guards' virility, to be eagerly helped up onto the metal walkway.

Smirtin quietly and slowly drew his giant scimitar and grasping it in his mouth, causing the timorous Errol to cringe, climbed up the piers which held the gantry as Ogadile stepped on to it, her paste smile directed devastatingly at the assembled guards.

'Excuse me!' She brushed them aside. 'This is a catwalk, isn't it?' she paraded her hip-swinging routine down the metal gantry, her boots clanking on the reverberating deck as the guards watched transfixed. She saw the unmistakably hands of her brother as he silently swung himself up and over the railings; then she turned and delivered a jaw-crunching kick to the nearest guard, who with windpipe severed, gasped ineffectually for air, before collapsing over the handrail. Smirtin took on the remainder; the swish of his scimitar cleaving the air as he decapitated three at a time, and Errol at the bottom did the mopping up, (the view was better).

'Excellent ploy!' Errol grinned as he wiped his blade across the beard of the nearest guard and the other two jumped back over the handrail to land beside him. 'You should be in movies.' He added, grinning obscenely at Ogadile.

'Poor sex-starved little munchkin.' The Genie seized the troubled actor by the balls and gave a hefty tweak, Errol's eyes watering.

'Funny,' she said, 'I would have thought from all your bullshit about your womanising, that you'd of been better hung!'

'Come on!' Bridget urged, 'let's get on with it...let's look for Luke!' They stepped over their acephalous, ensanguined assailants (former), and searched one cell and then another, but though there were many incumbents who bore witness to neglect and torture, there were none resembling the blond-haired youth.

Then as Jock passed one of the larger cells, a familiar voice spoke through the grille. 'Artist,' the voice spoke quietly, yet urgently, 'is that you? The artist who painted those beautiful paintings of the Garden of the Eon-beasts...'

'Emperor...' Jock stopped dead in his tracks. 'Emperor of the Eon, is that you I hear...my God, what have they done to you!' The man's face was hideously disfigured and the remains of harsh torture at the hands of the newly-risen cult affected his speech. 'We look for our son...we look for Luke, but as God is my witness, what happened to you?'

'I cannot describe the evil of these new mutants' the Emperor whispered.

'What of Neb Ankh?' Jock enquired, though he wasn't sure if he wanted to hear the answer.

'He is next door,' The Emperor nodded to the adjacent cell, 'but do not disturb him. He is in a deep depression and worried about the fate of his precious Garden of Eon-beasts. Now for your own sake, leave this place now!'

'I cannot leave without my son,' Jock stated flatly, 'do you know where he is...wait, I will get the keys from the guards. I will release you.'

'No, my friend,' the Emperor retorted, 'leave me here. I am finished, as is Neb Anhk. Find your son and exit this evil place...go down to the next level, he is down there I think...and may your God, and the technology of the Star People go with you...'

'Try below!' Jock shouted to Smirtin who jumped down the interconnecting ramp as if if were made of Lego and crunched heavily to the ground. He wrenched off the iron grilles with his bare hands, pulling out half the retaining walls to boot, but they were all empty. Then a faint voice cried out further down from the gantry: 'Father, Smirtin is that you?'

'He is down here!' Smirtin leaped over the debris of his own creation and ran full tilt towards the sound of the voice, checking out each cell, one at a time. In the last one he saw two white knuckles clinging to the iron bars of the grille.

'Luke!' Smirtin shouted 'are you all right? Stand back and let me get you out of there!'

Smirtin levered off the door in the grille, tearing it from its hinges as a white figure stepped out, peering out into the cavern, like a mole breaking ground.

'My son, my son!' Bridget ran up to Luke embracing him, 'what have they done to you? The evidence of torture could be seen on Luke's bare chest and his bruised body was a testament to the inhuman treatment he had endured in the recent days since his capture by the reborn Oracle and his clan. He was clothed in a loin-shroud only and his emaciated body was a shadow of his former athletic frame, whilst his unshaven chin made him look much older.

'I am all right.' Luke muttered, embracing both his mother and then Jock who stumbled down the slope to join them 'I am very, very hungry though...'

'Let us get you out of this foul place.' Jock, helped by Smirtin lifted the weakened youth out of the call, supporting him; he could barely put one foot in front of the other.

They helped Luke through the maze of the four passages and cautiously back up the stairs and into the Temple of the Eon. As they looked out onto the Grand Gallery, a strange premonition of fear gripped them; the place was not the same as they had left it. Instead of the balanced inverted pyramids of the Temple of the Eon, a new and menacing structure arose, its indeterminate surface gleaming in an ethereal, spectral light. Now stood only one giant pyramid, the correct way up, its irridescent apex towering up into the sky of the breaking dawn.

'They have completed the reconstruction!' Jock muttered, remembering Joruck's prophecy. 'The incubus has subsumed the structure of the Temple of the Eon into the Spectral Void...'

'What?' Bridget asked, unsure of her husband's meaning, but Jock bid her to be silent.

In the centre of this massive structure stood a raised dais on which a curious chair resembling a serpent stood and Luke's beleaguered mind urged him to think where he had seen it before. Then he had it: it was the identical chair that he had first seen at the cult's head-quarters in Elgin Avenue, that age ago; its serpent's head with the red ruby eyes that were charged with menace even from this distance; those eyes he would never forget.

Jock looked in vain for any trace of his paintings: there was none. Even the Grand Gallery was no more. Instead was only the translucent massive structure of the pyramid. Turning towards the crystal doors by which they had entered on their recent arrival, they stopped abruptly, for they were no longer there – only a wall of impenetrable crystal rose up from the iridescent pink floor.

Smirtin put his weight against the glassy wall, but there was no sign of give to it: it was a solid unyielding wall of some alien material. Nor was there any other discernible exit – *they were trapped*!

'How do you like my reconstruction?' a high-pitched effeminate voice echoed around the new pyramid, seeming to come from all directions. They turned around to see an emanation; that is a presence of a humanoid shape sitting in the chair on the plinth, but camouflaged by otherworldly ghastly creatures that flickered about it, nascent, as if ready to become.

'How do you like my eighth wonder of the world, this indestructible Pyramid of the Spectral Void, in which you will be our guests for all time!'

The diminutive, half-visible figure arose from his chair, his apparitions accompanying him and a group of purple robed men walked up onto the dais to form a circle around him, followed by an outer circle of orange robed younger men and women.

'We have effected the transition' the little man announced proudly. With the help o you progeny, we have brought our true followers home. The little phantoms you made such a mess of were...how shall we put it...a necessary sacrifice. But we are fully grown now...no splinter groups, just ourselves and our loyal followers.'

'Very cosy,' Jock held Luke and Bridget tight, trying to hold down the disgust that churned his stomach, 'almost like a family then?'

'Oh, the Artist who is several paintings short of an exhibition...we have found our voice at last. But let me tell you, you little being of clay...though you will live a million lifetimes in regret of your aiding and abetting our supreme fellowship, it is not for the likes of you, or your little army of retards to question the affairs of Masters of Space and Time!' the effeminate voice became charged by a deep guttural harshness which echoed around the vast pyramid as the orange robed neophytes stepped back a pace in terror. The flickering of the mutant's polymorphic forms of hybrid serpents rose up into the irridescent pyramid, but the faint, transparent flickering of this manifestation made it all the more menacing.

'I see you haven't managed to exorcise *your* demons!' Luke shouted at the shape-shifting Oracle.

'Oh, my little murderer,' the Oracle resumed his human persona, his voice still shrill with menace, 'it is *you* who cannot exorcise *your* demons! For though you unwillingly released the power I needed to garner those souls from the underworld - the dark gods - when you killed Ishtar, your little lover, you heaped an eternity of grief upon your puny soul in your pathetic fallacy of belief in a divine being...you traded the damnation of your soul to assist me!'

'Perhaps,' Luke countered, holding onto his parents shoulders and supported by Smirtin's stong arm, 'but I did it with the intention of preventing the viral plume of your evil madness from seeding in the minds of men elsewhere...and,' Luke shouted, '*I shall see you in hell!*'

'That you will,' the Oracle's sibilant voice was charged with venom, 'and you will start your journey there right now, along with your friends, by returning whence you came.'

'Take them below!' the Oracle commanded as a group of guards who had been standing in the shadows to the side of the dais emerged.

'*New Order, same henchmen.*' Luke spat as he was seized roughly and many heavy, mailed fists clubbed down Smirtin who was surprised from behind.

Chapter Twenty-Three
*** Below The Spectral Void ***

Many days and months had elapsed in the twilight zone of the dungeons below the spectral void. The flickering wall lights from within, cast their orange glow onto the prisoners who though in separate cells were in constant contact with one another, although growing weaker by the day. Even the black giant Smirtin had lapsed into a dark torpor, having tried without success to tear out the pinions which secured him in chains across his massive chest and legs; the jailers had taken no chances.

Now, with his body weight and musculature declining, he felt as weak as a kitten, feeding only on the slimy gruel of his daily meal, pushed through the grille by one of the guards who periodically prodded and poked him with his own giant scimitar, throwing mocking insults at him.

'There you are, big man...not so big as you used to be, now are yer?' Such were the taunts he had endured as he watched himself wither away and felt his strength ebb. He was unable to exercise, though at first he had tried to keep in shape by flexing his muscles against the restraints, but after a while he had relapsed and succumbed to a palsy of lethargy and depression.

Ogadile's dark beauty had waned and her pallor turned to a sour grey, her formerly lustrous black tresses were lank and dirty, covered in the oil and grease from the endlessly burning torches outside, with a hint of grey showing at her temples. The guards no longer berated her with lascivious remarks – their suggestions of how she could earn another bowl of gruel from them had long since stopped - as they joked amongst themselves, leering at her declining desirability.

Errol had cocooned himself into his own little introverted world, muttering to himself epithets of times gone by, when he was a master of his own schooner, sailing the high seas in search of nubile native girls. Now the guards had grown bored with listening to his far-fetched stories and no longer stood in rapt awe outside his cell, and he now recited his life story only to himself.

Luke had grown even thinner, his gaunt face graced by a dusty reddish beard, which grew long across his emaciated chest as he relived the eternal hell of killing his one true lover. His hopes of returning to the world of above and feeling the gentle embrace of Molly were dashed as he repented his crime in this world of Nethertime and had thought about dispatching himself - to be released by death - many times.

Jock and Bridget, sharing the same cell together had comforted one another as Jock looked at the protruding belly of his wife, sustained by his portion of gruel which he gave over to her; she was not long before delivering. And yet he fretted about the future of the twins to be; what would fate hold for them? The guards had sported with them, suggesting that the babies would be snatched upon birth to give the cult well needed women with which to promulgate their dark and evil clan. This was one thing though, that Jock, even though having grown weak and debilitated, would never countenance - yet the other option open to him, to kill them at birth, was unthinkable. Once he had suggested to Bridget that they release all four of them to heaven, but she had sobbed in such an emotional despair and repugnance of the idea, that he had not broached the subject again. Even so, there was not one second of his waking mind, which did not plague him in knowing what best to do.

He had prayed for help, or some direction, yet there seemed to be none forthcoming, and he had in desperation, set up a mode of communication, which was the banging of their gruel pans on the walls. In this Jock had sought to provide a link between their separate cells by means of his rather rusty knowledge of Morse code, which he had remembered from his brief spell in the navy, those long, long years ago.

The guards had been suspicious at first, then had laughed, returning to their game of cards, as they applauded one another in the fact that they're charges had finally gone mad. Luke had been the first to pick up on the signal, the sound of the banging had some sort of periodic logic, and it was a code. Then he had resurrected his memory, yanking it out of the morass of self-pity, to realise that his father was tapping out a message. The rudiments of Morse code he had learned as a boy scout in the land of his youth. He applied his mind to relearning it, until he was able to communicate with his parents.

Ogadile had joined in, then Errol who had known of the code in his previous life, and they were now able to communicate, apart from Smirtin who was beyond comprehending these strange intermittent signals. Instead, the black giant languished in his own torture - the ravishing of his powers - watching his muscles decline, the skeletal mass of his giant frame projecting from the withered flesh by the day.

'Dot, dot, dash, dot, dash...' 'The twins will be born any time now.' Jock had sent to Luke, Ogadile and Errol, who had tapped their futile encouragement, "be brave, hold on.' No congratulations; there was not room for rejoicing.

Then another message came from a distant cell, faint at first. But Jock picked it up and replied. 'Identify, explain, identify.'

'It is the Emperor of Eon,' was the reply that came back.

'Emperor' Jock sent back 'Is that you...are you all right?'

'I am alive' the reply came 'but only on a hog's breathe. Listen, I have to tell you what to do...'

'I am receiving' Jock sent back 'I am listening'

'Your amulet, your medallion...do you still have it?' Jock checked in his damp and dirty shirt, it was still around his neck 'Yes!'

'Then you must use it. You can only use it twice, once to travel from this place...and once more to return. You must await the birth and then take the babies with you, away from this place of evil...or they will be used by the cult...are you getting this?'

'Yes' Jock sent back, a ray of hope dawning in his hyperventilating breast.

'You can use the power of the amulet by reciting the incantation which begins with Neb Ankh...do you remember'

'Yes' Jock replied

'Wait until your wife gives birth, do not alert the guards that anything is different. When her twins come and you have the babies in your arms, give me the signal...I will direct my mind now to make contact with Joruck who will guide you on your way so that you may transfer effectively, and Neb Ankh, with whom I telepathise, will incant with me when the time comes ...do you know where you will go?'

'Yes' Jock sent back, ' I know where to take them!'

'Hold on to that image' the Emperor replied 'rehearse it in your mind...your place of arrival...and do not hesitate when the time comes, for the power invested in these tektites is non-terrestial and is very powerful magic!'

'Thank you, over and out' Jock closed the connection and whispered words of comfort and hope to the hyperventilating Bridget. 'I am in labour' she whispered, biting into the dirty singlet which Jock had taken from his body to give her extra warmth. Her body arched upwards as she lay on the rush mat which was their bed, her screams echoing around the cell and out into the caverns of the dungeons outside. The guards clattered up to their cells, their steel-shod leather boots rasping on the rock as they clustered around to watch.

'*Get away from here!*' Jock shouted, his voice strident as he tried to protect his wife from their leering gaze '*Do you have no dignity?*'

'They will be ours.' the Captain of the Guard gloated 'as soon as they come out of your proud little whore, they will be ours!'

'*Smirtin!*' Jock shouted 'Smirtin, help us now. We have need of you like never before!' The black man arose from his torpor, his former muscles wasted in a mess of dangling flesh. 'Forgive me!' he shouted, 'Forgive me for letting myself sink so low...I am with you, hold on.'

The colossus wiped his tear stained eye as he moved to the grille of his cell. Though his shoulders and arms were depleted of his former strength, he propelled his still weighty bulk at the grille and his restraining manacles snapped, catapulting him through the fractured iron so that he rolled out into the cavern. Resurrecting his indomitable will, he ran down the slope to Jock and Bridget's cell, leaping onto the taunting, lecherous guards to render them into a pulp with his hands, elbows, knees, feet and head flying around in a maelstom of bone-breaking, death-dealing mayhem.

Then, on seeing her taunters knocked into a pulp of their own depravity, Bridget gave one final agonising cry and the twins were born.

Jock was waiting with whatever garments he could muster to gather them up and present them to their exhausted mother.

'Now' the Emperor tapped 'do not hesitate, now...take them with you...you must hold your amulet up and recite the incantation...'

'Bridget forgive me, for you know what I must do... I will be back!' Jock whispered to the comatose mother, taking the two babies in his arms whilst holding the amulets between the three of them, then sitting crossed-legged on the earthen floor and reciting the incatation for astral travelling....

'Neb Ankh Sar Eff Jded Rhekit'

The Emperor and Neb Ankh repeated the incantation in unison with Luke, so that it echoed out through the cells and into the cavern as Smirtin collapsed on the corpses of the lifeless guards.

Jock clasped the newborn twins to his breast as the face of his wife, son, and friends and the murky depth of the dungeons dematerialised and they were borne up into the ether.

Chapter Twenty-Four
Miracle

Isaak had been pacing around his minuscule room. His eyes were tired as ever, having watched the transcript from the flickering monitor and trying to piece together the various links that he had established. He had been in communication with Joruck who had sent him a message, ecstatic that his operation on Bridget had been successful, and thanking him for his help in finding the genome, the key to delivering a treatment for such a delicate operation.

The two, Isaak and Joruck, were, though of very different origins, similar in many respects. Not only by their appearance, but they both lived in high-tech squalor and deemed themselves to be above mere mortals.

Through his transmissions from the cones, Isaak had gleaned some idea of what had taken place in the world of the Nethertime. He had followed, with many a misgiving and baited breath, Luke's killing of Ishtar, but that drastic and necessary action had been to no avail. For the incubus had resurrected into a new, more powerfull Oracle who had turned the Temple of the Eon into something resembling Fort Knox...the Pyramid of the Spectral Void.

Recently, Isaak had received an urgent transcription from Joruck, saying that he had lost touch with all of the assault party who had gone to save Luke.

'I can only attribute it to the fact that the Oracle has, in his highly mutated state, been able somehow to recreate a force field far greater than I have ever known. He is using the power of the Temple of the Eon to repel any time/space/matter protocol as he builds the Spectral Void into an impregnable fortress.

'How is that possible!' Isaak had replied

'He is one of us you know. Though he is one of the many who were expelled from our society...He is one of the Star people, yet a dissident, a subversive and a very alien and dangerous life form

''That much is evident' Isaak had replied

'The so-called Esoteric Oracle is the incubus of the third generation of mutants. Yet he has grown so powerful by subsuming the powers of evil, the ancient dark gods, which I admit we brought with us when we colonised your planet. He has grown to the point where even my own superior equipment cannot spy on him...he is a rogue mutant.'

At that level of desperation from the man, or alien more like, whom Isaak had come to respect, he had realised that there was little he could do and had sent him a transcript to that effect. There had been radio and brain wave silence for some time as Isaak's screen showed only a flickering image of the colossal pyramid of the spectral void, that voided any signals in or out.

Isaak was irate, and at somewhat of an impasse. He had played a part in the extermination of the cult, tricking them into astral travelling from their head-quarters in Elgin Avenue where they had been caught in a trap of marvellous ingenuity as Jock had triggered the volcano to erupt onto the Lost city.

Yet now it looked as if there was nothing either of them could do. This final chapter of the cult were ensconced in the impregnable fortress of the spectral void, and no one could get to them. Isaak fretted also about the fate of Bridget and the twins yet to be born...What would become of them. Were they also to be prisoners of the resurrected Oracle?

The monitor suddenly flickered into life. It was Joruck.

'I have urgent news' he exclaimed, a cats cradle of worry lines creasing his brow

'I have received a communiqué from the Emperor of the Temple of the Eon that was. He has used his final strength to send me this message and I fear for him. But his telepathic message is of the direst consequence...it concerns Jock and the newborn twins...he has escaped from the Spectral Void with the help of the tektite amulet bestowed on him by the Emperor, and he and the twins are astral travelling upon the ether, even as we speak. He has a lock on your homing signal that the Emperor patched through on Jock's departure. He will be arriving soon...this is extremely urgent...can you help?'

'I have no resources,' Isaak sent back 'I am alone here and...'

'*Do not retract from your mission!*' Joruck shouted back 'I have picked up his brain waves, he is desperate...he has new born babies, those of the one will...*You must help us now!*'

'Very well' Isaak replied weakly, shaken to the core.

'For the sake of your brethren, do this!' Joruck's face dissipated in a jangle of static waves. Isaac picked up the phone, 'Molly is that you...I have an urgent request...can you come?'

A thunderstorm raged about Portobello Road, sheet lightening zigzagged down onto the huddle of terraced houses as their occupants looked in concern at the spectacle in the sky above, for the night sky was devoid of cloud.

Molly sat on Isaak's bed, sorting through a large carrier bag of blankets, nappies, milk, bottle and a vast assortment of other needs, which she had hastily brought at her local chemist before taking the tube to Notting Hill Gate. Isaak was fixed to his monitor as strange patterns, not the normal static, oscillated wildly across the screen. He stepped through the shabby French windows onto the tiny balcony as the white bolts of lightening threw his aged face into a gaunt contrast.

The room was suddenly filled with an eerie green glow as the monitor blew up and the lights in his tiny hovel and in the street below fused; Molly rose in a tearful dread. The ghostly silhouette of a man, clutching a small bundle began to materialise in the centre of the room. Static charges of green fire emanated from his body, which radiated an otherworldly glow and appeared to smoke. Then stabilising, as if in a final presence, a man stood there and the sound of crying babies filled the room.

'Jock!' Isaak exclaimed, closing the French windows, 'Jock is that you?' The static grew less as the lights came on again and Molly and Isaak looked at the gaunt figure, his face hung with a frosty hoar as he walked as a dead man towards the bed, deposited his bundle of dirty blankets onto it and then slumped down onto the floor.

Molly went to the bundle of crying movement, unwrapping the still smoking package as Isaak tended to Jock.

'Oh my, look at this if you would!' Molly exclaimed, her eyes brightening as she looked down on the newborn twins, their straggly blonde hair twined about their unformed faces as they clutched each other and whimpered in their distress. 'There, there,' Molly coaxed as they gripped her fingers and she cooed at them, bending over them as a warmth of maternal bliss pervaded her being. With a skill she didn't know she had, but which came naturally, Molly held bottles to their mouths and they drank in great gulps, their tiny hands shielding their tight -closed eyes against the light. Steady now, she whispered as their crying abated and they looked up to her with their identical cornflower-blue eyes. 'Oh dear, I think we need a change, don't we?'

Jock was recovering, sitting up on the floor as Isaak poured him a glass of single malt whiskey, a good Irish brand that he was saving for a special occasion. Casting an eye at Molly he was relieved to see that she was not only coping, but relishing the task of calming the distressed twins.

'Thank God for women.' He toasted Jock, who though harrowed and gaunt, did not refuse the strong drink, and after a couple of gulps a glimmer of colour came back into his emaciated cheeks. 'Now then,' Isaak got to the point, 'you could tell me about your adventures, but somehow I think that would take forever...the urgent issue is, what do you want us to do with your twins?'

'I have money...But not on me.' Jock said, a furrow of realisation creasing his brow, for this was the real world, things had to be paid for.

'I'm glad to hear it.' Isaak replied. 'But we are not after your money old chap...we want to know how we can help you to deal with this these little ones.' he gestured towards Molly and the babies. She had just finished bathing them and putting fresh nappies on, her face flushed in the pursuit of her maternal abilities, which seemed to come so naturally.

'I have to go back.' Jock's worry lines came back as he fondled the tektite amulet he wore around his neck. 'I have to return to the dungeons of the Spectral Void to return to my Wife and Son! '

'That much maybe certain dear boy,' Isaak took another draught of the scotch as even his aged cheeks started to take on a flush, 'but what is the best that we can do for your beautiful daughters.'

'I have a brother,' Jock said, 'I have a younger brother who owns my estate...'

'Your estate?' Isaak raised an eyebrow 'oh dear me, I didn't realise you were aristocracy!'

'I'm not.' Jock retorted. 'I am talking about my so called brother, sir Marmaduke Merebrook, a man who had me dispossessed by seeding rumours about my own worth to our father. I was struck out of the will, disinherited. Hence I took the title of Jock Slater...artist and philander...'

'Oh I see' Isaak was humouring him. The man was a little deranged from his recent incarceration in the dungeons and his obviously harrowing experience of astral travelling.

'So what is your title, squire?'

'I am James Merebrook...of Merebrook Manor, eldest son and first in line to the hereditary title belonging to the late Sir Geoffrey Merebrook, my father.

'Can you prove it?' Isaak asked, a glimmer of disbelief still flickering in his eyes.

'No, I have nothing. No documents, no proof, only my money in a bank account, yet no cheque book or credit cards...for God's sake man! I have just returned from being away for two years in another dimension! My wife, my son and my comrades are rotting in the prisons of the cult, which you helped to try and destroy, but who are resurrected and now more powerful...if *you* do not believe what I am telling you, then for heavens sake, *who will*?'

'Shush.' Isaak quietened the distraught man, casting his eye back at Molly and the twins, who were now fast asleep in her arms and being rocked by the doting young woman.

'You are leading up to something, aren't you?' Isaak asked.

'Lend me money!' Jock said desperately. 'Lend me some money. I will write you a promissory note as I do not have any thing else and I assure you I will honour it...'

'How much do you need?' Isaak asked, his eyes narrowing.

'One thousand pounds' Jock stated flatly, 'that will give me time to reorganise myself, get to grips with this world again, my own world, and look after the twins until I can take them down to Merebrook Manor...'

'And then?' Isaak asked.

'Then I will deliver them to Marmaduke. He will not refuse his burden of guilt on having me disinherited...he will surely not do that? Then, once they are safe and cared for, I will return to Nethertime and join Bridget my wife to await our release, our salvation...'

'What salvation?' Isaak asked

'Both Joruck and Isis have predicted that these very special daughters of mine, the Twins, will effect our release in the future. They are of the one will, highly intelligent and telepathic...they will come to release us...it has been prophesied...!'

'A highly unlikely prognosis.' Isaak stated flatly. 'I can do no other than believe you however. Do not worry about the promissory note... I do not need money. Just to have been of service in destroying one chapter of the cult of decadents has been my mission. If what you say is true, and your beautiful Twins are destined to be the avenging angels in some future conflict – and I think that I have born witness to this - then it is my duty as de facto guardian of this present outpost, which was set up here to procure the advancement of humankind...It is my duty, but also my honour to assist you!'

Whilst the implications if Isaak's recent words were still registering on Jock's numbed mind, the old man stooped and pulled out a large trunk from under the bed, as Molly moved her legs to allow access. Isaak opened the trunk and both Jock and Molly gasped as they saw stacks of money, held together with elastic bands.

'One thousand pounds' Isaak said holding a wad up to the light, 'Take it and may God be with you...'

'Wait' Jock said hesitantly, holding one end of the stack of notes, 'you said you were here as a guardian...you mean...you are not one of us, don't you. You are a star person?'

'Aptly put my friend,' Isaak smiled, 'very politically correct.... yes I am here for a short time still...and then I will return to my own people. It has been long enough...and yes, in spite of my former rebuff, I have also heard via another source that your progeny will effect your release in the future and cause the downfall of the cult...for all time!'

'My God!' Molly swore 'and I thought you were just a pathetic old man.

'Old man, yes,' Isaak winked at her 'but pathetic, never!'

'You take this,' he said to Molly, handing her a similar stack of money. 'You have earned it, in your involvement in stamping out the Elgin cult. But now, if you were to assist Jock, or Sir James as we should call him, to help with the Twins as they travel down to Merebrook Manor, I would think of it as an investment in the future.

'When you put it like that, then how can I refuse.' Molly sighed, her arms around the Twins.

'Good luck with your endeavours,' Isaak raised his glass in a toast. **'Here is to your progeny, here is to the prophecy...and here is to the future!'** a strange light was shining in the old man's eyes.

✳✳✳

'Will I see Luke again?' Molly asked, her large green eyes were questioning as she sat feeding the Twins in the first class compartment of a train travelling down to Merebrook Manor.

'I have some harsh news for you.'Jock took a deep breath. 'Luke has changed. He is not the youth you knew. He was asked to make a terrible choice to try to avert the rebirth of the Esoteric Oracle. He has blood on his hands and on his soul, and cannot forgive himself for killing Ishtar.'

'*What!*' Molly's face blanched. 'You mean he *killed* that seducer, that harlot!'

'I am afraid so.' Jock replied solemnly. 'And that is why I urge you to forget him. He is far away in another dimension where I also must return, and I do not know how long before the prophecy of our relase becomes effective... if indeed it does! You are a young woman and you have your future to think of. But it is your decision, and if you choose to wait for his return, then so be it.'

'I see.' Molly choked back a sob as she looked at the indentical twins. 'When you return, tell him I shall always treasure the brief moments we spent together...he will be in my prayers.'

'I shall tell him that.' Jock hugged the distraught girl.

They detrained at the country station and took a cab; the taxi driver enquired, looking strangely at them in the mirror, 'Merebrook Manor, Sir?' as if expecting some further explanation as to the purpose of their visit, and looking hard at the carrycots.

'Wait for this young lady here, will you?' Jock stopped the taxi some way from the Manor and slipped the driver a ten-pound note.

Molly carried the carrycots one in each hand whilst Jock opened the estate gate and they walked silently through the grounds towards the house. They sat for a while on a garden bench, listening to the sound of the wind singing through the high treetops, feeling the sting of rain. With a tear trickling down her cheek Molly passed the twins in their carrycots over to Jock.

'Will I ever see them again, these beautiful babies?' she looked soulfully at Jock.

'You *will* see them, my dear child' Jock put his arm around the distraught girl. 'You will see them when you need comfort or need to know there is somebody out there that loves you...for they surely love you.'

Jock's eyes were over-brimming as he looked at the beautiful young woman. 'Perhaps,' he said, 'you will have children of your own. Perhaps we will meet up and be together again. But if not my lovely Molly, I want to thank you myself, but most of all on behalf of Luke, for helping us in this time of travail. You will never be forgotten!'

'You had better go now.' Molly whispered, trying to master her emotions! 'And when you return to Nethertime, tell Luke I will wait...'

'No' Jock replied, 'do not wait. You are a young woman and your need is strong. Do not wait. You will find the right person. You will have a family of your own. Think only that he loved you, as we love you.' Jock pushed a black bag towards her with his foot 'Take this,' he said 'it is only money, but it is the only way we have to repay your kindness...be well and successful in your life...I have many things to do.'

'You are going back aren't you' Molly grasped Jock and embraced him. 'You are going back to Nethertime...'

'I have to.' Jock said somberely. 'Wait here awhile, I will return.'

He took the carrycots and went down the drive towards the Manor, as the squall drove across the dark path. After a while he returned, and sat beside Molly.

'I have delivered them to my brother, Sir Marmaduke.' he said, his brow furrowed. 'He has vowed to care for them...'

'And your title?' Molly asked

'I didn't care to bring that up...only to secure his promise to look after my babies. If I ever return, I can pursue that claim, but it matters little to me, so I am Jock Slater, pure and simple. Now,' Jock clutched the amulet about his neck, 'you know you way back to the taxi, don't you?'

'Yes Sir James,' Molly whispered, 'I know the way back...do you?'

'I do.' Jock affirmed, holding the amulet to his breast.

'Neb – Ankh – Sar – Eff – Jded – Rhekit'

Molly was aware of a crackle of energy and a green glow to the side of her. She smiled in memory of the two beautiful Twins and turned to look at the seat beside her; it was empty. Molly picked up the black bag and made her solitary way from the grounds of Merebrook Manor.

THE END

OTHER TITLES IN THE TWINS OF TIME SERIES

THE TWINS OF TIME AND THE SEVEN SEAS OF TIME
ISBN 1905363907
THE TWINS OF TIME AND THE GOLDEN GROTTO
ISBN 1905363885
THE TWINS OF TIME AND THE BRIDGE OF TIME
ISBN 1905363869
KA KA RANISH AND THE TWINS OF TIME
ISBN 1905363915

SOME TITLES FOR OLDER READERS:

THE TRILOGY OF NETHERTIME

BOOK ONE: THE SACRED EYES OF TIME
ISBN 1905363923
BOOK TWO: THE OBELISK OF TIME
ISBN 1905363931
BOOK THREE: THE TWINS OF TIME
ISBN 1905363893

All these titles are orderable through your local bookstore or leading internet book sites such as amazon.com. Ebook editions are also available. Some of these titles are also published in gold-embossed hardback collectors' editions of one thousand, signed and numbered by the author, available only from **nethertime.com** or **twins-of-time.com**

ABOUT THE AUTHOR

I have spent a lot of my life travelling, and encountered some very strange events, which no doubt filter on down into my writing.

After leaving grammar school in England, I joined the merchant navy as a navigation cadet officer and sailed around the world, though my enthusiasm for painting was always with me, and after two years I jumped ship and enrolled in Art College. One year later I won a scholarship to the Royal College of Art in London. After getting an honours degree, I taught and exhibited widely, and then worked for the University of Chicago.

This was a challenging job - working in Egypt, recording the scenes on the eroded walls of tombs and temples in and around the Valley of the Kings - and it was to prove a lasting influence on my painting, poetry and writing. For in riding around the remote villages of Upper Egypt on my bike, my imagination was fired, and from that well of creativity emerged the characters and landscapes of the TRILOGY OF NETHERTIME.

But during this period, the surreal was not just confined to my fantasy novels, for many are the stories I could tell about being arrested for spying, robbed by camel-riding bandits and swimming the Nile in order to escape a pack of rabid dogs. These tales are too numerous for the telling here of course (maybe in another book)

After Egypt I lived for five years in the U.S.A. and Mexico, painting, writing, travelling and exhibiting, and ever amazed by the variety of wonderful landscape.

After America I lived in Scotland for ten years where I had the privilege of having Her Majesty the Queen and Prince Philip attend my exhibition.

But *the* event that changed my life was the birth of my twin daughters, Sophie and Laura who inspired me to start writing full time and are the protagonists in my fantasy series THE TWINS OF TIME.

Richard Turneramon

Printed in the United Kingdom
 by Lightning Source UK Ltd.
109819UKS00001B/199